FIRKETTLE'S FINEST

FIRKETTLE'S FINEST

A novel

Kenneth J. Hall

PARTRIDGE
A Penguin Random House Company

To order additional copies of this book, contact
Toll Free 800 101 2657 (Singapore)
Toll Free 1 800 81 7340 (Malaysia)
orders.singapore@partridgepublishing.com

www.partridgepublishing.com/singapore

CONTENTS

By the same author:

Chase your own strawberries,
The beginnings,
Learning Curve,
Old Asia hand

Dedicated to Mimin and the staff of Gleneagles Hospital Kuala Lumpur Malaysia, without whose care and attention I would not have survived to write anything.

PART ONE

Kevin Firkettle

CHAPTER: 1

Kevin Firkettle wanted to go back to sleep. Half of his brain knew full well that it was Monday morning and recognized that both it, and the alarm clock knew that without a doubt, it was time to get up. The other half though recognized that his body totally rejected the idea. The half that wished to veto any thought of instructing the body to move out from under his warm, teddy bear decorated duvet and face the week ahead, also sent quiet, but insistent messages to the logic centers and areas of Kevin's higher reasoning. Messages that spelt out in huge letters that in fact there was little point in subjecting his unwilling body to yet another week of pointless peering at a computer screen and attempting to juggle invoices with stock. A week of unmitigated boredom and drudgery. The querulous brain cells questioned why he needed to continue with this self-inflicted torture? Call in sick. Go on the dole. Hitch hike to Mongolia. Join a commune. Join The Foreign Legion. Join The British Legion. In fact, do anything other than stare at that screen of endless spare parts for cars for yet another inane five days. Kevin was aged twenty-five, and approaching twenty-six. For a person who had never known his parents, Kevin was remarkably incurious. Kevin having been discovered by accident by an observant refuse collector, who spotted the shoebox and the baby inside, on top of a rubbish skip at the back of a minor chain of super markets in Wandsworth. There was apparently a large tabby cat there too, with four kittens. Kevin liked to feel that the cat had adopted him, perhaps in the manner reminiscent of Romulus and Remus. They of course going on to found Rome. In any event, Kevin never founded a city, let alone an empire, and other than the cat, was never subsequently adopted by anyone. He did however have a name, if little else. As the words Kevin Firkettle, had been printed in large, if somewhat crude letters, on a scrap of paper pinned to his cheap and rather grubby blanket. For all of this somewhat bizarre start in life, he was quite well adjusted by generally held standards. In as much as Kevin had no criminal record, and was neither violent nor abusive. In fact, Kevin was a rather mild person. Which was probably just as well, as Kevin hadn't the build for street fighting. Nor the eyesight either, being as he was somewhat myopic and gangly. Further more he was neither an alcoholic nor a drug user. In fact, Kevin could be held up to be an example of 100% success for the British welfare state and a model of society.

The state having made little or no attempt to trace his antecedents, had just accepted him. Much in the way it accepted council refuse. It placed it in its appropriate place and processed it. So too, it did with Kevin. Kevin then from a very early age was conditioned to accept whatever life deemed to hand out to him without question.

At school, he had neither excelled, nor failed. Plodded, would have been the best description. Or perhaps, plodded in limbo, would have been even better. He had however managed to obtain four GCEs. This had then thus enabled him to find gainful employment. Consequently he had held down a regular job since he had left school. A totally meaningless and thoroughly boring regular job true. Still, one which due to his background of almost rote like conditioning of the need to become a worthwhile member of society, which did rather beg the question of what exactly had been his previous status, Kevin felt obliged to pursue. Irrespective of how much certain and disturbing parts of his almost unused reasoning and higher brain functions completely rejected the idea.

Kevin had discovered sex at the somewhat late age of twenty-three. Perhaps a more accurate description would have been that sex had discovered him. Sex in the form of Marlene Pervis. A cashier at a local supermarket. Marlene, who was a full year older than Kevin, and who lived with her widowed mother in an aging tower block council flat on The Isle of Dogs had her sights firmly fixed on the big time. That being to both her and her mother's view a nice little semi in an up market neighborhood and two point four children. Oh, and a Ford Escort. The small fact that the mortgage would be crippling, and that both of them would have to hold down full time jobs for the next twenty years and even one child would represent a financial burden of stupendous proportions, let alone a car, seemingly having not crossed either of the two women's collective minds. They, rather in the manner of persons who hold fundamental religious beliefs, also firmly assumed that their selection of life's chosen path was the correct one. Consequently, Kevin was subjected at regular intervals to the benefit of their convictions. Kevin, if not a willing and eager convert to their cause, at least was unresisting, being as he was the product of an institutionalized regime.

Marlene had previously been engaged to a merchant seaman at the tender age of eighteen. This state of affairs having arisen when she was convinced that she was pregnant. It subsequently transpired that the reason for the delay in her monthly period was due to the acquisition of a transmittable and highly virulent antisocial disease, rather than impregnation. Consequently, the jolly jack tar was crossed off the list of suitable suitors, and persons to whom cards will be sent at Christmas. On the credit side, Marlene got to keep the engagement ring. Thereupon, she took heed of her mother's advise and cast around for a, "Steady sort of person." A whole series of ardent male admirers followed over the next few years. All generally more interested in Marlene's local reputation as a bit of a goer, than marriage. Thus Marlene was caught between two lines of fire so to speak. The need to satisfy her urgent natural desires and the need not to get pregnant. Even Marlene could see that there was no future in continuing her lifestyle and took her mother's advise and whilst not wishing to give up her hobby all together, cast around for a long term partner with prospects. Also, a partner who had no local knowledge of Marlene's past. Kevin fitted the specification perfectly. Here now was her catch. With Kevin, she could safely become with child. Kevin would do the decent thing, marry her and devote the rest of his life to slaving away to support her and legal offspring. Marlene, being the sort of girl that was capable of learning from mistakes, confided in her mother. Her mother, whilst not, for the sake of propriety, making her suggestions too open, intimated that perhaps her daughter should employ her feminine charms to effect the desired result. Marlene did, with alacrity and Kevin was hooked.

There was however a small problem. One of Kevin's premature ejaculation. The first time that Marlene placed Kevin's unresisting hands upon her more than adequate bosoms, Kevin got a strange warm, wet feeling within his underpants. There seemed little that could be done about this, though give Marlene her due, she persevered. She tried stripping off and lying naked, her nipples erect and her dark triangle warm and inviting. Kevin promptly squirted around the place like a fireman attempting to extinguish a gorse fire. The second problem was that having ejaculated Kevin promptly lost all interest, and either wanted to watch TV or go to sleep. Marlene was to say the least was frustrated. Whilst Kevin, who in his innocence, still assumed Marlene to be the virginal maiden that she claimed, assured her that it was best this way as they could save it until they got married. Thus in true adult male format, avoided confronting the issue and prevaricated.

Kevin opened a savings account with a building society and attempted the fruitless task of trying to not only to keep abreast of inflation and the ever rising prices of the property market, but to surpass it. Meanwhile Marlene purchased a double sized, Taiwanese built, economy battery vibrator, replete with stimulating nodules, with which to defray her deep frustrations. More years passed. Her mother fretted over when her only daughter would wed and belabored the point at every opportunity.

Kevin labored at his computer screen seeing each day no matter how he saved, the gap between salary and house purchase widen. Consequently, life fell into a pattern, so reminiscent of Britain. Marlene's base, due to sitting eight hours a day at a super market cash out point widened. Her mother's views grew narrower in direct proportion to the visible evidence that her only daughter's prospects of wedded bliss were decreasing, to the point that her suggestions of the system to be employed became far less obtuse with each telling. The situation not being helped in any measure by Marlene being loath to explain in detail to her mother the fundamental problem that precluded her conception. More so as time progressed and her mother became more explicit and Marlene began to gather the impression that her late father had been a cross between Superman and a satyr. She reflected sadly that Kevin, whilst well endowed, had about as much chance of a bull's eye as a blind man playing golf. There was no way he would ever sink a hole in one. Marlene had been hoisted by her own petard. In pursuing her line for a semi, and the financial commitments that entailed, she had effectively delayed the date of her nuptial conquest. For try as he might, short of robbing a bank, there was no way Kevin was ever going to acquire sufficient funds for a small tent in Tottenham, let alone a semi. Consequently Kevin was, as had been his norm, seemingly plodding endlessly through his life, to no end. In fact, considering Kevin's back ground and Spartan upbringing, it was nothing short of a miracle, or very powerful genes, that gave him any incentive to continue upon his seemingly treadmill of futility. No wonder then that Kevin's higher senses, though ill defined intellect, screamed that he should if not remain in bed, at least take time to consider and conceptualize his life as a whole. Needless to say, conditioning proved to be the stronger force, and as per usual, Kevin got up. Not that the thought of matching an order for a left handed nylon grommet for an independently sprung track rod end, filled him with enthusiasm for the week's toil ahead, it did not. But generally, we all tend to be creatures of habit. So, lethargically and unwillingly, Kevin struggled out of bed to face yet another meaningless week of pure drudgery.

Kevin rented a bed-sit in Camberwell and shared a bathroom. His bed-sit had what had been fondly described by the estate agent as a dinerette. A galley on a rowing boat would have no doubt have been of larger proportions. So Kevin tended to clean his teeth in the sink, and favor an electric razor. He had purchased a microwave and this shared space on a chest of drawers with a mirror and a TV set. The chest of drawers also doubling as a refuge for both shirts, socks and tins of baked beans. One could say that Kevin was fully, if somewhat spartanly equipped. It was when Kevin was moving towards the small fridge with a view to checking upon his milk situation, that he noticed the letter.

The letter had been pushed under his door. This was not normal. Post was generally picked up by whoever and having extracted their own mail, the rest was dumped on a battered chair in the hallway. There, if not promptly collected, it tended to overflow onto the floor and be trodden upon. The landlord, a large and overweight gentleman from the Indian Sub Continent, periodically sorted through the discarded mail. Since apart from Kevin, the bed sits had a fairly flowing succession of occupants, most of the mail remained unclaimed and ended up in the dust bin. Obviously, someone had taken his letter by mistake, and then later, realizing it, had slipped it under his door. The fact that anyone else was even aware of his name was little short of amazing. That they had taken the trouble to deliver his letter, even more so.

Kevin did not normally receive mail. Other that the normal amount of junk post offering unbeatable offers, or the chance to win an exotic holiday in Central Asia, providing one first purchased a years supply of anti wrinkle cream or hand made Wellington boots with a built in modem. Kevin's mail only consisted of bills and overdraft statements. That or pleas for him to give generously to some obscure cause or another from starving gastropods to recycling one armed Latvian coal miners with gout. Kevin knew no one. Kevin had no relations. De facto then it followed that Kevin should not be receiving private mail.

Kevin picked up the letter with interest. It informed him in bold letters that the letter had originated from the office of Boggle & Boggle. Solicitors of Tunbridge Wells in Kent. Kevin was non plussed. He stopped and considered the envelope. He knew of no Boggle & Boggle, solicitors or otherwise of Tunbridge Wells. In fact, Kevin had never been to Tunbridge Wells. He wasn't very sure where it was and other than it was the sort of place in which monied people dwelt, that was the limit of his knowledge. Why then should he receive a letter from there? Kevin studied the address. Yes, certainly the letter was addressed to one Kevin Firkettle of his address. Kevin had a pang of anxiety sweep over him. Was he being sued? If so, then by whom and for what? No doubt for every penny he possessed and was likely to earn over the next forty years, screamed a warning voice inside.

Had Kevin inadvertently sent out a left handed grommet when a right handed one was required? Had this lapse on his behalf then resulted in some hideous multi vehicle pile up on a motorway somewhere? Was some council worker from Birmingham now suing him for lack of due diligence? Kevin hesitated, then, taking the bull by the horns sensibly opened the letter. If anything, the contents served only to confuse Kevin even further.

Dear Mr. Firkettle, the letter began. We, Boggle and Boggle are acting on behalf of the late Silas Firkettle, of The Black Badger, Houghton Springs Brewery, in the county of Westfordshire in respect of his will and estate. We believe that the deceased may have been your next of kin. There then followed a mumbo jumbo of legal jargon that solicitors the world over are so fond of using. Thus convincing the lay public of their professional competence and superiority, whilst at the same time giving subtle warnings of their legal powers and it being best not to question them. Kevin took a little time to wade through it all, but finally arrived at the nitty gritty. Namely that he should present himself forthwith at the offices of Messer Boggle & Boggle and upon proving his identity, he would promptly inherit his late relative's estate. Whatever that was, and where ever it was.

Kevin had to read the letter several times over, even looking on its obverse side for extra clues. None were forth coming, the back of the letter was tantalizingly blank and bereft of any information. Kevin found the situation both fascinating and at the same time disquieting. Nothing like this had ever occurred in his brief life's spell. His background and institutionalized upbringing had left him unprepared for sudden surprises. Life for Kevin had trodden an obvious and well laid out path. A path that had been laid out for him by his superiors and betters. All Kevin had to do was to get on with it and not complain. Now suddenly, and out of the blue Kevin was confronted with a totally new and unexpected situation. One that required Kevin to break with all normal routine and maybe even exercise a little bit of thinking for himself. It was this latter thought that Kevin found really daunting. It wasn't as if Kevin had suddenly won the lottery. "Here you are Lad, take your winnings and buy yourself a villa in Spain." No Kevin had to actually not go to work. Then he had to find his way to Tunbridge Wells and the offices of Boggle and Boggle. There he had to prove that he was actually Kevin Firkettle and what then? He received his inheritance? What inheritance? From whom? Did he have, or rather had, some distant uncle who had left him the sole inheritor of all of his possessions? What exactly were The Black Badger and Houghton Springs Brewery? Did he have any more relations? Would they all be gathered around a table and each have a share? The prospect appeared huge and daunting to Kevin. All of Kevin's training and past life experience screamed at him to push the letter back under the door, pretend it had never arrived, and go off to work as normal and forget all about "Uncle Silas".

It wasn't as if Kevin longed for or had any great desire to change his life style. He hadn't. In fact it had never occurred to him that any other life style existed for the Kevin Firkettles' on this world. No, he did as he was bidden and got on with life making the best of it. Anything else was for other people. Kevin in fact was to put it plainly, boring. Skinny, gangly, myopic and meek, with big feet and no interest in sports or pass times. A product of an institution and comprehensive school that at all times wanted to produce nice quiet round pegs that could be tapped into nice quiet round holes and let's not do anything that might lead to that boat being rocked. Kevin had gone along with that system for as long as he could remember. Even his relationship with Marlene he had never questioned. He neither found her attractive nor otherwise. Blond, courtesy of a cheap, propriety brand of hair bleach that in fact was a thinly disguised, watered down household cleaner. Garish red nails, large breasts and small body that was all too obviously running towards a weight problem in later years. She was a standard pattern too. Other than laying his hands upon Marlene's breasts, with the aforementioned consequences, this was the most exciting thing that had ever occurred in Kevin's whole lifetime. The letter however, had opened up a whole realm of new possibilities to him. Kevin suddenly realized that he was perhaps no longer alone in the world. Out there somewhere was his family. So awesome a prospect did Kevin find this, for the first time in his life he told a deliberate lie. Kevin called in sick and took the Green Line bus to Tunbridge Wells.

On the bus trip down to Tunbridge Wells Kevin again studied his letter. Who were his newly discovered relations? The benefactor must, Kevin thought, be some mysterious, unknown and possibly distant uncle. Perhaps he had some huge family out there? If so, the he would therefore only be due a very minor share of whatever there was to divide. Still, reasoned Kevin, a bit of something is better than a whole lot of nothing. He settled back in his seat and considered Boggle and Boggle. They were obviously a company of some substance and standing, having as they had sought him out from a backdrop of millions of nondescript persons. Their standing in Kevin's eyes grew the more he considered their ability to find him and the closer he came to Tunbridge Wells.

Tunbridge Wells is a pretty town and also a well heeled one too. Mercedes, BMW and Jaguar can be seen sitting in long, well kept driveways. Red brick and Georgian houses abound. Wealth is apparent. Solicitors tended to occupy rather plush premises in refurbished Georgian buildings on and off the High Street area. Kevin sought out the firm, subconsciously wiping his hands down his off the peg, well known chain store, trousers, and peeking at his shoes to check their rather lack luster shine. Kevin was then somewhat surprised to find that persons he questions knew nothing of Boggle and Boggle. In fact, it took him some time before he found someone that even recognized the address and knew the location of the street in question. It never occurred to Kevin to phone them. Telephones, taxis and restaurants were things that other used and not the Kevin Firkettles' of this world.

Boggle and Boggle, when he finally located them, turned out to be not quite what Kevin had come to expect within his own mind's eye. Not for them the carefully refurbished Georgian facade and fancy black painted wrought iron railings. No, Boggle and Boggle were obviously traditionalists. They did occupy an aged and weather beaten premises true. But not on the High Street or even within easy walking distance of the town's centre. No, Boggle and Boggle were housed in the basement of a seedy Victorian red brick that had not seen paint since the days of that good Queen's Jubilee. Tucked away tightly between an Indian take away and a newsagents whose specialty seemed to be that of a mail collection service and adverts placed by female osteopaths. Boggle and Boggle claimed not only to be solicitors but also doubled as a private detective agency. The original Boggle and Boggle having no doubt now long retired and passed on to whatever contentious and litigatious heaven, that solicitors the world over go to, once they have shook off their legal clogs. Kevin was seen by one of the more junior and perhaps the only remaining partner. A mere stripling of seventy or so years.

Kevin had never met a solicitor before and had assumed that they all followed the same role as purported by American and British TV. Dapper, neat persons, with razor sharp minds. The rotund, shabby, unshaven and rather scruffy gentleman in the shiny blue suit that sat across the desk from him in a huge and dusty leather chair did not fit easily into Kevin's preconceived ideas at all. Nor the huge fluffy black and white cat that shared the office with the aged incumbent. It sat dozing on a pile of dusty leather bound law books piled on the windowsill in the only patch of sunlight that crept into the unkempt office. When Kevin entered it turned one baleful yellow eye towards him, then ignored him and went back to sleep.

Each time the solicitor moved in his chair a million more dust motes sprang up to join their fellows in dancing in the lone beam of sunlight that penetrated the ancient office. The solicitor spoke and seemed to have difficulty with his dentures, that or the letter ess had escaped his mastery. He leaned over and extended a claw like hand, giving Kevin a limp handshake.

At school, Kevin had been forced to read Dickens and his mind was dragged back to some of the author's characters. The solicitor and his office were straight out of a Dickens's novel. Even the cat was Dickensian. All that was missing was a quill pen. If the office and its strange complement were confusing to Kevin, the outcome of the meeting left Kevin even more bemused.

It appeared that Kevin had indeed possessed a late relation named Silas. This venerable old gentleman having dwelled in the West Country and seemingly having held rather singular, if not down right uniquely odd views. For one he claimed to have been some hereditary Bardic Druid. Based on this claim he had followed some esoteric religion. A religion that required him not to cut his hair or eat meat. It did however require him to wear flowing robes, one ear ring, brew beer and seek out the company of nubile maidens. Not only had he claimed could his family and religion be traced back to Norman times and hence his name of Firkettle but beyond that even into Roman and prehistory times too. He had never married but had developed several relationships with his acolytes. Women far younger than himself. Exactly what transpired at that juncture was clouded in mystery, the upshot being that Kevin had appeared on his rubbish skip. His mother had it seemed, subsequently run off with a hot air balloonist whose luck and propane gas both ran out simultaneously somewhere over the North Sea, killing both of them in the process. Kevin felt profoundly depressed at this piece of news, but before he could assimilate it fully he was bucked up considerably by the next.

"Uncle" Silas claimed the right to make ale and cider. Nothing very spectacular about that in itself, but "Uncle" Silas, under some archaic charter dating back from William The Conqueror's time also claimed the right to sell his brews and more to the point, to be able to do so without having to pay the state one penny in tax or excise duty. Consequently, "Uncle" Silas had owned The Black Badger Inn and brewery. A hostelry that sold the cheapest beer in the country, and apparently some of the strongest too. Also a cider apple orchard of some size and a small bottling plant along with a natural water supply of sufficient purity and volume to satisfy all of the brewing requirements. Successive governments over the years, had attempted to tap this source of revenue and all had failed miserably. Boggle and Boggle for all of their apparent inefficiency but armed with William's Royal Charter proving more than a match. One government was sufficiently foolish as to try to limit the quantity of beer and cider produced, to that which could be sold only upon the premises. In this they had again been defeated. They had then attempted to limit the alcoholic content. Even there they had come unstuck, demanding a 2% limit, but having to settle for an expensive and litigatious 8.5% maximum. The Local Council had however managed to place a ban upon advertising. However, Boggle and Boggle were of the opinion that this and the 8.5% were both contentious issues. Since Silas had not been interested in expanding his brewing business, this situation had suited him admirably. In fact it would seem that Boggle and Boggle's only clients over the ages had been the Firkettles" and their litigations with HM Government. In each case Boggle and Boggle having both won the case and subsequent counter claims for false accusation, slander, loss of earnings, wrongful conviction and everything sort of treason with which they in turn had accused everyone from the local authorities to both church and state. The score to date over the ages standing at Boggle and Boggle umpteen. The others; zero. Mr. Wilberforce went on to hint that since Briton's entry into the EEC, all sorts of new possibilities of suing the state had arisen. These ranged from transgressing the laws relating to ethnic discrimination to that of attempting to impose regulations that contravened European food standards and freedom of religion. He had even rubbed his hands at the thought of such litigation. Assuring Kevin that he was looking forward to such future fees that could be milked from any unsuspecting politician who might be sufficiently unwise as to embark upon a path that crossed Kevin's now fundamental rights to brew and sell alcohol and practice his new found religion as he felt fit..

Kevin mulled over all of this in a bemused manner. He was still feeling profoundly depressed about being abandoned by his mother when suddenly the penny dropped. Kevin sat bolt upright. "Uncle" Silas was not his uncle. Silas had in fact been his natural father! He gasped at the idea. It was alien to all he had ever known. Somehow it did not gel; he could not get his brain to accept the concept. "Excuse me Mr. Wilberforce," Kevin leaned forward and whispered. "But am I to understand that the gentleman to whom you referred was in fact my natural father? I had assumed that he was some distant uncle" Kevin looked devastated and Mr. Wilberforce noted this.

Mr. Wilberforce beamed at him over the top of his spectacles. "Why certainly young man. Exactly. Just So. Dear old Silas was so to speak, your dad." He smiled benignly at Kevin and said, So, you inherit all of his possessions young man, and they are considerable." He nodded at Kevin, who continued to catch flies with his open mouth. Kevin looked perplexed. Many feelings flooded his body all at once. Mr. Wilberforce noted his concern. "Does it pain you to think that you had a father that never recognized you?" Enquired Mr. Wilberforce solicitously. "He never knew you know. If he had he would have taken you under his wing like a shot. I knew him very well and know that is true." Kevin said nothing and bit his lower lip. "Look." Said Mr.Wilberforce kindly. "You never knew him and he never knew you, so why don't you just think about him still as your uncle? Would that help at all? Just until you sort of get used to the idea. Uncle, aunt or grandfather, it makes no difference now. Legally that is. You inherit."

Kevin looked perplexed, and then realized that nothing had actually changed, other than now he knew the name of his father, and that he carried that name too. He looked at Mr. Wilberforce across the desk and nodded, "Yes, uncle Silas he remains. At least for the moment, until I can get my brain around it. I suppose that we all have to have had fathers somewhere?" He looked at Mr.Wilberforce who nodded in a kindly fashion. Kevin continued, "I think that I can manage an Uncle Silas for the moment. This is all rather a shock to my system. Could it just be our secret?"

"As you wish Kevin, as you wish. So uncle Silas it is and we shall continue to call him that." Mr.Wilberforce continued to look at Kevin in an avenuncular manner saying, "Best I tell you the whole story now."

Kevin nodded his agreement and settled back in his chair to discover more about his unknown past. The cat regarded him inscrutably over outstretched paws and yawned, as if to say, uncle, father who cares? Then it closed its eyes and returned to its dozing.

Silas had a sister. Some formidable tyrant of a woman who was wholly opposed to not only the demon drink, but her brother's individual religious views too. She also believed in a carnivorous diet and foxhunting. The woman's sensibilities being outraged at her brother cavorting in the summer's twilight naked around bonfires with nude and nubile young nymphs. She would have nothing to do with Silas and had married the Reverend Longstanton. An earnest and worthy gentleman of the church, some years older than herself. Seeking to purge her mind of her brother and to her viewpoint, his perverted ways, she had followed her husband to Africa. There to undertake missionary work and follow her hobby of slaughtering wild life. Africa at the time being the perfect place to do this as there was a surfeit of both wild life and unsuspecting converts at the time. Her husband also had a leaning towards placing a well-aimed heavy piece of soft lead in the odd passing elephant, and both flourished in their newfound paradise. During the week they shot at anything that was foolish enough to pass within range and on a Sunday they saved souls.

Life would have been both long and idyllic for both of them had it not have been for a faulty box of cartridges and two guns of the same caliber. They subsequently both came to a rather unpleasant end when they were mistaken for lunch by a hungry lion that obviously was unaware of the script. Namely that his regal mane should end up stuffed on the Longstanton's wall rather than stuffing himself regally with Longstantons.

Their passing was mourned by their flock, which steadfastly followed the particular lion. Diligently collecting its droppings. Taking care at the same time however, not to get too close. The idyllic pair, now inextricably interwoven, were buried in one box under an acacia tree in a simple, if moving service. The local wild life no doubt breathing a heart felt and collective sigh of relief as they got on with life without having to keep one open for stalking Longstantons.

They had however sired a son, one Timothy Longstanton. Timothy had been at junior public school when the news of the untimely end of his parents reached him. Some distant uncle on his father's side had claimed him for his own. If not with any marked degree of enthusiasm. Timothy's upbringing had then in many ways echoed that of his unknown cousin. In as much as he too became the product of a system. A totally different system however from that of Kevin's.

Timothy went from junior prep school to senior prep school to university. Whereas Kevin had plodded, Timothy had utilized the higher parts of his reasoning. Timothy had in fact devoted himself to logic and individual thought. To the extent that Timothy had managed to get someone else to do the work for him throughout his life. Timothy learned and understood the power of bribery, intimidation and blackmail at a very tender age. Timothy had his sights set upon a life of luxury, at someone else's expense naturally. The legacy had dropped into his lap like a gift from the Gods. Timothy immediately could see the potential for such a piece of real estate, and began in his mind to examine how best such a windfall could be exploited to his fullest advantage. Naturally he had claimed the estate for himself and had already begun exploratory feelers with parties whom he considered would be interested. However, now that Kevin had appeared on the scene, his claim was void, and Timothy saw the situation as being one where a usurper to the throne had in fact, stolen his rightful crown. Timothy's well kept and secret plans to convert his legacy into hard cash were all brought to naught. The news of Kevin spelt disaster for Timothy, and in one swoop he saw his dreams of an easy life snatched from his grasp.

Mr. Wilberforce of Boggle and Boggle, whilst informing Kevin that he had a cousin, went no further. He had been unaware that Timothy had schemes for dumping the brewery with all possible alacrity and of moving to South America. There to take up a new identity and exploit his newfound wealth and public school background. What he did tell Kevin was that there was a proviso in the will. A proviso whose terms and conditions had held no qualms for Timothy, as he had planned to grab the money and run. These being that to fulfill the terms and conditions of the will, Kevin had not only to take over the running of the Black Badger, he also had to adopt his late uncle's role as head of the faith, brew beer and cider, grow his hair long, wear an ear ring and live on the premises. Kevin was about to become not only a master brewer, but Lord Grand Master of The Lodge of the Sacred Domain. If Kevin agreed to these terms in writing, then an immediate sum of five thousand pounds would be transferred to his bank account. Kevin agreed. In fact for the princely sum of five thousand pounds, Kevin would have agreed to buy a wig, don the regalia forthwith and dance through Tunbridge Wells if necessary.

Mr. Wilberforce rubbed his hands again and intimated that he and Kevin were about to embark upon a ship of mutual gain. He presented Kevin with numerous and various documents that Kevin obligingly signed, wherever Mr. Wilberforce indicated. Kevin asked no questions. He was still totally bemused by the situation in which he found himself. Since all of his past life had in the main consisted of doing as he was told, he saw no reason not to continue in that vein. Kevin duly signed everything and anything placed in front of him by his solicitor. The last item however did give him cause to hesitate, and almost raise a query. It was Mr. Wilberforce's bill. Kevin had no idea that solicitors were allowed to charge so much. Mr. Wilberforce noted the pause in the up to then smooth flow of signatures. He took time to explain to Kevin that it was tax deductible from the company's profits. He beamed a little when he said this and then produced the company books. Kevin rapidly realized that not only had he acquired 5000 Pounds to his personal account, he had also acquired a seemingly profitable business with land and buildings too, along with one George Stoat, a long-standing employee. George it appeared came with the company as a non-optional extra. In other words, take the legacy and take George as well. He was on the books for life.

Kevin wondered what he would do with an old family retainer. The thought of employing someone filled him with apprehension. There again, as Mr. Wilberforce gently pointed out, George knew how to brew, and like it or not Kevin was now in the brewing trade.

Finally all the paper work was completed and Mr. Wilberforce sat back in his leather chair. The old solicitor was visibly more at ease now. He almost, but not quite hummed. The cat, via some strange lines of feline communication also knew somehow that the work was now completed. It stretched and gave a wide yawn and then jumped onto Mr. Wilberforce's desk and presented itself for attention. Mr. Wilberforce was quite obviously pleased. No doubt at the thought of all the possible lines of future litigation that were opening up for him. He tickled the cat's neck and the cat rubbed its head against him. Then suddenly the cat crossed the desk and jumped down into Kevin's lap. Kevin stroked the cat. He liked animals. Animals wanted attention and in return gave attention. Kevin had always longed for a dog. He would have settled for a cat, even a budgie, but the terms of his lease forbade the keeping of pets. Anyway Marlene detested all animals. She claimed that they made her itch and sneeze. The cat purred and settled itself down comfortably into Kevin's lap.

"Ah!

She likes you." Declared Mr. Wilberforce. "Do you like cats?" He asked, polishing his bifocals energetically with a large, if slightly grey handkerchief. He looked up expectantly.

"Yes." Said Kevin firmly. "I do, but I have never had one. The lease. On my bed-sit." He tailed off lamely, feeling somehow that it was his fault.

"Never mind young man. You can have as many cats as you like now. Probably own a few already in fact." He smiled benignly at Kevin, adding, "She's a good judge of character is old Asprophe."

"Err pardon?"

"Astrophy, that ball of purring fur on your lap."

"Oh the cat." Exclaimed Kevin, "I see. Um, why do you call your cat Astrophy?"

"Exactly!" Nodded Mr. Wilberforce. "Oh don't look so down, lots of people have asked the same question. But like I said, she's a good judge of character, and she likes you. Yes, we will get on just fine together. She wasn't too keen on that cousin of yours though." He left the statement hanging in mid air.

Kevin realized that he was supposed to take up the cue. "Why was that then Mr. Wilberforce?" But Mr. Wilberforce had produced a pocket watch and he was looking at it intently. "Good Heavens!" He exclaimed, "Is that the time? Time for lunch young man. Now where were you thinking of taking your solicitor for lunch then?"

Kevin hadn't actually thought of taking him anywhere and must have looked blank as Mr. Wilberforce prompted him. "Tax deductible you know." He nodded his head. "All you have to do is take a careful note of all expenses and send the receipts in to me once a month. I will take care of them. Don't worry you have an excellent accountant."

"Do I?" Asked Kevin, open-mouthed. "Of course. I tell you what, seeing as old Astrophy has taken such a shine to you, why don't I just give Bernstein and Shultz a tinkle and then you can take us both for lunch and you will get to know your accountant too." He picked up the phone and dialed a number. He held a short conversation, the outcome of which was that they would all meet in some restaurant.

Kevin began to feel more and more anxious. He tried surreptitiously counting what little money he had whilst it was still in his pocket. A fruitless and pointless exercise as he knew full well that the most it would run to would have been a pint and a sandwich in a cheap pub. There was nothing for it; he had to admit that he held insufficient funds. Nervously he said. "I'm very sorry Mr. Wilberforce but I didn't really expect all of this and I don't think that I have enough cash on me." He felt not only acutely embarrassed but guilty and ashamed too. He realized that he rather liked old Mr. Wilberforce and his scruffy and rather down at heel manner. He felt comfortable with him. Far more so he realized than if he had been dealing with some smart button down, up market model. He also liked the cat.

"Dear me, dear me." Clucked Mr. Wilberforce, "We new young capitalists, captains of industry and all that don't let little things like worry us."

"Don't we?" Enquired Kevin, now even more bemused with the newfound circumstances into which he fallen, "What do we do, I mean they do, or I do?" He shook his head in confusion

"Plastic?" Said Mr. Wilberforce kindly. "You do have a bank card I take it?" "Yes." Declared Kevin firmly, "But I never go into debt." He added equally firmly.

Mr. Wilberforce laughed. It was more of an elfish tinkle than a full-bellied laugh. "I don't think that even old Manni Bernstein and I together could eat and drink our way through five thousand pounds at one sitting dear boy. Don't worry, we won't break the bank. No point in killing golden geese etc. Oh, and it's tax deductible! I'll call a cab. You have no transport either I take it?"

Kevin shook his head and felt his face redden. "I may not even have enough for the cab fare, Mr. Wilberforce." He admitted sadly.

"Not to worry dear boy. I'll manage that, my treat to seal our new and long lasting partnership." He beamed some more. "Now you listen to Manni and follow his advice. Listen to me and follow mine. Listen to old George and follow his. Then you must read up on that religion of your "uncles" and maintain all of that. Add a bit too, if you feel like." He suddenly leaned forward over the desk and his voice and face took on a very serious tone. "That is very important, you understand, the religion bit?"

Kevin nodded, not knowing what Mr. Wilberforce was talking about. The cat stopped purring. Mr. Wilberforce must have picked up Kevin's slight hesitation, or maybe it was just the cat ceasing its loud purr. "The religion Kevin, it all hangs on the religion. The brewing, the sales, everything. You have to maintain the religion." He said very deliberately and seriously. "You did agree, and signed the documents. If not, then you lose the lot and that cousin of yours will inherit. We wouldn't want that now would we?" He looked at Kevin in a kindly and expectant way.

Having just become to his mind rich, the last thing Kevin wanted was to loose everything. He shook his head firmly.

Mr. Wilberforce beamed again and relaxed back into his chair. "Good, good." He sighed. "Just listen to old George and follow his advice. That way we will all get along just fine and everyone will be happy. In fact it will be business as usual." He beamed even more brightly at Kevin. "I can see that we will get along swimmingly. Not like that cousin of yours." A sudden dark look crossed his face. "Astrophy took one look and was off. Wouldn't stay in the same room as the fellow. Still that's all over now. He is, as the TV likes to say, history. Still Manni and I will tell you more over lunch. I'll call that cab."

The restaurant chosen was rather swish and overlooked a large swathe of grass, a sort of village green. Manni Bernstein was of about the same age as Mr. Wilberforce, but small, lean and very dark skinned. He reminded Kevin of some East End tailors with whom he had come into contact. Kevin had never been inside an up market restaurant before and the price of the food horrified him. Still, he reasoned, it's all tax deductible.

Manni and Mr. Wilberforce were obviously old friends, comrades in arms is how Mr. Wilberforce described themselves. They poured over the menu and ordered wine. Kevin just nodded at their suggestions. He had never eaten lobster before. He began to think that given a very short space of time he would come to terms with his new life style and enjoy it too. He wasn't used to wine and began to feel a little heady. Mr. Bernstein was telling him the history behind his late "uncle's" enterprise. It all seemed to hang on the religious hook. The brewing and Black Badger Inn all dependant upon his late uncle's observance of his strange creed. Without the religion, then all else fell too. It followed then that Kevin had to observe its rites and ceremonies. As it would appear that he was the only long-term follower, then he was free to add little improvements to the act of worship, but by and large, he was confined to past practice and procedure. "So young man, your first official ceremony will be Spring Rites." Offered Manni. "What does that entail?" Asked Kevin, feeling the need now to use big words.

"Mostly dressing up in ceremonial robes, then casting them off and dancing naked around a bonfire, as far I could ever ascertain. Oh, with an acolyte too, female gender." He nodded significantly. "I suppose that you do have someone with whom you can persuade to indulge in these ceremonies? It is important. I mean we could just hire a few babes for the night so to speak, but the local council is on to that one. Then that would invalidate the ceremony so to speak. We could be on a legal sticky wicket on that one. No you need some one you know. Your girl friend or something. Shouldn't be too difficult for a young fellow like you." He looked at Kevin hopefully.

Kevin immediately considered Marlene. She might not be too keen on prancing around a bonfire with local council officials looking on to check her validity so to speak. There again, she would be getting her marriage and house and a future too in return. Kevin nodded firmly, the wine giving him confidence. "Oh yes I have a young lady in mind." He declared firmly. He had taken a cigar when the waiter had offered a box and now, though a life long non-smoker, he puffed away at it expansively. His affirmation that he could supply nude, nubile dancing maidens to order seemed to place the minds of both Manni and Mr. Wilberforce at ease. The conversation turned to that of his mysterious cousin, Timothy Longstanton.

Timothy Longstanton had made a bad impression upon both Mr. Wilberforce and Manni Bernstein. He was not a person to be trusted apparently. The two gentlemen were of the opinion that Timothy would have grabbed what he could and ran. Thus leaving both themselves and the family retainer George Stoat high and dry. No; there was a nice little earner simmering away down in Westfordshire and all that it required was a legal heir who would continue in the family tradition. Namely brewing excise free alcohol, and undertaking odd religious ceremonies. Then there was money enough for all.

On a regular basis the local council or HMG attempted to break the stranglehold franchise that the Black Badger Inn held by attempting to point out where protocol had been ignored. To date however, all such actions had failed and the counter actions had been both successful and profitable. There was enough for all so long as no one rocked the boat. Timothy had been viewed as a positive ship wrecker. So with his head reeling from wine, cigar smoke and the whirlwind speed at which events were unfolding, Kevin left his Solicitor and accountant and having signed for the meal, was dropped off at the bus station. There to return to his bed-sit and reflect upon the strange turn that his life had suddenly taken.

CHAPTER: 2

Marlene was at one of life's cross roads. Kevin was to put it bluntly, a drag. Marlene could see that Kevin would never earn sufficient to enable him to keep Marlene in the style in to which she wished to become accustomed. There was the sex thing too. She felt that she could not confide in her mother. Her mother was a person who always worked upon the principle that a bird in the hand is better than.... and she was also unaware of Kevin's sexual failings. She would have stuck with Kevin as Kevin was so to speak, on the table. Why then throw the meal away, even if it was not too exciting and risk having to go down to the butchers again and sort out another piece of meat? Now however, Roger had appeared on the scene. Roger was the manager of the industrial cleaning team that was employed by the supermarket. Roger was twenty-seven and this was his first posting as a full-blown team controller. Roger's work consisted of coordinating his team of third world national bucket pushers and making sure that each location was sanitized as per contract. Which is certainly at least one step up from that of cleaning the place oneself. Roger played ruby. Roger owned a second hand car. Roger rented a small flat. Roger obviously had prospects.

Roger was also not unaware of Marlene's batting eyelids. Consequently, Roger had slipped Marlene a surreptitious, if not too subtle note. Indicating that he, Roger would not be too averse to slipping into her. He had asker he to telephone him. Marlene had done so. The conversation culminating in Marlene agreeing to meet Roger for a drink. The outcome of that tryst being not only a drink but a trip on to, "Some little club" Roger knew. Then followed a night of unbridled and from Marlene's point of view long frustrated lust, in Roger's bed. Should she now give Kevin the big E and move in with Roger, endeavoring to become with child ASAP. Or should she revert to her fiancé Kevin? To Marlene's mind there was no competition. Jolly Roger and his crew of mop swinging brigands held the day. Kevin was about to be blown away. The question was not so much one of should this course of action be prosecuted as one of how and most expediently? Kevin unwittingly and obligingly supplied the answer.

Kevin's trip to Tunbridge Wells not only gave him an inheritance it also left him with a second legacy. An unwanted second legacy courtesy of both tobacco and alcohol. Kevin had both a bad head and a bad stomach. He did not contact Marlene upon his return. Which was just as well as Marlene was once again romping around Roger's bed and making up for the wasted years. She had taken the precaution of removing Kevin's ring and having made up her mind to now remove Kevin, she phoned him at work and arranged to meet him in Mac Donald's that same evening.

Kevin had given long and careful thought as to how he would broach the matter of not only having Marlene move out of London. A prospect that he knew would not appeal. The "Countryside" in Marlene's view being a boring place full of dangerous animals such as cows. Dirty creatures from which milk came out of unhygienic udders, rather than nice clean bottles that were displayed upon the shelves of her place of employment. In addition, joints of meat wore heavy fur coats and wandered around unpredictably, rather than remaining static, sitting in a refrigerator done up appealingly in clear plastic wrap. No, to the Marlines' of this world, the countryside was full of flies, bugs, dirt and frighteningly empty green space. It was in a word, uncivilized. Kevin also wrestled with the other problem. That of the dancing naked around a bonfire bit. Kevin felt that the actual nakedness would be less of a problem for Marlene than the fact that Marlene would have to be barefoot on the grass. Well perhaps a pair of Wellington boots might be allowed giving Marlene's phobia to all things natural and terror of all things creepy. That certain town and or county councilors may be surreptitiously looking on. Kevin reasoned that they would choose to do so with discretion. So accordingly so would wish to remain hidden from view. On the basis of what the mind doesn't know, doesn't bother it, Kevin decided to leave that item out of the conversation for the moment. Best cross that bridge if and when he came to it. He could in all honesty claim that they were being spied upon, their religious ceremony interrupted and debased and no doubt Mr. Wilberforce would have a field day. So Kevin decided that first of all he would approach Marlene direct. If she demurred, then he would tell her about the inheritance. At that point he realized he would also have to explain about having to move to The Black Badger. Well maybe there was room for Marlene's mother too, perhaps that would be his trump card. Kevin was at heart was a kindly soul and had never thought to question if in fact he should marry Marlene. Marlene had after all chosen him and Marlene had a mother. To Kevin they were one and the same. Take one, take both.

Kevin met Marlene as arranged in Mac Donald's. Marlene seemed not to be at her ease, though reluctant to explain why. Kevin ordered the obligatory burgers and chips, along with fizzy drinks, not forgetting to collect various small sealed packets of tomato ketchup. Marlene had a fondness for tomato ketchup and if left to her own devices would smother everything on her plate with it. Kevin fussed around the plates and cardboard packets of fast food, finally sitting down himself. Marlene remained silent, as if wrapped in her own thoughts. Kevin, though having given the matter some considerable thought, had decided that a direct approach would be the best. He had steeled himself up, but confronted with an all but glowering Marlene, he lost some of his nerve at the last moment. He half wondered if by some odd quirk of fate if somehow Marlene had got wind of what he was about to propose. He was, he realized about to ask Marlene to leave her mother, her job at the supermarket and marry him. Not only that but to move out of her beloved London and take up residence in the countryside. There to embark upon a new life under circumstances that were unexplored territory for both of them. There was also the small matter of the rather odd requirements that also went along with the job. He considered now that bearing the above in mind, perhaps an oblique course would be more in order.

"Er, Marlene." He began. "I've sort of got this opportunity to move out of London."

Marlene who was at a loss as to how to go about breaking off her engagement to lackluster and no future Kevin if favor of glamorous and go getter Roger. Whilst at the same time maintaining the moral high ground saw her point of attack immediately. "What do you mean, sort of?" She said in a belittling tone. Then paused, adding, "Why do you want to move out of London?" She paused again waiting, her curiosity for the moment overcoming her assault strategy. "Move where?" She prompted.

"To the West country."

"Doing what?" Marlene just for one fleeting second decided not to burn all of her bridges.

Kevin considered his answer. Obviously Marlene was opposed to any move from London on principle. She was also in attack and domination mode. Attitudes that Kevin had never mastered. He could see that this was not going to be any easy task. He realized that he had lulled himself into a sense of false security. Persuading Marlene was going to be far more difficult than he had anticipated. He decided quickly that he had better down play the strings attached to his planned move and concentrate on the more positive aspects. "To run a pub." He exclaimed with a degree of enthusiasm that was not 100% genuine.

"Run a pub!" exclaimed Marlene in a depreciating and querulous tone, "What do you know about running pubs?"

Kevin felt vulnerable. "Not too much." He had to admit, "But I can learn." He added brightly. He smiled hopefully at Marlene. His smile was not returned by his fiancée.

Marlene now felt a self-righteous surge of confidence. She made an onslaught on Kevin's weakest point. His sense of self-confidence. "Who in their right mind is going to put you in charge of a pub Kevin?" she stated with distain. "Let's be sensible about this. All you know about is sitting in front of a computer screen and juggling with spare parts for cars. You don't even know what the parts are for and you couldn't fit them if someone gave you the tools. Now you tell me you are going to run a pub. You couldn't run an ice cream van." She paused for just long enough for her scathing comments to register, but not long enough for Kevin to mount a defense. She leaned forward and pointing her plastic fork at Kevin in a very threatening manner to emphasize he point, she continued. "Anyway don't for one minute think that I will spend the rest of my life with you serving beer to a bunch of drunken yokels and swilling down lavatories, because I won't. So if you want to run some pub out in the back of beyond;" She breathed a heavy and scathing breath. "God alone knows where. You can. But you can count me out!" Marlene felt almost vindicated in her viewpoint and sat back in the chair contented that she now had the whole situation well in hand.

Kevin was confused. Things were not going to his script. He had expected some reluctance on Marlene's behalf true, but he also expected to have been allowed to place his position on the table too. He wanted to highlight the strong points. Whatever they were. Marlene had taken up a position of total opposition and domination without letting him state the facts, massaged or otherwise. He decided on another approach. "Hang on Marlene, let me explain." Explanations however were the last thing Marlene wanted to listen too. Kevin had offered her an opening, now she was going in for the kill. Kevin was obviously about to embark upon some hair brained scheme that he had read about in some Sunday supplement. A scheme for which he was not only totally unqualified but patently unsuited too. Kevin could not be allowed to run down to the shops safely, let alone run a pub. Here was Marlene's chance to rid herself of him once and for all. The thought of Roger became even more appealing. Marlene went for the throat. In a superior tone, and gathering her self together at the same time, she declared in a loud and very firm voice "I'm not interested in listening to any explanations Kevin Firkettle." She arose from her chair in almost regal manner. "I am not going to live with you in some country pub and that's final."

"But you don't understand Marlene. This is very important, I have to go there." Kevin looked up at his bristling fiancée and knew that he was sinking fast. He tried one last desperate effort to appeal to Marlene's better nature. He might just as well have asked a fox politely to replace the chicken and smooth down its feathers.

"Fine, then you go by yourself my lad!" With wonderful drama she removed her engagement ring and let it drop onto the plastic tabletop. It spun there and then dropped off onto the floor. Kevin bent down to retrieve it and when he had, Marlene was already half way out of the door.

Kevin felt very embarrassed. He felt as if everyone in the restaurant was looking at him. In point of fact no one was. Alternatively, if they were it was only with passing interest. Should he dash after Marlene? He was undecided and naturally the longer he remained there, the greater became the distance between them. Kevin also felt very alone in the world and depressed. He was at a loss as what to do. He was committed to going to the West Country by the terms of his inheritance. He had accepted the 5000 Pounds. Some of which he had already spent on an expensive meal. Kevin decided to remove himself from Mac Donald's and attempt to clear his brain. He needed to assimilate this new turn of events. Life was moving far too fast for his liking. Kevin wanted to be quiet, but the thought of his empty bed-sit did not appeal either. So, mustering as much dignity as he could and slipping the ring into his pocket, Kevin walked out of Mac Donald's with a view of finding some place quiet where he could collect his thoughts and plan his best course of action. Kevin walked, the early spring night was fresh, and the sky clear. He walked, with no particular direction in mind as he considered what to do. He was committed to the terms of his late "uncle's" will. It followed then that he had to leave London. Marlene was totally opposed to such an idea. He also had a very desperate need for someone to take the lead part and star in the nude dancing role. He had considered that Marlene would not be too happy about that but now he had no one. Furthermore he did not feel that he had any prospects of finding anyone. Should he place an add. in a newsagent's window? Mr. Wilberforce had cautioned against enlisting the services of persons unknown. What was he to do? He had absolutely no idea. Kevin also realized that under the terms of his inheritance if he didn't come up with the goods, and fast, then he was going to find himself heavily in debt. Debt worried him, he squirmed inside. He mentally ran over the cost of the meal, wine and cigars and shuddered. Kevin realized with a start that he was more concerned with his inheritance than the fact that he had just had his fiancée walk out on him. Kevin gave that some thought, and felt sad. In fact Kevin began to feel very sorry for himself. He could see that no only had he lost Marlene, he was about to loose The Black Badger too. Kevin wandered on, deep in melancholy thoughts, oblivious to direction, passers by and traffic.

Kevin had walked; wandered would have been a better description, for well over an hour and he now found himself on Hungerford Bridge. He stopped in the middle of the bridge and leaning over the railing looked down into the dark Thames water rushing below. The tide was flowing swiftly out to sea. The streetlights were reflected in the black and rapidly flowing water. Kevin wondered wildly just where a sealed bottle thrown into those waters would land. On some far distant shore? He found himself thinking of palm-fringed beaches and white sun lit sands. Perhaps if he jumped into the Thames he too would end up on some exotic beach. No such luck, he realized. More like his bloated, dirty and grossly swollen body would be washed ashore on to the mud banks of Erith Marches. There to be pecked at by the gulls until someone noticed it. If in fact anyone ever did notice it or, if they did, bothered to report the fact. Kevin was not a very good swimmer. In fact Kevin realized that he wasn't very good at anything. He thought that he couldn't have been a very attractive baby, and must have failed even at that early age. Why else would his mother wish to leave him in rubbish skip of all things? His job was uninteresting. His life was uninteresting. He would never have been able to save sufficient for a small house. Not that it mattered much now, as he had no reason for buying such a home. The thought of a cozy home made him feel even more depressed. What was worse was that now, for the first time in his life that he had any prospects; they too were being snatched away from him. He hadn't even been able to hang on to Marlene. He hadn't even been able to explain to her, such were his inadequacies. Kevin had no idea what to do and he had no one to turn to for help or advice. Kevin knew at that moment that he was totally alone in the world. No one cared for him, and he was a failure. Even when things were handed to him on a plate, he still could not get his act together and become an organized person. The Thames began to look positively inviting.

"If you are going to jump, give me your loose change before you go." Kevin became aware of someone standing beside him.

"Er, sorry."

"I said. If you are going to jump. Can I have your loose change please? It's a waste otherwise and I'm hungry."

The owner of the voice was a small, young and skinny looking girl with long brown hair. She was dressed in a blue denim jacket, jeans and trainers. Kevin was again at a total loss. "I wasn't going to jump." He declared hotly.

"Huh! I've seen black holes looking brighter than you pal." The girl, who would have been around eighteen, rubbed her denim-clad arm across her snub nose, and sniffed loudly. Kevin couldn't make out if she had a cold or was making some social comment with regard to himself. "Well?" asked the girl. "Are you going to jump or not? I can't hang about here all night." Kevin felt as if he were taking part in some surreal film. He couldn't get a grip on reality. "Do you usually hang around bridges waiting for people to jump and ask them for their loose change?" Kevin hadn't realized that suicide could be so popular. He had a sudden vision of lines of people patiently waiting their turn to jump and this odd little, elfin like girl tugging at their coats as they teetered on the edge of the rail and eternity.

"No! Of course not. It's just I'm a bit down on my luck too and thought if you were about to take a dive then you might as well give me your loose change. What sort of a wrist watch have you got?" Kevin, being conditioned, as he was to comply with demands, obligingly showed her. "Huh! Cheap old thing, still, better than nothing. Got anything else of value?"

Kevin suddenly felt overwhelmingly sad. "An engagement ring."

"Oh!" said the small creature, visibly brightening, "I'll have that." "No you won't!" Exclaimed Kevin defensively.

"Well it 'aint going to be much use to you down there and fish don't wear them. I could hock it for cash and get something to eat." She sounded accusing, "Let's have a look at it then."

For once Kevin felt that he had been pushed too far. "No" He declared firmly, realizing that perhaps for the first time in his life he had made a decision that contradicted a demand made upon him. The small girl sniffed again. "Why did you want to jump then?"

"I never said that I did!"

"OK. So let's assume that if you were going to jump, then why? Not of course that you were about to do such a thing. I mean, like have you eaten?" "Yes." Agreed Kevin.

"And do you have a place to sleep?"

"Yes." Kevin had to agree again.

"And have you got any money?" Again Kevin had to nod his head. He began to feel a little foolish.

"So, let's examine your situation. By the way, is the law after you or have you just committed some heinous crime?" Kevin shook his head to both questions.

"Right then. Full stomach, place to sleep, money in pocket, 'aint just murdered his mother with a meat axe, and the law 'aint after him. Oh, yes, one other. Have you got some incurable disease?" Again Kevin shook his head. "So why the bloody Hell do you want to jump off the bridge then?" She looked up at him in obvious amazement and shook back a stray wisp of hair.

"It's a long story." Said Kevin defensively.

"Ah! So you were about to do a flyer then." Her small pert face, devoid of make up took on a self-congratulatory air.

"Yes. No. I don't know!" Kevin was confused.

"What's your name?" She had asked him in a gentle voice that somehow conveyed a genuine desire to know rather that being just a formality.

"Kevin. Kevin Firkettle."

She scratched at the side of her mouth with an index finger that was all but swallowed up in the sleeve of the oversize jacket as if considering this piece of information. "Funny name that." She said finally, "Still I'm Vicki. Vicki Heart. Pleased to meet you Kevin Firkettle." She offer him her diminutive hand and said at the same time, "Now seeing as how I have just saved your life, in a manner of speaking and I'm hungry. Furthermore you have some long story to tell. How about you and I finding some nice little Indian curry house, and you buy your aunty Vicki a plate of curried chicken and rice and tell me all about it?" Without waiting for an answer she linked her small arm through his and led him away from the railing and the swirling waters beneath. They walked in silence for a while, Kevin finding that he had to measure his much longer step against hers. Marlene had never wanted to hold hands in public; Vicki appeared to fit with ease into the crook of his elbow. "Where do you live?" Vicki asked him breaking the silence.

"Camberwell." Answered Kevin, "Camberwell Crescent actually."

"So why are we walking to the north of the river? Daft that." She sort of swung him around in mid step and retraced their steps back over the bridge. "Cheaper south of the river anyway." She declared as if that explained everything. They continued walking in silence.

At the end of the bridge they wandered until they found a curry house. Vicki examined the menu displayed outside. "Not too exciting, still it will do. Oh, I never thought to ask if you liked curry. Not that it matters, you have eaten anyway, come on." And with Kevin mumbling something about liking curry she bundled them both into the cheap and rather down at heel restaurant. She chose a table and indicated that Kevin should sit down too. "Take your anorak off." She ordered, "Let's have a look at you." Kevin did so without a murmer. Cor! Not much there to feed the fish on is there? You sure that you have eaten? I mean like this year?" She laughed. It was an infectious giggle and again she brushed away the loose hairs that constantly fell over her face.

Kevin felt defensive and also strangely dominant. "OK Rambo, take that denim jacket off and let's have a look at Miss Universe. It's too big anyway."

"Yes" She agreed, smiling, "But I got it second hand in a charity shop." She removed it and Kevin saw that she was wearing a thick knit grey, polo neck jumper that also seemed to be too large. She saw him looking at it and nodded her head. "Yep, I think the person that owned the jacket owned the jumper too. Still it's warm, and I might be glad of that later to night." The waiter, a rather unhygienic looking individual from the sub continent, wandered over and in a disinterested manner and placed two equally grubby looking menus on the table in front of them.

"Chicken curry, rice and garlic narn bread." Said Vicki without bothering to pick up the menu. The waiter nodded, and looked expectantly at Kevin.

"The same." Kevin said quickly, feeling embarrassed.

"Drinks?" Asked the waiter in an disinterested tone. He chewed at the nail of a none too clean index finger of his right hand. Vicki looked at Kevin. Kevin looked at Vicki. "Nah!" She said. "Too expensive in these places, we'll nip round the pub afterwards." She handed the waiter back the menus and dismissed him with a sort of a shrug. He wandered unenthusiastically off back towards the kitchen area.

"Not exactly your wild swinging scene and food fare of Europe is it?" Vicki looked around the dingy restaurant. They were the only patrons. The decor was grubby red flock wallpaper and the paint was grimy. A couple of very sad and the worst for wear pictures of elephants and turbaned people waving what looked like large umbrellas, decorated the walls. Along with adverts for mini cabs. "Don't suppose they get much trade until the pubs shut." Said Vicki, taking in the surroundings. "Well Kevin, you certainly know how to impress a girl on her first date." She laughed her infectious laugh again and Kevin grudgingly warmed towards her. He began to take stock of her and she noticed.

"Fun sized." She said, "You know, like little mars bars." She made a face and wobbled her head, smiling as she did so. "Don't you really have anywhere to sleep?" Asked Kevin genuinely.

"No. And don't go getting any fancy ideas about slipping me into your bed and slipping yourself into me." She gave him a quizzical look and wagged an admonishing finger.

"I wasn't." Said Kevin, feeling accused. "I just wondered, that's all. Why? What happened?"

"OK." She agreed. "Seeing as how you are buying the food, I'll tell my tale of woe first. Then we will decide whose tale is the worst and the winner gets to jump off the bridge. Deal?"

"I'm not so sure about the jumping bit."

"Coo! Haven't we moved on?" Her face became serious and she adopted a tourist guide type of voice. "Tajh Mahal Restaurant. Gateway to sanity. One hundred meters but light years away from Hungerford Bridge." She laughed again. Kevin began to realize that her demeanor was infectious. She also had a cute smile. He studied her closer. She was small, tiny almost. Her nose was a mere snub and her hair brown and long. Again she caught him looking at her. "Look all you like." She said impishly, "It won't make them grow. Wish it did." She sniffed and stuck out her diminutive chest. Kevin felt embarrassed. "So my story. Right. What can I tell you? Council flats north of the river. About a hundred miles north. Father that used to knock me mum about, oh and me too. Run away at 15. Got caught and returned. Run away again, but was a bit smarter this time, 'till I met Leroy that is."

"Who's Leroy?" Asked Kevin. He felt a little uneasy and wasn't sure what he was getting into.

"Leroy was half Jamaican."

"What was the other half?" Asked Kevin in all innocence.

"Bleeding evil mate." We used to nip over to Amsterdam and bring back the wakki bakki. Then the police got wind and raided our gaff. They grabbed Leroy but I wasn't in and a friend got the word to me. So I skipped fast and hitched a ride down here. Driver thought that he was on to a good thing, but I managed to persuade him otherwise."

"How did you do that?" Asked Kevin, now all big eyed.

"Easy. I smacked him one with a lump of wood. Then used my last pennies to get into the Smoke and loose myself."

"So you really have no money, haven't eaten and have no where to go!" Kevin was amazed at the small strange creature. She reminded him of a Jack Russell terrier. Small, but not prepared to concede an inch.

"I already told you that. Right that's my tale. Your turn. Oh, hang on the nosh is coming. Best save it until I have stuffed myself. I won't be concentrating otherwise."

Kevin sat back. She was hungry he realized. "I can't really eat all of this." He offered, "Would you like some?" He offered his plate.

"Wish I could Kevin, but I've only got a little stomach. I need to eat little and often. Stick it in a doggy box. I'll eat it for my breakfast. That bread too." She pointed with a loaded fork that was half way to her mouth.

"No need for that." Kevin found himself saying, "Ill make you breakfast."

"Will you now? And just how much is that going to cost me?" She looked at him suspiciously.

"Nothing." Kevin exclaimed. He disliked the implied accusation. "I just thought that since you have no where that the least that I could do would be to put you up for the night. That was all, honestly." He had an almost pleading look on his face.

She laughed. "I believe you sunshine. Thousands wouldn't. But I warn you any funny funny and I'll rip your ears off!"

"I believe you. I really do." He said earnestly and he meant it. He knew instinctively somehow that he had a tiger cub on his hands. However, he also felt protective too. In fact Kevin realized that a completely new bunch of feelings was flooding through his body. He liked the small girl, but at the same time was a little frightened of her. A tiger cub he thought again. She really is like a tiger cub. Vicki was mopping up the last of her curry with the remains of the narn bread. "Right Kevin, will the funds run to half of lager and then I will listen to your tale of sorrow and desperation?" She pushed away her plate and the waiter who had been hovering came over.

"Oh the funds will more than cover it." Said Kevin expansively, producing his credit card and wondering at the same time why he had chosen to say that. Did he have a need to impress Vicki he wondered? Then suddenly he saw that compared to her, he had no problems. Vicki however was looking at him carefully, as if assimilating this new piece of information. She waited quietly and a little vervously as the waiter checked the card. When it was accepted she seemed to relax but remained silent as if waiting for an explanation from Kevin.

Kevin had noticed her anxiety and reassured her, "It's quite Kosher, honest." She continued to look at him from across the table biting her bottom lip as if wanting to believe him. "I'll explain everything to you in the pub." declared Kevin. He stood up and helped Vicki into her jacket. He wanted to put his thoughts together. He found Vicki disturbing whilst at the same time intriguing also he realized that he had not really assimilated his own situation. He thought that maybe if he explained everything to Vicki, then it might at the same time become clearer to himself.

There was a pub close at hand and a rather nice one too. The lounge had secluded tables and Kevin felt relaxed. Vicki wanted half of lager. Kevin sat her down and took her jacket from her. Hanging it carefully on the back of her seat. She looked at him with an odd, and as if perplexed frown on her young face. "Don't frown." Said Kevin, "I'm not about to go through your pockets."

"If you find anything I'll share it with you." She joked. He face lighting up into her impish smile again.

"Perhaps I can share something with you." Kevin found himself saying cryptically.

"Depends on what you want to share." Vicki replied sharply, adding, "I have already warned you."

Kevin felt defensive. "Nothing like that, stop worrying. Let me get the drinks and I will explain." He returned and sat down. "It's like this." He began. I have, sorry, had this fiancée, Marlene. She only likes living in London, but I have to move and she won't move with me."

"So that's why you were about to sling yourself off the bridge?" Vicki looked incredulous. "She can't have loved you Kevin." She added seriously. "Honestly, I know it may not seem like it right now, but you are better off without her." She leaned forward and patted Kevin's arm in a motherly manner. Kevin found himself liking her concern. "No, there is more to it than that. Like I have never seemed to be able to get anything right. I was an orphan and I never had a home, and I thought that I was going to have one with Marlene. Then I got this inheritance."

"I thought you said that you were an orphan?" Vicki looked suspicious.

"I am. I was. I mean some strange uncle died and left me all of his money and business. However, to inherit it I have to move to some equally strange village in the West Country. It's pub, you see." He ended lamely.

"Hang on Kevin. Let me see if I have this right? You were brought up in an orphanage, right?" Kevin nodded. "Then out of the blue you find that you had some rich uncle who snuffs it, leaving you all of his worldly. Considerable worldly?" Kevin nodded again. "But to collect the bank roll, you have to move out of London, right so far?" Kevin continued to nod. "Then this bird of yours Marlene, don't want to move and gives you the Big E?" Kevin nodded his agreement." So you contemplates learning to swim in concrete Wellingtons?

.... It's a bloody psychoanalyst you need mate, not midnight swimming lessons. Gawd Almighty!" Vicki exploded, "Spends all his life with nothing, except some dumb bird. Gets a great wallop of money slung at him, along with a country pub no less and wants to top himself. The prosecution rests its case Me-Lud. It's the Looney bin you need Kevin Firkettle and that's straight. Christ If I had been your bird I would have moved to The South Pole!"

"Would you have? Honestly?"

"Too bloody true mate!"

"There's a bit more to it than that."

"I'm listening."

"Well there is this other cousin, Timothy Longstanton. I'm first in line, but if I don't follow the terms of the will exactly, then he will get to inherit, instead of me."

"So follow the terms of the will, dummy!" she looked at him with an exasperated face.

"That's were the problem arises." Complained Kevin, looked hopeless again.

"I'm still listening."

"Well this uncle of mine had some charter that allowed him to brew and sell beer without paying revenue to the Tax Man. This is all tied up with some strange religion that he headed. Providing I follow the customs and practices of the religion, then I too get to brew the beer, oh, and cider and sell it."

"Ah, and you don't know how to brew beer? Is that the problem?"

"No, not exactly. There is some old boy employed down there too and he is apparently the master brewer. No there seems to be no problem there. It's something else and I have accepted 5000 Pounds on account that I will undertake the terms and conditions of the will."

"So do just that Kevin!" Vicki was getting even more exasperated and showing her confusion.

"I have to get my ear pierced." Exclaimed Kevin as if that explained everything.

Vickie looked at him as if he was some alien life form. Then she leaned over the table and patted his hand in a comforting manner. "It doesn't hurt Kevin, honest. Anyway" She quipped, "It could be worse. Circumcision for instance or castration even." She grinned at him.

"It's not the ear ring that bother me." Said Kevin in an exasperated tone. "It's the religion bit Vicki. I have to dance naked around some bonfire."

"Bloody Hell Kevin! Exploded Vicki. "For all you have at stake, do it! Even if CNN and ITV are there with a satellite link. You can't be that shy! Christ, buy a plastic donger, if you are embarrassed, and glue it on!"

"It's not me I'm bothered about." Kevin almost wailed, "I have to have a partner. A female partner."

Vicki seemed stuck for words. "So hire one you dope!" She finally managed to splutter.

"I can't Vicki. It has to be some one I know. I can't just put an add. in the corner shop. So, no partner equals no inheritance equals having to pay back the 5000 Pounds. Now do you see my problem? Marlene wouldn't do it."

"Did you ask her?"

"Well, no, err, not exactly. She didn't give me time. As soon as I mentioned moving out of London she slung the ring back and dumped me." Kevin sat back in his chair looking hopeless. Vicki looked at him with a slight frown decorating her pert face. "Let me see the ring Kevin." Kevin dug into his pocket and passed the ring over the table to her.

Vicki placed it on the third finger of her left hand and stretched out her hand examining it. "Nice." She murmured. "Too big. Podgy fingers that fiancée of your has." "Yes." agreed Kevin grudgingly, "She has a bit more meat on her than you have."

Vicki looked at the ring on her hand for while, saying nothing. As if sizing up the situation. Finally she closed her hand and leaning over the table asked Kevin in a quiet voice, "How many people know her and also know you and about the legacy?"

"No one." Answered Kevin immediately. "That was why I wondering if you see your way clear to helping me and then I could help........" He tailed off hopelessly.

Vicki sat back in her chair and looking squarely into Kevin's face said bluntly, "Let me see Mr. Kevin Firkettle. I think that you are proposing that I substitute as your fiancée, move down to where ever with you. Get my kit off and dance naked around some dodgy bonfire in the moonlight. That way you get to keep the pub and all that goes with it. Right?"

Kevin looked embarressed and muttered, "The thought had sort of crossed my mind."

"All this on the basis that you bought me a plate of curried chicken in some scruffy cafe and half of lager?" Vicki looked astonished.

"I suppose so Vicki." Mumbled Kevin miserably. Kevin was dropping deeper into despair. "I didn't know what else to do. I didn't mean any harm honestly. I wouldn't have tried anything else. I like you. I think you are nice."

"Think I'm bloody easy more like." Replied Vicki tartly, but she had an impish glint in her eye. A glint that Kevin in his anxiety didn't notice. He took her at face value. She continued in the same admonishing tone, "You have some nerve, you have!"

"No Vicki, really. My intentions were honorable. "Protested a now floundering Kevin.

"Honorable he says!" Vicki wagged a small and delicate finger at him, "And then he suggests a bit of woodland romping!" She sat back and waited but Kevin just squirmed in his seat. Vicki again looked at the ring, extending her left hand and turning it slightly so that the stones glinted. She looked up and in a matter of fact voice enquired. "What do I get out of all of this then. Apart from a nasty cold and stinging nettles on my bum!" Vicki was openly smiling now, but Kevin hadn't noticed, such was his anguish.

"I don't know, I hadn't thought that far ahead. What do you want?" Kevin's voice was taking on a tone of desperation.

"I quite like the ring." She said, and turned her small hand in and out of the light some more.

"You can keep it." Stated Kevin firmly.

Vicki looked at him and grinned and quickly added, "That and three square meals a day. Some new clothes, oh and a bit of makeup and a little rucksack.

"A rucksack?" asked Kevin, with a bemused look on his face.

"For the clothes Kevin." explained Vicki as if talking to a three year old. "I only have these." She held up her small arms adding, "Unless you fancy slipping back to my place and dodging the Dope Squad to collect my gear? No I thought you wouldn't. You are learning Kevin Firkettle." She sat back, then added as an after thought. "Oh and five hundred quid and no hanky panky. Deal?"

"You mean that you will do it?.... Really?" Kevin was obviously taken aback.

"Well let's put it this way. You take me back to your place. Let me have a bath and swill out my naughties, and then very much depending upon how you behave yourself, you have a surrogate fiancée. By that I mean in spirit only. I have no intention of throwing in my body too, small as it is." She offered her hand across the table. "Shake partner." She said. Kevin duly shook the small outstretched hand.

They drank up and with Vicki hooked into Kevin's arm headed for a bus stop. "You know Kevin." Vicki stated seriously, "It's a relative cosmology in which we dwell."

"Pardon?"

"I said. It's a relative......"

"Yes, I heard what you said. I just wondered what you meant."

"I meant that I once saw a programmed on TV. A documentary about these Indians living in the Amazon. One Indian said that all he really wanted in life was an aluminum cooking pot and a decent machete. Sort of puts things into perspective don't it?" "I didn't realize that you were a philosopher Vicki."

"Ah you have lots to learn yet my son." She looked up at him and laughed. "I'm going to have to put some cotton around this ring. That, or never open my left hand again. You know Kevin, you're a right little ladies man you are. Dump some poor maiden, and get engaged to another all within half an hour and even use you same ring too. I can see that I'm going to have to watch out for you and your smooth talking." She hit him playfully and Kevin laughed ruefully too.

The bus dropped them off at Camberwell Green and they crossed the road and entered Camberwell Crescent. Large Georgian houses, three stories high lined each side of the street. "Here." Said Kevin, indicating one of the houses that was pretty well indistinguishable from any of its neighbors. They went inside and Kevin unlocked his bed-sit.

"Oh very salubrious Kevin Firkettle." Vicki surveyed the untidy scene that confronted her. "Yes, I keep meaning to tidy up, but there seems no point."

"Yes Kevin. Right first things first. Got any clean sheets?"

"Yes." "That's a good start. where are you going to sleep Kevin?"

"On the floor I suppose." Kevin decided that if he moved the table a little then he could fit in between it and the dinerette.

"Good. Got any toothpaste? I have my own brush." Kevin nodded. "Clean towels? Shampoo, soap, Soap powder?" Kevin nodded again. "How about an old shirt?"

"An old shirt?" Kevin was obviously confused.

"Yes Kevin. A clean, shirt. These are the only clothes that I possess. I want to have a bath, wash my clothes and go to sleep. So a nice clean shirt would be ace. Tomorrow I will take a sub from you and buy some little girly things, like we agreed. OK?"

"Yes." Agreed Kevin He liked the way that Vicki took charge of things. Kevin was not good with open-ended situations. He found a plaid shirt with long sleeves and handed it to Vicki. "This OK? Vicki?"

"That will do the trick nicely Mr. Firkettle. Now point me in the direction of the bathroom and I will ablute myself." "Whilst you do what?"

"Have swill Kevin, have a swill." When Vicki returned, wearing the shirt and a towel wrapped around her waist and carrying her meager washing, Kevin had made up the bed and a place for himself on the floor. "Off you go Kevin, and don't forget to clean your teeth. She smiled at him mischievously, and Kevin did as he was told, without demur.

Vicki was in bed when Kevin returned; he turned out the light and tried to make himself comfortable on the floor. He felt cold and the floor was very hard. He thought that perhaps next day he would invest in a simple camp bed and a sleeping bag, meanwhile there was nothing to be done except make the best of it. Kevin was used to making the best of it. He wriggled, trying to find a better position. There were none.

"Are you alright?" Vicki's voice questioned him from the bed above him.

"Yes." Lied Kevin.

"Isn't it cold and hard down there?"

"Just a bit, but I will manage for tonight. Tomorrow I will buy a sleeping bag and a simple camp bed for myself."

"Honestly?" Questioned Vicki. "You will do that?"

"Well it is cold and uncomfortable down here." "You are strange Kevin Firkettle."

"How do you mean Vicki?" "You just curl up down there in the cold, with your clothes on and don't complain."

"But you told me to, and that's what we agreed."

"Yes, I know, but I was being careful. I didn't know if I could trust you." "Of course you can trust me." Kevin sounded as if he couldn't understand why there should be any question about trusting him.

"I know that now Kevin. So just as long as you behave yourself, you can come and sleep here next to me. There is plenty of room. I'm only little, but you have to wear something."

"Can I honestly? It is cold and hard here. I've got a pair of shorts and a clean tee shirt."

"That sounds just fine to me. You put them on and I promise not to peek. Then I will curl up next to the wall and you can curl up to me."

"Your hair smells nice." Said Kevin. "It's still damp. God alone knows what it will look like in the morning. Still better clean and untidy than neat and filthy."

"I think Marlene would have preferred the other way around." Mused Kevin.

"Yes, well she would have been happy in this place then. Tomorrow my lad, when you are out earning an honest copper. I will clean this pig sty up. I don't think that it has seen soap and water for many a long year. Oh and don't forget to give in your notice. I don't want to live here any longer than necessary."

"How do you mean Vicki?"

Vicki turned over on to her stomach and rested her elfin like chin in a small cupped hand. The tee shirt was far too big and she had to push the sleeves up. It was undone at the neck and her long, damp hair hung down each side of her face. She looked at Kevin seriously in the darkness. "You really are a lost soul aren't you?" She asked. "No, shhhh." She placed a small finger on his lips. Kevin remained motionless. "I'm not at all sure that you will survive on your own Kevin, and I have decided that for the moment anyway, I rather like being your fiancée, so I propose this. Tomorrow you give in your notice, I clean up here. You leave me with some cash and I will see to the food and do the shopping. Can you drive? Good, so can I. We are going to need a car, or a van, or something cheap and reliable. You need to go to the bank and get them to contact your Mr. Wilberforce. Better still get him to write to your bank and establish that you are a man of substance.

Then you borrow from the bank for the car." Kevin automatically shook his head, saying, "I don't like going into debt."

"Kevin, don't be foolish, you will need transport. Therefore it will pay you to get a good second hand diesel vehicle. It will be tax deductible, you see. Shhhh

.... You also give notice on this dump. Tomorrow. Then just as soon as possible we load up the wheels and head out for your pub. Don't worry, I will look after you."

Somehow Kevin believed that she would. Instinctively he felt that he could trust this small, strange 18 year old girl who had appeared like a guardian angel from out of no where. He felt at ease in her presence, more so that he ever had felt with Marlene. Also he was in bed with her and she wasn't all over him like a rash and also he realized with wonder he wasn't experiencing any problems either. Whereas Marlene had been a solid woman, tending towards the bovine even, Vicki was tiny. For the first time in his life Kevin felt secure, and he liked it. Suddenly though he was flooded with fear, one day Vicki would walk away. This was after all only a business arrangement. Something with which to abide by the terms of him inheriting The Black Badger and all that went with it. "How long will you stay?" He found himself blurting out, his anxiety being betrayed by the tone of his voice.

Vicki looked at him in the darkness and asked in a quiet voice, "How long can I stay Kevin?"

"As long as you wish, Longer." Kevin's face and tone rang true.

Vicki looked at him in the gloom, and smiled. She brushed his face gently with her hand. "I tell you what Kevin Firkettle. I will stay for as long as you need me and you are kind and respect me. How's that?"

"Good!" Exclaimed Kevin. Then you will be around for a long time and I will like that. He sounded relieved.

"Yes, may be I will." She replied and turning over she cuddled her small body into his, taking his right arm and placing it around her. "Had you ever thought about time?" She asked.

Kevin was perplexed by this sudden shift in the conversation. "How do you mean Vicki?" He found that he liked cuddling her and that it seemed quite natural to be lying in the same bed and discussing time.

"Well what is it? I mean we talk about time as being a measurement of the Earth's rotation and we say that we can't travel through it of faster than it. But that's all to do with definitions and a lack of definition on our behalf. If I phone you from here and you are in Australia then your time and my time are different. For you I could be calling from yesterday, so effectively I have, or my voice at least has moved through time. But the transmission was at the speed of light, which we are told is a limiting factor. Since time is the same for both of us, but also at the same time different, is it a constant? Interesting isn't it? Now you think about that and go to sleep."

So Kevin did, and as he had been conditioned throughout his life to do as he was bidden he went to sleep, secure in the knowledge that Vicki would remain close to him to guide and protect him. All he had to do in return was to be kind to her and respect her. He knew that he would have no problem in the respect bit and he wanted to be kind to her. Somehow with her at his side he felt that there would be no problems in looking after either of them. Kevin was experiencing security. He snuggled deeper into the bed and fell asleep with ease, perhaps for the first time in his life, content and unafraid.

CHAPTER: 3

Timothy Longstanton was annoyed. Not only was he annoyed, he was frustrated too. Frustration comes about when one's life is not going according to one's plan. When one's best efforts are thwarted by the actions of others. When fate seems to conspire against one. All of which appeared to Timothy's mind to have happened to him. Timothy was not used to being thwarted by fate or anything else for that matter. Consequently these feelings were both new and alien to him.

Timothy had grown up in the sure and certain knowledge that he was a superior being. Not just by the comparison to himself and the African children, the progeny of his father, the Rev. Longstanton's flock, but to other mortals too. Timothy had been sent to a minor public school in England. Minor public schools striving all the harder to prove that they are superior institutions, capable too of producing, patronizing, pretentious, and disdainful products. Thence naturally, Timothy automatically moved on to university. A long standing English tradition that works basically on the lines that if the father could afford the horrendous fees and the boy the rigors of the system, then anything that survives should then be groomed for leadership. As either it would be a narrow-minded genius that ignored physical discomforts in pursuit of whatever esoteric topic that had taken its fancy. Alternatively, a shifty, devious and untrustworthy individual, capable of personal survival at the expense of others. The former generally becoming research scientists and the latter forming an admirable and satisfactory stockpile of future politicians and Free Masons. Since by the law of averages, most fell into a category that was placed somewhere between the two extremes, this large group was again split. The heterosexual dunderheads heading for the army and those with a penchant for members of their own gender, being absorbed into the Foreign Office. Any remaining were generally beyond redemption, so ended up either as sophisticated confidence tricksters or in the church. Timothy fell into this demographic grouping and seeing no quick fortunes to be made by selling salvation, opted to live by his wits. Or more to the truth, had opted to live off the backs of others. Thus upholding the very foundations of British aristocratic tradition.

At public school he rapidly discovered ways and means of survival. By a combination of subterfuge, blackmail and deviousness, he played the strong against the strong, and exploited the weak. All to his own advantage. University merely offered greater and more sophisticated opportunities to expand upon knowledge thus so far gained and enabled him to continue to exploit others for his own benefit. Upon leaving the hallowed halls of learning, Timothy graduated to the world of finance and was mopped up by the city. The result was now Timothy had been involved in some shady dealings in the city and a bit of dodgy antique business that involved the importation of certain "Ethnic" artifacts. Artifacts that invariably vividly depicted human beings in the act of going about the furthering of their species. This being a small but highly lucrative market of dedicated devotees. There was also rumor that there had been some association with himself and a very dubious character of Middle Eastern origins and a shipment of illegal arms. Though this was strictly a rumor only. As a consequence of which his ventures had not escaped the notice of both Scotland Yard's Fraud and Special Brach. Timothy, had no wish to be detained at Her Majesty's Pleasure. The mere thought of having to live cheek by jowl with the lower life forms that populate the planet being far more of deterrent than any stigma attached to incarceration. Timothy knew that what he needed was a fast injection of funds. This would then enable him to skip the country and set up anew. Somewhere where the police were less sophisticated, more amenable to bribes, but in a country with a pleasant climate and an upper class that aspired to an aristocratic life style, based upon European, "Values" In other words, some place where Timothy could play his cards of affected accent, background and ostensible wealth to the maximum. He thought that South America would fit the bill nicely. After all they knew how to keep their peasant population impoverished and in their place. Fortunes were to be made stripping away the jungle and raising cattle to satisfy the appetite of North Americans for beef burgers. And there were no fiddling little petty restrictions regarding environmental damage, or displacing native peoples. One just hired someone to shoot them. South America held very definite attractions for Timothy.

He had long been aware of weird uncle Silas and his little gold mine. Not that uncle Silas had exploited it as such. No, basically all uncle Silas had wanted to do was to be left alone by the authorities, all authorities, and allowed to make a living brewing beer and cider. He had seen no positive advantages to paying out any of his self generated earnings to anyone else in the form of tax. He had his own water supply, bought his electricity, had cess pit drainage and paid his phone bill. He owned the land and so had his family for eons before the local council had ever come into being. Why then should he pay them anything? They made no contribution to the generation of his wealth. Similarly. why then should he pay the government revenue on his beer? If he made it for X and sold it for X+ so as to enable him to purchase the necessities of life, that was fair and honorable. However, he saw no reason for having to sell his products for X++++++, so that Whitehall could pocket the +++++ at the expense of his customers. He was quite prepared to pay road tax, he used the roads. Insurance was sensible and Income tax could be avoided. That was just an unpleasant irritation. He paid Bernstein and Shultz to sort all that nonsense out. No uncle Silas just wanted to be left alone to brew his ale and pursue his hobby of dressing up in flowing robes, only later to cast them aside and prance naked around a bonfire with some equally nude maiden. In private, on his own land and out of view of prying eyes. All pretty harmless, albeit perhaps a little eccentric.

Timothy had been under the impression that he was the only heir and thus would eventually inherit. Uncle Silas however detested Timothy. Silas had believed in hard work and reaping the profits of one's own labors. To live on the backs of others, was in his view exactly what governments did, and his views on supporting them were well documented. Timothy, to his mind fell into the category of parasite. Equally though, the old man did not want to see his family tradition and possessions fall into the hands of the detested government by default. He needed an heir. Patently, the old man had been unaware of the very existence of Kevin. Had he have known, then no doubt Kevin would have been groomed for the role of worthy successor. As it was Silas had only been able to resort to placing conditions in his will that he felt would force Timothy to continue the tradition. His natural greed overcoming his desire to exist without lifting a finger and having others support him.

Mr. Wilberforce, of Boggle and Boggle was well aware of which way the winds were blowing and thought to himself that all of those maidens over all of those years, should have at least produced something somewhere at some point. It was he, of his own volition that instigated the search for another contender to the will. As he too had no time for Timothy, who he regarded as not only being a waster, but dangerous. Timothy, he thought, would have got rid of the Black Badger, the brewing and George too. In doing so robbing he, Mr. Wilberforce of an income. Apart from which, he, Manni, George and Silas all went back a considerable number of years and he had been very fond of the old man and his eccentric ways. Several of the court battles that he had fought on Silas's behalf had become classic test cases, and were recorded as such. This gave him pleasure, as he knew that he had left his mark on history. Furthermore he had enjoyed the challenge and got quite a kick out of besting the finest that both local council and government department had been able to throw at him. He also recognized that with Britain's full entry into the EEC, vast amounts of power passed to Brussels, this in turn offering a whole new range of opportunities. No, Timothy was to his mind a shallow, parasitic waster. Not even a cardboard cutout of Silas.

Timothy had indeed planned to convert all of his inheritance into liquid assets as fast as possible. In fact he had two breweries interested in buying him out lock, stock and barrel, so to speak. Since neither was aware of the other's interest, Timothy had planned to sell the property to both! Simultaneously! Then to skip out fast with his profits and anything else that he could lay his hands upon and that wasn't screwed down. All of this now lay in ruins with the surfacing of Kevin.

Who was this Kevin? This cuckoo in the nest who had managed, without apparent effort, to usurp Timothy of his rightful inheritance. From whence had he sprung to place a huge spanner in the works and frustrate Timothy's nefarious plans? What was known of him? Timothy decided to do his homework. He had discovered Kevin's address by the simple method of purchasing a CD ROM of all registered voters. This he ran through his lap top. Though as yet he had not met Kevin and would not have recognized him had he jumped out and bit him. This, Timothy reasoned was not good. Any army depended upon good intelligence and full and up to date information of the enemy if it was to pursue a successful campaign. So Timothy set about first of all recognizing his enemy. He thought of waiting in his car, but it was a bright yellow and black, two door Taiwanese Speedo, and rather stood out. So Timothy hired a non descript van from a rather seedy establishment in Brixton that asked few questions. He waited patiently in Camberwell Crescent, and at a distance took photographs with a long-range lens. As Kevin was the only white person that emerged from any of the similar looking terrace houses, Timothy abandoned the camera on his second day of vigilance and followed on foot. Thus Timothy now had a face and body rather than a mythical entity. Timothy knew that if he was to best Kevin, then he had to learn all about him. So Timothy set about leaning, and the more he learned, the less he liked it and the more insubstantial did Kevin become. In fact there seemed to be nothing about Kevin to learn. He was almost a non-person. Nothingness, a Nonentity. In fact in many ways Kevin had managed to achieve for himself exactly what Timothy would have wished for him self, total anonymity. Timothy was bemused, and then he saw the way to turn this to his advantage. If Kevin almost didn't exist, why then should he exist at all? Who would miss him? Who would complain? Kevin, Timothy decided was wholly expendable. Therefore, Timothy set about planning the demise and elimination of Kevin, permanently. Once that was achieved, then he, Timothy could step forward and claim what he saw as being rightfully his. This struck Timothy as an admirable solution to his problem. Now all that remained was to decide upon the most expedient method. There again, he would have to be very careful. He had motive, and the police forces of Britain took a pretty dim view of the disposing of a fellow human. Irrespective of how useless that person was in the eyes of the disposer. No he would have to achieve Kevin's demise in such a way that he was in no way connected. Food poisoning would seem to offer a neat solution. Kevin would be introduced to botulism, or salmonella, e coli or something equally fast and lethal. How though to obtain the necessary pathogens? That posed a problem. Timothy gave the matter some thought. He reasoned that such pathogens would be kept under close control. After all they are not the sort of thing that the local supermarket is likely to stock along with baked beans and marmalade. No, they would be held in medical laboratories, along with drugs and things. Drugs! Of course! Get some junkie to break in to a lab and steal the germs for him. That was the answer. Or was it? Wouldn't some needle jabbing, fried brain, loony be the last person to entrust such a mission? Why not then just settle for drugs alone? Who would be taking too much notice of some loner that took an overdose? So what if he had no previous form for taking drugs? Maybe this was a first time? A sort of congratulatory shot in the arm for winning the Silas jackpot. Yes, the more Timothy thought about it the more the idea appealed. It was neat, simple and plausible. Kevin, perhaps a secret drugs user, had, in the first flush of wealth indulged his habit, but a little too enthusiastically! What Timothy needed was a pusher, a Mr. "Let me lay some smack on you brother" person. Then, once Timothy had acquired the necessary toxin, he planned to disguise himself and purchase a pizza. Having then doctored a pizza with a liberal helping of some product from the Columbian rain forest, he would deliver it to Kevin. He would make up some cock and bull story about it having been paid for, not able to take it back, etc. Who would refuse a free pizza he reasoned? Furthermore all suspicion would then fall upon Kevin. He would be unconnected. All he needed was a good alibi to cover the time of the delivery. Timothy began to plan in earnest and look around the clubs scene for a suitable drugs pusher. He soon found one. Timothy arranged to meet in secret with "Big Earl Winston"

Kevin woke up and for a second wondered why he was in bed with some small body curled up beside him. He moved and the small body slowly uncurled itself, sat up and rubbed a pair of sleepy, dormouse eyes to him. The events of the previous evening came flooding back to him, as Vicki turned a sleepy face towards him. Her hair he noticed was actually a tinge of russet, and her eyes were bright blue. She smiled at him.

"Hello Kevin, and how are you feeling this morning?" Asked the small, sleepy face, hiding a yawn with the back of a hand encased in a too long sleeve...

"Fine." Replied Kevin automatically, and at the same time taking stock of the small body all wrapped up in an oversize plaid shirt. He liked what he saw and considered that the shirt looked far better half on Vicki than fitting himself.

"Has the label fallen off?" "Pardon?"

"I was wondering if my label had fallen off. You are staring at me." Vicki pulled a face at him.

"No, I was just looking at you and thinking how pretty you are." Kevin blurted out, wondering at the same time why he was disclosing his thoughts. "I thought that your hair was brown, but actually it's sort of red."

"Ah! So lust rears it's ugly head does it? I had better cross my little legs before this monster takes advantage of my poor little body." Vicki drew back in mock horror. "By the way the correct method of complementing a lady first thing in the morning is to comment on her hair's charming shade of natural auburn. Not to tell her that it's sort of red."

"No! Honestly. I wouldn't do anything like that! I'm not like that!" "What? Complement a lady first thing in the morning? Churlish you are my son, right churlish."

"No, I mean, your hair is lovely, and I wouldn't.

.... You know what I meant!" Kevin suddenly felt more confident. "Like I said, I'm not like that." He realized that Vicki was winding him up, but Vicki had a few more punches to throw. "Oh aren't you then. Queer are you?" Vicki's face had a look of mischief about it.

"No." Kevin was confused.

"So I'm not good enough for you is it? Rather have Big Marlene is it. Only fancy big women?" Vicki pouted.

"Yes. I mean No. I mean, I mean, I don't know what I mean, but what ever it is I mean it's not to hurt you. Honestly Vicki." Kevin tried to cover his confusion. "Any way I never got around to doing anything with Marlene. Not that I couldn't." Kevin added quickly and defensively.

Vicki gathered the shirt around her throat and rolled onto her stomach so that she could look closely into Kevin's eyes. As last she had the night before, she placed her small chin on top of her hands, resting her upper body on her elbows." So I am quite safe then am I?" She asked Kevin seriously.

"Yes, of course you are." Kevin's voice had a ring of open honesty about it, but Vicki pretended that she hadn't noticed.

She waved a small finger at him. "Now Mr. Kevin." Her face and tone were serious. "Last night I had nowhere to sleep, and you took me in. Also you behaved yourself and were the perfect gentleman. I do thank you for that and I am happy to go ahead with our business deal if you are. If however you have had second thoughts, then I understand. You can have the ring back and I will be on my way."

"No Vicki, please stay. I need your help and I like you. I will keep to my side of the bargain, honestly. I won't molest you. Honestly." Kevin's tone rang with sincerity.

Vicki considered his words for a while and then as if coming to a decision said, "Good, I would like to stay and yes, I like you too. I feel that I can trust you. Just as a matter of setting the rules straight though, we need to trust each other. No relationship, commercial, political or matrimonial can exist without trust, you understand that?" She looked at him seriously.

"Of course I do Vicki."

"Right so that means that we have to be honest with each other. That means no lies, ever Kevin. You understand, lie to me and I will be off so fast it will take my shadow a week to find me, and you never will. You must never lie to me ever Kevin." Her face was very serious.

"I won't" Agreed Kevin.

"You agree too quickly my friend." Declared Vicki. "Give it some thought and then tell me in all honesty if you can play by my rules? I promise never to ask a question to which I don't want to hear the answer, but if I do, then you must answer me honestly."

"I agree." Stated Kevin firmly, "But the same applies for you too Vicki."

"Deal." Said the small girl seriously and offered her hand. A hand that Kevin shook.

Vicki rolled onto her back and played with the long ends off the shirt. She flopped the loose sleeves. "OK Kevin Firkettle, your first test question. Did you ever have sex with Marlene?"

"No." Answered Kevin honestly.

"Why not?" Asked Vicki suspiciously.

Kevin took a deep breath. "Well it wasn't that I didn't want to, or that she didn't want me too either, but it just sort of never worked." "You mean you are impotent?" Asked Vicki incredulously.

"No, just the opposite I'm afraid. Look this is very embarrassing. I mean, it's not every day that I find myself in bed with a pretty young lady discussing my sex life, or the lack of it."

"Consider it as therapy then." Vicki's voice had an impudent ring to it, but Kevin didn't notice. "Come on explain to your aunty Vicki."

"I just got too excited and it was all over for me before it ever got a chance of starting." Kevin shrugged and made a face.

"So actually your are by definition a virgin!"

"Unfortunately yes, but not through lack of trying not to be." Admitted Kevin rather sheepishly.

"I see. Oh well no problems there then. Just wanted to know, you know I was just wondering after last night, you know. Thought that perhaps you preferred boys." Vicki's face had an impish grin to and then suddenly she flashed her wide eyed honest look. "Not that it matters. Just thought that maybe that was why you broke up."

Kevin was confused. "But you asked me not to bother you."

Vicki rolled over again, "Yes I did didn't I? And you, bless your soul were the perfect gentleman. Thank you Kevin Firkettle, A girl is safe with you to look after her." She kissed him lightly on the lips, "Come on my good and honest man time to get up and plan our day. You go and shower and I will try to find us some breakfast. Lord but I had better get some organization into this midden." She kicked at him below the bedclothes with a small leg, and Kevin found himself obeying without question

Vicki found some bread and made toast and tea, but the milk was off, so she dumped the tea and settled for instant coffee, black. She packed a still bemused Kevin off to work with instructions to give a weeks notice, meanwhile she would, "tidy up the pit." As Kevin was leaving she brushed back a stay wisp of hair and turned her elfin like face to him. "Kiss" She ordered. "After all I am your fiancé." Kevin hesitated. "Are you sure you are not gay?" Asked Vicki in mock anger, placing her small arms on her hips. The plaid shirt was far too large. Kevin obediently pecked her on the cheek.

"You are funny." Was all he could manage.

"Better funny than queer!" She retorted, and bundled him out of the doorcalling after him, "And don't forget the ear ring, or do you want me to hold your hand?"

Kevin found himself going to work with a smile on his face, and a light heart. He was giving them a weeks notice. He was getting his left ear pierced. He was going to buy a van. He had broken with Marlene and now Vicki had burst into his life. It was all very confusing, but exciting too. He had never ever in his life before made snap decisions. In fact he had never ever made a decision. Suddenly Kevin realized that there was a whole world out there waiting to be discovered. Kevin would have normally, backed away from such a portal, but now he was eager to step across its threshold and discover what lay beyond. Just as long as he had Vicki behind him to guide and back him up. Kevin knew that he would never really have had the fortitude to embark upon this venture alone. It also came as a shock to him to equally realize that not only would it never have worked with Marlene, he was secretly rather glad to be shot of her, and her mother. Vicki was fun, full of surprises and also very resourceful. He felt that he could depend upon Vickie and Kevin made a silent promise that he would do nothing that would jeopardize their relationship. Kevin knew that with Vicki, then all would be well, without her, he was lost.

He gave in his notice to a startled Mr.Coggings, and wandered off whistling. Kevin had never been known to whistle before. But as it drew time to go home, Kevin was filled with anxiety that Vicki would not be at home. The feeling grew stronger, feeding on themselves and Kevin phoned his bed-sit. Vicki answered, guardedly. "Oh it's you. What's the matter now? Has your shoe lace broken!"

"Um, no." Kevin paused, now reassured, at a loss. "I haven't had my ear pierced." He added, as if that explained his calling. "It was too late, but I will, I promise.

"Well, what's the problem?"

"Nothing. I just wanted to make sure that you were alright, and if there was anything that you wanted me to pick up on the way home?" Kevin improvised.

"That's very nice of you Kevin. Thoughtful no less. No everything is OK at moon Base Alpha. Just fire up your starship to warp five and get your self home here lover boy. Your aunty Vicki is lonely."

"Warp eight for you Vicki" Kevin found himself saying happily.

When Kevin arrived home, he found a whole new look Vicki. She had tied her hair back into a ponytail and was wearing the jeans she had on the previous evening. However, she had tied another of Kevin's shirts around her. She looked like a clean and bright, but rather scruffy elf. "Kiss" She demanded and lifted her pert little face to him. Kevin kissed her gently on her forehead.

"This place looks clean." He commented, taking in the order and tidiness.

"I don't know when it was last cleaned, but I found dinosaur eggs under the bed." Laughed Vicki.

"As long that's all you found." Replied Kevin.

"Ah, yes, well that and the unopened packet of condoms, also covered in dust, I put them in the drawer. Along with the Playboy mags! Some of those women must have been inflated at a garage!" She sniffed and turned on her heel.

Big Earl Winston studied Timothy and listened in wonder as Timothy did his best to street talk. Who was this middle class, white, weirdo that was trying his hand at jive talk? The accent did nothing to improve matters either. He had been told that Timothy wanted some special stuff, but along the line, like Chinese Whispers, the tale had changed as it passed from hand to hand. Anyway, Big Earl was a third rate drugs dealer, and mostly happy pills.

"So Brother." Timothy was saying, in carefully modulated upper class tones. "I'm looking for real stuff. I want you to lay some 100% Columbian pure my way, my man. Stuff that will kill a donkey. I want to ice my brain. You dig?"

"Obviously, thought Big Earl to himself, the punter was looking for designer drugs."

"I want to blow someone away. For real. You dig?"

It sounded to Earl that the crazy had been dumped by his bird, was going to hold a party and he wanted some pop some pills with his friends to forget the chick.

100% pure Columbian indeed. Who was this nutter? Who ever he was he knew nothing about the drugs scene that was for sure. Equally he was too stupid to be a cop. No this was just some, well-heeled upper class twit who wanted to show off. Fine, that would cost him. Earl had just the stuff. He handed Timothy a packet of powder.

"Guaranteed to maim the brain?" Asked Timothy.

"Ever last cell my man." Replied Earl, with conviction.

"This will blow a person away?"

"With just one puff. So make sure you cut it good."

Timothy parted with a large sum of money and pocketed his goods.

"What you sell him Earl?" Joey his minder asked out of curiosity.

"That rough shit that Reggie knocked up in his garage and gave those kids the heebie jeebies."

"Jeeze Earl! That would give an elephant nightmares!"

"Certainly would Joey my old son. I think that it's time you and I took a little holiday. They tell me Spain is very nice this time of year and extradition is so tricky from there." Big Earl Winston, though black as the ace of spades was a Southwark born and bred cockney, and spoke like one too.

That night, Timothy finalized his plans. First he would go to the cinema and take note of the film. Then the following night, he would go to the same cinema and cause some confusion at the box office. Nothing big, just enough for the cashier to remember him. Once inside, he would slip out again. Then he would don his disguise, and purchase the pizza. Then taking up yet another disguise, he would deliver the pizza to Kevin. Kevin would eat it and become history. How unfortunate. Timothy rubbed his hands at the thought.

Camberwell Crescent is a long road that runs roughly south, parallel to the train lines. Its houses are all depressingly similar. Three storey Georgian edifices, most with out visible numbers. In fact the whole numbering system is odd, starting as it does in the twenties. It has been known to give Postmen problems. One of the large houses is a hostel for those unfortunate members of society that have fallen upon hard times and have no other shelter. It offers a bed and a hot bath. TV and the facilities to wash one's clothes, plus simple, wholesome if not wildly exciting fare. It also has very strict rules with regard to what may or may not be consumed or brought onto the premises. Drugs and alcohol being among prohibited items. Its inhabitants often have difficulty in coping and coming to terms with both their mental state and their position within urban society. Some have been known to spend the day in happy contemplation of the rigors and pressures that have befallen upon mankind in the western world in the twentieth century. They occasionally, when overwhelmed with ponderous and portentous deliberations with regard to the direction that mankind is heading, had been known to sit on wooden benches, thoughtfully provided by the Borough Council, on the Green itself. And, with only a bottle of meths for company, while away the daylight hours in reflective and introspective thoughts. Occasionally breaking their meditations to accost a passing stranger with a request for a modest donation, with which to sustain their cogitations.

Some days later Timothy went to the cinema, and Kevin took Vicki out to a pub.

Vicki had bought a short, dark blue, denim skirt. It was decorated in white stitching with an embroidered flower upon it and the edge of the skirt had been carefully machine frayed. There was also a matching jacket and white blouse. On her tiny feet she now wore neat white, high-heeled shoes. She had tied her auburn hair back into a ponytail and held it in place with a small white ribbon. Kevin thought that she looked enchanting, but managed to contain his true feelings with a, "You look neat. I like the outfit."

"I nipped down to Peckham Market and bought it all there. It wasn't expensive." A swift worried frown crossed her small face. "I'll pay you back Kevin. Honest." Kevin looked at her, and laughed. "No you won't."

"I will. Honestly Kevin. Out of the five hundred that we agreed upon." She looked openly at Kevin, as if willing him to believe her. "I don't want you thinking that I am taking advantage of you."

"No, I meant, you don't have to repay me. You cleaned up the room, and cleaned everything too. And you cooked for us. I like it. It really looks neat. My treat, honest."

"You mean that?" Vicki looked at Kevin with a slight degree of wonderment.

"What? The present or the you look beautiful bit?" Kevin realized that he was getting better at this and smiled to himself.

"Both!" Declared Vicki firmly. "Yes, both. Oh, and thanks for the meal. Usually I only have frozen stuff. What was that I ate?"

"Sweet potato, pineapple and chicken livers in ginger, oh and a few other odd veggie and a chili." Vicki smiled, "The late and not lamented Leroy did have his uses, I learned a bit of Caribbean cooking. Other than that nothing good ever came out of that relationship. Do you really think that I look pretty?" Vicki did a twirl.

"Yes Vicki. I honestly do. Let's go for a drink and I can show off my beautiful fiancée to the world." "Mmm." Said Vicki quietly. "I think that you are sweet talking me Kevin Firkettle. I can see that I will have to be on my guard. But thank you anyway. No one has ever told me before that I looked beautiful. Cute maybe, but never beautiful. You may continue my man if you so wish, this maiden will not complain." She gave Kevin the benefit of her most magnanimous of smiles.

Kevin and Vicki went by bus to Lewisham and to a pub that was well known locally for its live Country and Western bands, as they were walking to the pub, Vicki suddenly said, "Kevin, I'm only small and I don't drink very much. It makes me either silly or morose, and I don't want to be either with you. So please, no trying to get me drunk, it will only sour things between us. You know, you didn't buy that camp bed did you?"

"Oh, I'm sorry Vicki. Look never mind the pub, some place will be open and I can still get one and a sleeping bag too. I didn't know that it was still necessary. And I won't try to get you drunk, or myself, for that matter."

"Kevin you say the sweetest things. Come on, dead dogs and divorcees it is then and forget the bloody camp bed" She took his arm in a familiar manner that Kevin found himself enjoying.

They spent a happy evening together and Kevin found himself really enjoying Vicki's company in a manner that he had never experienced with Marlene. He also enjoyed looking at her. He found himself comparing her to Marlene and decided that he by far preferred Vicki. He wondered why and decided that Vicki was pert and prettier. She was also bossy, but not in the commanding and patronizing manner of Marlene and her mother. He found that he rather liked her confident and bossy manner. He also had a sneaking feeling that decisions that Vicki made were for their mutual benefit, whereas decisions that Marlene or her mother had made had in the main been for their benefit. He felt comfortable with Vicki, and not threatened. He also found himself feeling protective, though at the same time he realized that Vicki was far more capable at looking after both of them than he was at looking after either himself or her.

"Penny for them Kevin." Vicki's pert and cheeky little face gazed at his from across the table.

"Just thinking about how my life has changed since I met you. I feel like I have known you for ages, but it's only a couple of days actually. Strange isn't it?" "And do you feel that it's changed for the better?"

"Very definitely so. You are very bossy, but somehow you are bossy with a smile and what you say makes sense. So I am happy to follow your lead Vicki Heart. Heart is a good name for you. I think that you have a big heart."

"Hiding behind these little boobs is it?" Vicki grinned and stuck out her diminutive chest.

"Why are you always going on about your boobs Vicki? You are built just right. I think so anyway. Big knockers would look silly on a small body like yours. No, you are just perfect."

"Kevin Firkettle, have you been having lustful thought about my body then?"

"NO Vicki! I only........."

"Why not then? What's wrong with it?" Vicki feigned mock anger, and then laughed. "Oh your poor face. I'm teasing you Kevin. I do that because I feel safe with you. You are a strange man but I trust you." She patted his hand gently. "You're a nice man too Kevin, I'm glad I found you in time."

"So am I Vicki. You are like a little tiger cat. All sweet and pretty, but you have sharp claws and are not afraid to use them."

"And you Kevin are like a wildebeest."

"A wildebeest?" Asked Kevin incredulously, scratching his head in wonder as he spoke.

"Yes Kevin A bewilderbeast!" Vicki laughed and Kevin laughed with her. "Now, since my word is gospel, transport. What have you done in that department? It's not my business, and it's your money, but we are going to need wheels."

"I phoned Mr. Wilberforce. He had a word with Mr. Bernstein...."

"Mr. Bernstein?" Queried Vicki.

"Yes, you know, our accountant. Manni Bernstein, the one who came for the meal in Tunbridge Wells."

"Ah yes." She paused. "Our accountants?"

"Well I thought that we were partners, so I just said our. Ok if it bothers you. My accountant, but that sounds too grand and snobbish. I prefer our, if it's OK with you Vicki. I mean, we are supposed to be engaged."

Yes, we are, aren't we Kevin. Mmmmm, I wonder if I like being engaged to you?" She looked at Kevin quizzically, squinting her eyes up, and then batting her eyelashes. "I shall have to watch my grammar and say is not rather than 'aint. Mmmmm. Mrs. Kevin Firkettle, mien host of The Black Badger. Firkettle, Firkettle. Not so sure about the name, sounds too much like a hard water problem." She laughed, "Go on, you were saying?"

Kevin had remained silent whilst Vicki had teased him, and he paused a fraction longer, as if considering the implications of her words, then mentally shaking himself like a wet dog he continued. "Manni said that there was some transport at The Black Badger. It seems that we have some enormous, ancient and antiquated truck, lorry, or something. So I asked Mr. Wilberforce to write to the bank manager and explain my new circumstances. Manni told me that a small van would be in order, and that he had been telling Silas for years to purchase one. He phoned the bank, sent a fax and a covering letter. I see the manager tomorrow, do you want to come along too?

"Do you want me to come with you?"

"To be truthful Vicki, I was going to ask you anyway. I will feel more confident with you by my side. It was your idea as well." He paused and looked hopefully at her adding, "Please."

"Of course I will come with you. What to wear? What time is the appointment? Where is the bank?"

Kevin told her and sketched a small map.

"OK, don't worry, I'll meet you outside. If I get up early and nip off to Peckham again, the stall I bought this from has smart trouser suits too. I'll get one. If that's OK with you. This blouse will be fine and the shoes. We can forget about handbags. And you had better look smart too Kevin. This is important. Just as well you didn't have the ear job. Still there will be time after the bank"

They returned home, discussing their strategy for the following day blissfully unaware that Timothy Longstanton was at that very moment watching a film and plotting the total destruction of Kevin.

When Kevin returned from the bathroom, Vicki was again dressed in his too big, plaid shirt and she had carefully placed her clothes on hangers. "Stick this on the curtain rail Kevin, I don't want it to get creased and it's too high for me. You will be peeking at my bottom otherwise." Kevin laughed and hung her clothes as demanded. "Let's see what you will be wearing." Kevin showed her his suit. "That's OK. Shirt? Mmm. Not exactly the trendy executive, but solid and dependable. Tie? GOD NO! That one is better. Yes, you will do. Oh shoes and socks?" She held his shoes up in one hand and inspected them. She nodded grudgingly, instructing, "Socks OK, but give the shoes a clean Kevin, OK?" Kevin nodded. "Now If I stick everything in the launderette tomorrow in Peckham. I can get my togs, whilst they are washing, then get them dry. Come back here. Skip out and meet you. Zip back again, do the ironing and sort out the evening meal. How's that grab you partner?"

"It's marvelous. Do you always plan ahead like that?"

"I'll let you into a secret Kevin." Vicki said succinctly. "Most people do. People with busy lives that is Kevin. Like normal people Kevin."

Kevin thought about that and Vicki climbed into bed. "I never did." Said Kevin slowly. "I never had too!" The thought dawned upon him. "I just did as I was told. People said do this and do that, and I just did."

"And was that how you became engaged to Marlene?" Asked Vicki in a small voice. "Doing as you were told."

"I suppose so." Answered Kevin, with a degree of wonder creeping into his voice. "It was her mother's idea."

"I should have known." Sighed Vicki resignedly. "And poor old Kevin just went along with it. You are free now Kevin. Don't you know that. It has all been handed out on a plate to you. All you have to do is reach out and take it. You have to make your own decisions now Kevin, and with that comes a degree of responsibility too, so reach out and make the right choices."

"But I don't know anything about beer and brewing or pubs for that matter, and Mr. Wilberforce told me to follow the advice of George. Isn't that what I have always been doing?"

"No Kevin You have been doing as you were told without thought or question. Mr. Wilberforce told you to listen to George and follow his advice. That's very different. It's also good advice by the way. No, now you have to decide in your own mind what advice to take and which path to tread, and lucky old you.

.... You have a ready made business with which to do it, and three solid persons who will do their utmost to help and assist you to succeed."

"Three?" "Wilberforce, George and Manni."

"But what about you Vicki?"

"We were just temporary partners Kevin. Remember? Remember our agreement too? I never promised to be around for ever did I?"

"No Vicki." Replied Kevin in a small voice. "You didn't. But I had hoped that you would stay around."

"We'll see Kevin. We don't really know each other very well yet. People change. Right now you feel you want me around, but once you are on your feet and a businessman, it may be different. I might just be a nuisance to you and your ambitions then."

"Oh I don't think that you would ever be that Vicki. I like you too much."

"Well we will see. I tell you what, I'll stick around until such times as I think that you still need me. How's that?"

Kevin thought about it. Then replied, "I think that will be just fine Vicki. I really do." He made himself more comfortable in the bed. "Tell me about yourself Vicki and Leroy."

Vicki sort of shuddered. "Are you sure Kevin? Remember I will only tell you the truth. You might not like it."

"I don't think that you are a bad person Vicki, and yes, I do want to know."

Vicki took a deep breath, and lying on her back began. "When I finally ran away from home for good, like most young people, I headed for London. I had no money, no job and nowhere to stay. Pretty soon I got hungry and tired. I tried to find a job, but could not. Then I got scruffy and a bit smelly too, so the prospect for work diminished accordingly. It's easy to drift into a strange non world, full of people like oneself. You sleep in a cardboard box. You live with junkies and winos. It's dangerous for a young girl. I was at my wits end and hungry. You must understand that I was hungry. I had tried to steal food from supermarkets, but they have security cameras and anyway scruffy people tend to get watched more. So I though that the only way was prostitution. I was a virgin you understand. I met Leroy. Leroy was kind to me, well at first he was. Like you he took me in, and fed me. Then he got me a passport. He never touched me Kevin but took me over to Amsterdam. There I was introduced to the drugs scene, the marketing end! I used to smuggle hash into the UK. Just slip over and bring it back in. Then Leroy showed his true intentions. He wanted me to go the game in earnest. One little virgin for sale with small tits but an unused pussy. He was all for hiring me out to the highest bidder. You get the drift?" Kevin nodded, but remained silent. Vicki took it as a signal to continue. "His reasoning was that if I had considered going on the game for food, why not for hard cash? You see Kevin, I trusted him, I suppose that I thought that I loved him and now it turned out that I was just a saleable commodity. I didn't feel very clean. I had smuggled hash, because Leroy had told me to. Like you, I hadn't given the matter much thought. Suddenly though I realized the risks that I had been taking for what? For Leroy? Now he wanted to sell me off. That was the reason he had never bothered me sexually. He had always planned to set himself up as a pimp. I refused."

"What happened?" Asked Kevin quietly.

"Leroy is pretty big. He raped me. Simple as that. So I did a runner and phoned the police. No doubt now Leroy is trying to explain away the funny white powders and pills. I hitched that truck. Smacked him one when he came on too strong and ended up here with sweet old you. Now, right now; I'm useful, I can be your legs person, and keep house for you. Then I have agreed to do the moonlight-dancing bit. But you will grow Kevin and I will get left behind. You won't want some nude dancing, ex drug running nearly prostitute for a partner. Then I will have to move on. Until then, I will be nice to you and hope that you will be nice to me, because Kevin Firkettle, right now I have no place to go and you are all I have. Now I am feeling a little bit sad and I might even cry, but I will try not to as I would only be crying for myself. So if I could just curl up like this and you could see your way clear to cuddling me I would feel a whole lot better." She turned away from him, curling up into a ball and taking his arm she placed it gently across her. "Good night Kevin Firkettle."

"Goodnight Vicki." Kevin replied and gently kissed the back of her head. "Don't worry, I won't bother you, and I won't let anyone hurt you either. Ever."

CHAPTER: 4

Timothy Longstanston had given thought to his disguise and had purchased two theatrical wigs. One long and blond, the other shorter and red. He also bought spirit gum and a blond beard and mustache. In other and separate small shops, he acquired a reversible red/blue anorak, old jeans, blue and white trainers and a large base ball type hat with a long bill, all second hand. These he placed in a hold all in the back of his car along with a pair of small sharp scissors, suitable for trimming a moustache, false or otherwise and a large hand mirror. He was ready.

That night, donning the long blond wig and carefully trimmed facial hair, he went to the cinema, and took careful notice of the film.

Kevin, unaware that plans were being made for his demise blissfully went about working out his weeks notice. He confused his colleagues by smiling and whistling. When asked what had caused his new demeanor, he just smiled enigmatically and said nothing. Soon word got around that he had given notice and a rumor started that Kevin Firkettle had won The National Lottery. Finally Mr. Coggings asked him outright and Kevin just shrugged non committedly and replied, "Something like that." However, he refused to be drawn further as he was sensible enough not to place himself into a position whereby he could be critisised.

Vicki, visited Peckham market again and purchased, after some fearsome haggling, a smart, light brown trouser suit, along with matching shoes. With her hair tied back and wearing a tan headscarf, she waited for Kevin in strengthening spring sunshine, on the pavement, outside of the bank. Gaining several admiring glances as she did so. Kevin duly arrived on time, and Vicki immediately taking both his arm and control, steered him via the large glass doors inside. There, before Kevin could complain, she went straight to an unoccupied part of the counter and announced quietly that they had an appointment with the manager. After a short period of time, they were ushered into the manager's private office.

The manager was a lean gentleman in his mid fifties, and he had obviously been well primed by Mr. Wilberforce. He had a file open on his desk, as, with an expansive wave of his hand and practiced smile, he indicated them both into chairs in front of him. He offered them tea or coffee, "Only instant I'm afraid." He said, giving a rather disarming, "What can I do?" kind of look. "Tea would be lovely." Stated Vickie, "Milk, but no sugar please." She smiled sweetly. The manager spoke into a phone, giving instructions to one of his minions, then, replacing the phone he sat back into his chair. With his very best smile he said smoothly, "So you have inherited a small but lucrative business, I gather?" He looked at them in a friendly and expectant manner. Kevin nodded silently, but Vickie, again seizing the reins and smiling in a very disarming manner said, "Yes, actually we have." She paused, and then continued, "My fiancé's late uncle left him a brewery in the West country." She waved a small and delicate hand in the direction of the open file on the desk. "But you would know all of that." Not waiting for a reply, she continued in a positive tone. "We are keen to move down there and take command, so to speak. We know nothing of brewing, but we have retained the services of the Brewery's Master Brewer. There is a regular market. We thought to do up the pub some and try to attract outside trade. Expand the catering side maybe. Naturally we will need some transport and we were thinking in terms of a transit size van, diesel would be best. Then it can double for the move and also the commercial needs of the business. We can use it as a run around too; the ground clearance will be useful if we need to drive along unsealed lanes to make any deliveries to farms etc. And there again it would be more sensible to have something of a robust nature in the winter months. Kevin's mouth dropped open, Vicki noticed, so turning to him askeded, "Those are our feelings aren't they dear?" Kevin paused and Vicki surreptitiously kicked and at the same time looking intently at him, prompted, "The ground clearance Kevin, remember how those were our feelings?"

Kevin's first attempt at vocalization turned at to be a squeak, which he hastily converted into a cough. "Yes, yes, those were our feelings." He finally managed in an almost normal tone.

"And very sensible too." Nodded the bank manager. "Yes, I can see that you have thought out this move. I can see no problems in advancing you credit to purchase such a vehicle, Umm, were you thinking in terms of a new unit?" He waited, whilst Kevin looked at Vicki for guidance, she shook her head, and Kevin, taking his lead turned back to the manager. "Umm, no, but a newest second hand unit with a guarantee." He looked back to Vicki who nodded brightly. There was a knock on the door and tea and biscuits arrived. The remainder of the time was spent with the financial details, and the manager's suggestion that although they were relocating, they could still retain the use his branch and he would see that things ran smoothly. Anyway they were taking a loan from his branch, so why not remain with him etc, etc. etc. Such are bank managers the world over, positive grovellers if they smell the scent of money and ruthless tyrants if they fear a loss. Kevin duly signed where indicated and as if on some magical merry go round, found himself back on the pavement outside the bank with Vicki still holding his arm.

He looked at her in awe, "How do you do it Vicki?" He managed at last.

"Do what yer Burk?" Was Vicki's reply.....

"The bank thing. The manager. The van?"

"Well someone has to get this show on the road Kevin. Come on the van we are buying is in the showroom waiting for you and your cheque book. First of all though, it's hole in the ear time lad. Grab that cab." And pursing her lips effortlessly she gave a piercing whistle that would have stopped a double decker bus dead in its tracks.

Timothy Longstanton's next ploy was return to the cinema next day, dressed as himself. Then passing over a 10 pound note, he politely asked for change for a twenty. When confronted with his original tenner, he was profusely apologetic, and begged forgiveness for his stupidity. The cinema was one of those multi theatre types that show several films. All of which begin and end at roughly the same time. The foyer was busy, which was as Timothy had hoped. He took his seat, but then made a move for the gents. Once inside, he dived into a stall, locked the door, donned the short red wig, and removed his short dark raincoat, placing it in a plastic carrier bag. Substituting the raincoat for the red side of the anorak. On the pretext of buying popcorn he left the theatre and mingled with the crowd, slipping out quietly. He had parked his hired van a short distance away and he made his way back to it. Once inside, he drove away quietly, only stopping some distance away to again slip on the blond wig and having switched the anorak for its blue side, he then purchased the pizza and drove on to Camberwell Crescent and Kevin's planned demise.

Timothy had now changed into his Pizza delivery disguise, the blue windcheater and baseball cap. He had also struggled into blue jeans and blue and white trainers. He felt the part and practiced his "Rough Boy" street talk to himself as he drove towards Camberwell Crescent. The pizza he had purchased came complete with its own heat retaining, polystyrene box. This he placed inside his own carton that he had fashioned himself and decorated with colored pens purchased from a large supermarket. Being careful to carry out all procedure whilst wearing surgical gloves. The drugs, which came in the form of an innocuous, white powder form, he had carefully placed on the top and mixed it in with the tomato paste, and then added an extra topping of Mozzarella. He had also taken the trouble to, "Liberate" some traffic cones. Since Britain's' entry into the EEC, there seemed to be a surplus mountain of traffic cones, and all were usually, it seemed, conveniently left on the M25 for anyone with a mind to do so, to take. He had taken the trouble to mark his desired parking spot earlier with the afore said cones. By 19-45 Timothy was parked in the Crescent, pizza at the ready and he began to put his plans into action to remove Kevin Firkettle, once and for all. Pulling his cap well down over his eyes he stepped out of his hired van on to the deserted street to deliver the lethal Pizza.

It was at this point that the first doubts crossed his mind as to the invulnerability of his scheme. Timothy was unsure as to which of the seedy, down at heel, identical, grubby, three story Georgian Terrace houses actually housed Kevin. Now he knew that he had the correct side of the road and was close to his target. Timothy looked along the street in confusion and at the depressingly similar facades. Each cast in a deep shadow by the yellow street lights and weary looking plane trees that edged the roadside. He decided that it was the one with the blistered paint and broken knocker. He was sure that was the house. It was after all the most run down of a singularly run down set. That would be Kevin's lair, the dirtiest and cheapest.

......
He passed the aged, blackened railings and mounted the four dirty steps, glancing as he did so into the dingy basement. Not that he could make out much due the grime on the windows and curtains that would seem not to seen soap and water since the opening on the building. He looked for a bell, none was evident. He tried the knocker, but without success, it hung loosely from one screw, but the actual knocker mechanism was rusted solid. Timothy ripped it from the door in disgust. How like Kevin, he thought, to live in a pigsty like this. Thus; he deserved to die. The universe would be a better place without the Kevin Firkettles' of this world. He clouted the door with the now free knocker as if to emphasize the thought to himself. Nothing happened. In frustration, Timothy wielded the knocker like a hammer and delivered several solid blows, imagining as he did so that he was striking Kevin's exposed scull. He rapped again impatiently. After all, his master plan had not included delayed door openings.

Kevin, now sporting a gold ear ring, actually lived next door, but was out with Vicki having finally taken delivery of their all but new, white transit van and was at this very moment happily driving back to Camberwell Crescent with Vicki. Capital Gold blasting out of the speakers to keep them company. Kevin had supposed that one just went in, paid for the van and drove out. Not so, he discovered. It had to be registered, that took time but the salesroom did that for one. Then there was insurance, again the salesroom could assist, but Vicki had insisted that they visit a few agents and brokers first and get some quotes. Her intuition in this had again proved to be correct from a financial standpoint. Then they had visited a jewlers that also pierced ears and Kevin sat nervously as a small gold ring was inserted into his left ear. Thus had passed most of the afternoon. Then the van had to be serviced and it was almost six o'clock before they finally drove it off the forecourt. Since there was the usual London Traffic, Vicki had suggested that they eat out and a Chinese restaurant had been sought. Hence they returned to Camberwell Crescent just as Timothy was belting the front door with the now totally independent knocker. However, the house whose front door Timothy was trying to demolish, although horribly similar in it's depressing frontage and air of desolation to the one in which Kevin resided, was in fact the house next door. A house that had been purchased out of necessity, by a grudging and parsimonious local authority. A house that reflected the resentment of city councilors in having to maintain and fund such a dwelling. It was in fact, a half way house for recently released inmates of her Majesties pleasure. Sparsely funded as it was from the public purse, it lacked dignity, facilities and anything that even vaguely resembled hospitality or charm. It did however have a reasonably leak free roof, and could offer clean, if only tepid water, a small bed and basic and rather Spartan fare. Into this haven of prosperous and genteel living Timothy Longstanton arrived with a large, and more to the point, free pizza.

Ray, "Fingers" Malone was equally frustrated. He had just spent a fruitless ten minutes or so trying, without success to scrounge a cigarette from a fellow boarder. Ray was a person that was solidly hooked on the daily nicotine habit. He was often wont to be heard saying that doing bird was one thing, going without a fag something all together far more unpleasant. He heard the knocking on the front and had ignored it. Then a thought crossed his mind. Maybe the person outside smoked. Ergo, he, Ray might be able to persuade him, or her, to part with a fag. So, waving a hand in dismissal of his contemporary, Ray started up the stairs to the front door.

"Happy Cat Pizza" rapped off Timothy, "Kevin Firkettle ordered this prepaid Pizza. He proffered the package.

"D'you smoke mate? The unshaven, lean and sallow face looked at Timothy hopefully around a suspiciously and carefully controlled cracked open door. Timothy stared back at the unkempt face and dingy all but obscured interior." Just typical Kevin he thought in disgust. What a dump! He was brought back to the present by the face asking hopefully, "Fags, You know, I need a fag mate, gasping I am." Timothy nodded dumbly and reached for his cigarettes, saying in a robot like voice, "Kevin Firkettle ordered the pizza, is he there?" A scrawny hand took two cigarettes from the proffered packet and then grabbed the pizza with the other hand. "Yes mate." said the face, "He's inside." The head nodded back over its shoulder. "I'll give it to him. Thanks." The face smiled a toothy grin and closed the door. Timothy Longstanton was left standing in front of the now firmly closed door. A broken knocker in one hand and a bemused look on his face. A white transit van pulled into the curb. Cut its engine, slid open the doors and Kevin and Vicki stepped down. Timothy looked aghast, as ignoring him; they went to the house next door, speaking excitedly to each other as they fumbled for a key. "Right lad!" said the small female imperiously. "Tomorrow we phone Boggle and Wottsit and get the directions for The Black Badger, and Saturday we are packed and heading westwards and a whole new life by nine o'clock. We will take the M4 to the M5 junction south, that much I do know for sure. We can stop at the service station there and have breakfast and double check the route" Was all Timothy caught before their door closed.

Meanwhile Fingers had taken his prize into the, "Lounge" "Anybody for pizza?" He enquired nonchalantly. The inmates looked up in interest, catching the characteristic scent of heated cheese. Hands appeared. "Hang on, not so fast my lovelies. One slice three fags, OK?" Fingers took a slice of pizza and munched upon it reflectively. Cigarettes appeared at lightening speed. Fingers retreated up the stairs towards his shared sleeping accommodation, taking his cigarettes and another slice of pizza with him. He paused at the door to the shared bedroom, and decided to continue upwards where a door gave access to a small flat roofed area. Fingers sat down on the flat roof with his back resting against a chimney. He looked down over the low retaining wall of the flat roof and out over the Crescent with its dejected and listless plane trees and dirty pavements. He lit one of the cigarettes he had acquired and carefully deposited the remainder in a battered tin which returned to the inside pocket of his jacket. He munched on his second slice of pizza. Soon he was joined by three other inmates, and then another two. They also sat down, backs to the chimney and gazed down over the Crescent.

As the drugs took, effect their conversation turned to birds, and flight and became almost philosophical in nature. Soon they were joined by another boarder. All now seemed to hold deep and firm views with regard to Bernoulli's theorem and aerodynamics in general. Someone spoke of Icarus, describing how he soared too close to the sun and gently, one by one they too attempted flight. Each stepping confidently off the roof's edge.

The resultant mess, noise and general mayhem of seven smiling, and obviously oblivious men, crashing helplessly to the pavement 3 floors below brought the presses of Fleet Street to a halt. Front-page headlines were changed. Tabloids had at least three days of copy out of it. Whilst the more serious minded spoke at length about drug rehabilitation programs, several MPs saw it as a wonderful chance to cash in and make their faces seen and score political points. Next-door Kevin and Vickie were hardly oblivious to the event as ambulances and wailing police cars rushed to the scene of carnage along with TV crews. Timothy however, cursed Georgian architecture, Kevin and the world in general. He had stood non plussed at the door whilst Kevin and Vicki disappeared into the house next door.

He stood for a second on the pavement and looked across at the large, white, transit van from which his victim had emerged. Who was the girl he wondered? They were obviously working together. Not only that but they were bound for Westfordshire the very next Saturday morning. Then the penny dropped. Kevin had a girl friend? A wife perhaps! Know nothing; non-attractive, non-person Kevin had a partner. A female partner. Not only that but a smart and pretty, young and attractive female partner. This was not something for which Timothy had planned. Damn! Thwarted again! Now he had to dispose of two persons...... It was whilst Timothy was pondering upon this new turn of events, that he heard the sound of voices on the roof above him. He quickly began to retrace his steps towards the hired van and having collected the traffic cones, he sat and lighting a cigarette pondered the events. He decided that he wanted a second look at the houses and work out why he had chosed the wrong one. He drove up to the end on the crescent and turned around. It was whilst he was opposite Kevin's house the first body came crashing down. Timothy removed himself from the scene with all possible haste.

Timothy realized that now he was faced with a new set of circumstances. If Kevin was heading for the Black Badger, with a pretty young girl in tow, then from the few scant words Timothy had overheard, obviously Kevin had some idea of keeping the business alive. This was also a new thought to Timothy. He had assumed that Kevin would sell off the property as fast as possible and run. Timothy did rather tend to view persons other than himself within his own and rather dubious light. That would at least give him some breathing space Timothy reasoned. On the other hand there were now two persons to remove, rather than one. Timothy was unsure of what to do, but felt strongly that he should do something, more so in light of the seven mangled bodies and an unfortunate cat, victim of collateral damage, which at that very moment were being hosed off the pavement. Timothy decided that he would switch back to the Sports car, and drive down to the junction of the M5 and M4 on Friday night. He could stake out the service station, maybe in the meantime even attempt to improve upon his alibi for this evening. He had no definite plans, but he would be closer to both of them and could observe and await his moment to strike. And so, as Vicki and Kevin packed their meager possessions in readiness for Saturday's trip to Westforshire. Then snuggled down together under the Teddy bear decorated duvet. Timothy Longstanston was already planning his rout for the M4 out of London and the heading for the River Severn and the M5 junction service station.

Saturday, the trip out of London, once they had again run the gamut of Police and news reporters was uneventful. Their main topic of conversation had been, "What had happened?" Neither knew. Their first inkling being the noise of police and ambulances outside of their front door. They had no wish to dwell upon the scene of carnage, and were impressed by the amount of blood a human being can contain. The police very quickly established that they were not witnesses and could offer little by means of explanation. So having taken particulars and the address of the Black Badger, they were passed over. Vicki was visibly upset as indeed was Kevin, but he felt that he had to put a brave face on matters, and steered Vicki firmly back inside the house and into his flatlet. He also found that Vicki was not averse to cuddling very close to him under the duvet and this he found comforted him too.

The next morning they both wanted to leave as fast as possible and put all of Camberwell Crescent into a closed folder, but they stuck to their plan and carefully closed up everything in the flat.

Saturday brought early morning spring sunshine. It was bright and cheerful as they headed out past Heath Row and then followed the airborne jumbos heading west. The transit gave a nice steady note and lumbered along at a steady and effortless 65 mph. Vicki had tuned into a local VHF station, but quickly changed stations when the newscaster began to again dwell upon and relate the previous events in the Crescent.

"No White Van driving Kevin." She admonished when Kevin overtook a large and slow moving articulated lorry.

"Oh come on Vicki, he was doing all of 45! In the middle lane too. If anyone is a White Van driver, he is, sorry was."

"Oh, just go quietly please Kevin; I'm still seeing all that blood. Let's stop at the Severn Junction for a late breakfast please"

"OK Boss, Severn Junction it is…. Where is it? I have never done this sort of thing before."

"Where it has always been dopey. In between Wales and England" Vicki quipped, smiling a forced cheerfulness, then adding in a conciliatory tone "Just keep going straight and it will appear, don't worry Kevin, even we can't miss it. Take no notice of me Kevin I am just upset and excited all at the same time, I really am."

"Are you Vicki? Excited I mean. I'm a bit scared. I mean how are we going to manage?"

"We shall do exactly as Boggles and Wotsitts suggest, and dance naked around bonfires, drinking beer that George has shown us how to make; easy." and she smiled impishly at him but still with a forced air of happiness.

"I think it is only the acolyte that has to do the nude bit." Murmured Kevin glancing at her and then nodding firmly said, "Yes, only female nymphs are required to shed their kit and frolic. Grand masters look on and ogle" He gave her his best leer.

"Yes, I can see this is going to have its moments. Will that be with or without pubic hairs Oh Grand Master?" Vicki gave him her serious face.

"I believe that's optional." Kevin replied equally seriously.

"Huh! The things a girl has to do to make a living." Vicki sniffed, "Just make sure it's a warm night, otherwise you won't be able to tell my tits from goose bumps." She wriggled and laughed, and placing her hand upon Kevin's leg said with a ring of pure honesty, "I like being with you Kevin Firkettle, dancing or no dancing, this going to be fun."

Joe and Harry Scruggs were very annoyed. Joe and Harry made a nice little earner skipping over to France in their Transit, filling up with cheap wine, beer and cigarettes, and then taking the Channel Tunnel train back to England. All totally legal under the rules of the EEC. Even transporting their cargo all the way back to the West of England was not outside the law. Selling the goods however was most certainly illegal. Not that they admitted their intentions of so doing to Her Majesty's Custom and Excise Officers at Folkstone. No, they steadfastly maintained that they were having a party, a wedding party and all of the large quantity of what would be highly taxed bottles and cartons jammed into the back of their white Transit, were in fact, solely for that use. "And no officer, certainly not. Sale of the aforesaid was furthest from their mind." When it was pointed out that this was the third load in 18 days, their only reply was that it was a very big party that was planned. A closer look into their finances then revealed that both of the gentleman in question were claiming to be unemployed and drawing the relevant Social Benefits. Their cargo was impounded, pending further investigation, along with a warning that the van too could be confiscated if they were found to be guilty of smuggling.

With the very real possibility of penal servitude hanging over their heads, the brothers were, to say it mildly, more than a might testy. This then turning to a massive sense of injustice. "Bleeding Frogs don't pay half what we do. We're in the Common Market 'aint we? Bleeding Government is ripping us off brother, and that's a fact. Bleeding cheek, taking the load even. French tax was paid. Bloody illegal is what it is brother. We'll get a good brief and sue the gits..." And so, with annoyance at HM Customs and Excise turning to the government as a whole and life in Britain in general, the brothers, also driving a white Transit traveled towards the Severn Junction westwards on the M4.

Timothy had driven westwards on the M4 for some time into the night, and was now strategically parked at the M4/M5 service station with a good view of all incoming vehicles. He was also tired, and cramped. Taiwan made Speedos being more conducive at attracting females and then taking them to a suitable hotel, rather than accommodating copulation or sleeping adult males. He was also aggrieved. He felt a sense of injustice that his plan to eliminate Kevin had failed. He was also annoyed that Kevin now seemed to have some attractive young girl in tow. It did not fit in with the image of Kevin that he had acquired. That meant that somewhere, he Timothy had neglected or overlooked some facet of Kevin's mentality. That then indicated that he, Timothy was incorrect in his assessment. That also went to annoy him further. He was so engrossed in his introspective analysis of himself that he totally missed the brother's van enter the service station. He did not however miss Kevin and Vickie's arrival. He stealthily followed them into the restaurant and watched them order breakfast. He purchased a newspaper and over it, carefully observed them. He decided to follow them, and if the opportunity occurred, to involve them in a lethal accident. When they made a move to continue their journey, Timothy rushed to place himself ready to follow.

"Harry! Whose this twerp in that yellow peril sports car? He's been on our tail for miles now!"

"How the Hell would I know?" Replied Harry, turning to look back over his shoulder and through the rear windows. "Some baby driver. Lose him Joe." Joe put the hammer down, and his foot went to the firewall. Transits' are not renowned, or built for speed and acceleration. Their van lumbered forward. Timothy with ease, increased speed in accordance. "The buggers speeded up! I'll slow down." Timothy obligingly decreased his speed to match theirs. "The daft sod has slowed down too. Do you thing he's following us? Customs maybe?"

"Try speeding up again Joe." Harry adjusted the nearside mirror to get a better view of the small yellow sports car immediately behind them. "Don't look like Customs to me Joe. Too poncyfied. Wave him on."

"Nah! Don't want to let him know we've twigged him, I'll turn off at the next junction." He did, and Timothy doggedly followed. "He bloody well is following us! Who is he?"

"He could be one of the Fowler gang. Maybe he thinks we still have a full load and he and his old man are out to hi jack us?"

"If he can find anything in this van Harry, I'll share it with him, his old man too." Joe grimaced.

"Not the point brother is it? If it is Old Man Fowler up no good, we had better sort this fast and mark this punter's card."

"So what are we going to do brother?"

"Well Harry, I reckon that he has to make the first move. I mean we have a full tank, and we are now heading for nowhere, with nothing on board. Let's see what this git gets up to. I think that I will take us a quiet ride in the countryside brother."

Timothy had no exact idea of the location of the Black Badger relative to his present position. However, he had a sinking feeling that it was not in the direction in which they were heading. He tried to visualize the map of Westfordshire and he could not understand why they were now going generally south, when he felt sure that they should be going much more to the west. The sinking feeling turned into near panic when it dawned that he might have been following the wrong white van. Being unable to see the occupants from his position, he decided to overtake and spot them in his rear view mirror. Timothy accelerated and began to close up for overtaking. The brothers however had by now taken a small secondary road with high hedges each side, and overtaking was not built into its design.

"Hi up Joe! The bugger's making his move, he's trying get alongside."

"Bloody Hell Harry! Is he crazy or heavy? Then as the thought exploded into his brain, "He could be a hit man for the Fowlers."

"Jeasus! Joe he's going for broke." Cried Harry, as Timothy slipped alongside the van. He looked up studying the occupants very carefully and not smiling. They were two men and defiantly not his targets.

"That's it Harry, he's marking us, Bugger this." Joe spun the wheel right catching Timothy neatly on the nearside front tire and spinning him at speed into the hedgerow. He disappeared from out of Harry and Joe's vision and both brothers heaved a sigh of relief.

"Any damage Harry?" enquired Joe solicitously after a short time.

"Don't think so. I'll stop and take a gander." Harry pulled in. He cut the engine and stepped down. "Can't hear him any." He shook his head and shrugged his shoulders. He looked at the front offside. "Bit of dent and scratch." He kicked at the wheel. "Nothing I can't fix brother

Wonder what he's like?" A thought occurred to his brother. "What if he wasn't a hit man for Old Man Fowler?" Harry Shrugged, "Serve him right for driving like a twatt in a poncy car!" He shrugged again, "Come on, let's get offski and clean up this paintwork before we get incriminated."

At the point where Timothy's car had left the road, the hedge was rather thin, which was fortunate. Not quite so fortunate was the fact that the land sloped away very steeply and was wooded. Timothy's little sports car, whilst designed with lightness and acceleration in mind was not designed to either fly, or take on 100 year old beech trees, head to head. Plastic disintegrated, thin, carefully preformed panels took on an altogether different shape, glass shattered into a thousand fragments and the small, yellow, sports car ended up being welded to the tree. There was a sizzling sound as water from a smashed radiator boiled on pieces of hot engine and the sound of a deflating, punctured airbag. Then silence.

PART TWO

The Black Badger

CHAPTER: 5

Vicki had been studying the map. "Men don't listen and women can't read maps!" Kevin said smugly. Since leaving the service station and with some food and coffee inside her, Vickie's spirits had risen, as if with the sun. It was after all, a glorious spring day. "Speak for yourself only Sunshine!" was Vickie's quick reply, "Take the second junction left from here, it will lead onto an "A" road. I will keep you informed of other changes in our route as we progress." She looked at Kevin confidently. "Hmmmph!" Exclaimed Kevin, "Captain to Navigator, course confirmed!" and he laughed.

They proceeded at a leisurely pace, following Vickie's map reading. Eventually and in due course they arrived at the small market town of Scrumpton Bridge. This centre for local government and rural tourism boasted not only a bypass, but two bridges and a rather nicely designed riverfront. That and the road to Frothershome with its giant Tesco Super store and petrol pumps seemed to be it. Although the map did mention a small industrial area and a housing estate. Both no doubt tucked tastefully away somewhere in the region of the now defunct railway line and old gas works. The town was rather like a place that time had forgot and since the opening of the new bypass, that is exactly what in fact, time had done. Situated as it was in rolling, rich agricultural countryside, it tended to only come to life on a Tuesday, which was market day and when the pubs remained open for at least 12 hours. The Government had done its level best to assist the finances of the town by installing a local tax office, obligatory Job Centre (For non existent jobs) and instigating training courses in Information Technology (For which there was no demand) The population of 15,000 or so souls living in the main by either working for local government, Tescos or were unemployed. Many of the latter then displaying a remarkable degree of entrepreneurism by either working for themselves, or servicing the blossoming British black labor market, whilst at the same time diligently collecting their unemployment benefits. The remainder of the workforce opting to commute to Frothershome to turn an honest coin. Not that the area appeared in any way depressed or run down, on the contrary, life seemed to be good for the dwellers of Scrumpton Bridge and its environs.

A quiet back and scenic road wound its way out of Scrumpton Bridge and eventually, after many twists and turns through delightful countryside entered the village of Houghton. Village was perhaps too brave a term for Houghton. It did have a village green and school, even a cricket club and small sub Post Office cum shop. A Norman church with a square tower watched quietly over the collection of houses, now mostly owned by the more financially secure members of society, and its graveyard, neatly kept graves, bore witness to the passing of time. Of The Black Badger however, there was no sign.

They stopped at the Post Office and bought an ice crème each and made enquiries. The Black Badger, it would seem, laid along "Houghton Springs Lane" The lane being next to the cricket pitch. A narrow, tree shrouded, green tunnel, which followed a tiny stream that ran along the right hand side of the road, gurgling and cascading its way down the gently ascending roadway. Wood pigeons fluttered nosily from the trees that overhung the road from each side, as they carefully navigated its narrow and blind bends. Houghton Springs Lane continued to rise gently, passing fields and more clumps of woodland. Then it entered a steeply sloping, wooded valley. The stream left the roadside abruptly, turning right into the wood and towards what appeared to be a small cliff face that could just be seen through the trees. The trees on their right hand side suddenly gave way to an old orchard whose spring buds were just appearing. Further on in the distance stood a cluster of stone buildings. All tucked attractively below the wooded slope.

The largest of the buildings had a wooden sign with a badger painted upon it and the words Houghton Springs Brewery could be clearly seen. Next to and separate from the brewery stood the Black Badger Inn. They had arrived! They drew into the car park in front of the Black Badger. Kevin switched off the engine and both of them looked at the place that lay bathed in late afternoon spring sunshine and was to be their immediate home.

The Black Badger Inn consisted of a large, solidly built stone pub that stood back from the roadside. Next to which stood the brewery, which was contained by its own low stone wall and separated from the pub by a large cobbled yard. The stones of the walls were covered in patches of lush green moss and the odd weed. It had an air of genteel poverty, of having seen better days and immediately Kevin was reminded of Mr. Wilberforce and his cat Astrophy but Vicki clapped her hands in joy, "It's wonderful!" She had declared, as Kevin drew into the yard and switched off the engine. "Marvelous. All it needs is some paint, a clean up and a bit of renovation and it will be perfect. We could do tours of the brewery. How real ale is brewed, bar meals and some Bed and Breakfast. We will soon be on the tourist map!"

"Hmmmmm, not to mention romping naked around bonfires on warm evenings. That should boost the trade and the local digicam sales!" Reflected Kevin quietly, more to himself than Vicki. He opened his door and stepped down. He went around the front on the van to help Vicki, but she had already alighted. She stood viewing the buildings with her small hands held together in front of her and a look of pure joy on her face. She spun on her heel and laughing exclaimed to Kevin in an excited voice. "It's wonderful!" As they both stood there, taking in the scene together, a door in the side wall of the brewery opened and a lean, straight-backed man in blue overalls stood there looking at them. He had a pipe wrench in his right hand and Vicki, with a burst of inspiration called out, "Hello. Are you Mr. Stoats?" The man nodded, but continued to stand there looking at them both. His face, under a flat cap, neither smiling nor not smiling, no emotions showing. "This is Kevin. Kevin Firkettle." She added, "And I'm Vicki." The man continued to observe them. He seemed to be of undetermined age, anywhere between 50 or 60. Vicki looked up at Kevin and giggled, "Maybe they don't speak English here." She murmured. A large black and white collie dog appeared beside the man, and it too looked at them with a baleful eye. Undeterred Vicki pressed on. "Are you Mr. Stoats by any chance?" she enquired. The man nodded solemnly. "Oh good!" exclaimed Vicki, but now beginning to hesitate due to the man's lack of response. "Mr. Wilberforce told us that you would be here." The name Wilberforce seemed to move the man to action and he very deliberately shut the wooden door behind him and came forward, the dog following at his heels. As he came closer it was clear that though he was not a young man, he was evidently very fit for his age. Kevin proffered his hand and smiling said, "I'm Kevin. Mr. Wilberforce told me that you knew all about brewing and running this place, and that I am to listen to you carefully and take your advice. I know nothing I'm afraid, so I will have to depend upon you totally if we are to make a go of all of this." He waved a hand to encompass the brewery and inn, and looked a little hopeless.

George Stoats seemed suddenly relieved for some unknown reason as he shook Kevin's hand, but he still seemed guarded. Vicki meanwhile had been making friends with the collie. "He's beautiful." She said, patting the dog that now stood firmly erect with its eyes partially closed and its tongue hanging out. "What's his name? Ohh and I'm Vicki, I'm Kevin's fiancée." She sort of smiled as if in explanation and shrugged her shoulders whilst offering George Stoats her tiny hand in greeting.

"He's a she and called Gyp." Remonstrated George Stoats, but quietly and without malice, though no expression crossed his face. He continued in a quiet but guarded tone, still expressionless. "Pleased to meet you miss and you young sir." He paused, then as if coming to some private decision, said, "So you were thinking of carrying on with the business then were you?"

"Oh yes, most certainly we are." Said Kevin emphatically, "And please Mr. Stoats call us Kevin and Vicki."

George looked at both of them quietly, as if sizing them both up. A few long seconds passed and Vicki fidgeted and patted the dog with more vigor. Finally George, looking straight into Kevin's eyes asked evenly, "So will you be needing me and the missus then?" "God! Yes!" Exclaimed Vicki. "You're not thinking of leaving us are you?" "Please don't do that!" almost shouted Kevin. "Everything depends upon you Mr. Stoats. Mr. Wilberforce said that you sort of came with the brewery and we just assumed that you would want to keep things running. We had hoped to expand a little and try to get more trade you see. I honestly know nothing about beer." They looked at him and then at each other helplessly, knowing that their fortunes hung with this strange, quiet, expressionless man. A moment passed and then unexpectedly George Stoats smiled. A quiet and somewhat care worn smile true, but definitely a smile.

"Well I expect you knows how to drink it lad!" George looked at them both again, but this time in a far friendlier manner. Gyp rubbed herself against Vicki and she unthinkingly patted the dogs head. "Well seeing as how Gyp has taken a fancy to you, and these old bones might still be useful, I reckon as how I'll stay."

"Oh thank you Mr. Stoats." Blurted out Kevin. His gratitude and relief evident in his both his tone and body language.

"And you had better call me George young man, you too young lady. Now I think you had better come over to the pub and meet the missus, her name is Beth by the way and she has a bit more meat on her that us lot." He turned and led them into the Black Badger. Gyp following behind.

Like the rest of the buildings, the Black Badger had seen better days. It was in need of paint and furnishings, but was spotlessly clean. The dark oak seats were chipped and worn in the simple bar. As they walked through the lounge, the soft furnishings either sagged or needed reupholstering. The curtains were clean but faded. The horse brasses were all brightly polished, and the bar clean but the pictures on the walls were in a sorry state. The whole atmosphere was one of age and full usage rather than neglect. Rather like an old pair of favorite shoes, clean and polished, but still old and worn. "Beth." Called George in loud voice from somewhere in the back. "Come down here gal, I have someone to meet you." He reappeared and a few moments later his wife Beth appeared.

Beth, was as George had said, a person with more meat on her than they had. Not that she was obese, but well rounded in a Rubenesque manner. She looked to be the motherly type, friendly and with a winning smile. She was also dressed for work in an apron.

"Now Beth," began George as a way of explaining, "This here is the new boss Mr. Kevin Firkettle and the pretty young lady that Gyp has taken a fancy to is his fiancée Vicki." He looked at Vicki and on her cue, she replied.

"Vicki Heart, Pleased to meet you Mrs. Stoats." She looked at George, "Mr. Wilberforce didn't tell us that you were married."

"Oh aye miss, for many a long year now." He looked at his wife and smiled. "Mr. Firkettle was saying that he wanted to carry on with the brewery Beth." He looked contented and nodded to himself as he spoke. "Tells me that he knows nothing of brewing but wants to learn." He stroked his chin as he spoke and seemed to be thinking of times long past.

"Yes I do, if you will teach me please, and please call us Kevin and Vicki." Kevin looked at both of the older people earnestly, and then took off his glasses and polished then vigorously on a tissue.

"Really? That's what you want?" Beth looked happy but incredulous. She paused and looked intently at Kevin and Vicki. They in turn looked at each other, but it was Vicki that broke the silence and took charge.

"Shall we sit down?" She asked quietly and led them all to the nearest small table. When they had all sat down she, bit her lip and then spoke. "I rather get the impression that you are both surprised that Kevin and I want to continue the business." She held up her small hand as Beth started to speak. We were told by Mr. Wilberforce about your husband being here, but he made no mention of yourself." Beth suddenly looked apprehensive. "No matter" Continued Vicki, "You are both most welcome. In fact, to be very honest we cannot survive here and run the business without you. It is as simple as that. Now what is your problem? Please be frank with us. I have put our position to you. If in fact you intend to leave, then we have to radically rethink our situation." She sat back waiting. Kevin was obviously out of his depth and just looked from one person to another, try to gather clues.

"Well Miss." George began quietly, "Me and the Missus live in the cottage attached to the brewery. Old Silas was not a great one for business expansion and we all rather ticked over. Since he was all tied up with that religion thing, it took up his time and he never was one for making money for monies sake. When he died, we knew that there was some chap called Timothy Longstanton ready to inherit. Old Wilberforce and Manny said that he was a total bad lot and would have sold up this lot as fast as possible. Now just where that would have left me and the missus I wonder?" He looked at them quietly and Beth twisted her apron in her hands. Kevin suddenly and quickly replied. No one was expecting him to take the lead, but he spoke quickly and firmly, and with great sincerity.

"No one is throwing you out. Never! It will not happen as long as I have any say in the matter. I, I mean we, need you, and you need us. So we will all work together and share the profits. I never had a home, or a family. I met Vicki and she was all I had. Now I have a home, a business and hopefully two loyal employees to aid and assist me. I know nothing of brewing or running a business. But I want to learn. I want to learn more than anything else I have wanted in my whole life and I truly hope that together we can make a go of the Black Badger and Houghton Springs Brewery." He ended and looked a little flushed and embarrassed. It was after all the first real decision that Kevin had made in his life. Certainly it was the longest speech.

Vicki looked up at him in a mixture of admiration tinged with sadness, "Well done Kevin." Was all she said and she placed her small right hand on his arm and squeezed. Even Gyp sensed that some thing important had passed and she got up from the corner and strolled over, placing herself between Vicki and her master George.

George quietly arose from his chair. He offered Kevin his outstretched and work hardened hand. "You have a deal young man." Were his simply words, "Take our hands Beth. We can trust this man, he has the same mould as old Silas, and as God is my witness, he never lied nor broke a promise." Beth stood and laid her chubby hand on that of her husbands, smiling happily as she did so. "Come on young lady, you are part of this too aren't you?" George looked at Vicki, who in turn bit her lip and looked at Kevin, who nodded his assent vigorously. "To the Black Badger. May she be successful?" Said George in a loud voice, but Vicki started to giggle. "It's just like The Three Musketeers," she burbled uncontrollably, "All we need is hats with feathers. No honestly, I mean no disrespect. "She had caught George's stern look. "I honestly agree with all that has been said and I am proud that Kevin spoke as he did and I know that he meant every word." She continued breathlessly, "And I want to do everything I can to help, it's just I could see us all in the bar mirror and I just started to giggle. I think it was nervousness at being included, and I really do thank you for wanting me included." She looked up at Kevin and impulsively, stood on tiptoe kissing him lightly, saying softly, "You are an honest man Kevin Firkettle." Kevin for his part could not hide his embarrassment and unashamedly blushed. He resorted to further spectacle polishing to cover himself and his feelings. "Tell us about old Silas, and what is expected of me please." He said, more in an attempt too change the mood of the conversation.

George sat back, "How about a few sandwiches for lunch and a pint of Black Badger? Beth will do us some cheese and onion and I'll draw the beer. You do drink Miss as well as giggle I take it?" he looked at Vicki with a friendly twinkle in his eye. Vickie made a wry face and nodded saying, "Just a half please." Beth got up and went out of the room, followed by Gyp, who had obviously recognized that food was about to be produced. George pulled two and a half pints of dark brown beer. Each had a frothy white head. He brought the drinks over on a tray, handing Vicki hers first. "Try putting yourself outside of that then." He said firmly. He stood back and took a drink from his glass, looking expectantly at both of them. Vicki drank and looked up with a frothy moustache, "I like it!" she declared with a smile on her face. "I could soon get the hang of running this pub!" She drank again with obvious enjoyment and wiped the froth from her upper lip. "It's really nice Kevin, better than larger." George snorted in obvious distain that his best ale should be compared to some inferior drink. Kevin nodded and looked at his glass that had retained its pristine head, "Very nice indeed." George seemed satisfied. "I want to learn how to make this stuff.' He said seriously, as he tapped the glass in front of him whilst George sat down. "Silas." George muttered, "Where to begin?" He took a swallow from his glass as he considered the question, then seeming to have found the correct starting point began his narrative. "We were all in the army together, old Silas, Wilberforce and Manny too. National Service it was called and we were all in Malaya together. That's were we got to know each other. Silas was always a one for the ladies. Well those little Asiatic girls were something I can tell you." He smiled to himself as if remembering fond memories. "Before I met the Missus, you understand?" He looked at them both as if needing approval before continuing his story. They both nodded back on cue. Satisfied George pressed on. Well Silas was always going on about his heritage, rights, and things. I never took a lot of notice until he started on about beer. I had been apprenticed to a brewery you understand. Then Wilberforce got interested and Manny was a one for figures and accounts. It all sort of grew, and next thing I knew was I was here helping Silas, Manny was doing the accounts and Wilberforce was fighting off the enemy, so to speak. Now I recon as how in the beginning he did the religion bit just to keep the business going and as an excuse for a bit of romping. He was always a great one for romping was Silas." He paused and gave then an old-fashioned look. "Then he seemed to get more into it, I don't know if he was just believing his own line of thought or if he really did believe? Who knows? Does it matter? He never did anyone a happoth of harm. He never knew about you Kevin." George looked at Kevin seriously. "Honestly, if he had he would have had you here like shot, believe me. When he died I got to thinking that surely there must be some heir some place other than that useless vermin Timothy. I Spoke to Wilberforce and he had been thinking along similar lines, and it was him that sought you out. And a Damn good job too, if you will pardon the expression Miss Vicki?" He sat back in his chair, and then looked up as his wife arrived with the sandwiches. "By heck lass, that didn't take you a minute!"

"Oh I was doing some for our lunch anyway when you called me. So, was just a case of cutting some more." Beth placed the plate of Sandwiches on the table in front of them, along with some paper napkins. "Just dig in; there are more makings in the kitchen if you need." She sat down, "Now, what have I missed?" she asked expectantly, as she helped herself to a sandwich.

"Not a lot gal. I was just telling them about how all of this came about. That's history now. What we need to do is concentrate on our futures." George rubbed his chin and looked concerned.

"But surely that is not a problem?" Kevin paused, and then added not so confidently, "Is it? I mean is it a problem? We were told that really all we had to do was continue with the religion thing, and Vicki and I will handle that and you brew the beer and I suppose you run the pub and we are your apprentices...." He tailed off lamely and both George and Beth looked at each with concern written all over their faces.

Vicki picked up the worry vibrations emanating from other couple. "Please, just what is the problem? If we don't know, we can't help solve it. If it's the dancing naked bit.......

"She looked at Kevin and shrugged, "I have already agreed to do that. I don't suppose that any prying eyes will want to be seen, so I think I can just forget about them. Unless that is you will be there with a video camera George?" She laughed as Beth bristled.

"That he will NOT young lady!" She said firmly but with a friendly smile,

"Aye, more's the pity." Reflected George a little sadly. "No Miss that's not the problem."

"Then please tell us what is." Begged Kevin, now starting to get agitated. George took a mouthful of sandwich, and then a swig of beer. He wiped his mouth on a paper napkin and sitting back, he seemed to consider his words carefully. "It's like this." He began. We have been under attack from the government in the guise of Customs and Excise since we began, but Wilberforce has not only kept them at bay, but has had questions asked in the House about our Chartered rights. No, the Government is not a problem. Just as long as we keep a low profile, they have pretty well given up bothering us. It's only when we get a new lot, like this New Deal Democratic bunch with Billy Boom at the helm, we start to feel any heat. Then it's only new brooms etc and after a bloody nose or two, they sink quietly back into their swamp again to lick their wounds and hope that Wilberforce doesn't embarrass then too much. Usually they quietly pay up in out of court settlements and try to look dignified. No, our problem is much closer to home." George paused again, collecting his thoughts and gyp stirred, looking up over her shoulder at them before again settling down to snooze. "Down in Scrumpton is a soft drinks company owned by

Maxwell Crump. Crump's Cola is his main line. He has his own bottling plant and deep well. The water table is depleted and he is having problems with extraction. Now he can't take from the river, the River Board won't let him. It's a salmon and trout river you understand, National Park and all that stuff. He can't go deeper, not another aquifer. He can't draw from a shallow borehole as the water table runs on towards Frothershome and he would be taking their water with major consequences. So basically our Maxwell is stuck with limited production and no chance of expanding his business, and our Maxwell has big ideas."

"Why doesn't he just up stakes and move the whole works to a better supply?" Asked Kevin, looking as if he had solved the problem at one fell swoop.

"Expense lad. Expense." Cautioned George. "Rumor has it that Young Maxwell is in over his head now and is caught between the rock and the hard place. Not enough cash to move and not enough water to supply an expansion that would pay for the loan he took out for the new bottling line. No our lad wants Houghton Springs. That way he could move directly here, and use our bottling line to tide him over whilst he transfers his plant here. Plenty of room, plenty of water and then there is also Councilor Cynthia Blenkingsop. Widow of the not so late and lamented Colonel Montague Chisem-Blenkingsop of "The County Stores Sporting Goods." Firearms for the gentry etc." and Master of the local foxhunt. He and Silas crossed swords very early on when Silas refused the hunt point blank to cross his land. The colonel near on had apoplexy. I don't think he ever forgave Silas. Anyway the upshot was that the silly old sod fell off his horse and broke his neck, and good riddance too. Left the lot to that damned wife of his, who has carried on the grievance ever since. And it's not helped any by her being a member of the "Soldiers Of The Divine Order" A right potty crowd that would make Cromwell's Puritans look like a bunch larger louts. She wants us closed down and run out of the county and possibly has joined forces with Maxwell. My suspicions are that she will stop at nothing to have us closed down and Maxwell will resort to underhand means if he thinks that he can get away with it." We have been having a bit of problems with the well pumps. Their shed go broken into, but Gyp here raised the alarm. Whoever did it had no knowledge of pumps. So I suspect that friend Maxwell hired some local yobbos from Frothershome to do some damage, but they only knew about hitting things with hammers. Not that it would have not been sufficient mind you. But our pumps are submersible and only the pipe work and cables show The pump house actually only holds the switchgear panels and it's not a brilliant idea to go smacking 380 volts cables with a hammer. That doesn't mean that they won't try again. And now we have the EEC sticking their nose in"

"In what way?" asked Vicki, who had been listening intently.

"Well since Britain joined in 1992, Brussels has been issuing directives left, right and centre. The paper work is huge. But since we are a traditional brewery and only use hops, malt, water and yeast and that is what is specified, I don't have too many worries there. No our problem is one of brewing plant and bottling plant standards. Maxwell is well aware of this and I recon that he will try to get us closed down on public health grounds, him and that Cynthia Blenkingsop. She is really in flap about the dancing and bonfires bit. Work of the Devil is how she describes it. Children of Satan cavorting in our pristine fields sort of thing. So you see we are under siege. We need to keep the pub going, if we fail to brew for more than four months, we forfeit the rights under the charter. We can't run this place and guard against willful damage, not enough manpower. We need to dance the Spring Rites and the EEC could suddenly inspect us at any time any ideas how we can cover all fronts so to speak?" He sat back, blowing out a deep breath. "That and our house and livelihood and Timothy Longstanton too...........

You can see as how me and the Missus have been on tender hooks."

"We need help." Said Vicki firmly. "Spring rites are no problem. Kevin can mug up on the ritual and I will willingly dance naked until I drop if it will keep this place afloat. Lookers on or no lookers on!" She added firmly, "Though frankly what they would find voluptuous in this little body is beyond me, but we will do our best. Won't we Kevin?" She looked at him.

"Certainly will Vicki." Was Kevin's equally firm reply. "Now just where can we get some manpower?" He looked at George and Beth for clues.

"We can't afford it. Simple as that." Declared George flatly. "That and the damn rules governing employment these days."

"Part time then." Said Vicki, not to be dissuaded.

"Oh aye, we can get plenty of part timers, but they are all on the dole, and won't give that up and their Bingo. Cynthia and Maxwell would have a field day. All they have to do is get an injunction banning us for operating for 4 months whilst the courts decide if we were guilty or not. Then it's all over whether we win or loose the case."

"When do we open for business?" asked Vicki in a practical manner.

"Well we are not governed by opening hours either Vicki." Said Beth in a motherly tone. But some regulars folks usually drop by about six o clock."

"And we have to do the deliveries too. I have put them on hold due to not wanting Beth to be alone here after the break-in." Stated George.

"Right said Vicki, taking command. You and Kevin get the van loaded and draw me a map. Give me firm instructions as where to go, in what order and what to expect when I get there. I will start on the deliveries. Beth, you do what ever you usually do and George can introduce Kevin to the subtle secrets of making beer. That is a start, we will worry about other things later." She got up from the table and looked at them all expectantly.

"Well, I'll be!" Murmured George, looking at the miniature Vicki's stance, "I should watch that one young man, has a mind of her own and that's for sure." He nodded his head and Kevin smiled.

"Yes, I know and she is usually right too, so I for one will follow without argument. Come on George; show me how to load our van."

"Well we have our own truck, but I dare say your van is far better, come on lad, let's get to it. Loading it is, and I will get you started and then draw Miss Vicki a map and tell her all about our local farmers and their oddities."

It was late afternoon before Vicki returned. A diminutive figure driving a large white Transit. As she drew up into the front on The Black Badger, she switched off the diesel engine and slid back the driver's door. Kevin, who had heard her arrive, appeared at the side door that George had used earlier in the day. Gyp came bounding out and ran to meet Vicki and receive his affectionate patting. "There's a good dog." Said Vicki, fondling the dog's ears.

"How did it go?" asked Kevin, "Did you get lost?"
Vicki shook her head, "No, I just followed George's map and directions. It was fun, and some people gave us stuff." She indicated into the van where Kevin could see two gutted rabbits and a large black plastic bag. "Wood pigeons." Stated Vicki blithely, "And there is an apple pie and a cake and that sack at the back contains a salmon that I am assured is out of season, but sort of got stranded on the bank and it was a shame to waste it!" She gave him a quizzical look and shrugged her shoulders. "They are really nice people and I would have been back sooner, but always had to have a

natter and a cup of tea. Everyone wanted to know who I was and what was happening." "So what did you tell them?"

"Business as usual and plans to clean the place up etc. I thought that was the best line. Well, it's true." She added defensively, "And I told them to tell all of their friends too. That should give old Cynthia Silly person or whatever her name is and Mucky Maxwell food for thought. Come on unload these empty bottles for me." She indicated inside the Transit that was stacked with crates of empties. "It's too heavy for me, but better ask George where first." She looked at Kevin as she took the two rabbits and Gyp followed her every movement with acute interest and sniffing nose. "I only drive, collect money, goodies and spread rumors." She added, as if in explanation. "Come on Gyp, time to lean how to be a sexy barmaid." And taking the pair of rabbits she headed for the door into the Black Badger, escorted closely by Gyp, leaving Kevin behind standing in the yard. A Kevin totally bemused by her dynamic attitude. He scratched his head, blinked through his glasses and then, doing as his past conditioning had molded him, turned back into the brewery to locate George and instructions as to where to place the empty crates.

Beth it seems, having taken Vicki at her word, had carried on as per normal. That it seemed included cooking an evening meal for them all. "Only a steak pie and chips with a few peas I'm afraid." She said in an apologetic tone, "But I can put Nancy Greenway's apple pie in to warm and do us some custard." Nancy Greenway it seemed was one of the regular customers who had some arrangement regarding apple pies and discount on bottles of Black Badger. As indeed it seemed did most customers. Payment in kind being part and parcel of the business. "Those pair of rabbits will do nicely for a stew and pie too. I'll just pop them in the freezer; we'll have that half salmon tomorrow."

Vicki had settled herself down into an easy chair in the kitchen by the AGA range, and was drinking the cup of tea that Beth had handed her. The kitchen was spacious and had a large pine table in the middle. A welsh dresser, also made from pine and quite as antique as the table, dominated one wall. Mugs hung from its hooks and decorative plates looked back at her from its shelves. A large china cabinet stood against another wall and there were cupboards and shelves too. All holding their own particular items. The kitchen was obviously Beth's work room, and the command centre. Beth caught Vickie' appraisal.

"There is a cold larder too where we keep the ham and bacon, and also the veggie." She pointed to a door behind her. Then continuing without break and in a rather nostalgic tone, "Silas used to like to do the books in here, on the table there, but there is a proper office. And a typewriter." She added with a touch of pride. "Oh by the way, I put all of your stuff, not that there was very much." She smiled gently, "In the master bedroom." She smiled again in a knowing and motherly manner. "It's the only room with a bed you see." She paused and looked at Vicki, "Well I know how you young folks think different from us old 'uns, but there again we had plenty of practice with Silas." She laughed. "He was quite a character you know, but he was a kind man and never set out to hurt anyone. Just had his odd little ways. Your Kevin reminds me of him you know. Not so much the looks, but the gentle nature. I think you made a wise choice of husband there lass." And leaving Vicki to ponder her words she went towards the pantry area, saying as she went. "Why not have a bath Vicki, the range gives us yards of hot water. Then we can eat before the rush starts. Not that there is much rush these days, but the locals don't like any sudden changes."

Kevin enjoyed the meal in the cozy kitchen. Not just the food. Which after having done some manual work, to which he was not familiar and not built for either, gave him a healthy appetite, but the atmosphere too. This is what a real family feels like, he thought silently to himself. This what I have been missing all these years. He looked fondly at Beth and George and then at Vicki sitting beside him. "Penny for them." Said Beth. "You were miles away lad. Has that man of mine been working you too hard? He's not got the build for humping barrels around George and no more has the lass for that matter. Lord I have seen scarecrows fatter than these two."

"No, honestly." Kevin protested, "I was just thinking about the Black Badger." Vicki looked at him and he had the strangest feeling that she knew that his answer was not 100% true, but she said nothing. "It's the diversion of labor." Began Kevin to hide his true feelings. "I just can't see how we are going to cope without extra help. There's just too much work."

"There is certainly a lot of work, that's true. There again we don't get a lot of customers. Most of our trade is delivery to the farms and such. We can cope with things as they are but not any expansion and frankly we only cover expenses now. If you are talking expansion, new equipment, more customers, that means a lot more bar sales. Which means higher production rates in the brewery. And then, yes we are short staffed. Even counting your help in the bar and Kevin in the Brewery, we would be hard pressed. Now we will have to bring ourselves up to EEC standards it seems and work night shift too to guard the plant. Then there is the need for new barrels, they don't come cheap and look around the bar. We can't expand without some investment in new furnishings." George tailed off. "I'm no defeatist, but those are the practicalities of the matter." He held up both of his hands, palms open to wards them.

"We need a business plan." Stated Kevin firmly. "And more help, certainly in the short term for security, if nothing else. I shall phone Wilberforce first thing tomorrow and get him to talk to Manny. We need some capital to tide us over for a short spell, even if we have to take a bank loan." Vicki looked at him in amazement, but no one else noticed her slack jaw as Kevin continue. "We will also need a decent computer and access to the internet." He looked around the table and was met with approving nods. Vicki quickly regained her composure and turned her look of amazement into an open mouthed nod too.

"I will lock Gyp up in the pump house tonight. She will set up a racket if anyone comes lurking around and that should frighten them off. More so if I let fly into the air with barrel from the shotgun." Stated George emphatically.

"You be careful George. We don't want any accidents." Said Beth in a worried tone.

"Oh I dare say I will take the pellets out first gal, claim I was shooting at a fox anyway."

Vicki had remained quiet throughout, as if embroiled with her own train of thoughts. They were disturbed by the bell in the bar ringing. Beth looked at the large clock on the kitchen wall. "Now I wonder who that can be?" She declared. "It's too early for old Tom. You clear away here love." She said to Vicki, "And I will go and see."

"May I come?" asked Kevin hopefully.

"I don't see why ever not Kevin. It's your Pub after all. Maybe it's your first customer." Kevin followed Beth into the bar.

Sitting at a bar stool was a man that looked to be in his early thirties. He had unkempt dark hair and he wore thick-rimmed spectacles that gave him a bookish air. He smiled a winning smile as they came in behind the bar. "I hope that you are open." Began the young man. Kevin took in that he was wearing a tweed jacket with leather patches at the elbows.

"We certainly are." Replied Kevin in his best "Mien Host" manner. "What can we get you?"

"A pint of your Black Badger please." Said the man, who had started to search through his pockets. He finally produced a curved pipe and a pouch of tobacco. Beth had taken a glass and was pulling energetically on the beer pump. The dark, frothy liquid streamed into the glass and formed a firm head.

"Can't recall seeing you here before." She said in an open voice. "Passing through are you?"

The man was now busy tamping tobacco into his pipe from the pouch. "No, not at all, I live over the hill in the old Grange." He struck a match and began to suck noisily. "Peter is the name. Peter Goodbody." Clouds of fragrant smoke that had a strong scent of toffees filled the air.

"I thought that was some Government place for refugees or something?" Ventured Beth. "Can't say as how you quite fit into my idea of a foreign refugee somehow." She left the sentence hanging. Peter took a swig of his beer.

"Hey this good stuff!" he exclaimed, looking at his glass. "I heard about this place on the web, on a real ale site, but no one seemed to know much about you. Do you have your own website?" He looked at them waiting for an answer. Beth looked completely blank, but Kevin stepped in.

"Not yet, but we are considering it. We have to be careful as we are not allowed to advertise."

"Are you not now?....

Well you could claim that it was just information of general interest. Home brewery etc. I'm sure that you could get away with that if you were careful." He relit his pipe and puffed again. "Pity really, this is a damn fine brew. Anyway to answer your question. Quite correct, English to the marrow. I run the place."

"What sort of a place is it then exactly?" asked Kevin, now also curious.

"Oh a sort of half way house sort of thing." Kevin visibly shuddered at the term half way house as visions of bloody pavements filled his brain. He shook them off quickly, but no one seemed to have noticed and Peter was saying. "When they are accepted as political refugee status and have no family or friends and damn little English too, the Government places them with us at the Grange. The idea is that we find them part time work, and the Government subsidizes the factory or what ever. That way they are introduced into the British way of life, get to assimilate the language and culture, make friends etc. etc. Stops them from falling prey to unscrupulous property owners and starting new ghettos in the inner city areas. Remember, most of these people are from rural backgrounds."

"Just a sec." said Kevin. "Let me see if I have this correct. You have spare manpower. You need to place this manpower where they can learn all about the English way of life, and the Government will subsidize their wages?"

"That's about the gist of it. Snag is, the Government, in it's infinite wisdom, decided to locate us down here, just about as far away as one can get from any industry of any size. Except in Frothershome that is. But they have more labor than they need...."

"He shrugged and looked a little hopeless.

Kevin looked excitedly at Beth. "Peter, oh by the way I am Kevin and this is Beth. Now Peter I might just be able to assist you. It just so happens that we do need some help right here and as soon as possible."

"My word! Is that so, well I will be only too pleased to help, but you have to know a few things about your prospective temporary staff." He again paused to relight his pipe.

Kevin said to Beth, "Please ask George and Vicki to come in on this, it will save me having to repeat it all again later." Beth nodded and trotted away. "Just hold fire Peter until the rest of the team arrive. I have inherited this place and we mean to make a go of it, but we are short handed." Beth reappeared with George and Vicki. Vicki was drying her hands on a towel. "This is Peter and he has something to tell us." Stated Kevin simply.

Peter explained that he was the head of the Refugee rehabilitation centre that was Government funded. That his refugees all consisted of Kharzinistanies and pretty well all had little idea of English. He had been selected for the job of head of the centre as he had majored in Kharzi, as the language was called and Central Asian studies. "At least I can communicate with them if nothing else." Was his comment. He went on to explain how the Government's plan was to place the refugees in local industry and heavily subside the companies that accepted them, explaining the reasoning behind the move was one of integration into the British way of life. "I mean," he said in a forthright tone, "What could be more English than a country pub and a real ale brewery too no less. You could employ some men for all the heavy work in the brewery and no doubt one of the women in the kitchen, maybe a young girl too to help out?" He looked at then hopefully, adding, "Honestly with the subsidies in place the cost to you really would be negligible." They all in turn looked to Kevin. Kevin was suddenly aware that he had overstepped his mark and all of his natural fears, built up over the years flooded back. He was not used to making decisions. Decisions had always been made for him. He was a follower, not a decider. Kevin began to panic. He licked his lips, and hesitated, realizing that all eyes were upon him and he had to make a decision. He looked at Vicki for assistance, but she just looked back quietly. Kevin had no idea of what she was thinking, did she approve, or was this just a wild idea, a drowning man clutching at straws? Kevin began to sweat and had a sudden compulsion to flee. He looked at Vicki again, but could not bring himself to ask her what she thought. Then Vicki imperceptibly gave a tiny nod and Kevin felt a flood of relief wash over him. "Yes" was all he could manage, and all the others nodded their assent too. Kevin sighed a great and heartfelt sign of relief. He had made a decision and it was accepted as being the correct one. He suddenly felt buoyant and clapping Peter on the shoulder said. "Thank you Peter, that drink is on me and the next one too!" He looked at George and Beth for approval, but they were both smiling at him. Only Vicki had a distant and sad look in her eyes.

CHAPTER: 6

They had spent the rest of the evening serving the local regulars that usually came with each weekend. They were farmers in the main, and remained in the bar. However, the lounge held a smattering of folks from other walks of life. All, in each group, except Peter seemed to know each other. Takings were not enormous, but Kevin could see that there was potential for expanding the business. Especially in the food sales area. He had spent a lot of time talking to Peter. Peter had been at pains to explain in detail how the regulations operated and strange to say, they seemed minimal from Kevin's viewpoint. Most of the paperwork falling upon Peter's shoulders. "Got to make it attractive you see?" Had been Peter's explanation. The up shot of it all was that The Black Badger provisionally agreed to take two night watchmen, two men for the brewery and a further two female staff to generally assist and clean the place up. The male helpers could work both in the brewery and outside too. Given time, Kevin had observed, even the orchard and grounds in general could be addressed. "Damn fine gardeners you know!" Peter had stated. "They just love to get into the soil. Would have your grounds spotless in no time and if you wanted them to grow vegetables? Well just give them a share of the produce as an incentive and you could be self sufficient I dare say." Beth then observed that she could do with a young girl for general helping out and an older woman in the kitchen if they were going to start to serve proper meals." So it was finally decided that the new staffing would be: Two watchmen on the night shift. Two brewery hands. two female staff and Two adolescents to act as general handy men and gardeners. The Black Badger had grown over night by over 300%!

The last customers left the Black Badger at about 11-30 pm and they closed up by midnight. George taking Gyp down to the Pump house for the night and doing a last minute check of all doors and windows on the brewery. Silence descended upon the Black Badger, broken only by the hoot of a pair of barn owls that had long nested in the brewery store shed and hunted rats and mice for a living. "If we put some owl boxes up in other places, we might get another pair to live here." George had observed. "Been meaning to do it for years. Ah well, we have some help tomorrow, so that's the sort of job that can get done now I recon. A vegetable garden is a damn fine idea Kevin. Any of the farmers around here will dump us a load of cow manure from their winter stalls for a couple of crates of beer. You leave that to me, I'll sort out the lads and the gardening bit. There is a large plot that is well overgrown and has not used for years up beyond the orchard. We could get some potatoes, carrots and greens in no trouble if we have help. Might even get that old greenhouse functioning again and grow some tomatoes too." George gave Kevin a very satisfied look and almost hummed to himself. He nodded and commented, "We aren't lacking for tools either, plenty in the old shed." And he went off with Gyp to do his rounds.

Kevin and Vicki were tucked up in the one huge bed that had belonged to Silas. The Teddy Bear duvet somehow looking small and out of place among the heavy, dark oak furnishings of the large, old fashioned bedroom. Vicki had been very quiet all evening and Kevin sensed that something was wrong, but he could not work out what was the problem. He was worried that he had made some gaff. However, try as he might, he could not recall having said or done anything that would have given Vicki cause for offence. Kevin tried to rekindle the happiness that she had shown when they first arrived.

"What's the matter Vicki?" he asked, "You don't seem to be as happy as when you first came. Is it something that I have done? I mean I tried to do as you would have wanted. Have I made a mistake? If so, I am truly sorry. I would never deliberately hurt you. You must know that by now" The last sentence had a slight note of panic in it, mingled with sincerity.

Vicki was silent at first but then said quietly, "No Kevin, you did very well, I think that you made the only sensible choice that was available to you."

"But you are still not happy with me are you Vicki?" His voice held a note of concern and unhappiness in it, but also a hint of non comprehension too.

"Is it important to you that I am happy Kevin? I mean really important?" She lay quietly beside him on her back, speaking softly but very seriously.

"Yes! Yes Vicki, it really is" Kevin replied quickly and earnestly. "I want you to be happy, it's very important to me."

Turning slowly on to her stomach, she raised herself up on one elbow. Vicki cupped her small chin in her hand looked down at Kevin with a wistful look on her face. As if she was thinking about distance things. She was still wearing Kevin's plaid shirt and she pulled at the collar as she quietly considered the face that looked back up at her. She and traced its outline with her small hand. The sleeve of the far too large plaid shirt fell and brushed Kevin's face as she quietly let her hand drop beside his head. A full moon was shining brightly outside. They had not bothered to draw the curtains as Vicki had commented on how pretty it was, and its clear light bathed the bedroom in its pale white glow. Colors faded into softer tones, and vision was foreshortened and slightly blurred. She pulled at the long sleeves of the plaid shirt that belonged to Kevin with her free hand, and then pushed a stray wisp of hair from her eyes. "Kevin,' she began seriously. "We had a business arrangement." She laid a small and delicate finger on his lips when he tried to protest. "Yes we did Kevin and you have kept your side of the bargain like the gentleman that you are. However, remember that I told you that you would grow? Well I didn't expect it to be quite so fast Kevin. No," She placed her finger on his lips again as he began to protest.

"Shhh, listen to me please. Just look at what you have achieved today. You have taken this place over. Seen that it has great potential. Sorted out the problems and started expanding. You have taken charge Kevin. You made decisions. Important decisions. All on your own. You will soon be making a lot more." She sighed as she looked down at him in a sad and friendly manner, and then continued as Kevin listened. "I will keep to my side of the bargain but I know that I will be left behind in all of this once the road in front of you becomes clear. There won't be a place for silly little run away girls with a Midland's accent in your life Kevin. It will be a completely different type of lady you will want sitting next to you at breakfast. So that is why I am rather quiet. I hope that we can remain friends Kevin, but even that will be difficult once someone else enters your life." She shrugged her small shoulders, "It was a nice dream for me Kevin Firkettle, but I know that was all it was. When I saw this place I loved it, but I know that it cannot be. Dreams are dreams Kevin, and I can't be part of yours. It's a pity, I like it here and I liked you as you were. I knew all along that this would happen. It was just that I hoped it would have taken longer and we would have more time together." She tailed off and rolled over on to her back again.

Kevin was silent. He considered what Vicki had said and he realized that he was losing her. He fought down the rising panic and tried to marshal his thoughts and emotions into some semblance of order. He took a deep breath and began. "Vicki, I haven't known you for very long. You came into my life out of nowhere. Just the same as the Black Badger. To me you and this place and George and Beth are all sort of one thing. I felt like I belonged here today when I ate at the table with you all. It was like as if I suddenly had a family. I have never known that ever before in my life. I liked it, it was a good feeling. We were all pulling together and solving a mutual problem together."

"Yes!" Intervened Vicki. "I could see that, but they are your family Kevin, I'm just the outsider."

"That's not how Beth and George treated you!" contradicted Kevin, "They were very nice to you!"

"I didn't mean like that Kevin. Of course they were nice to me. It's you and me I'm talking about."

"What have I done?" queried Kevin incredulously. "You just said that I had behave correctly!"

"KEVIN. Let me spell it out to you. I feel that you will soon be very capable of standing on your own two feet and won't need me. Then I will be in the way. OK? Understand?" She had again raised herself up on her stomach to look at him but her face had changed and now looked defiant, but at the same time as if she was on the verge of tears. She rolled on to her back again with a resigned sounding sigh escaping from her lips.

"What a load of Bloody nonsense!" exploded Kevin hotly. He raised himself up and looked firmly down at Vicki in the moonlight. "I could never have made any decisions without you standing behind me. I don't have that kind of strength and confidence. I have never made decisions before. I have never had to. They terrify me now; I have to look at you for guidance. Anyway, anything positive that comes out of this venture is tied very firmly to you. I owe you Vicki and I always will. I will never forget that. We all shook hands remember, one for and all that stuff? You have a stake in all of this.

"Exactly Kevin." Vicki said quietly from her prone position beside him. "And anything you do for me will be out of gratitude?" It was half statement and half question.

Kevin rolled over to look at her more closely and placed one hand each side of her head.\. He thought how small and vulnerable she seemed lying there in the big bed in the moonlight. He paused, still looking intently into her elfin like face, its edged blurred in the moonlight. A sudden deep and overwhelming compassion came over him. Feelings that he never knew he possessed flooded his very being to the core. He tried to consider his thoughts, but could not manage any logical train of reasoning. What was firmly pushing its way to the front of his mind that this was a very important moment in his life and if he made a mess of it, the consequences would be dire and lasting. Kevin knew that there was no turning back and that he had to follow his heart. He paused and looked at her some more in the soft moonlight. Then not knowing where the words came from and touching Vicki's hair gently, said he said quietly and firmly to here and with deep sincerity. "You are very beautiful Vicki. The moonlight highlights the auburn tint of your hair, and I want to be able to always to see you like this beside me. I am nothing without you Vicki Heart. I don't understand you or what is happening in my life, but one thing I am absolutely sure of is that I need you beside me." And he gently kissed her on the lips."

Vicki froze, for just a moment and placed her small arms around him. "Kevin Firkettle, you are an old smoothie and have a way with the ladies." She admonished him gently. "Do you mean that? I mean REALLY mean that? The for ever bit?"

"Yes Vicki I do." Replied Kevin, "I just cannot imagine my life without you being there. You are just perfect. Any decisions that are made I need to make with you. Vicki. We can make a go of this place together. I can learn from George and you can learn from Beth. Eventually they will have to retire but not before I have all the secrets that George possesses. Anyway we would need to keep them on and they don't have any other place to go, so I guess that George will become a sort of consultant."

Vicki giggled, "George a consultant. I can just see him in that flat cap and boiler suit of his, handing out his business cards!" She laughed some more and snuggled down into the bed still holding Kevin close to her. "So what's the plan then?" She asked.

Kevin snuggled down beside her and holding her small body close to his said, "Well, first of all we get the help and set up the night watchman thing. Then we clean up the place to EEC standards, dance the dance, and look to open up the trade some more. Whilst at the same time leaning the trade ourselves."

"Yes Kevin, I know all that. I mean our plans you and me?"

"You mean marriage and babies and all that sort of stuff?" Kevin relied as if it was a new concept.

"Yes Kevin, all that sort of stuff as you so succinctly put it."

"I dunno." Was Kevin's response. This has all sort of taken me on one leg sort of thing. I hadn't thought that far ahead. My first hurdle was to try to stop you from deserting me and leaving me stranded. I don't mean just The Black Badger, I mean in my life. Honestly Vicki I have nothing without you. You are everything to me. I can see that now. You are the single most important person in my life and I can't understand why it took me so long to understand that fact."

"You mean like a whole week or so Kevin?" Vicki looked at him and giggled, using her mock serious voice. "It took me a whole ten days or so to get you to work out that I am the best thing since sliced bread.......

WOW! Where do we go from here I wonder?" She waited expectantly.

"Get you a new ring I suppose would be a good start." Was Kevin's answer.

"No; actually that would be a bad start." Contradicted Vicki. "Beth would notice immediately and there is no point in getting one the same now is there? Let's just get this one made smaller. It's a nice ring anyway and I do like it." She brought her small arm up from under the duvet and waggled her fingers. "It's just that it keeps slipping off, even with wool wrapped around it."

Marlene would never have stood for that!" exclaimed Kevin

"NO! I dare say she wouldn't.' Countered Vicki quickly, with an edge to her voice.' There again, I AM NOT MARLENE! So please no more odious comparisons and her name is henceforth taboo. More so in bed! It's called jealously if you didn't know Kevin Firkettle. And by the way, I still think Firkettle sounds like a descaler" She sniffed for effect, but secretly smiled to herself and snuggled even closer.

"OK, OK, just trying to be helpful." Said Kevin in a conciliatory tone. "So we keep the ring. Just as long as you are happy with it." He looked at her in a questioning manner.

"That's it?" Said Vicki, looking incredulous. "Just, "We keep the ring?" Nothing more. How romantic can this boy get when he asks a girl for her hand in marriage?"

"Well I did say that your hair was auburn and not sort of red like." Offered Kevin. "I am learning, but I'm not much good at these things."

"Hmmmm," signed Vicki, "How about kissing me and telling me that you love me, and that you will never leave me, and will always take care of me? How about that bit Kevin?"

"But you know all of that!" Protesyed Kevin.

"SO TELL ME AGAIN ANYWAY!" Vicki demanded, kicking him under the bed clothes with a small foot. Then adding in a more gentle voice, "I'm not really as tough and strong as you think Kevin Firkettle. It's just I have had to learn to fight my corner and just like you, I too need love and attention." She pulled him towards her and whispered in his ear, "Do you know what two people who love each other do in bed together Kevin?" She whispered softly.

"Do you love me Vicki?" Asked Kevin as if the thought had just occurred to him and pulling away a little so that he could see her more clearly.

"Yes Kevin I do. I don't know why but when I thought that I was losing you, I realized just how important you were to me."

"Oh I knew that you were important to me from the first night that we slept together."

Vicki laughed, "What a romantic! Could you rephrase that statement please?" She hit him playfully.

"Well not like, oh you know what I meant. Anyway, I only know that I always want to be with you and I know the rules, so I also know that I didn't feel this way with, "That OTHER person." See? No names. So, if that is love, then I love you too Vicki, but I don't really know what love is as there hasn't been a lot of it my life."

"So Kevin, what do you suggest we do about this situation, and I mean right now. Here and now?"

"Umm, I don't know. I mean I don't know what you want me to do and I don't want to do anything that will hurt you."

"Well since this is a magic bed." She looked at him seriously and wiggled her bare toes against his leg "Yes it is. Just think about all of those young maidens who met their fate here with uncle Silas." She tailed off looking at Kevin with a sparkle in her eyes. "All that roggling."

"All that what?"

"Roggling Kevin, making love. SEX you dummy. Kevin Please, kiss me and make love to this nearly maiden who is frantically panting and will be a total push over!"

"Vickie!" Cried Kevin in alarm. "You know how I told you it was before." He looked at her in a mixture of confusion and worry.

"Kevin Please try. Look I'll take my panties off." She slid her hands under the bed clothes and wriggled. "There, all ready to go. Honestly! I never thought that I would end up begging for someone to give me a good roggling." She laughed, "Oh come on Kevin, let's just cuddle and kiss and see what happens, sooner or later it will all work out." And she held her small body close to him murmuring," Just cuddle me first Kevin and tell me again that you love me. Let Uncle Silas do the rest. I'm sure that he is looking down at you right now and approving of all your actions."

Vicki was the first to wake. She lay in the large bed, still cuddled up to Kevin. She stirred and gently stuck her tongue in Kevin's ear. He mumbled, and then laughed, pushing her small hand away as he did so. "You know what happens when you do that." He complained in mock earnest.

"Mmm, I know. I was sort of hoping that it would happen again."

"I think that it might." Said Kevin with interest, "In fact I'm sure that it will."

"Oh good." Said Vickie lazily. "Take me, Take me." And she giggled. "Steady Kevin, I'm only little, you don't want to go breaking anything before it's all run in. It doesn't come with a maker's guarantee." She giggled, saying, "Slowly please. Mmmmmm, that's better."

Maybe somewhere old Silas grinned.

"You look well this morning Vickie." Was Beth's comment as she poured hot water into the large china teapot that stood on the range, "You must have slept well. She gave Vicki a very old fashioned and knowing look and smiled contentedly. "He's a nice young man is that fellow of yours. Very sensible. When were you thinking of getting married then?" She looked at Vicki with her head turned a little to one side and her tongue just touching her bottom lip as if in anticipation."

"Why? Do you fancy the job as bridesmaid?" Vicki gave a twirl and held out an imaginary skirt, laughing gaily as she did so.

"Just a wee bit too old for that job lass, but you would make a lovely bride." She said wistfully, more to herself than to Vicki. Adding, "George and me were never blessed with children." And bringing the teapot over to the table, she placed it firmly on an old blue colored ceramic tile.

"Well we haven't set a date yet." Said Vicki, in a practical tone. "We were sort of hoping to get this place set up first."

Beth looked at her in a kindly and motherly manner, "Don't leave it too long lass, no magic left then."

"Oh Beth, there's all sorts of magic here." Vickie's eyes sparkled. "I'm sure that there is plenty left." She swept her arm around the room in a large circle and her eyes sparkled even brighter in happiness and she laughed.

"My word, we are in a good mood this morning! It must be Silas's bed!" She laughed too, adding, "Oh there was a lot of magic happening in that bed I can tell you." She started to pour tea, smiling to herself as she held her thoughts.

"There still is Beth." Said Vicki quietly. "Believe me, there still is."

Their conversation was cut short with the arrival of both Kevin and George. They were in deep conversation and didn't really pause as they sat down at the table, saying good morning to the two women as they did so. Beth was busy at the range cracking eggs and turning over thick rashers of home cured ham in the pan. The two men involved her in their conversation as she cooked. The up shot being that she and Vicki would put together a list of things that needed to be done to revitalize The Black Badger in order of priorities and each would supply an estimate of costs. This included opening up the spare rooms, of which the old Inn seemed to have abundance. Vicki assuring them that catering for bed and breakfast would be profitable. George and Kevin performing a similar exercise with the brewery and bottling plant. Peter Goodbody was due at nine o'clock with his promised labor and assorted obligatory Government forms all completed as far as possible and ready for signature.

Peter duly arrived on time with four older men, two young men who looked to be about eighteen or perhaps nineteen and two women. The older men all wore heavy black beards and seemed to be all in their early forties. They were also wore dark red colored turbans on their heads. Peter had explained that they were all members of some small religious sect that had been pushed out of their home turf by the larger and more dominant tribes that were still embroiled in a civil war in Kharzinistan. Kevin was reminded of pictures of Pathan tribesman and tales of the Khyber Pass. Certainly these men favored baggy trousers and high leather boots. All they needed was some long barreled flintlock carbines and they could stand in as extras on a Hollywood set, he mused. The male labor force was divided into the guards and the day shift. The two young men were obviously not traditional and wore tee shirts and jeans and denim jackets. They were a breezy, friendly and good looking pair and both sported dark, but well trimmed beards. Travel arrangements were made, and all the other odds and ends that are required for who would do what, when, where and how etc. Basically two men would stand watch at night and the other two who had carpentry skills, would help in the brewery and be general handy men. The two lads were going to be in the main responsible for the grounds and garden. The two watchmen went back with Peter and the two women were placed with Beth. One was a pleasant looking woman in her mid thirties and the other a young girl, some relation and about 19 years old. The older woman was wearing a dark dress but the younger jeans and a tee shirt. Nobody seemed to have any great command of spoken English, but all seemed to understand quite well. The two older men were both keen and friendly and George was obviously happy with his charges. "You done well there boss." He said smiling at Kevin, "We won't have any trouble with these two. Both strong as oxen and happy to work." Kevin felt relieved, and realized that George had called him Boss.

"I don't feel like your boss George." He ventured. "I know so little and have so much to learn in such a short time."

"Well fact of the matter is that you are the boss lad, and you are doing a good job. As to whether you feels like the boss, is up to you. All I can say is that you doing a good job so far."

Kevin noted that he had been demoted to lad again and the praise was only conditional. "I will do my very best George. For all of us. And with your and Beth's help and Vicki pushing me from behind, we will make a go of all of this." He stood back and waved a hand to encompass his empire.

"Ay, you have a fine lass there Kevin. But she is strong willed, so best to give her a loose lead." He nodded in a knowing way. "I recon that we can set those pair of young lads on the orchard today and setting out a vegetable garden up on the top beyond the trees as soon as possible. If they can drive I might even manage to wangle a tractor and cultivator." He winked at Kevin. "That will save some manpower." He pointed to an area that was out of sight, beyond the orchard. "It's a nice level patch, sheltered by the hill here and the apple trees and has high hedges on three sides. South facing, good land too and a real little sun trap. It has been dug over for years, so no great hardship to open it up again. There used to be beehives up there. But they are all stripped down and in the outbuildings now. You might fancy starting up a hive or two? Then we can make mead again. Years since we made mead." He reflected, with a fond smile on his face. "Old Wilberforce will love that. He had a ding dong battle over the classification of mead. It weren't cider, that's for sure but was it beer?" George pushed back his flat grey cap and scratched his head, smiling. "Now that was the question? Government said it weren't beer. Local council agreed. They thought that they had us by the short and curlies..... Ha! Old Wilberforce had set it all up before we even fermented the brew. Ran circles around them all he did. Meanwhile we weren't allowed to sell a drop. Customs confiscated the lot, barrels and all. Old Wilberforce just smiled and bided his time. Then he produces some legal document going back Lord alone knows how long. Henry the Sixth or some such time. Anyway, we won. Then the Customs had dumped the brew and the cross petition started. We claimed for the barrels, loss of earnings, and cost of the brew. Every thing sort of slander. They settled out of court, as usual. Went off to lick their wounds little knowing that we had only used the old barrels and the brew was not up to scratch anyway. We did very nicely out of that one thank you." He doffed his old cap to an invisible Government and Customs officer. "So Bees is it? Right time now you know. I know were we can get a brood. The high hedges keep them safe and make them fly high, so no dangers. We can get the men to disinfect the hives and get Ambrose; he's our local beekeeper, to set us up with a couple of broods. Good for the apples too."

Kevin looked blank, and shaking his head said, "Why not?" Just as long as I don't have to get close to the bees. I mean who will look after them?"

"Don't you fret any boss. My Beth loves the little fellows. A right dab hand she is with bees." And he smiled a happy smile, whilst Kevin noted that he again been raised in rank. I'm beginning to work this all out, he thought to himself. Any decision that I agree with, that George wants me to make and I am the boss. Anything that I might decide wrongly and I am only the lad. So all I have to do is move between boss and lad and I should be on a non collision course. It will probably be the best choice anyway if it's concerning the brewery. So having to his own mind solved a dilemma as to which way to jump, Kevin went about leaning the mysteries of the old brewery plant.

Beth's day was equally productive and she set the young girl busy cleaning out the spare rooms and taking down old curtains, washing windows and deciding with Vicki what should be the color schemes, whilst the older woman was put in charge of making a clean sweep down stairs and helping to prepare the meals. They all sat down together to eat in the old kitchen and Kevin marveled at how his family had grown. The men appreciated George's brew and the women quietly sipped at their glasses smiling whenever they caught Kevin's eye. The younger girl blushing, and was it seemed, the butt of several remarks poked at her in fun and in their own language by the men folk. Vicki looked on and smiled to herself, as did the older woman too.

Peter arrived around six o'clock with the watchmen and then got into a deep conversation with the Kharzi refugees in their own language. He looked at Kevin and shrugged his shoulders at his charges, with a sort of "I don't know" look on his face.

"Problem?" Asked Vickie, "Have we made some dreadful gaff and offended their culture or something?" She looked worried. "I hope not. We got on so well together and we do need them. They all seemed happy and keen to work too." She left the question hanging in Mid air and looked at Kevin with a "What did you do?" expression on her face. Kevin looked blank and said, "We all got along just fine."

"No! No! No!" Assured Peter. "It's just the opposite actually. "They want to know can they live here? They like it here. They like you and are very happy to work here. They just don't want to run back and for to the hostel." He looked questioningly at them and opened his hands waiting for their response. "They have so much more privacy here, I guess. Or maybe it's the old village and family thing. The hostel is very institutional."

Vicki stepped in asking, "Assuming that we had no objections and that we could house them. Could they stay with us?"

Peter scratched his head. I suppose so. I mean I can't think of any reasons, legal that is, why not. I mean it really is integration isn't it? That is after all the Government's stated aim. It would certainly solve a transport problem. Right now I have to use our mini bus and skip back and fore twice a day. Not that it a problem you understand. But it does take time. I'm free to pay reasonable expenses, so a breakfast etc. is no problem. Then there is the heating, water too. I can fix all of that. Of course from your point of view is the advantage of being able to stagger their off days. We could move their beds and lockers here in your transit. No, I can't think of any objections from our end. In fact, it would suit me better. It really is up to you." He waited for their reaction.

All eyes again turned towards Kevin. Kevin did not panic as he had done previously when confronted with a decision. He said to Peter, "Excuse us just one moment Peter whilst I call a meeting of the board." And he indicted to the others than they should meet in the other room, around the kitchen table. Once inside the kitchen and with all members present Kevin addressed them. "Well we have a proposition that we allow the Kharzinistanies to live here." He held up his hand to stop comments as he had not finished. "Yes, I know that there is nowhere for them to stay, but assuming that there was. What are your feelings on the matter?" He sat back in his chair and waited for responses to his question.

Vickie remained quiet but George and Beth started an animated conversation between them selves. Finally George turned to Kevin and said," Well, me and the Missus have no objection and think it might even be to our advantage to have them all here, but that does not solve the problem of where to house them all." He waited and looked at Vickie. She just nodded and indicted that she had no strong feelings one way or another and was happy to go along with any decision.

"So assuming that we can solve the accommodation problem, you both feel that we should allow them to stay?" He looked at George and Beth, who both nodded saying, "Yes, if we can solve the accommodation as you said."

"Any suggestions?" Enquired Kevin, looking hopeful.

"Yeees, maybe." Offered George, looking at his wife. "I was thinking that we could clean out the old brewery offices. Give it a coat of paint. It has two large rooms upstairs and a smaller one next to the main room downstairs. It also has a fireplace, and the jackdaws have failed to nest in the chimney as yet. The men could have the upstairs rooms. Two are on night shift anyway. The women could take the downstairs room. It won't take that much cleaning up and if you are thinking of refurbishing The Badger, Well, I dare say we can cut the carpet oddments here and there. I mean, it's no Ritz hotel, but it's dry, warm and has a toilet. WE could easily put in a shower. They would all be together." He looked at his wife, who nodded.

"It might just work." Beth said seriously. "But it needs a fair old clean up and paint job, that's for sure. There again would they want to be all together?"

Kevin spoke, "So assuming that the Kharzis agree, then we are all in favor?" He was met with firm nods from all around the table. "OK, let's talk to Peter."

They spoke to Peter, who in turn spoke to the Kharzis. "They are happier staying as one group." He explained. "It's the tribal thing I suppose." So all together, as one group, they inspected the old brewery offices.

"You know." Said Vicki, looking the rooms over for the first time. "It really could be quite nice." The Kharzis obviously agreed and it was decided that Kevin would take a trip into Town with George and purchase all what was necessary to begin the conversion and then let the Kharzis loose on their new home. Peter promised to supply beds and bedding and cupboards. He claimed that he had a lot of unused stuff at the centre.

A few days passed by and life had begun to form a routine in the Black Badger and brewery. George had shown them the brewery transport. It consisted of an aged Morris Minor with a split windscreen and a side valve engine. It did actually start, but from the amount of smoke coming from the exhaust pipe, the engine was consuming equal parts of oil to petrol. Kevin shut it down and viewed it sadly.

"Ay." Agreed George, looking at Kevin's face. "She's a right old bag of nails. The truck's even worse!" He added helpfully.

The truck was indeed in a very sorry state. It was an old Second World War Army vehicle that had been stripped and converted to carry barrels. It had been modeled upon an old brewers' dray and at one time must have been a bright machine. Painted as it had been in reds, blues and greens. Gold colored, Gothic lettering, edged in black ran down the length of the vehicle on each side. Proclaiming that it was the official transport of Houghton Springs Brewery. Whilst, over the cab was a painted a large black badger. Kevin shook his head sadly. "Pity really." He reflected. "Good job we have the transit!" He looked at George, "How did you deliver to the farms George?"

"Oh we stopped delivery a long time back." Commented George, off handedly. "Vicki's was the first in ages!"

"No wonder the farmers were so pleased!" Exclaimed Kevin. "You set us up George! You planned for us to take over and move forward from the start!"

"Maybe, maybe not." He scratched his head, pushing back his cap. "A lot depended upon you two." He smiled secretly. "Knew from the moment I set eyes on that little lass of yours that things would work out. So what will you do with these old relics? Put them to good use same as me and the Missus?" He laughed.

"I don't know George. I would like to restore them, but One. I don't have the skills and Two. We don't have the money. But I would love to see it all repainted in its original colors and carrying our beer." Kevin looked wistfully at the dilapidated lorry. "They aren't eating anything and my guess is that they are worth money, so I guess we will just put them on to the back burner for a while." He took one long, last look at the old lorry and followed George out.

The men had all but finished the painting of their new home and Peter was bringing the beds and other stuff in drips and drabs, using the transit. The two young men had set to in the orchard with a will and a local farmer had turned up with a tractor and rotovator and not only dug out the garden, but had also at the same time rotovated in a considerable amount of farm manure too. George had laid down another brew, the bees had been ordered and word had got out that the Black Badger was under new management and that real food was now also on the menu. More people started to come in at lunch time and then the evening trade picked up too. Soon Kevin and Vicki had a whole new circle of acquaintances. All of whom soundly approved of the developments at The Black Badger. However, in Scrumpton Bridge, not everyone was so enthusiastic.

CHAPTER: 7

Maxwell Crump, of "Crumps Cola" to name but one, was not a happy soul. Maxwell, a heavily built, sour faced man with cauliflower ears and a mean temperament, had invested heavily in a new bottling line for his soft drinks factory. A factory that was placed next to the old gas works and had, in his father's time, been advantaged by the rail link. The rail link, along with the production of gas and his father, had long since ceased to exist. Now the depleted deep water aquifer, from which Maxwell drew his soft drinks water, was going the same way. Maxwell had not thought to ever question from whence his supply of liquid wealth originated. It had satisfied his father's needs and so, to his reasoning, it should satisfy his. Or so Maxwell had assumed. Unfortunately, with the growth of Frothershome, to the north and the new light industries there, the existing deep water table, from which Crump's Cola drew its water, had been placed under great stress. More being extracted than was being replaced.

Frothershome had been designated an "Expansion Area" by the New Deal Democratic Government of Billy Boom, "Silly Billy," as some called him and under his government's tenure, expand it had. Offering as it did virtually free light factory space and other generous, but not so obvious perks in the guise of light tax and heavy subsidies to any Japanese, Chinese, Taiwanese or other foreign company wishing to avail themselves of the opportunity under the New Democratic Government's scheme to make a fast buck. All on the basis of employment in a rural area and maintaining low unemployment statistics. The employees in turn being subject to income and many other more subtle taxes. Thus contributing to the subsidies that

tempted the foreign companies to set up shop in the first place. It could
be argued that they were in fact paying for their own employment to a
large extent. But since the arrangement seemed to suit both sides of The
House Of Commons (Many MPs having stock in the companies concerned)
the situation was quietly resolved by allowing the industrial area to tap
the shallow water table that ran from Scrumpton Bridge north, under
Frothershome. However the situation was not being helped much by both
towns drawing drinking and domestic water from the River Trolop which
in turn depended upon the shallow water for a natural replenishment. This
extraction of drinking water having been hotly contended by the river
board management. They had however been under great but quiet and
subtle pressure from Whitehall and a confidential compromise situation
was quietly agreed. Since the River Trolop was a noted salmon and trout
water, and an area of outstanding natural beauty, all extraction was strictly
controlled and regulated. Hence, any shortfall in domestic water needs,
also had to come from the deep water table. In short, though no one had
noticed it, Scrumpton Bridge and Frothershome were about to run dry.
The Government had bigger fish to fry and larger problems on hand than
one puny, acne scarred soft drinks manufacturer with an "Almost" police
record, and rights to draw heavily upon an already depleted water supply.
Maxwell was dumped.

The only other fresh, sweet water supply was Houghton Springs. This
lay on a totally different aquifer complex that was quite extensive in depth,
but very localized and that all lay firmly in the hands of Houghton Springs
Brewery and its owner, Kevin Firkettle. Past brushes with Houghton Springs
Brewery were legion and not even The New Deal Democratic Government
felt that it was politically opportune to take them on again. More so on the
basis that they needed to requisition the brewery's water supply to subsidize
Scrumpton. This being due solely to the Government's shortsightedness in
the first place. A whole can of worms of vested interests, deals and nefarious
alliances could then come to light. The opposition and tabloid press would
have a field day. No, that was the last thing HMG wanted. So best let
Maxwell go to the wall. In any event, he openly supported the opposition.

Maxwell however, needed to get his hands or rather his pumps on Houghton Springs. The Government for their part, were far more interested in obtaining Yen, Rinminbi or Taiwanese Dollars, or anything else for that matter, rather than assisting a sole, small businessman survive. As Billy, "The man of the people" was so fond of saying, Maxwell just did not see the big picture. Maxwell could not have given a rat's arse for the big picture. All Maxwell could see was the slow demise of Crump's Cola and various other brands that he bottled for other companies. That in turn ending his extended holidays in the Caribbean and cosmetic surgery for his wife. Not to mention Mandy and the Pied de Terre in Birmingham. Maxwell felt that he had been stabbed in the back by the damn socialists. He also felt very aggrieved that instead of Houghton Springs Brewery dying a decent death along with the demise of Silas and thereby opening up a slot for he, Maxwell to exploit. He had been robbed of his livelihood. Maxwell Crump was a deeply disgruntled soul.

He had, on several previous occasions approached old Silas with a generous offer to buy him out lock, stock and beer barrel. Each time however, Silas had shown no interest. This had frustrated Maxwell even more, as he had felt that since for once in his life he was being reasonable, then the cards should by rights, fall his way. Maxwell having fallen into the trap of thinking that if he believed something strongly enough, then it would happen. More so since it was, to his way of thinking a logical and sensible move on behalf of Silas. Maxwell just could not understand why Silas should refuse his offer. Maxwell grew bitter and he had waited and waited and waited thinking to himself, "Will the old boy never die?" But, finally, Silas had passed on to the Great Brewery in the sky and even better, no heir was around to step in and take his place.

Then word finally filtered through of Timothy Longstanton. Maxwell quickly made Timothy an offer. Timothy accepted. Unknown to Maxwell, Timothy was happy to accept any and all offers in the fond hope that he could sell to as many people as possible and skip the country fast with the profits in tact. However Timothy now had somehow just disappeared.

Maxwell could not reach him by telephone. The landline just rang and rang and the cell phone said unavailable. Houghton Springs brewery had some new owner and the word was out that expansions were planned. Also that the new owner was not just blood line to Silas, but followed the same strange religion and had a nymphet on hand ready for the Spring Rites ceremony too. Thus Maxwell fumed in frustration.

Maxwell was a well-built individual, and had often been in trouble when he was younger. Nothing too serious, a bit of bullying here, a few fights there. Always with smaller children and youths. All of which had been taken care of by his father who was a Freemason and had various friends in the police force. He was also friendly with some local Magistrares and often played golf with them. Maxwell was not a Free Mason, didn't play golf, nor did he have friends on the Bench or in the Police Force. In fact, the opposite was true. Maxwell had a record of aggression and traffic offences and had always sailed a little too close to the wind with regard to legalities. Consequently Maxwell reverted to form had done what to him was the obvious. Once Silas was dead, he had imediately began a campaign to frighten George and Beth into leaving. His objective, to obtain the water rights by default. If no heir was present, then the brewery would fall to the state and be placed up for auction, or some distant relative in Tasmania would turn up. Either way, the place would be run down and vandalized in the interim period. Maxwell would ensure that happened! He even considered arson as an option. Thus, he would purchase the plant all nice and legal for a song. Since he had no interest in continuing brewing, this would stand in his favor with regard to both Government and local Council. What Maxwell had neglected to take into consideration was the abilities of the yobs he had hired. Two young trouble makers in their last year at the local comprehensive school. Nor that in the process of carrying out the plan, that they might come in contact with large quantities of Black Badger ale. As a consequence of which be well intoxicated when they attempted their acts of vandalism. That coupled with no knowledge what so ever of mechanical plant, had resulted in what was actually minor damage. This time Maxwell would not make the same mistake. He decided to hire some heavy boys that he knew from one of the clubs in Frothershome. Maxwell had decided to pull the gloves off.

Councilor Cynthia Blenkingsop was the widow of the late Colonel Chisem-Blenkingsop. Actually, he had risen to no higher than Captain in the Catering Corps in the regular army. However upon taking his discharge Captain Montague Chisem–Blenkingsop had been obliged to join the Territorials, maintaining his rank of Captain. He had inherited Blenkingsop's Meat Pies upon the death of his father. The Territorials were in need of catering services from time to time. As were local gentry for weddings and such. Soon Ex Captain Chisem-Blenkingsop was riding with The Hunt and driving a Jaguar. His rise to Colonel in the Territorial Army being due to a combination of Free Masonry cronies, useful contacts and his discount rates for friends, rather than any military ability. The good Colonel had enjoyed life to the full. Making full use at the same time of his ability to purchase alcohol in bulk and at reduced rates. With the passing of years, his figure grew fuller and his nose redder. His moustache more flamboyant and he was in many respects a well known, and well liked, county figure in the mould of Colonel Blimp. He studiously attended all functions, speaking banalities and the obvious in well-modulated tones and upsetting no one in the process. He was a popular figure, who offended no one and gave every occasion a certain Je ne sais quois. Always available, providing drinks were free and never without a glass in his hand. The latter trait being his ultimate downfall. He had come to an untimely end whilst trying to simultaneously swig whiskey from a hip flask and negotiate a fence on his hunter. The horse stumbled and the poor colonel, resplendent in Pink, fell, breaking his neck. His loss was mourned throughout the county and immediate arrangements were made to find another caterer and source of cheap alcohol.

Cynthia Chisem-Blenkingsop came from landed local gentry. A small, plump, matronly energetic widow just into her fifties, she had enjoyed the prominence that came with the social standing of her hailing from a well established, local farming family and her husband's rank. Becoming a county councilor had really been a foregone conclusion in her life. She had been quite a good councilor, outspoken, patronizing and arrogant true, but for all of her failings, honest and reasonably sensible. She had also been quite devoted to her husband, who had been some years her senior. She had seen herself in the role of Squire's wife and had spent her time breezing around the county opening old people's homes, charity auctions, dog kennels and campaigning to keep the cottage hospital. However, upon the demise of the good Colonel, the poor lady had become quite distraught and somewhat unhinged. To the extent that she had turned to religion for her sanctuary and succor. The religion of her choice however, was not that of the local parish church. Had that have been the case and she had gone about spending her spare time placing fresh flowers in aisles, polishing the brass work and arranging the parish fete, no doubt all would have been well. Cynthia however had fallen under the spell of, "The Soldiers Of The Divine Order." A rather radical sect that had its origins in The Bible Belt of America. Her conversion coming about by answering the door on a Tuesday afternoon to a couple of well-dressed and politely spoken young men. Well dressed and politely spoken young men being at a premium in the UK at the time. Young men who had quietly but insistently pointed out to Cynthia the error of her thinking, the evils of demon drink, and the regretful state of public morals. They had continued in this vein and had finally ended up criticizing pretty well everything that even hinted of enjoying oneself even in moderation. This all being classified under the heading of The Devil's work. Since Cynthia's marriage had been childless and not actually included too much sex. The good Captain being away most of the time with his troops then later with his Free Mason friends and finally with a bottle. Cynthia was both a frustrated and resentful person. The Soldiers Of The Divine Order found fertile ground in which to plant their seed in Cynthia. The seed took root and bloomed not so much into a tree as more primary jungle. The outcome being that Cynthia was now a bulwark for temperance and abstinence. There being none so fanatical as the recently converted.

It had been Cynthia who used her influence upon the council to obtain land and planning permission for the sect's temple. A small, uninteresting, breeze block structure with cement rendering, but with a fine high pulpit from whence a steel eyed, sharp featured preacher could look down upon his flock and thunder at them about the loose moral behavior of mankind and the Hellfire and brimstone that awaited all sinners. Sinners in their mind being a loosely classified group of any persons not holding to their particular beliefs. So a pretty harmless bunch of non conformist nut cases. Or they would have been had it not have been for Cynthia being both a member of their sect and a councilor and holding strong views regarding public morals and alcohol.

Houghton Springs Brewery was a thorn in her side. Not only did it produce the demon drink. It did so in blatant contention of Customs and Excise statutes. If that wasn't enough, the owner did so under some heathen charter. A charter that gave him the right to brew his pernicious libations at will, providing he continue his depraved cavorting with young, nude, nubile young women. Cynthia bristled in righteous indignation at the mere mention of The Black Badger. Coming from good puritan stock, she had always held firm, if somewhat muddled views regarding sex. Sex was something only to entertained whilst in the holy bond of marriage. Not that she had ever done much bonding. Cynthia was a complete hotch potch of confusion. On the one hand totally frustrated sexually and yearning to be ravished. Realizing at the same time that the chances of such were pretty slim. On the other, lashing out at the very thing she yearned for most, to assuage her frustration. All around her she could see other people enjoying what she wanted most, but due to circumstance and social position was prevented from participating in herself. With the demise of her husband and rapid conversion, she had fallen upon he knees and thanked The Lord for striking Silas down and expressed her fervent hope that he would burn in Hell for all eternity without the option of parole. Maybe not quite the forgiving sentiments expressed in The New Testament, but ones to which Cynthia whole-heartedly held firm. At last! She thought, The Black Badger has been smitten by the sword of The Lord and shall not blight the land from this time henceforth. No more will naked females prance and flaunt their bodies in heathen licentiousness. She had thus proclaimed so from the pulpit even, (experiencing hot flushes as she did so.) Calling upon the congregation to raise up and rejoice. Which, being conditioned to do so, they obligingly did. Now the word was out, not only did Silas have an heir, but a young heir too, and one that promised to not only continue in the grand and debauched manner of the late Silas, but possibly eclipse him to boot. Difficult times make for strange bedfellows, and the unlikely alliance of Maxwell Crump and Councilor Cynthia Chisem-Blenkingsop, was about to be born.

Both Maxwell and Cynthia were fully aware of the date upon which the Spring Rites Festival was due to fall. Both also knew that should the ceremony not be performed, then this would offer an opportunity to bring Houghton Springs Breweries production to an end once and for all. Both then, each in their own way, went about sealing the fate of Kevin's livelihood.

Cynthia took the course of action that required Divine intervention. Accordingly, each night she fervently prayed that there would be some freak of weather that brought in a sudden snowstorm with a chill factor of -40C on the night of the Spring Rites. Thinking happily to herself, "That should nip them in the bud." Or possibly that should nip their nipples in the bud, or whatever. The more she conjured up in her mind's eye the picture of young bodies coupling in the damp grass, the more unsettled she became. Young women with firm young bodies and men built like stallions. It was all too much, and dreadfully unfair too. There she was, a fifty one year old widow, childless and having known no man except for the drunken fumblings of her husband. Who she had passionately adored, but with whom she had been unable to communicate. Left now high and dry on the shelf with little to which to look forward. There had been Silas, well over sixty, still pulling young girls, brewing and drinking with impunity, and cocking a thumb at God, the Government and the local council too. Now the whole scene was about to begin all over again, but this time with a fresh generation. Cynthia did not know if she should take to the bottle, religion or the night ferry to Amsterdam and the nearest sex-toy shop. She settled for religion.

Maxwell took a more practical route and planned to sabotage the breweries water supply. To this end, he hired some heavies.

Cynthia, now fully convinced that her prayers would be answered and the ceremony prevented from taking place by spiritual intervention, took it upon herself to involve the local press. Her logic being that if the ceremony upon which the charter stood were to be unilaterally abrogated, then proof would be required. The press, smelling that once again, the old antagonists were heading for the ring and someone would get a bloody nose, took interest. Quietly they ran a book in which they gave Councilor Blenkingsop odds of 10:1 against placing the knock out blow. Anyway, now that there were new performers dancing naked, a few nymph like, but decorous shots might liven up circulation. They were after all in the business of selling newspapers for a living. Whilst all these machinations were being conducted at a local level, somewhere along the line, someone in Whitehall goofed and cats came leaping out of the proverbial bags.

Whitehall was getting some stick from the electorate regarding asylum seekers. The tabloid press would have one believe that every cross Channel train was laden down with illegal persons of other religions and skin color. Each lashing themselves to the underside of the wagons, with if not the blatant assistance of French police placing a finger on the knots, then certainly standing by in the role of deaf, blind mutes. "The Floodgates have been opened." Shouted one headline. "Hoards unleashed." Blazoned another, not wishing to be outdone in the hypo bole department. Consequently, good asylum news was in short supply. Peter Goodbody's placing of Kharzinistanni refugees in not only erstwhile employment but actually, "Embedding" them in a small rural community, was a Heaven sent gift. Embedding being the buzzword of the moment. This was not unnaturally seen as a major achievement, and one, which the New Deal Democratic Government should exploit. The small fact that the embedding had been of major assistance in the prolonging of the existence of Houghton Spring's Brewery and the Black Badger as a thorn in the Government's side being overlooked in the process and general exhilaration of the moment. They notified the National Press. Suddenly someone within the corridors of Whitehall did their homework and the consequences were understood. The Government realizing that they were now skating on dangerously thin ice. Any minor digging would reveal the past concentrated attacks upon

Silas and abysmal failure to shut him down. Equally embarrassing now was the situation in which the Government was subsidizing the Black Badger to employ the refugees and aid Houghton Springs Brewery. This would be picked up with gusto by the opposition and exploited to its full. Billy Boom shuddered at the possible headlines. "Government uses cheap foreign labor" would be the very least he could expect. With an election looming, the last thing Billy Boom, Leader of The New Deal Democratic Party wanted was this particular can of worms to be opened. He called a private Cabinet meeting at Number Ten. So totally unbeknown to Kevin, he had become a hot political issue and possible the cause of a change in Government.

MI5 and 6 ran a thorough check on his background. Nothing untoward was found. Kevin was a nobody, a nothing, a nonentity. The girl was a total mystery. No records seemed to exist for her. Or so the reports stated. The small fact that a laptop containing all their information gathered thus far, had been left on a tube train and stolen, was quietly ignored by both services. So they smoke screened fast. Camberwell Crescent offering a beautiful opportunity. There was the strange incident that had occurred in the house next door, they reported to HMG. However, they added, no evidence was found that linked either of them to that unfortunate circumstance. The police had concluded that it was some drugs turf related; gangland killing that had gone wrong. Since only ex convicts had been killed along with a stray cat, The Met had breathed a collective sigh of relief. Said good riddance to bad rubbish and got on with more fruitful occupations like catching speeding motorists with hand held radar units. In fact it was proven beyond all question that they, Kevin and Vicki, were not even in the area when the fatal pizza was delivered, but driving their recently purchased van. Certainly, a question hung over the head of Timothy Longstanton, but he was now discounted, as he no longer had any connection with the Black Badger. Furthermore, he had been involved in a road accident that was miles away. Thus her Majesty's Secret Service dispensed with Kevin as being a threat to the country. Anyway, they were fed up with running stupid errands for the lot in power.

Now though, the British Real Beer Drinkers Association was mentioning The Black Badger on their web site and counterparts in Europe were showing an interest too. Before they knew where they were, Billy could see The Black Badger as being front-page news. There was no way of capping the story, so what could he do to capitalize on the situation? Billy, as usual went for the 180 degree about face, with subtle built in provisos. At the slightest hint of past failed actions and Governmental embarrassment, he would act. Blaming all previous actions upon the opposition and a local council that was not a supporter of his party. He would take a trip to The Black Badger, be photographed quaffing a half pint in the company of the, "Where ever they came from" refugees. Suitable spin could then be applied and Billy would come out as a staunch supporter of, "The Little Man and ethnic minorities" Religious tolerance could be played up and nude dancing definitely played down. Meanwhile, under the new EEC food and drink regulations, some nook or cranny could be utilized to shut them down once and for all. Thus could Europe be blamed and spin applied so that Billy was seen as having to fight against superior odds, brought about by the previous government having surrendered its sovereign status to Brussels. It wasn't an ideal solution but the best they could cobble together at short notice. So unbeknown to Kevin, he was about to take centre stage.

Kevin and Vicki were taking the Spring Rites very seriously. Kevin had donned the ceremonial robes and had Beth make necessary adjustments in their fit. He was a good deal slimmer than Silas had been. He felt that he looked quite impressive in the white robe and blue and gold trimmed red cloak. The very high white wizard's hat with the green tassels was a bit over the top, he felt but he was too superstitious to either dump it or remove the tassels. He practiced in front of a mirror. He had made up some fine sounding gibberish, which he accompanied with lavish sweeps of his ash thumb stick. Whilst holding the leather bound copy of the rites in his other hand.

Vicki had bought some clear plastic slippers. These were to protect her feet from stones and sharp objects whilst performing the dancing. She had taken to rehearsing with Kevin up stairs in front of the mirror and insisted in performing nude. "I must feel the part." She had asserted. Standing on tiptoe, with her arms held high above her head and fingers clasped. She studied her reflection seriously and stuck out her small chest so as to obtain maximum effect. "I'm glad that I trimmed the pussy hairs." She said more to herself than Kevin, viewing her small body in the full length mirror and attempting graceful ballet like, stylized movements. Sooner or later though, such cavorting always ending in laughter and Silas's magic bed as Vicki now called it. And so, as Cynthia prayed for rain and snow, Maxwell assembled his two heavies and made plans of destruction. Kevin and Vicki celebrated their love for each other and practiced their role. The Kharzistanies learned the dark arts of brewing and the two young lads worked diligently both in the garden and orchard, setting hives and seeds. George and Beth steadily upgraded the Black Badger using whatever labor was available and the two watchmen did their rounds at night. Meanwhile the Black Badger prospered, and the bars gathered more customers especially at weekends when Beth found that she had to begin to consider table bookings. Billy Boom had laid his contingency plans and the local press was getting ready to secretly photograph Kevin and Vicki and the Spring Rites. Everything seemed on hold, except for Maxwell and his henchmen.

Now, though it had registered at some level that The Black Badger had employed foreign labor, in the manner of the rather insular British, they had been discounted and left out of the equation. The two watchmen were never seen. Being asleep by day and outside in the dark at night. Anyway, one Kharzinistani in the dark looked much the same as another to a local. Certainly, the younger, local lads were aware of Melchi, the young girl and spent fruitless hours trying to impress her. Melchi for her part smiled a lot, looked wistful, giggled and moved on. Labor was divided and sometimes Vicki waited on tables and sometimes Melchi and also Vania, the older woman. Beth was very much responsible for menu and cooking, though both of the younger women were quite adept at cooking too and very soon could copy all of Beth's standard fare. Rabbit pie and chips with peas, gravy and a pint of Black Badger being a favorite meal with the customers.

It was the day before the Spring Rites Ceremony was due. Kevin was feeling nervous, but Vicki was unperturbed. "No one will be there Kevin."

She admonished him as again she practiced in front of the mirror. "And if they are, it will be my little body that will interest them." She did a twirl and then wiggled her slim hips provocatively.

"That's exactly what I mean!" Stated Kevin firmly. "I don't like the idea of you prancing about naked Vicki."

"OOPS, sorry my Lord and Master. And there was this small maiden thinking that you enjoyed it." Vicki pouted at him, adding dejectedly," Why?" Don't you think that I am attractive enough?"

"No, Yes. I mean that's not the point. I don't like you doing it in front of an audience." He looked at her hotly adding, "You seem to like the idea."

"Ahah! So you are jealous Kevin Firkettle. So just what is the oint Kevin? You being jealous, or the survival of all of this lot?" She cocked her head on one side. "Are you really jealous Kevin?" She bent forward lacing her clas ed hands between her closed legs and leaning forward to out at him.

"Yes!" said Kevin firmly and pulling her gently towards him he bent his head so as to bring his mouth close to her ear and murmured, "I love you Vicki and I hate the idea of you flaunting your somewhat less than voluptuous body for all and sundry to see."

"Somewhat less than voluptuous is it?" Vicki giggled and wriggled closer to him. "Well you could still employ Marlene……

"She left the sentence hanging in mid air.

"Well maybe I will have to think along those lines later." Said Kevin seriously.

"You Bloody Well Won't!" Said Vicki sharply. Turning her small face to address him. "If anyone is cavorting naked with my husband, it will be me Kevin Firkettle! You make no mistake about that!"

"I was only being practical." Protested Kevin.

"Seriously Kevin, let's just get this one over first. Honestly, I recon that there will be no one there and if there is they will be well hidden and not want to show themselves. We are committed to this path and too late to turn back now. We both knew exactly what was involved and accepted it. So no more complaining. Just lie down here with me on uncle Silas's bed and make love to me and tell me how jealous you are............

But leave out the less than voluptuous bit please. Maybe if you kiss them, they will grow? Worth a try anyway." And she pulled him towards her. "Just a moment Kevin. Do you think that you could take that hat off first?"

The first sign of trouble came at about one o'clock in the morning. Gyp started barking furiously and there was some noisy and excited conversation in Kharzi, beneath their bedroom window. Kevin sat up and rubbed a bleary eye. Vicki sat up too, her small breasts poking over the teddy bear duvet. "What's going on Kevin?" She asked him in the darkness.

"Dunno. Can't see a thing. Put the light on Vicki, I drew the curtains as there was no moon and it is overcast too. I had better find out what the problem is."

"You be careful." Pleaded Vicki. "They all sound pretty excited. Maybe they are fighting amongst themselves." But Kevin had already slipped into jeans and a pullover and was heading for the door. Downstairs He met George, who had also been woken up by the noise."

"Quiet Gyp." He ordered, as the dog's barking grew more frenzied. They put on the outside light and upon opening the door was confronted by the largest of the pair of Kharzi watchmen. He stood over a very frightened white man, who he held firmly by the hair. A large curved knife, inches from his throat. The man on his knees was obviously terrified and he rolled his eyes and tried to speak. Gyp, picking up on the general tenor of the scene was barking, growling and snapping. The Kharzi watchman, calmly tightened his grip and knife closed in and touched his prisoner's throat. The man immediately though better of speaking and continued to roll his eyes in fear. The watchman went into a stream of Kharzi, indicating with his head back towards the quarry and pump house. George quieted the watchman down with pressing down movements of his hands and then gently placing his hand upon the knife, pushed away from the man's throat.

"OK, what's the story?" he questioned the man.

"Honest mister." Began the man with panic in his voice. "We were just minding out own business and we were jumped by two of these fellows."

George deadpanned him back. "Where?" was all he asked.

"Back down there." The man attempted to indicate with his head, but the Kharzi tightened his grip on his hair ever so slightly, and the man had second thoughts as to the prudence of the move.

"Back down there at one thirty in the morning? On foot?" George added. "Not a very likely tale." He looked at Kevin, and out of sight on the risoner, winked broadly at him. "Best leave him to our friends Kevin. He is obviously lying. I dare say that he will want to tell the truth before they finish him off. Then they can deal with him in the same way as they delt with the other couple."

"What other couple?" almost screamed the man.

"Oh didn't your boss tell you? Tut, tut. Now I wonder why that was? Just why do you think that we employ these heathens? Slicing up little lads like you is child's play. Then they eat most of the evidence! The pigs finish off the rest. No lad, you just keep pleading your innocence and we can all go back to sleep." He clapped his hands together as if that was the small matter solved. "Yes. Take him away and eat him." He spoke to the Kharzi but was careful enough to use a deep local brogue, understandable to the man, but not the Kharzi.

"I'll tell the truth." the prisoner pleaded.

"I don't suppose he cares too much." Observed George. I mean he has his breakfast so to speak. "What do you think Boss?" He turned to Kevin. "Shall we just pretend we heard nothing? Or are we interested enough to hear the whole sordid tale? Up to you?"

Kevin took his cue and kicked at the yard, looking down as if in deep thought. He pulled at his chin with his right hand. "Snag is George, what shall we do with them if they decide to tell the truth? I mean we can't really let the Kharzies eat them then can we? I mean, it's not playing the game is it?" He had done his very best at an upper middle class accent. It would not have fooled the BBC, but there again, the captive had more pressing things on his mind that regional tones. Before he could follow the line of thought any further, the man pleaded with him.

"Look guvnor. I'll come clean. Just get this heathen off my back. Me and Blakey will leave the county. Honest. Like we were never here."

"Hmmmm............" Offered Kevin. "Maybe you will and maybe you won't. Can we take the risk? I tell you what George. Let's go and see what the other one is like and then make a decision. He is still alive I take it?" He looked at the man who was still on his knees and held by the hair, and had a sudden sinking feeling. What if in fact The Kharzis had killed him? They went to the pump house, the man stumbling ahead of them, held in the light of his guard's steady torch beam.

The pump house was situated below the small, moss and fern covered cliff face. The small stream gurgled out of a small cave and wound it's way out towards the road. The pump house drew it's a waters from this source, but deeper inside the cave. The other Kharzi, also dressed in a turban, leather waistcoat and baggy trousers tucked inside high soft boots, was sitting quietly beside the prone shape of a fallen man. Kevin's heart dropped, missing several beats as it did so.

"Bloody hit him hard enough to kill an ox!" protested the first man. "Dare say his scull is all bashed in." Then as if realizing that if in fact his companion was dead, then to remove any evidence, he would be shortly joining him, he sort of gasped and croaked and fell silent, biting his bottom lip.

George bent over the body and inspected it by torchlight. "Best tell us what happened." He said quietly, getting up with a very serious look on his face and looking at the now visibly shaking man. He looked meaningfully at Kevin, and held up his hand, stopping Kevin, who had come forward to inspect the prostate figure at George's feet.

"Maxwell Crump hired us." Whispered the man, Me and Blakey. We were to smash up your pump house. He never said nothing about guards, let alone bleeding cannibals. Honest Mister, just let me go. I won't say a word. Never come back here ever."

"Ahha! Friend Maxwell. Well I have been waiting for him to make his move ever since he bungled the job last time."

"He told us that he had hired school kids to do the job, but they got drunk and messed up."

"Well he hardly going to tell you that if you get caught you stand the chance of being eaten now is he?" George looked at him in scorn. You're lucky pal, your mate is sleeping but should wake up with a nasty headache, but his scull is not depressed. Now how did you two get here?"

"We have a van back along the road pulled into a field." Offered the man.

"Well boss, what do you think? Kill this one in cold blood and feed him to the troops, or let him collect his sleeping friend here and make a run out of the country?"

"I don't know." Prevaricated Kevin, relieved that the accomplice was still breathing. I mean, they would save having to feed these guys and the pigs for a few days."

"Maxwell gave up half up front." Pleaded the man. "You take it, please boss." He dug into his pock and proffered a wad of notes. Falling to his knees as he did so.

Kevin looked at George for just a brief instant and caught George's scarcely imperceptible nod. "Yes, OK"

The man almost sobbed in relief and shuffled forward on his knees to offer Kevin the money. "On two conditions." Stated Kevin firmly. Refusing the notes in the outstretched hands. One, you take this man to the nearest hospital in the next county as fast as possible. He fell whilst getting into your van. Understand?" the man nodded eagerly. "And two. That you never come within 200 miles of The Black Badger again. For if you do, rest assured I will not treat you so kindly next time my man." Kevin maintained his best upper class accent. The man on the floor groaned and tried to sit up, holding his head as he did so.

"What hit me?" He questioned, looking at the fresh blood on his fingers in amazement.

"You fell out of the car. Drunk you were. Drunk as a skunk. I'll get some whiskey inside of him." The first man offered, trying to raise his fallen comrade. "I've got a bottle in the van. Come on Blakey, let's skedaddle sharpish." He managed to raise the man, but fell back with the effort. "Our men will help you." Offered George, "And see that you move out in the right direction."

"Don't worry boss, we 'aint never coming back. They won't kill and eat us once you have gone will they?" He looked worriedly at them.

"The boss always keeps his word. So just remember that and keep to your side of our agreement. Otherwise we will hunt you down. These man take a very dim view of persons who have no honor. They don't even credit them the right to be eaten. Well not by humans anyway."

The man shuddered, "No fear of that boss. We'll keep stum and do like we have been told." George indicated that the Kharzis should help the duo, which they did, but not at all gently.

"Well, well well!" Pondered George quietly. "I suspected Maxwell Crump before. It had all his clumsy finger marks about it. Now we know. We shall have to think about what to do about friend Mucky Maxwell. George rubbed his chin reflectively.

"How badly hurt is the other man?" Asked Kevin, anxiously.

"He should be OK boss but needs to see a doctor in case he has a concussion." George seemed to dismiss the man from his thoughts. "There won't be any more problems Boss. What shall we do with the money?" He indicated the wad of notes in Kevin's hand.

"Use it to make the Kharzi's living accommodation better I guess. I don't know. Maybe we should call Peter tomorrow and let him handle the situation. Frankly, I was worried that our side had killed the other guy. That watchman seemed quite happy to slit throats at the drop of a hat!"

"Yes, Boss, I recon that we need Peter to have a quiet word with them ASAP. We need protection, but we don't need bodies! Well, enough excitement for one night and you have a big day tomorrow. Best get some sleep." They heard a car engine start, and Gyp barking. Then shortly afterwards the two watchmen returned. Kevin thanked them for their diligence and said that he would get Mr. Peter to talk to them all later in the day.

Kevin returned to Vicki and found her downstairs with Beth and the two Kharzi women. Kevin and George recounted their story to allay the women's fears. Though the two Kharzi women seemed not too perturbed. Eventually they all went back to bed, but neither Kevin or Vicki slept well.

When Peter arrived, again the story was retold, this time however it included the Watchmen's version. Kevin and George expressed their fears that a far more serious situation could have resulted and asked Peter for advice. Peter explained to the Watchmen and all of the others too, that whilst they were there to protect the interests on The Black Badger, restraint could be used, but that fell far short of hitting an intruder over the head. The latter course of action would seriously jeopardize their continued stay at the Black Badger. This obviously caused some conflict of interests with the security guards, but if those were the rules of engagement, so be it. Peter was at pains to apologize and went on to explain that from the Kharzi's point of view, the Chief had needed protection and protection was what he got. Peter spent more time explaining the laws of the UK, confusing them even more perhaps. When Kevin handed Peter the money though, indicating that he should take it. Peter said to the Kharzis that the money was theirs and how would they like to split it? There was a flurry of excitement. The Kharzi's went into a huddle and spoke quietly among them selves. Finally, they came to a conclusion and through Peter asked Kevin to hold the money for them as they had something planned for a future date. When pressed, it transpired that Mulchi, the young girl wanted to marry one of the two younger men and it seemed that Vania, the older woman had aspirations towards one of the brewery team too. The money, it was decided by popular consent would be used for the celebration. Vicki and Beth looked at each other when this item of news was broken. Then the Kharzi's went into another huddle and called Peter over to join them. Several times, they looked at Kevin and seemed to be in deep and serious conversation. Finally, Peter nodded to them and walking back to Kevin said. "Well, you seem to have made a big hit with them all Kevin. Not you alone, but all you." He looked at them with a smile on his face, and continued. But seeing as old Kevin here is the boss, they look to him for leadership. Now two of them wish to marry within the group. Do you have any objections?" He looked at Kevin keenly.

Kevin looked a little blank and indicated that really it was up to them who they married and not his business. "Ah! But it is your business Kevin." Admonished Peter gently. "They are here, far from home in a strange country. You have given them refuge. You have provided food and shelter. You have become their leader so to speak. And." He paused for effect and then continued dramatically, "In the absence of a traditional leader, it is up to you to allow this marriage to take place. Your word is final."

"Hang on Peter! Just a moment. You mean that if I am their leader I have the right to agree or not to this or these marriages?" Kevin looked amazed and Peter slowly and seriously nodded. "And if for instance I was to say no?"

"Then they would not marry, providing you were their accepted leader." Explained Peter.

"So if I am not their leader, then I am not involved and they are free to do as they feel fit?" Kevin smiled as if he had solved the problem.

"Nope. Then they could not marry, as they would be bereft of the Leader's blessing. Tradition old bean. Simple as that."

"In other words, I have no choice and have been railroaded into becoming their tribal Leader, even though I cannot speak a word of their language! Jeepers Peter! You be their chief or whatever. At least you can communicate with them! It takes me all my time to stop them from bashing trespassers over the head! I don't need all of this!

"Kevin, what can I do? They want you, not me. It's an honor."

"It's an honor that I don't need Peter!" Kevin looked at the others for moral help. Vicki was almost laughing outright.

"I don't know lad." Said George. "Might not be such a bad idea. I mean you will have some moral control over those two." He nodded towards the two security guards. "And I don't see as how we can continue to work as a team if you don't."

"That lass wants to marry Dimas." Offered Beth, she seemed not to be in the least surprised and on a first name basis too. "Why she and Mulchi have been planning this for a long time. It was only now that their future seemed more secure that they could see a light at the end of the tunnel, so to speak. You have to let it go ahead Kevin."

"Of course you do Kevin!" Said Vicki firmly. "Take the Chieftainship and tack it on to the role of Grand Master or wizard or whatever you are. It's not a major problem." She stifled he urge to burst into laughter. "Maybe you can add some more tassels on the hat?" She forced herself to hold her mirth in and winked at Beth who giggled in return.

Kevin noted that with his objection he had been demoted to lad by George. He also realized that if the Black Badger was to run smoothly, he needed no bad feelings within the team. More so at this critical point in their development. "OK." He surrendered, "Tell me what is involved. Anything for a quiet life. Just as long as I don't have to eat the sheep's eyeballs or anything." He looked at all of them with an, "I Give up" expression.

"Not really sure." Stated Peter in a hesitant tone, "Have to ask them I suppose." He nodded back at the Kharzis and then wandered back to them and started talking. Finally turning back to Kevin. "Well, it all seems pretty straight forward as far as I can make out. They will get them selves organized and then come and present you with their allegiance. Simple as that. Then they request your permission for these four to marry, you say yes and that's about it. Not so bad as you thought was it?"

"And no sheep's eyeballs?" Enquired Kevin Peter shook his head.

"No sheep's eyeball's." He assented. He looked at the Kharzis and gave them thumbs up sign. They all immediately began a babble of excited conversation and both women smiled happily at both their intended husbands and Kevin.

Vicki slipped her arm around Kevin and squeezed him murmuring, "Did you ever read The Astrix Comics? Maybe you get to be carried around on a shield." And she burst into suppressed laughter, that was in the general mood of happiness, was not noticed.

CHAPTER: 8

It was late in the afternoon of the day of the planned spring rites festival that Maxwell decided to check on the Black Badger's pump house himself. He had not heard from his two hired thugs and he was worried. Maxwell Crump had inspected the pump house from the outside. There were no signs of a forced entry. There were however some recent blood stains on the concrete outside the pump house door. The pumps themselves were not running. Obviously the only present water demand was for domestic supplies at the Black Badger. The water, he knew, was pumped up to a high concrete tank situated close to the orchard and well up the slope so as to supply pressure. This tank must be full and the pumps would only start when the level in that tank dropped. Even as he stood there, the pumps cut in and the soft sound of water flowing through the pipes could be heard. Maxwell cursed. His thugs had either failed, of just absconded with the money he had paid them up front. Maxwell cursed again. He looked about him to check that his presence was undiscovered. He stood silent, waiting, but the only sounds were those of wood pigeons in the trees in the woods above. He had taken the precaution to hide his car well inside Battle Woods and he had walked through the trees to the springs. The weather was warm, the day had been sunny, and Maxwell was sweating, but the early chill of a spring evening was cooling the sweat unpleasantly on his body. He decided to climb to the top of the wooded hill and try to quietly locate the proposed scene of the Spring Rites. He knew that there should be a bonfire there ready for lighting. Maxwell slipped along the edge of the brow of the wooded hill, keeping well with the undergrowth and tree line for security. He tried to find the ready made bonfire. Sure enough, there it was, over in the far corner of the top field. Maxwell cursed some more. He settled back into a secluded spot to think and light a cigarette. It was whilst he was smoking that noticed a furtive figure sneaking through the trees to his left. Maxwell silently observed. It didn't look like one of the refugees, in fact Maxwell was sure that the man was carrying a camera. The man also slipped down into hiding. Maxwell pondered the development. He could not move without attracting the other man's attention and he didn't want that. Obviously the guy with the camera was some voyeur, hoping to photograph nude young girls. Maxwell had a little think about that too and came to the conclusion that since he was stuck there, he too might just as well enjoy the show. Maxwell settled in to wait. After about fifteen minutes Councilor Cynthia Chisem-Blenkingsop appeared. She was evidently well prepared and she carefully unfolded some plastic sheeting. This she placed in position just inside the edge of the woods and she also settled down to wait. Maxwell smoked another cigarette and waited to see what developed. Obviously the other pair were both unaware of each other and himself.

Next to arrive were two young foreign looking men. They lit the fire, and once it was well established, disappeared back down into the woods, in the direction of the Black Badger from whence they came. Maxwell decided that the two young men were in fact the rumored employees. Some refugees or something. Apparently The Black Badger had a couple of women working there too. A good looking youngster and a some neat thirty year old too. Maxwell decided to pay The Black Badger a visit. After all, he had every right to buy a pint of beer. Maxwell began to plan his moves. Maybe he could pull one of the women, bit close to home, but it would save nipping up and down the motorway to Birmingham all the time. Cheaper too, and no doubt the woman, being a refugee would glad of a few quid and happy to keep her mouth shut and legs wide open.

His fantasizing was cut short by the arrival of Kevin. Kevin all dolled up in his ceremonial regalia. Maxwell shook his head, muttering to himself, "Bloody weirdo!" as Kevin solemnly proceeded to walk around the fire speaking some strange language and alternately banging his stick upon the ground and stopping. Then to throw open his arms to the four cardinal points of the compass. He then proceeded to throw some powder on the fire that produced a bright green/blue flame. Then to continue in similar manner, as he circled the now well burning fire

Kevin and Vicki has set out together. He dressed in his robes, and carrying the stick, hat and large leather bound book. He had been given two bags of powder by George, who had winked and told him that one contained some copper compound and the other powered magnesium, of the type used in theatricals. "Just in case there are any lookers on Boss." He had said secretively. "No need to tell Vicki, just adds a bit of color, so to speak." Kevin was experimenting with the blue/green chemical first. He rather liked its effect and whilst shouting some more gibberish, threw on a second handful. It produced a most satisfactory whoosh and a very pretty colored flame. Kevin began to enjoy himself.

Vicki had worn a diaphanous gown, that reached almost to her knees. She had then slipped into her already oversize anorak. "Catch me death." She complained and gathered up the gown carefully over her jeans "I hope that fire is nice and warm. Won't be able to tell goose bumps from my tits at this rate!" and she wriggled deeper into the anorak. She giggled. "Go on Kev do your thing and then we can both shoot back down home and have a nice cup of tea. And for Gawd's sake keep that stupid hat on straight or I swear I shall wet my self. Not that it will matter as I won't have my pants on." And she pushed him ahead of her.

Kevin did a few more passes and Vicki, still hidden, hissed at him from the foliage at the edge of the woods. "Hang on Kev. It's colder than I thought, I must have a pee." Kevin worked his way around the bonfire again making more signs with his stick in the air and apparently evoking Gods, Spirits or whatever. Then turning towards where Vicki was hiding he threw his arms open wide and shouted in a loud voice, "Appear wood nymph." He brandished the leather bound book in one hand as he did so and waved the thumb stick about in the other. Vicki appeared in her transparent gown. The breeze caught it and Kevin thought how pretty she looked as she danced around the fire, arms making graceful movements.

Maxwell took notice. "Not bad." He muttered, "Bit on the skinny side, but I wouldn't chuck it out of bed." He glimpsed the cameraman surreptitiously taking shots.

Vicki danced some more and Kevin did a fair imitation of The Sorcerer's Apprentice. He began to really enjoy himself and threw some more of the powder on to the fire. Vicki twirled around and then shed her flimsy, transparent robe. Kevin, now well into his role, evoked the Gods of the Spring Rites. He waved his stick, whilst at the same time trying to keep the high, pointed hat from falling over at an angle and blocking his eye sight. He was making a mental note to place a headband inside to make the hat fit better when he noticed a movement out of the corner of his eye. He turned his head a little too sharply and the hat tilted down and slipped over one eye. But he had taken in that Vicki, who was on the opposite side of the fire, had her back to the intruder and was unaware of her presence. Not for long. Cynthia Chisom-Blenkingsop strode purposefully out from the edge of the woods, brandishing a large wooden crucifix, shouting at the top of her voice, for them to cease their pagan incantations immediately. Maxwell took notice and wondered just what the councilor was doing. The cameraman grinned to himself and refocused his lens.

Cynthia was making a great deal of noise and she was visibly annoyed. She strode up to Kevin and knocked off his wizard's hat with her crucifix screaming, "BEGONE, YOU SERVANT OF SATAN!"

"Steady on!" exclaimed Kevin, more in surprise than annoyance. "Watch what you're doing with that cross lady!" He avoided another attack, and bent to retrieve his hat.

Vicki had stopped dancing and ran around the fire to Kevin's side. "Push off you stupid old bat!" She cried, "Mind your own business."

"It's The Lord's business. It's my business. It's everyone's business." Declared Cynthia, in very loud and dramatic tones. "You are the embodiment of Satan!" She pointed the cross at Vicki.

"No she's not!" Said Kevin hotly. "She's my fiancée, and you are trespassing, so piss off and leave us alone, you stupid cow!" He tried to push Vicki behind him.

"Easy Kev, this fire is bit hot on my bum!" Complained Vicki, trying at the same time to get from behind him, but not come within range of a wild eyed, cross waving Cynthia. Kevin too was keeping a watchful eye on the cross. It was he noted, rather robustly constructed out of a hard wood with a pretty solid looking metal Jesus nailed on it.

"You may well gaze in awe upon our Lord." Declared Cynthia solemnly. She again threatened him with the cross. "For it's the Devil's work you are about. Be gone vile serpent!" She shouted at the top of her voice and she held the cross like a club above her head. "For the Lord shall conjure up angles with heavenly armor to smite you down, Satan's Spawn." Her face was now purple and her eyes all but popping out of their sockets. The camera clicked again and again.

"Oh go and conjure yourself up a psychiatrist, you stupid cow." Said Kevin firmly. "I've had enough. Come on Vicki, get your clothes on." And he took Vicki's hand and threw the two bags of powder into the fire. The blue/green powder, of which there was still a little remaining, ignited immediately. The magnesium powder, which was as yet unused, took about two seconds before it ignited with a huge flash of brilliant white and blinding light. At that moment the two Kharzi guards appeared, wearing as they did, high boots, baggy trousers, leather waistcoats and turbans. Cynthia, who had been looking directly into the fire at the time, had staggered back away from the minor explosion. As she regained her sight, she was confronted by a large cloud of white smoke and by what appeared to her already agitated mind, to be two savant's of Satan. No doubt direct from the fires of Hell itself, and willing to do their Master's bidding. In her already frenzied state, it was just too much, and she dropped into a dead faint.

"Bloody Hell. Said Kevin fervently, "Where did you two spring from?

"Maxwell too was amazed at the timing. He fully realized that this was some simple magicians trick, but he gave Kevin full marks for pulling it off. This new owner was going to be a difficult nut to crack if he planned this far ahead.

The newspaperman was all but wetting himself in mirth and knew that he had some marvelous photographs. He, Like Maxwell, ducked down into the bracken and remained stationary.

Vicki left the scene with as much dignity as she could muster and out of sight of the others, slipped back into her jeans and anorak. Kevin looked at the prone woman at his feet. He shook his head, saying. "Oh pick the silly cow up." And he stumped away back towards The Black Badger, calling out to Vicki as he did so. Cynthia Chisem-Blenkingsop was rather unceremoniously slung over the shoulder of the larger of the two guards. They all plodded back towards The Black Badger in an extended group, down the slope and through the budding trees. Disturbing wood pigeons as they did so. During the trek, the councilor came round, but seeing that she was being carried on the back of a presumed Genie or whatever, no doubt heading for the underworld, she mumbled incoherently and promptly passed out again. The two Kharzis ignored her and purposefully continued unhurriedly. Gyp appeared to greet them and wanted to join in the new game. She jumped up at Cynthia and tried to nip at her skirt. Everyone ignored her and discouraged she wandered off to chase squirrels or other more interesting doggie pursuits.

At The Black Badger Kevin went to change and found Vicki in the bedroom also changing into fresh clothes. "Who the Hell was that I wonder?" asked Kevin in wonderment, removing his cloak.

"Buffy The Vampire Slayer is my guess." Offered Vicki unhelpfully. "I thought that cross was a wooden spike. Gawd! Kevin, you might have warned me! Nearly catch my death of cold, goose bumps all huddled together for warmth. Next thing out leaps Aggie the Witch waving a cross and calling me all sorts. What do you do? Sling some bomb on the fire and POOF! The two demon kings appear. No wonder the poor cow fainted! As for me? Well I'm left standing there nuddi. Nigh on frozen on one side and my bum getting third degree burns on the other and pussy exposed for all the world to grin at. I tell you Kevin, it's hard to maintain one's dignity with out pants and bra. Even more so when you are toasted"

"I'm sorry Vicki, I really am, but honest, I haven't the foggiestv who she is."

"Oh come on sweetheart, get that fancy dress outfit off and we will try to get the bottom of all of this. I thought that perhaps there would be a couple of voyeurs and actually I rather got a buzz from that. But I never expected the pantomime.

.... Watch out. He's behind you... Then as for the two Kharzis. Well the bosses bit of stuff is just not supposed to reveal herself to the workers. What The Hell were they doing there in the first place. Bloody Hell Kevin!

We should have sold tickets!" and she laughed. "It's all a bit ludicrous. Oh Kevin laugh. Just look at your face!"

"I'm not happy Vicki. I don't like the idea of you being caught in the act so to speak by the Kharzis and I want an explanation for that. Then you say you liked the idea of flaunting yourself. I'm not happy Vicki."

Vicki went over to him and placing her arms around him said softly. "No damage done Kevin. We will sort out the employees perks and I'm sorry for saying I enjoyed it. Actually I didn't say that, but it was my first performance in public so to speak and I had centre stage. It was different. I love you, you silly old thing. Anyway, no one can claim that the Spring Rites were not observed.

.... If you will pardon the pun." And she kissed. "Come on lover boy, explanations are required from the staff."

Down stairs, in the kitchen Cynthia had come around. They found her sitting in a chair drinking a cup of tea. When she set eyes on Kevin and Vicki however she again began to rant and rave about Satan, Hell fire and paganism and had to be restrained physically by Beth. "Best you go away." She said to them both, waving a hand at them, "The ambulance has been called." And she returned to trying to calm an obviously highly agitated Cynthia. Kevin and Vicki sought refuge in the bar.

Maxwell had waited for all of the others to leave the scene, and then quietly made his way back to hidden car. Maxwell sat quietly in his car and pondered. The man with the camera had looked vaguely familiar. Maxwell lit up another cigarette and then, having searched through his memory banks, remembered who the man with the camera was. Of course! Arthur Smallpiece. That's who it had been. Maxwell nodded his head to himself and started the car. Maxwell suspected that should they meet. Then he would be recognized by Arthur. He thought that discretion was called for, so decided against going into the bar of The Black Badger. Instead, he switched off the car's engine. He waited patiently in his car for about 15 minutes and then drove away in the opposite direction. Arthur Smallpiece however, had surruptiously followed Kevin and the others back to the Black Badger. He had quietly entered the bar by the front door and was now sitting on a high stool at the bar and nursing a half a pint on Black Badger. Arthur Smallpiece or "Half a Story," as he was known locally, was not renowned for either his journalistic scruples or accuracy. Why ruin a good story with the truth? Being Arthur's motto. Arthur however had decided that he would have a drink in the bar, as if just passing and dropping in. Maybe he could get to have a word with the new owners. After all, they had no idea who he was. He sat down at the bar on a high stool and called for a half a pint. Kevin served him.

"Are you the new owner then?" Enquired Arthur innocently.

"Yes." Replied Kevin, holding out his hand. "Kevin Firkettle."

"And are you related to old Silas then, or just bought the place?" Arthur wanted to lull his victim.

"I'm his son actually." Said Kevin, realizing at the same time that this was the first time he had admitted as much. He had always regarded Silas as his uncle and had told Vicki that too. In fact everyone believed that Silas was his uncle and here he was telling a total stranger that Silas was his father!

"Son eh? Oh, no wonder you are making a go of this place."

Kevin knew that he had made a mistake and began to back peddle. "Actually everyone thinks that I am his nephew, so I would be happy if you kept it to yourself please."

"As the grave Kevin as the grave." Arthur gave his best honest look. A difficult task for a scrawny little man with a receding chin and scraggy moustache. He looked a little like a ferret peeping over a toothbrush. "As the grave." He muttered again with added sincerity. "But isn't there something about religion or something tied up with running this place?" he sipped his beer as he spoke and eyed Kevin over the top of his glass.

"Yes, there is." Declared Kevin, a little pompously. "I am now the Grand Master and leader of the Druidic bards."

"Indeed, indeed!" Said Arthur, as if being very impressed.

"In fact we have just completed The Spring Rites Festival." Kevin was feeling good, this was after all the first time in his life that he had anything to shout about and he had a receptive audience too.

"So you are now the Grand Master and as such claim all of Silas's old rights and intend to expand The Black badger?" He waited and as Kevin nodded quickly interjected with, "I can see that the pub food has been added, and very good too. Do you have any more ideas for expansion?"

"Well we would like to attract tourist trade, B and B, that sort of thing. Maybe people would like to see a working brewery in action." He improvised. It was then that he noticed that Vicki and George had joined him behind the bar. He had no idea how long they had been standing there. "This is Vicki, my fiancée." Declared Kevin, we will run The Black Badger together.

"Evening Arthur." Said George in an unfriendly tone. "How's the paper? Still poking your nose in where it's not welcome and taking Photographs?" He turned to Kevin and Vicki. "This is Arthur Smallpiece, known locally as Half a Story. He's our local Paparattzi! Best say nothing to him. Even when he's right he still has to lie!" Arthur, knowing that his cover was blown, whipped out a small digital camera and took a couple of shots before they could stop him. Then shouting thanks and goodnight, he rushed from the bar leaving the other seated patrons staring at his flying mackintosh as he barged outside.

"Bloody Hell!" exclaimed Kevin, a newspaperman? George nodded glumly.

"I think that I let cats out of bags." Said Kevin morosely. He looked at Vicki. She stood her ground and stared back at him with a stern look on her small face and then she said firmly.

"OK Kevin. In the back, your aunty Vicki wants words with you lad." And she stood with one hand on her hips and with the thumb of the other indicated the kitchen. Kevin's heart sank and without a word he passed by her in the direction she indicated.

Vicki redirected Kevin upstairs with a, "Forget the kitchen, too many ears for what I have to say." Kevin plodded up the stairs and Vicki pushed him into the bedroom. "Sit down." She ordered. Kevin sat unhappily on the edge of the bed. "Right Kevin Firkettle." Vicki began in a quiet but very steady voice. "As I recall we had a pact, never to lie to each other. Correct?"

"Yes." Agreed Kevin.

"So old Uncle Silas is in fact dear old dad. Correct?"

"Yes Vicki, but I can ex........"

"No you cannot Kevin." Said Vicki quietly. "How long have you known this?"

"Since the beginning I suppose…. Well Mr. Wilberforce sort of didn't tell me direct. I think he didn't want me to feel unwanted. Then I found it easier to think of him as my uncle. In fact I only sort of recognized that Silas was my father this evening."

"So who was your mother, come on Kevin, I want to know all about you. You have been keeping secrets from me right from the start Kevin. Look Kevin, I love you. I trusted that you would tell me the truth. There is a principle at stake here Kevin and if you cannot see that, then you are not the person I believed you to be. Remember what I said about trust?"

Kevin nodded his head miserably. "I didn't think of it as lying to you Vicki. I just didn't like the idea of being dumped by my parents. It seemed simpler to keep thinking of Silas as my Uncle. I still do actually. I can handle an uncle Silas. Do you love me Vicki?"

"Unfortunately for me, yes I do." She sat beside him and took his hand. "I understand your reasons Kevin, I really do, but I don't like finding things out second hand so to speak. More so in public with the local press present. Now think please, if that man was a reporter, he will have been at the bonfire and has all the photographs. The Sunday Papers will be crawling all over this place soon. Which may be good for tourist trade, but not so nice for me. So Kevin just how are we to handle all of this?"

"I don't know Vicki but if you love me, then I'm sure that we will struggle through."

"We need one story Kevin and one story only. Silas was your father, but he didn't know it. I am your fiancée and also your acolyte and business partner. We have the right to dance about in seclusion on our land, observing our religion without interference from others. We will say no more and no less. We will not explain our religious beliefs to anyone. We don't have to. I think that we can work this to our advantage Kevin. I dare say page three of any national daily will engender more interest that my tiny tits." She laughed, "But Kevin no more warnings about not keeping me fully informed." She kissed him lightly. "I need to trust you Kevin I really do need that. Please think first love. OK?" Kevin nodded his agreement. "Now, please, the whole story." She sat waiting and Kevin related all that he knew of his past.

Down stairs the arrival of the ambulance had provoked some interest and it was Vicki who decided to take the lead. She gently, and without elaborating said to the local customers, that they had been performing The Spring Rites Ceremony and that suddenly Cynthia had jumped out and tried to stop them. She added that without the Rites Ceremony the Black Badger would have to close. Sympathetic and understanding nods circled the news. "Bloody old busy body!" said someone and more nods and agreement followed. The conversation turned to Arthur Smallpiece and his more well known misinterpretations of the facts and soon it was business as usual. It was George that solved the riddle of the two Kharzis. "I sent them to keep a lookout for unwanted visitors but I must have been a wee bit too late." He explained. They were well down the bank and out of view of you and the bonfire. They heard Cynthia's yelling at you two and jumped in to the rescue sort of thing. All in good faith Miss Vicki and I do apologize. It's that idiot Half a story that bothers me."

"Oh George, don't worry. I'm not that bothered. Poor old Kevin is taking it hard though and by the way Silas was his father not his uncle."

"Oh we both knew that Miss." Said George blithely, looking at his wife. "If the boss wants to call old Silas his uncle then that's fine with us. I mean, they never met. I dare say it's easier for him to think about Silas that way." He looked kindly at Kevin. "He was a nice old boy you know. He never knew about you. If he had, you would have been here at the double. We knew that you existed from Wilberforce, and we realized that the news would be a shock to you. No, the nephew is that useless lay about Timothy Longstanton. It's a pity old Silas never knew about you, he would have liked you lad. He would certainly approved of you too Miss Vicki." George looked at them both and Beth nodded in agreement.

"He was a good and honest man, and he would have loved you both." Said Beth echoing her husband's sentiments. "He would have been really proud of what you are trying to do with The Black Badger and how you are helping the immigrants too.

"I feel a bit ashamed." Admitted Kevin, "I kept calling him my uncle when I knew that he was my father. However, I still seem to think about him as uncle. Odd isn't it?"

"Well, we just called him Silas, so why don't we just do that and think of him as that?" Beth looked at them in turn.

"Silas it is then." Exclaimed Kevin, "Our mentor. Let's drink a pint of in his honor."

"Better still." Said Vicki. "Let's start a whole new tradition. A free pint of Black Badger on Spring Rites night? That should draw the crowds and give us some support. But no peeping." She added laughing.

CHAPTER: 9

The local Press was a weekly paper. Arthur knew that he had some good photographs and that the story was worthy of being picked up by the more sensational of the Sunday papers. A deal was cut and the local press ran the story, but unpublished photographs were sold along with the story to a Sunday National. At the Black Badger, nothing much happened. Vicki was the butt of a few friendly comments coming from the regulars. Such as, "Sorry lass didn't recognize you with your clothes on." Sort of thing. Which she took all in her stride. There was never any malice behind the remarks and all were of the friendly banter nature. However, when the Sundays' got hold of the story, the phone began to ring and reporters from London arrived. This didn't really bother The Black Badger any as it was all free advertising. The story was, surprisingly enough, handled in quite a reasonable light. Small independent brewery fights for survival and religious freedom etc along with complimentary comments and photographs of having offered homes and employment to refugees. The paper in question, having had a long-standing disagreement with Billy Boom and having no time at all for The New Deal Democratic Party. In fact, The Black Badger came out with medals if anything. The Real Beer drinkers phoned and a gentleman named Andrew Ashbow paid them a visit.

Andrew was a slim built man, in his forties, who favored casual wear. He was apparently, a well respected member of The British Real Beer Drinkers Association and he joked with them about his unfortunate initials AA. "I have endure all sort of stick over that!" He declared smiling at them over a tankard of Black Badger. He complimented George on his excellent brew. He stated that he had been taking a keen interest in developments at The Black Badger and he wondered if he could be of any assistance? It transpired that Andrew was about to be involved in the development of a Rural Folk Museum that was to be based about 20 miles away. This all being something to do with European Cultural Heritage and funded from Brussels. They took Andrew on a tour of the brewery and bottling line and he showed particular interest in the old truck and Morris Minor car. He made Kevin an offer. Donate the Morris Minor car to the Museum and allow the Dray to be rebuilt and painted at the museum's expense and placed on display too. In return, he informed them. It could be possible for the Museum to organize a grant. The funds allocated being to assist in the refurbishment of the brewery. It was after all a traditional, rural, and working industry. Exactly in fact, the type of enterprise that the Museum and its cultural organization wished to promote and maintain. Then in the summer, when there were county shows etc. The dray would be placed on exhibition and free samples of Black Badger Beer would be given. This in turn would give The Badger free advertising without infringing any laws. The Museum would also print and display free literature about The Badger and if Houghton Springs Brewery wanted to then charge some small admission and tour fee. Then that was up to them. To Kevin it seemed like a good idea. He contacted Mr. Wilberforce who was enthusiastic. Mr. Wilberforce even made a trip down to see Andrew and discuss the legal aspects. He then visited The Black Badger and stayed for two nights. He was very impressed, and his approval was evident.

"Well, well, well." He declared. "Things are moving ahead. Well done young man! Old Silas would be proud of you all. The Badger has never looked so spic and span" That and other compliments and the thought of all the fresh litigation that may result had Mr. Wilberforce positively glowing and beaming in anticipation. "Manni tells me that the balance sheet is looking healthy, young Kevin and that your prospects are rosy. You seem to have found your natural place in life!" Mr. Wilberforce almost hugged himself in glee." Naturally, George and Beth were happy to see their old friend again and they spent a long time reminiscing with their old compatriot. Mr. Wilberforce left all too soon. However, it was very obvious that he and Manni approved of all things done to date and that the Badger was heading towards financial stability. The only blight being the state of the bottling line and the cost of its replacement. Even so, Mr. Wilberforce seemed not too dismayed, "I have a lot of faith in you Kevin." He confided, "Maybe at the worst, the bottling will have to cease for a time. Until we can afford to service he loan for a new line. We will have to talk to Manni later. Meanwhile, you just keep on brewing and serving beer and meals." He clapped Kevin on the shoulder and having made his farewells to George and Beth, left them to return to Tunbridge Wells and Astrophy.

The Kharzis began to prepare to accept Kevin as their surrogate tribal leader and again the same Sunday papers picked up on that. In fact, everything in the garden was running beautifully. More and more people were visiting The Black Badger and the profit margin was increasing now that full meals were being offered. Kevin used the office computer to print rather attractive menus. He included some photographs of the brewery and a short outline and history. Andrew helped with the presentation and was careful to include the breweries connection with William's Charter. He also cleverly mentioned the ancient religion, but in such a way as to leave the reader tantalized with a lack of information and wanting to find out more. In short, The Black Badger was advertising itself, whilst legally not doing so and only offering information. The Real Beer Drinkers web site also spread their name far and wide and letters began to arrive with foreign stamps and postmarks. Kevin had thought of building his own web site but was cautioned against it by Mr. Wilberforce. He wanted to check all angles and build a water tight case before Kevin embarked upon such a venture. No doubt hoping that some authority, local or national, would be foolish enough to try to close the site down and thus again be involved in expensive litigation. However, both the local council and the government were keeping very low profiles for the moment.

Not all persons were quite so enthralled by the blossoming of The Black Badger. Maxwell Crump for one fumed but was powerless to intervene. Councilor Cynthia Chisem-Blenkingsop had taken refuge in a home for those suffering from nervous breakdowns. She still awoke in the middle of the night screaming that Satan's Imps were carrying her away. That and wild dreams of sexual fantasy, that she secretly rather enjoyed, haunted her nights. She was however sensible enough to keep the information regarding the sexual dreams to herself.

In Whitehall however, Billy Boom was not a happy soul. The last thing he wanted was for any spotlights to be switched on over Scrumpton Bridge or the Frothershome area. Far too much was at stake. Now it seemed that the National Press was giving far too much publicity to Houghton Springs Brewery and who knew where that might lead? He called in his henchmen and together and in total secret, they plotted Kevin's downfall. The past records of battles with Silas Firkettle were studied. Litigation was ruled out and covert operations considered. Finally, they put together a top secret plan. Houghton Springs Brewery had to be closed down. If not it would only be a matter of time before the whole water shortage situation and its reasons became public knowledge. If that happened, the Opposition would have a very big stick with which to beat "Silly Billy and his boys." Under normal circumstances, since basically no one in the country knew or cared about Scrumpton Bridge, they may have survived. The national interest levels now however, had placed Scrumpton Bridge firmly on the map. More so since in its environs was the cheapest pub in the country. Selling real ale too. No Houghton Springs Brewery had to go and its water source be taken over for the greater good of the country. The spin doctors would do their work. The beer had to be condemned as unfit for human consumption. But at the same time the spring water had to be labeled pure and unadulterated. But how? If the brewery could be forced to cease production for a four month period, then they were home and dry. The obvious angle of attack would be via the EEC. If the EEC could condemn the brewery for any reason, then Billy Boom had won. Not only that, he could point accusing fingers in the direction of Brussels and bemoan the fact that the previous Government had devolved so much power to Europe. To achieve this objective, a secret slush fund was activated. Money taken from the public purse and held in a bank in The Cayman Islands for such dire emergencies was activated and plans were made to sabotage the plant biologically. Two ex MI5 operative were brought out of retirement to achieve this aim. Kevin was now, both unwittingly and unknowingly part of "The Big Picture."

Billy Boom did not want to just close the brewery for good; he needed a watertight excuse for doing so. The EEC would provide that. The Home Secretary's son Lawson Squitter, was a member of the European Parliament. He was the sole owner of, "Lawson's Laxatives" whose motto was, "We move the world." The Foreign Secretary dropped huge hints that Lawson was looking to expand his patent medicine business and was looking for a suitable location to build a new plant. This installation would be subsidized by EEC funding, providing it was placed in an area of high unemployment. Houghton Springs would fit the bill nicely. It had a good water supply, was in a rural area and the employment of immigrant labor could also be exploited both for profit and political proper gander. What was needed was not to do anything that damaged the purity of Houghton Springs water; rather the bottling line would be targeted. If this could be closed down on health grounds and the storage of the draft beer too. Then all it would take would be a few months of non production to sink The Black Badger forever. This would be the task of the ex MI5 operatives. Unpleasant but not deadly microbes would be inserted into casks and bottling line. Suitable money would change hands via offshore accounts with certain persons in Brussels and instructions would be given to certain persons who would be involved in the inspection on Houghton Springs Brewery and The Black Badger. Maxwell Crump could sink or swim, no one cared. Lawson's Laxatives would, after a suitable period, come in to "rescue" the area from further unemployment and the Kharzis would be "saved" along with the reputation of the Government. The spring's water could then be exploited to the full and a local water shortage postponed. Laxatives after all required far less water than beer to produce. Also they were not consumed in similar quantities. Then all would once again be in order and it would be business as usual for The New Deal Democratic Party and rip off Joe Public unabated. All in all, a very satisfactory solution. Billy rubbed his hands together as he practiced his best open look for the public in front of a full length mirror. He grinned to himself. What was his salary as PM? He did a quick mental calculation and thought about a second term in office and what his pension would then be upon retirement. Civil Service pensions being based upon the amount earned in the last year of employment. He rubbed his hands in glee, he could skim the pot, more so if he could wangle a parliamentary raise in salaries. The two ex MI5 agents were briefed.

Maxwell was in a quandary. He could see all too well that the writing was on the wall for "Crump's Cola." Unable to obtain more water, his production was limited. Without an increase in production, the new bottling line was not running to its design capacity. Thus he was not reaching the profit level anticipated when the line was purchased. Purchased with a bank loan that was now eating into and posing a drain upon his rapidly dwindling reserves. Maxwell fully realized that unless he could boost production, he would go bankrupt in the foreseeable future. When that happened, and it was a when and not an if, he would lose everything, including his girl friend in Birmingham. Maxwell was a desperate man. He needed Houghton Springs to be shut down once and for all. He also needed not to be seen as having been involved. He pondered over Timothy Longstanton. Surely he too now would be feeling the cold winds of winter blowing around him? Timothy had wanted to sell the brewery to him, but had now disappeared. Where had he gone? Why had he gone? Timothy, he reasoned, must be a very unhappy man to have seen his realizable capital asset stolen from under his very nose. Not only that but it was now a thriving business. Maxwell decided that his only course of action would be to establish Timothy's whereabouts and attempt to inveigle him into his plans too. Obviously Timothy now held no claim to the brewery, but what about receiving payment for its destruction? Maybe Timothy would enjoy leveling the playing field so to speak? There again, if the present owners just happened to perish in the destruction.... Timothy would inherit. Hence all suspicion would fall upon Timothy. If he was arrested and found guilty, then eventually the brewery would come under the auctioneer's hammer. Maxwell pondered some more. He could see that he too had a motive for wanting the destruction of The Black Badger and all that went with it. With the exception of its water supply. He needed to cover his tracks under deeper cover. He had an inspiration. What if he could involve The Soldiers of the Divine Order? Maybe pretend to show an interest in their foolish nonsense. But at the same time give some excuse for wanting his wish to convert to remain secret for the present? This way he might even have two arrows to his bow. If he failed to locate Timothy, or Timothy was not interested in assisting him, then Crazy Cynthia and her bunch of loonies could carry the can and he would have to burn the place down himself. Not the best solution he thought, but when needs must, the Devil drives. Maxwell went about trying to discover what had happened to Timothy Longstanton.

Timothy had survived the crash. He woke up to find himself inextricably interwoven with both his car and the tree. He sat there dazed. Actually that was all he could do, as he was firmly jammed between seat and a collapsed airbag. He wasn't in any great pain, if anything he was rather light headed. He wondered if in fact he was still alive, or had passed the veil. This then set him wondering if he was now doomed to spend eternity trapped within the sports car? He tried to turn his head to look around him but his neck hurt and his head didn't seem to want to turn. He gave up. His car appeared to have crashed horizontally into the tree at some height up its trunk. Actually that was exactly what had happened. The car had gone through the hedge in the first instance. This wickerwork of tangled, but carefully cut and plashed branches, absorbing some of the energy. It had next encountered the outer branches of a large forked branch of the very substantial beech tree. These again had slowed down the cars pace. It had slid along the branch, tearing off various bits and pieces of its underside along the way. Each removal absorbing energy. The airbags had inflated. The seat belt held Timothy in place as the windshield shattered and the roof was opened up like a sardine can. Finally, the car stopped dead against the trunk and was now sitting firmly upon the forked branch. The front end having performed exactly as designed, with each part bending, buckling or collapsing as intended. With each deformation absorbing impact energy. Timothy was alive, but injured badly. He was also trapped half way up a tree and all but out of sight of the road. A road that was not heavily used. He was lucky that the driver of a large, and passing furniture van had spotted him. The only reason being that the driver was alert and positioned high up on the vehicle. He had been on the lookout for a side road on his right that led to a farm. The new occupants having used his company to move their possessions. He saw the bright yellow of the sports car and stopped. He could not park at that point, so he continued some further distance until there was a straight piece of road. There he pulled in as best he could. Having first of all switched on his hazard lights, he climbed down to investigate. He called the emergency services on his cell phone and in due time Timothy was extricated from his metal tomb and taken to a regional hospital for treatment. When he was in a fit state to talk, the police established his identity. Timothy decided that it would be sensible not to mention white transit vans. This, he thought might in turn lead the police back to Camberwell Crescent. Then to Kevin and his white transit. Better to be quiet and invent a whole new mythical truck that has pushed him off the road. As a consequence, the police did not connect him with Camberwell Crescent, and his story of a short break in the country was accepted. "Broke more than you expected sir!" quipped the friendly constable. Timothy would have squirmed but squirming was out of the question due to various weights and plaster casts. Timothy had in fact had a very lucky escape. Several broken ribs that were more painful than dangerous. A nasty whiplash injury that required a plaster collar. A broken right arm and strained spine that needed traction. Along with various cuts and heavy bruising and several stitches in odd places here and there, were the totality of his injuries. For all that Timothy was enraged. He saw all this as being directly attributable to Kevin and Timothy harbored dark thoughts of what he would do to Kevin once he was mobile. Boiling in oil would be far too good for Kevin. He pondered crucifixion and brooded.

The hospital had a diligent volunteer visiting team of dedicated middle class and middle-aged women. Women with no husbands or children to distract them and far too much time on their hands. These well-meaning matrons, took it upon them selves to visit those unfortunates in hospital who had no relatives close to hand. Their objective was to bring cheer and comfort into the lives of patients and break up the monotony of the daily routine of a national health establishment. One of these ladies adopted Timothy. Not that her presence was welcomed by Timothy. He would far have preferred to have been left in peace to plan the slow and painful death of his cousin. Instead of which, his detailed planning was interrupted my some idiotic old hen who plastered him with platitudes and prune juice. "To keep your bowels open." She declared in a firm and stern voice and placed a straw between his teeth and ordered him to drink. Timothy hated prune juice, but grudgingly accepted that it was preferable to soap enemas. The indignity and discomfort of which he had already endured. So he did as he was instructed by the fearsome female clad in baggy tweeds who hovered over him. He noted that her matching tweed hat was embellished with a long pheasant's feather. She also sported quite a reasonable moustache and she reminded him rather of Robin Hood. Timothy, in a passing moment, wondered what she looked like naked. He shuddered and sipped the prune juice. Even that was preferable to thoughts of this Amazon nude. His visitor had obligingly brought him a supply of Sunday papers. Of the tabloid kind that Timothy so hated. They were after all designed for consumption by the proletariat. Not that Timothy could sit up and read. Had he have been able to have done so, then he could have had the lady leave them beside his bed. He could then have disposed of them with all alacrity. No, she decided to sit there and read them to him. Helpfully showing him the pictures too. It was during one such session that Timothy, to his horror and dismay, saw a picture of his cousin staring back at him from an inside, double page spread. Yes, without doubt, it was the accursed Kevin. A Kevin who now seemed to be mien host of a prospering Black Badger. Another photograph showed the now recently decorated outside of the pub at night, all arrayed in colored lights. The Black Badger Inn board, positively gleaming in a spotlight and fresh coat of paint. A Black Badger that was about to work hand in glove with some rural folk museum and with access to EU funding too, no less. Timothy was appalled. The Real Beer Drinkers had put Houghton Springs Brewery firmly on the internet map. Bed and breakfast was offered, along with a tour of the brewery. Bee hives were busy producing honey for mead. Apples were being grown for cider. Fresh vegetables from the extensive garden were used on the daily menu. The employment and integration of unfortunate political refugees was highly commended. And now, to crown it all "Kevin The Nobody" was being hailed as a local, in situ, de facto, tribal leader. The article went on to talk about forth coming marriage ceremonies between his "People" and how Kevin would officiate with a local registrar in attendance. A New Deal Democratic Party spokesman in Whitehall was lauding Kevin for his humanitarian efforts. They also took the opportunity to emphasize how they were supportive of freedom of religion and individual rights etc.

"Bloody Hell!" exploded Timothy, "That idiot Billy Boom will give him a bloody knighthood next." After all, he thought viciously, both Bob

Geldorf and Mick Jagger had received one each. His visitor lady looked at him severely. She was not used to such language. She tutted him. Timothy quickly reversed his attitude and sought to sooth her disapproval with a fast. "He is doing a wonderful job. A knighthood is far to small a recognition. Nominate him for The Nobel Prize I say." He tried to nod but the plaster collar around his neck prevented any movement. So he settled for a sickly sycophantic smile instead. The dragon lady seemed mollified and went on to explain in some detail local stories that lauded Kevin and The Black Badger. Timothy inwardly seethed.

Maxwell was trying to find a method that would enable him to track down Timothy, but at the same time not be seen to be doing so. He decided in the interim period to visit Cynthia. He found her sitting quietly in an easy chair in the grounds of the hospital. A private establishment that preferred to be called a retreat. This being used by well heeled alcoholics, and drug users to de-tox. It was a quiet and peaceful place that also offered a full menu. Obesity patients, not being part of the hospital's cliental. He sidled up along side of her and greeted the councilor. Cynthia recognized Maxwell but could not fathom out why he should be visiting her? She immediately went on guard. Maxwell, who could hardly claim that he was just passing and dropped in, went for broke.

"Mrs. Chisem-Blenkingsop," He began. "I don't know quite where to begin, and this may all sound so foolish, but I think The Lord guided me here."

Cynthia was hooked, "Get a chair." She said. "Sit here and tell me all about it." So Maxwell fetched a chair and sitting next to Cynthia went on to explain his dream in which an angel of The Lord had appeared to him and ordered him to seek out Cynthia. Naturally Cynthia was enthralled. She had after all been chosen to do God's bidding. Proof of this was that Maxwell Crump, not exactly known for either his strong religious leanings or philanthropic nature was wishing to be instructed in the ways on The Soldiers Of The Divine Order. Here indeed was a repentant sinner, languishing in darkness, and she Cynthia, had been chosen to lead him into the light. Cynthia was beside herself with both exhilaration and religious fervor. Maxwell, was pleased that the old bat had been such a push over. He was careful at this stage to make no mention of The Black Badger. So, after withstanding one and half hours of Cynthia's exhortations and halleluiahs, He stifled a yawn and slipped away on some pretext or another, promising to return the very next day. Once out of sight of Cynthia, he pulled out his cigarettes, lit up and taking a deep lungful decided that a quick trip to Birmingham and a night with randy Mandy were in order as much needed reat and recuperation.

After a night of clubbing and sex, and a long lie in bed with his voluptuous, young mistress, Maxwell returned to visit Cynthia. This time he had developed a plan and decided at the next meeting he would obliquely slide The Black Badger on to the agenda for discussion. When he eventually did so, he was more than gratified by the reaction. Cynthia went ballistic! She ranted and raved to the point that Maxwell had to calm her down in case they attracted the attention of the hospital's staff. He expressed firm views that reinforced Cynthia's opinion of, "That Devil's Spawn" at Houghton Springs. Maxwell, apart from having to endure the nonsensical religious ramblings, was happy and to all intents and purposes home and dry with Cynthia.

His search for Timothy eventually called for him to check hospitals. He posed as a cousin from America and adopted what he fondly imagined was an American accent. His search in the London area proved fruitless. Then, in a moment of inspiration, he wondered if Timothy had thought to see The Black Badger for himself. The local regional hospital obligingly confirmed that they did indeed have a patient named Timothy Longstanton, who had been involved in car accident. When Timothy was informed that he had a visitor, namely his cousin. Timothy was assaulted with feeling of rage and curiosity in equal amounts. He had firmly made up in his own mind to dispose of Kevin as fast as possible and also as painfully as possible. He agreed to see his cousin.

When the person claiming to be his cousin arrived, Timothy was at a loss. Thoughts of other unknown members of his family flashed through his brain. Just how many more of them are there? He wondered. This is going to turn into a serial killing! He had after all, only spoken to Maxwell on the phone.

Maxwell was to the point. He disclosed his true identity, and then began a rambling account of Kevin and the growing Success of The Black Badger. He concluded with remarks that he was disappointed that Timothy had not been able to claim his inheritance, and wondered if he was in business with Kevin? If so, was there any chance of them selling the brewery to him, as he was still interested.

Timothy immediately recognized a fellow traveler in Maxwell His whole demeanor screamed lies and nonsense. Timothy went about using his subtle skills, honed to perfection over the years to discover just what, exactly, Maxwell really had in mind. Maxwell, he decided, was in financial difficulties and needed the brewery. He pondered upon this for a while, trying to work out what exactly was it that Maxwell needed so desperately? Not a brewery, he knew nothing about brewing. Anyway, unless the beer was sold tax free, there was no profit in a micro brewery. Apart from which, there was the religious angle too. No Maxwell could not be interested in making beer. Did one of the big boy brewers have designs on Houghton Springs Brewery, he wondered? If so, why had they not come forward years ago? There had been no evidence or mention of such enquiries. Timothy mulled some more and then it dawned. Of course! It was the water that interested Maxwell. He decided to confirm his suspicions. "Running short of water are we?" He studied the nails of his left hand in a disinterested manner. He looked up at Maxwell and said in an offhand tone, "Just a whisper on the grape vine old boy. You know walls have ears etc."

Maxwell was aghast and his expression told Timothy that he had hit the bull's eye. "umm, err, No. Umm not exactly.." Spluttered a flustered Maxwell.

Timothy looked at him directly and said in a quiet and sotto voice, "Oh come on, don't try to fool me Maxwell Crump. You are running short of water. The whole world is running short of water." He paused and studied his victim. Maxwell squirmed visibly. "The question is old boy, what are you prepared to do about it?" He waited quietly as Maxwell, obviously greatly at unease attempted to formulate a reply.

"What would you suggest?" was the best he could manage. Timothy knew that he had Maxwell exactly in the palm of his hand.

"Mmmm, I would have to think about that. Neither of us want to be implicated do we?" Maxwell pricked up his ears at the word we. Timothy, he decided was also wanting to shut down The Black Badger for his own reasons. Now all Maxwell had to do was to find out to just what lengths Timothy was prepared to go. He breathed an audible sigh of relief. Naturally, Timothy made a note of this and also Maxwell's more relaxed body language. Well, well, well, he mused to himself. Old Maxwell is not averse to seeing Kevin's body dangling from a gibbet either. Timothy paused, as if considering a weighty problem. Finally he said, "I think that it is time that you stated your case old bean. I mean, it was you that sought me out in the first place and now, low and behold, you turn up here at my bedside. You obviously need my help. The question is, just how much help do you require and how much are you prepared to pay for it?" He waited for Maxwell's reply.

Maxwell looked around him. He had taken the trouble to draw the screens around the bed and as Timothy was in a corner bed and the one next to him was unoccupied, he reasoned that a quiet conversation would not be noticed in the general hubbub of visiting time. He peeked around the screens to check that they were not overheard. Satisfied, he leaned close to Timothy and said in a barely audible voice, "How about if I said that I wanted the place destroyed?"

"Ahha," murmured Timothy, neither disagreeing or otherwise. "And the owner?" He looked at Maxwell with a slight smile on his face.

"Whatever." Said Maxwell and looked directly at Timothy.

"So my dear cousin has upset you too I see." Timothy looked smug. "Well my friend, you toddle off now. We don't want to raise any suspicions by being seen together, and just as soon as I am out of here, I will contact you by cell phone. We will only use cell phones. No written words. No land line conversations or physical contact ever again. Is that understood?" Maxwell nodded his assent. He quietly arose and left, carrying with him a feeling that he was fully in control of the situation. Now to go to phase two, he thought to himself. Butter up that old bat Cynthia and her bunch of God bothering crazies. Behind him and unseen, Timothy mentally hugged himself, the casts and other medical encumbrances preventing him from doing so physically. Here at last was an opportunity to dispose of Kevin and lay the finger of suspicion and motive firmly at Maxwell's door. Timothy began to plan in earnest.

Back at The Black Badger, trade was booming and George was having to brew more often. The bottling line was prone to problems due to its age and was hard pressed to keep up with demand. New bottles had to be purchased and labels printed. The Real Beer Drinkers were suggesting that Kevin adopt a personalized black bottle, and thus identifying his product with ease. A couple of well known national super markets were wanting to stock a trial sample of Houghton's Black Badger and it seemed sensible to upgrade the label a little but at the same time maintain a traditional feel about the product. They thought to employ the services of a marketing company, but further investigation revealed that the cost would be prohibitive. Andrew Ashbow came to their rescue and via friends, offered some rough designs. These, whilst not being too far removed from the original label, were certainly more up to date in lettering, color scheme and information. A design was chosen and the printer notified.

Kevin, whilst not having a full blown web page, did have a business email address. Soon he was having to devote some time to answering letters from not only persons in the UK seeking information, but oversees too. Vicki decided that she would take over this task. The Black Badger was firmly on the map and UK tourist organizations began to voluntarily offer information about Houghton Springs. Mr. Wilberforce was delighted, having first given Kevin a standard reply that kept them well within the ban on advertising. Whilst at the same time giving a full description and history that left the enquirer in no doubt as what exactly to expect. He was no doubt anticipating fresh legal battles and damages. To his disappointment though, no one seemed interested in taking him on in open court.

The Kharzis were busy preparing for the forthcoming marriages of both Vania and Mulchi. They indicated that they would organize everything and suggested July the 14 as a suitable date for the ceremony. If any assistance was required, they told Kevin, then they would shout. Kevin observed that they seemed to be arranging things quite adequately alone and as such were best left to their own devices. Peter Goodbody and Andrew Asbow assisting with guest lists and Kevin offering to fund the whole operation. The local and National press were duly informed.

"Wonderful!" Cooed Mr. Wilberforce, "Marvelous advertising and not a thing the powers that be can do about it!" He rubbed his hands in joy at having again poked a stick into the hornet's nest and left it impotent to retaliate.

It was mid May and the weathermen were promising a hot summer. The dust had settled over the Spring Rites and it was yesterday's news. Cynthia had emerged from her retreat and though quieter and seemingly preoccupied with other thoughts, had returned to her activities as a local councilor. The reason for her preoccupation was in fact Maxwell Crump. He had taken up his role as convert in waiting, so to speak and was busy receiving instruction, in secret, from Cynthia. He visited her twice a week and was sure to adopt his best charming attitude. Cynthia was flattered. She took to making fruit cake and biscuits for his visits. She began to experience a re-occurrence of her dreams of sexual fantasy. Only now, she dreamed that she was being ravished by a large, naked and very hairy Maxwell, in a most satisfying manner. She even took to going to bed earlier so that she could enjoy her fantasies to the full. Though she did so with a very guilty conscience. She was also torn between thoughts of blatant lust and her puritanical religious beliefs. She more she attempted to push away her rising sexual urges. The more vivid became her dreams. She found that she was experiencing hot flushes and sweating palms at the thought of Maxwell's arrival for instruction. She realized that the only real instruction that her body was interested in was far removed from the tenants of The Soldiers Of The Divine Order. She took to using expensive perfume and went on a diet. In fact, Cynthia found that her whole bodily reaction to Maxwell highly disturbing. Disturbing, whilst at the same time very exciting.

Maxwell however was having his own problems. Both his wife and girl friend were giving him an ear bashing. The latter pushing him for a commitment and to divorce his wife. The former complaining bitterly that Maxwell was never at home. Between his wife's complaints, and Mandy's moaning and having to put up with an obviously besotted Cynthia. Plus the need not to upset her in any way and maintain his role of eager convert. There were also obvious and pressing financial problems too. Maxwell in short was having a hard time. Thus he found himself spending more and more time with Mandy in an attempt to get away from and deny reality. Mandy enjoyed the sex but that in turn only made her press her case for recognition even harder. She became more and more voluble about Maxwell's continued reluctance to divorce his wife. Maxwell actually had no intention whatsoever of divorcing his wife. Such an act he knew would beyond all doubt set the seal on his financial ruin. So, at a loss as to what to do, and being a man, he did nothing and continued to seek sexual escape with Mandy and butter up an ever increasingly enamored Cynthia.

In The Black Badger, they were all sitting around the bar, as had become the custom and mulling over the general situation when Vicki came up with an idea. "Let's have a Mid Summer's Festival." She said, out of the blue. "Plenty of time before the wedding and no nude dancing." She declared firmly. "That would have to done strictly in private and at unannounced dates in future." No, since Houghton Springs Brewery was now well on the map, a straight forward ceremony to celebrate Mid Summer's Day and also to encompass the "Religion" in a more public manner. Thus adding verisimilitude to the very reason for the existence of The Black Badger. "We could use the paddock field next to here and bring in a band." She said brightly, looking around for support.

"No we couldn't." Stated George, in a matter of fact voice. She and Kevin both noticed that Beth was also shaking her head. "You'll be celebrating Mid Summer's Day alright." George looked at them both in a very serious way. "That is if you want to keep this place open."

"Oh Gawd! Muttered Kevin, not more calling upon The Dark Forces and risking disembowelment at the hands of Crazy Cynthia?"

"Ceremony, yes. Cynthia, no." George waited.

"OK, OK what do I, I mean we, have to do now?" Kevin had a totally resigned tone in his voice.

Just the bonfire and dance routine on the evening before mid summer's day. That's all." He looked at them both and Kevin turned to Vicki and shrugged his shoulders in an almost Gallic manner.

"It all comes down to you Vicki, I'm afraid."

Vicki sniffed, "OK Captain. Kit off and wriggle!" She sniffed again and said in a miffed and sotto voice, "I still think the idea of a festival and band in the paddock is a good one."

Again George shook his head, "No Miss. Vicki, there is not enough parking area as it is. So if you did anything in the paddock you would have to use it as parking too. Then you would have placed traffic between the pub and the customers. A child might be injured. It's not worth the risk Miss. No, a better and long term solution would be to knock out part of the roadside hedge and have a proper car park made. Then we could turn the present cobbled yard, which is only used as a parking area now into a nice little, safe, walled garden with tables and chairs. There any children would be quite safe. "He eyed them both keenly and waited for their reaction.

Vicki considered what he had said and slowly nodded her head. "You are quite correct George." She stated. She turned to Kevin saying, "He is you know. That cobbled yard is, or could be a valuable asset as an outside extension. Put some shrubs in tubs there. Some creeper, well plenty already, growing up the walls. Tables and umbrellas, what do you think Kevin?"

"Excellent idea. Apart from one small thing." He looked at Vicki with a quizzical expression. "Cost my love. That would require a proper car park being built. That would cost money. Money right now we don't have. Any extensions will have to wait until we have this bottling line sorted out." He looked resignedly at them all.

It was Beth that then spoke. "We could start by having some nice flower baskets hung around the place. Then we could place some tables, just six maybe, right outside in front." She waved a hand in the general direction. "Next to the stone wall and the car park. We could put another six or so along the side next to the Paddock. It is still separated by the stone wall" She pointed towards the front and side walls of the bar that faced the road. Safe for children and easy access for us to serve customers that fancy sitting outside. We could put some shrubs in tubs at the end to hide the wall that joins the side on the house. Maybe a trellis too and some climbers? We will put car parks and yard conversions on hold behind the bottling plant problems." She smiled at them. "We could still have some small recognition of Mid Summer's Day though. Just a free bottle of Black Badger with every three pints bought. Maybe have a crememorative label. One we can use every year? Oh and string the Xmas lights up too."

Kevin looked at Beth and nodded. "that's a great idea and it sounds like the best compromise we can have at this point. What do you say George? Flowers, lights and tables is it? For the moment anyway"

George nodded, "Aye, best we can do for the moment, but the way this place is moving we will have to do something about parking soon or The Council will be around our necks. It's our land, and our hedge, so we can convert any time we like. That paddock is not classified as agricultural. So no planning permission is required. Start asking for quotes boss. Then if The Council starts making a fuss, we can say that we have the situation in hand, and prove it. The money can wait until someone gives us a bill!"

Quietly recognition of Mid Summer's Day was leaked, but no mention of any ceremonies was made. Enquiries regarding the cost for a car park were requested and the tables, flower baskets and shrubs were taken in hand. None of which escaped the eye of Billy Boom and his henchmen. They grew progressively more worried as week by week; Houghton Springs Brewery seemed to be gaining celebrity status. Certainly on the internet at least. He did his homework and knew that Kevin would have to hold a mid summer's eve ceremony. Since that would go ahead irrespective of what he did. Billy decided to just make things as difficult as possible for The Black Badger. He quietly started to push the EEC to instigate an inspection and primed his ex MI5 men to be on stand by. A rather unpleasant but not terminal bacterium had been obtained and was sitting quietly multiplying, in a secret, government-funded laboratory.

Quietly too, and mostly via the internet, enquiries began to come in by Email asking if any ceremonies would be forthcoming? Moreover, requesting details. Each request being softly fended off with that any ceremonies were of a strictly private nature and for followers only and not Joe Public at large. "Can't have a bunch of larger louts yelling Get them off!" Quipped Vicki. Maxwell received the news on the grape vine too. Maxwell went into high gear and began his manipulation of Cynthia. He also informed Timothy. The Soldiers Of The Divine Order, thundered from their pulpit, but they were only preaching to the converted, it had no impact whatsoever. Cynthia naturally grew more and more frustrated.

Timothy Longstanton thought that the Mid Summer's eve ceremony would be a most opportune time to burn the whole place to the ground. After all, he reasoned, everyone will be causing commotion around some bonfire or other. Not only that but the loonies that he had seen reported in the press would no doubt be out in full force too. What better opportunity? He began to refine his plans.

The bottling plant was still giving endless problems, but somehow George managed to keep it running. Kevin began to juggle with the cost of a new plant against trying to renovate the existing unit. It was a fruitless task. They needed a new bottling line. "Nothing for it." He declared at lunch one day after a particularly grueling morning of keeping the line running. "We will have to have bank loan for a new line and that's a fact."

"Can we afford it?" Asked George glumly? "It's not like buying a mouse trap."

"Frankly, no we can't but I can't see that we have any options. What we need is good second hand line. I will try looking in the web after lunch."

The Kharzis had been working at a steady and methodical speed and renovations and improvements were ongoing. They had been growing vegetables and tomatoes and also sprayed the apple trees. Beth looked after the bees and they went about their business of pollination and everything was neat and tidy. The Black Badger hummed with activity, meals were served, beer drunk and local deliveries made. Preparations were well under way for both festival and weddings. In fact, everything other than the bottling plant was running smoothly. The old boiler had passed its mandatory inspection and the steam required for the brewery could be raised without a hitch. All pumps and plant now gleamed from having all the copper work polished and the brewery was spotless. The old wooden floors had been sanded and treated to a coat of industrial grade polyurathane. The walls had been washed and then painted with white emulsion. Even the supporting wooden pillars had been sanded and varnished. The windows had all been cleaned and their sill repainted. In fact the old brewery positively shone.

Visitors were taken on tours and free samples drunk. Those that imbibed too heavily were offered bed and breakfast and Kevin began to see lights at the end of tunnels. It was then that they received a letter from Brussels. It seemed that the EEC inspection team would arrive on mid summer's eve too. Kevin could do nothing about that and decided to take a walk up around the fields above the old orchard and plan his meeting with the EEC representatives. It was lovely morning and he called Gyp to accompany him. It was only when they reached the top field and noticed that a few of the neighboring farm's sheep had broken through the hedge, that the first inkling of trouble ahead arose.

CHAPTER: 10

Willie Clayton was fed up. Congress and the Senate had cut off his funding. OK, he still had the CIA secret funds but the head of the CIA had pointed out to Willie just how much it cost to run an aircraft carrier. The gross national budget of several small countries was considerably less. So now he was haggling with the CIA to get back the illegal funds that he had given them in the first place. The CIA were naturally loath to hand over any money and The President couldn't very well make too much fuss over funds that were in fact both illegal and clandestine.

The outcome had been a face saving exercise for all concerned.

Congress being well aware such funds existed. Yes, the USS Terminator could take up position. But under no circumstances was it even to point its weapons anywhere, let alone arm or fire them. Probably end up shooting down Concord, or worse still. One of those cheap package tour jets owned by that gentleman whose name sounded like a chutney company. That really would stir things up. The gentleman concerned, having sufficient money to finance his own private war in retaliation! No, navy planes could fly around, carefully, and certainly not in a manner that could be in any way construed as being provocative.

Since both Senate and Congress had rather been piped to the post by Willie's premature mobilisation action, it would now seem foolish to stand down without gaining a few points. But the sooner that America was taken off this present war footing, the better. As it was the National Parks were full of survival groups all shooting at each other. Which, in the general view of things wasn't viewed as being such a bad thing, as it took their minds off shooting members of the Senate and Congress. But they were also shooting deer and other animals out of season and pretty soon, once all of this present turmoil was over, someone would have face the wrath of the conservation lobby.

Then there were the marches on the White House to contend with.

Every freak in the country was bearing arms and shouting from his corner. Frankly the Government was amazed at the weaponry that some of these freaks were toting. No one would have been too much surprised if some group or another produced a small thermo nuclear device that they had purchased from a mail order company. Legally too. Naturally with all this firepower now out on the streets, shootings, bank raids and general mayhem were the order of the day. Britain, whilst under the threat of immanent attack, was peaceful by comparison. Some Boston newspaper statistician had already produced figures that detailed the over all cost to the American taxpayer in damage and lost revenues.

And not a shot had been fired. Willie had wanted to charge him with treason, but had been advised against it on the grounds of right or wrong, the legal costs would have been enormous. That and the case would have dragged on for years. He fumed over the fact that he was President and he couldn't even sue some jerk. This job wasn't quite so good as he had imagined, he mused.

Now, Willie had been instructed in no uncertain terms. By both upper and lower houses. Go over there, get the best deal possible.

Which would mean sharing things some with the Brits and leave the advisors to sort out the details and proclaim a victory. Meanwhile the Terminator could be down played and eventually slipped into the role of protecting the blasted sea weed from outside interference from an unnamed foreign power. North Korea or Libya springing to mind as being likely candidates at whom to point fingers. Generally one could point a finger at either of them and blame them for anything. No one ever questioned it. Then, depending on how well he pulled it off would depend if he got impeached. Both the Tribune and The Post were down in Florida chasing up some leads with regard to some break in some place. There was also the matter of Lulu.

Willie had worked out that if he was going to survive this little lot then maybe, just maybe Lulu could be of assistance. If that donkey dick of a British PM fancied her, well maybe he could use her as a bargaining chip. For sure all the stupid cow had done since she returned was talk about Bloody Toni and the size of his prick! He was also pissed off about the way she now called him, "Little Willie." So Congress had cut off his funding and it felt like Toni had been instrumental in cutting off his balls. Furthermore, if he didn't pull this deal off, he would get impeached. No doubt that would suit his hatchet-faced wife who had threatened to run against him in the next campaign. All in all, The President of the United States of America was not a happy camper.

Naturally, upon arrival there were the jolly handshakes, and the plastic smiles, for the benefit of the press and TV. Once that was over, Willie said he was tired, it would be a big day tomorrow etc.

and he took himself off to bed, only to find that some dick head had placed Lulu's bedroom, way down the corridor.

Bradford was sitting in the cellar. He carefully checked each of his bugs in order, listening quietly. Toni and Heigar, the rhythmic sounds of sleep. Meddlesome too. Someone had placed Lulu in the bedroom he had assumed would have been used by Gobbleton, but Gobbleton had made other sleeping arrangements. Lulu seemed restless.

It was time to test the signals. He dialled Peter on his mobile phone.

"OK Pete, fire one."

Back in the farmhouse Peter transmitted the first signal. Toni woke up and instantly went into smarm and charm mode.

Toni was a little confused. He knew that he had to be nice to someone, but no one was talking to him. He had no input. Toni had been programmed to react. He had never been programmed to produce any original thoughts of his own; thus he reacted to the only stimulus that was around. The gentle snoring of his wife Heigar, as she lay on her back in a huge, floucey nightdress. "Had I ever told you that I find the sound of your nocturnal, nasal breathing mellifluous?" Heigar slumbered on. Toni continued, having prompted no reaction. "To lay here next to you and listen to happy buzz saw noises, reminds of a spring day, walking in the woods in my youth. The chirp of crickets, the happy hum of be....."

Heigar awoke. "Shuddup!" She scrabbled around in the dark for her hand held console and groggily punched the sleep button. Toni collapsed.

Peter relayed the information about Heigar's signal to Bradford.

"Pay dirt! What's next Brad?"

"Hang on Pete. We have isolated two signals. Smarm was the first and sleep must have been the last. That leaves us with three to decode. Press number two." Peter activated Toni's earnest and sincere programme. Toni woke up again.

"Heigar. It is my firmly held belief that the cornerstone of our British way of life, fundamentally is that of a secure family relationship. It is upon such foundations that the new social order, as offered by The New Deal Democratic Party, can and will move forward. All pulling together, not ignoring our duties, but as of one, keeping our eyes firmly on the future. The heartland's behind us, pushing us forward, ever striving......."

"Shaddap!" Heigar again hit the sleep button and Toni, obligingly, went back to sleep. Heigar was annoyed and she muttered to herself, "I swear I'll kill that raving queer Meddlesome if he doesn't get his programmes sorted out and the glitch removed from the system.

I'll send him off to Austria tomorrow on some pretext. That idiot Gobbleton can stand in and monitor Toni. Anyway it's about time he earned his corn instead of spending all of his time shagging that skinny oriental bitch. Can't see what he sees in her. More meat on a butcher's pencil." All of which Bradford took a careful note.

"OK Pete. That was the Earnest and you can trust me role. I guess that Heigar must have pushed the sleep button again. Try him on the third signal." At the other end, Peter placed Toni into confident and aggressive in mode.

Again Toni awoke. "Heigar. It is the right of every husband to expect a certain standard of behaviour from his wife. Therefore, I feel that it is only fair to give you advance notification of my intention to have sex with you....."

"Swein Hunt! Slaffen fur Christ's sake!!" Again she hit the sleep button, and again Toni slept.

"That one is, "Pushing my point" Mode." said Brad confidently.

"Now I wonder what the last one is? Go for it Pete."

Heigar registered the fact that the bedclothes were rising in response to Toni's erection. She reached for her console, but was too late. Toni was upon her, and her floucy nighty was up around her face somewhere. She tried flailing her arms but it was of no use. They got caught up in all the ribbons and roses. OK, she thought, maybe it's just sex that is overriding the programmes. After all Freud had pretty well proved that it was a dominant driving force. Since Freud had originated in her neck of the woods, Heigar was inclined towards believing in his theories. Maybe let him wear himself out some. Release some testosterone. Then switch him off. Heigar decided to lay back and enjoy the experience. Once Toni slowed down some, and she felt it was time, she would suggest another position. Then make a grab for the console and switch him off.

"What's happening Brad?" It was Peter.

"Would you believe that the PM is going like pile driver? That is sex mode, from the way he is grunting and the bed is bouncing."

"What's Heigar doing?"

"Laying back, dreaming of the Tyrol, edelweiss, and enjoying it by the sound of it."

"Shall I switch him off Brad?"

"Naw! Not yet. Let me get signal strength on old Heigar's moans.

If we time it just right, we can switch him off just as her bubble is about to burst. That really should frustrate her!"

With perfect timing, Peter hit the sleep mode and Toni collapsed on top of a very upset Heigar!

"Mein Gott in Himmel! Wass ist wrong mit you?" Heigar struggled to uncouple herself. "Enough!" She cried. "You sleep on your own." And she dragged a recumbent Toni into the passageway, leaving him lying on the floor, and stomped back to bed, rearranging her night dress as she did so.

"What's happening Brad?"

"Dunno Pete. I think the old cow has dragged the poor sod off some place. We really must have pissed her off. Maybe next time I had better rig the place for sound and vision. Hang on, that's the bedroom door closing.

Old plastic smile Toni must be out on the landing. Let's wake him up again."

"Which button Brad?"

"Sex was pretty interesting. Fire up his hormones again."

Peter obliged.

Lulu was upset. Toni had been fantastic. The last time she had enjoyed sex like that had been with two East German discus throwers in Minsk. Even they though, and both together, could not match up to Toni's standards. She wondered idly if all Englishmen were built along the same lines and if her choice of adopted country required rethinking. Still, Willie's willie was better than no willie at all and he was sort of sweet. She decided to try and pay him a visit. He had been pretty grumpy with her of late. She had tried to explain that it had not been her fault. She had even claimed it as having been rape. Willie however had rejected this out of hand on the basis that she had been enjoying it too much! Lulu slipped quietly out of her bedroom and ran slap-bang into Toni. Toni responded as he had been programmed to do, and pushed her back inside her bedroom. Lulu couldn't believe her luck.

"Oh Toni!" She murmured as she willingly led him back to her bed, closing the door behind them.

"Bloody Hell Pete! The old ram is screwing Lulu."

"Shit! What shall I do Brad?"

"Nothing Pete. She's telling him that he is all man and she has never stopped thinking about the last time! What last time is that I wonder? He puts it about a bit does our Toni. No wonder Heigar sticks him out at night. He's like a old tom cat!"

Willie Clayton couldn't sleep. The Brits never had air conditioning and their beds were too soft and the pillows too hard.

Furthermore he was jet lagged. He decided to check out Lulu's bed, Maybe if he rolled around with her for ten minutes or so, then he could sleep. He got up and padded off in his silk dressing gown. He didn't bother knocking on Lulu's door, and went straight in. He pulled up short at the sight that met him. "Jesus Toni! Don't you ever stop?"

"Quick Pete. Smarm and charm mode!" Peter switched programme.

"Willie! How nice to see you. Just let me put this away." Toni stood up, "Lulu, close your legs. It's regarded as impolite in front of a visitor. Come Willie. Let's sit over her. Now how can I help you?"

Willie Clayton was caught flat-footed. This guy could not be for real. He found himself replying as if in a daze, "Well for beginners, you could start by ceasing to shag my woman every time my back is turned!"

"Willie, don't be foolish." Toni declared expansively. "Believe me. That's only my way of furthering East West relationships. It's nothing. Anyway, she enjoys it. Why don't you take advantage of our old English hospitality whilst you are here? Go and shag Heigar.

Fatslobe's wife too, if you like. Get her sober and she would probably enjoy it."

Willie was completely bemused. "What is this? Some kind of Limey tradition? Pass the host's pussy?" Willie was tired, annoyed and he didn't understand the Brits. Furthermore he didn't want to.

"Exactly Willie. It's an Old English Country House Weekend. Very traditional. Sometimes we play sardines first. Get a willing little housemaid in a dark cupboard with three of you, and boy can you have fun.

Willie considered Toni's words. This guy is for real, he thought.

Maybe it is some crazy old Limey tradition. I mean they dressed up in funny clothes and chased foxes and everyone knows that they are inedible. Who knew what these weidos got up to inside the confines of their own homes? And his brief was not to upset them. He decided to play along and see where it led. "Can't say I fancy Fatslobe's wife.

Too skinny for my liking."

"Well there you are then. One can not say that about Heigar."

Willie mulled on that statement. Was this guy offering swapsies?

That big wife of his was a fair piece of ass. Willie went on a fishing trip. "You're right there buddy. Fair piece of meat that woman of yours. And you say this is an old English tradition then?"

"Give us sincere and earnest Peter." Bradford had been monitoring the conversation.

"Absolutely Willie. Trust me. I can say with all sincerity that you are welcome to work your way into her affections at any time you wish. Host's hospitality and all that. Nothing would please me more than to see your aspirations fulfilled in that direction."

"Third programme now Peter. Let's push the point."

Toni clapped his hand on Willie's shoulder. "You go for it old friend. Come on, up you get, and up you get, if you get my meaning."

Toni gave his grin for which he was famous. "Get in there and give old Heigar a good poking. She'll love it. So will you old boy. Goes like a train does my misses." He ushered The President out of the door.

"Stick him back on sex Pete, I'm switching bugs to see how Willie gets on."

Willie had meanwhile slipped into bed with Heigar. Heigar was sleepy. "Toni, sleep yah?" She reached for the console and realised that it was not Toni. Heigar stopped in mid move. Her Logical Teutonic brain examined the possibilities.

It was a mistake. Dismissed.

She was about to be raped. Dismissed. Too quiet. Anyway, she never got that lucky.

Someone fancied her. Who?

"Heigar, it's me."

Good God! It's The President. Well, that's OK then. He would never have to tell because of the fifth amendment.

Heigar settled back to have completed that which Peter had so recently and rudely interrupted.

After 30 minutes Peter placed Toni into sleep mode, and everyone in both households went to bed to sleep. With the exception of Willie and Heigar. Good old Toni had been quite correct. She did go like a train. Willie Clayton, when he did finally go to sleep, slept soundly.

Both He and Heigar had silly smiles on their faces.

Next morning the old relationship between America and Britain was back on line. Meddlesome was controlling Toni and Toni was behaving perfectly. Heigar decided to delay sending him to Austria for two reasons. There was no way that from a political point of view that he could have disappeared at a time like this, and any way Toni was behaving normally.

They decided that perhaps it was his biological needs overriding the programme. Well, that could be sorted out quite easily. Anyway she didn't want the boat to be rocked. She wanted Willie to hang around as long as possible.

Gobbleton had been down inspecting the seaweed and declared that there was mounds of the stuff, all washed up along the foreshore in front of the farm. Toni was steered away from the question of ownership and they decided to all stroll down after breakfast and look at the stuff for themselves.

"Looks like it's hardly worth a small rowing boat Willie, let alone The Terminator." Toni was in charm mood. He playfully kicked at the piles of seaweed with his foot. He was on walk a bout and for the press and TV was wearing jeans and an open neck shirt with the sleeves rolled up and his famous silly grin. He did a lot of waving.

"You know Toni, you could be right. We don't actually know if this stuff is all that it is cracked up to be. It looks pretty nasty, and smells odd too. Can't say I'd fancy sitting down to a plate of it myself." Willie Clayton poked at a pile with a stick. "How about if we get the scientific boys to have a look at this stuff?"

"Yes Willie. Exactly what I was thinking too. Oh Lord! Here comes Gerald and his performing ferrets." All TV cameras had now focused on the arrival of Gerald Fatslobe. He stood a little above them all on the riverbank, wearing his country gentleman's outfit. Tweeds and gum boots. A ferret peeked out of each lower side pocket in his jacket. He waved his walking stick in greeting in their direction. "God! I hate it when he up-stages me Willie. He's so fat he fills a wide screen TV all on his own." Come on; best get over there before he says something stupid. Gerald however had more important things on his mind than just getting his face on TV. Gerald had found that his pigs quite liked eating the strange seaweed. Maybe all of his financial problems with regard to pig feed costs could be solved overnight. Thus his negotiating position with Al Arrod would be strengthened.

So the Summit continued, and eventually drew to a successful outcome. Having decided that the Vietnamese would remain as a token force to protect the seaweed. Assisted by the Free Welsh Army. The four academics having been promoted to Brigadiers, the six work experience lads becoming

Sergeants and mad Baron De Lacey not being mentioned. He having seemed to have disappeared off the face of the earth, along with his little tank.

Willie was happy sleeping with Heigar. Lulu was happy sleeping with Toni. Who now seemed to be operating on his own at night quite well without external stimulus. Meddlesome could get some sleep and Gobbleton continued to make his own arrangements.

Myreg breathed a sigh of relief and went back to spitting, waving his arms, poking Rhonan Phillips and collecting his allowances from the Welsh Assemble.

The USS Terminator steamed into Portsmouth on a Good will visit and school children were given rides in munition lifts and allowed to play virtual reality war games called Hunt Saddam.

The World breathed a sigh of relief. The Swiss all appeared, if a little sheepishly, from out of their nuclear shelters and the French lifted their ban on the Channel ports. Bogus asylum seekers again began to flow. Africa carried on starving. The Chilli Chicks released a controversial record called, "The sea weed in my face." Which was banned by the BBC. Thus guaranteeing it a place as number one in the charts, and generally things returned to normal.

Te'Upp was not so happy. She had planned on dumping Gobbleton as fast as possible and returning to her beloved Vietnam. Hanoi however had other plans for her. For Vietnam to be acting as a peacekeeper now became a liability. Not only was there the cost involved, the troops were also being exposed to unnecessary, decadent Western trappings.

Such as a 24-hour supply of electricity and indoor plumbing. Plumbing of any nature being a novelty. Not only that, they were developing a taste for chips, Worcestershire sauce and pizza and ignoring their sacks of rice and salt fish. Since they were actually employed to guard the seaweed, it made it a little difficult for Vietnam to cultivate the samples already sent and then to proclaim to the world that it had been their discovery all along. No, something more subtle was needed. Gobbleton provided the answer.

Hanoi knew full well that Gobbleton was under the impression that Te'Upp was Taiwanese. Also, that Gobbleton thought that he would soon be retiring to some oriental love nest with Te'Upp. Hanoi saw how to exploit this loophole. What if Gobbleton could be brought to Vietnam, whilst under the impression that he was in fact going to Taiwan? As long as Te'Upp was with him, he would not be suspicious. Once in Vietnam, then some statement could be cobbled together to the effect that he had defected to the worker's paradise and given them the secrets of the seaweed. That only there could the seaweed be grown under true socialist conditions. To be given freely to a starving World. All blame would then be focused upon him. No mention then would have to be made of any deals and political trade offs that resulted in Vietnam feeding the starving third world in the process. Much better that way. Vietnam didn't have to provide an excuse for possessing the weed. All blame would fall squarely upon his shoulders.

Te'Upp was instructed to remain faithfully by the side of her lover.

Later would she receive instructions as how the journey was to be effected. Te'Upp voiced her objections. As a freedom-loving daughter of the glorious revolution, she could not in all honesty remain at the side of the capitalist exploiter for the rest of her life. She was going to add, fat, hairy pawed, groping, and suffering from halitosis, but thought better of it.

Hanoi was understanding. They fully realised the sacrifices that their comrade sister had made and sure, she could dump the slimeball, once he was on Vietnamese soil and had made his confession and had appeared to the world on a suitably doctored piece of video footage.

Meddlesome, though sleeping better was not of a forgiving nature.

He began to plot the demise of both Heigar and her father in earnest.

A skiing accident would be best. If he were to secrete some small waterproof explosive charges above the Schloss Kutzanburnz, along with a radio controlled firing device. Then later, when the snow was around, he would detonate them. The resultant avalanche should remove all traces of both Heigar, father and evidence. The idea appealed to him. He gave it closer and more detailed thought. Once they were out of the way, he would install his own computer system elsewhere and then have sole control of Toni. Then he would deal with Gobbleton too.

Gerald meanwhile began to feed his pigs on the seaweed in earnest, allowing them to wander along the foreshore and forage for themselves.

Te'Upp had persuaded her Gobbie to come to Taiwan. She depicted their idyllic life together. A house by the sea. Overlooking the azure waters. The sound of wind chimes. Sunshine and servants to wait upon them and her Gobbie in a silk dressing gown, with a dragon on it. She also dressed in silk, awaiting upon the every whim of her Lord and Master. Anyway, now that Taiwan had the seaweed, time was running out for them both. Either come with her, and rest in her arms. Or stay and face the inevitable scandal. Gobbleton said that on the whole, a life of ease and nuptial bliss with her in Taiwan was preferable to a long spell of porridge in Wormwood Scrubs, and promptly enquired as to when would they be leaving?

Secretly they slipped aboard a ferry for Ireland and from there, equally secretly boarded a Vietnamese tanker in Wexford. Gobbleton was on his way. Te'Upp was not looking forward to being cooped up with him for the voyage, but consoled herself that it would not be long before she was rid of him. Then she could claim her hero's accolade of The Ho Chi Minn Medal for service to her country and settle down and marry some decent political cadre from within the party.

Back in Pembrokeshire Gobbleton's disappearance was noticed.

Meddlesome was suspicious, but kept his own council, awaiting events to unfold. Nothing happened. It was as if Gobbleton had been swept from the face of the earth. Meddlesome immediately suspected Heigar.

Yes, it was obvious! She had done away with Gobbleton and he would be next. Meddlesome decided to eliminate Heigar and her father, before he too suffered a fate similar to that of Gobbleton.

The general feeling in Britain however, was that perhaps Gobbleton had drowned. The Cleddau was dragged. More seaweed was disturbed and washed up on Gerald's foreshore. The pigs flourished.

The scientific team produced their conclusions. The seaweed was indeed some new species. It did indeed only grow on Blue Stone. It was absolutely useless as a food base. Apart from a very unpleasant taste and slimy texture, it had no nutritional value what so ever. It did have some very odd strings of hydrocarbon molecules that as with any hydrocarbons contained energy. There was no way though, that a human gut could break them down. You might just as well try feeding people on sawdust. In fact, sawdust on the whole tasted better. They got ready to go home. The seaweed bubble had burst.

The world groaned. A couple of African leaders, wanting to take the heat off themselves, and their Mercedes cars and personal Swiss bank accounts, promptly accused the West of deliberately suppressing the truth in a racist bid to keep their populations oppressed and in debt. Since most of their population's could neither read nor write and were too busy trying to scrape a living, and knew full well that the boss man was crook. It tended to get ignored.

The Vietnamese UN force got ready to go home, but at the last minute decided to defect en mass and seek political asylum. Back in Hanoi, Gobbleton, not speaking Chinese and still being under the impression that he was in Taiwan was wondering why there were water buffalo carts in the main road and no BMW saloons. Te´Upp was called before the Central Committee and asked to explain how it was that not only was the sea weed useless, they had just worked out how much the policing exercise had cost, and there were insufficient funds within Vietnam to foot the cost. Not only that, all of the troops employed had opted to remain in the UK. Far from receiving her accolade, she was banished to a worker's collective for re education through labour and worse still, instructed to take Gobbleton with her.

The only one who breathed a sigh of relief was Kenu. He went and lit a few candles and incense sticks in the small Shinto shrine he had built in his garden and he banged a gong quietly, so as not to disturb his sleeping and ever attentive Brenda.

Life in Britain returned to much as it had been before the Summit. The Vietnamese had joined forces with the Free Welsh Army and were swapping recipes for salt fish and lava bread on S4C TV. All of the arms, with still the exception of Mad Baron De Lacey's little tank, had been quietly handed over to the British authorities. Since there was no where to house this latest batch of asylum seekers, all other Government designated hostels etc. bursting at the seams. It was decided to leave them at Gerald's farm. Gerald saw the advantage of this. The Vietnamese understood pigs had time on their hands and the British Government had to feed them. Gerald effectively had a free work force. Not only that, but he could be seen as being philanthropic too. Willingly allowing his farm to be used to house poor, unfortunate asylum seekers. He quietly made all his other staff from cook down to farm labourer redundant.

The scientific team was still hanging around. No one was quite sure what he or she was doing, and if asked, no one understood the answers. Obviously they had not used up all of their funding and would remain until such times as they did. So they were ignored and allowed to carry on with what ever they were up to.

The Vietnamese slipped into the farm and the community with grace and ease. They set themselves up a whole cottage industry in manufacturing coloured kites, candles, polished stones and carved driftwood. All of which they sold at a Sunday market in Haverfordwest.

Being small, neat and polite they were also a hit with the local girls. Something that didn't go down too well with some of the local lads. But after a couple of skirmishes in which the Vietnamese bounced the much larger and heavier local boys around like ping pong balls, and then apologised for doing so, it was though better to accept them. So they formed their own football team and applied to play in the local league.

It was the Vietnamese who first reported the change that had come over the pigs. They had been harvesting the seaweed from across the river each day. The pigs preferred it fresh. The pigs had quietened down, so much so as to have become almost docile. They were jolly and fat. They were no longer displaying any signs of nervousness. They approached you to have their snouts patted, or their backs scratched and grunted appreciatively if you obliged. That could have been put down to all of the extra attention that they were getting from the attentive Vietnamese. But it seemed to be more than that. The pigs quite obviously were happy and contented. So much so that none of them had exhibited any signs of BDS. The pigs were no longer prancing around, farting and defecating in all directions. Furthermore, they no long stank. In fact, they no longer smelled bad even.

Obviously something had happened. The scientists, with both time on their hands and funds available, decided to satisfy their enquiring natures and began to investigate.

It was discovered, to the amazement of the scientific group, that the pigs were all free of BDS. Had the disease died off of its own accord? The mysterious prion having vanished? Or was the seaweed something to do with it? That having been the only variable in the equation. The scientists were intrigued. Both they and Gerald decided that it would be best for the moment to maintain silent and keep the information quietly to themselves. No point in setting any premature hares running.

A paranoid and agitated Meddlesome had visited the Schloss Kutzanburnz. He had done what checking of the programme that he could without a total shutdown. He had found nothing. No further aberrant behaviour had been observed in Toni. Heigar and her father were both of the opinion that an excess of testosterone had caused the sudden glitches and the programme going haywire. It fell upon Heigar's lot to then reduce his hormone balance and maintain them within controllable levels. Meddlesome had not given up on his plan to rid himself of both Heigar and her father though. He took to taking long walks around the castle. Something that arose the suspicions of the Herr Professor, who unbeknown to Meddlesome, spied upon him through a pair of ex SS Panzer Division binoculars. Tracking his every move. The good Herr Doctor having no love for Meddlesome. Since Meddlesome obviously only regarded him, the famous and about to be World recognised Herr Professor, Doctor Frantz Kutzanburnz, as just some custodian of that electrical monster in the cellar. The Herr Professor puffed himself up in rage and frustration. He knew that limp wristed Englishman was up to no good, but what exactly was he planning? He followed Meddlesome's wanderings with renewed and intense interest. Reminding himself how much he hated perverts, and gypsies, and people with long hair, in fact the list was almost endless. Still, soon he would be famous and together; he and his daughter would control Europe. Via, Toni, of course. Then the World would sit up. Oh yes. There would be no room for limp wristed Meddlesomes in his New Order!

Meddlesome during his walks mulled over the problem with Toni and his hormones. There were obviously only three answers. Change the programme for one that over rode his urges. Supply a substitute for Heigar once she and her father had been safely disposed of. A substitute that would really have to be introduced soon. Or castration! The latter certainly held appeal.

On the other side of the Atlantic, Willie was not so happy. The seaweed had proved to be a fiasco and an expensive one at that. Lulu wasn't the same. Hardly surprising when one considered the amount of punishment that her body had been absorbing. The effects of which were all too apparent to Willie. Those Damn journalists were still sniffing around in Florida and Impeachment was on the cards. Willie really had upset both houses when he had mobilised without their consent. Now the bean counters were busy producing costing's. Willie began to cast around for something to take the mind of the people away from him and onto something else. He almost wished that Iceland would plant a flag on his shores.

Gobbleton was equally unhappy. Taiwan had somehow become Vietnam and his delightful little submissive Te' Upp had transformed into a bullying midget. Also the promised house by the sea and life of luxury had not materialised. Now she had informed him that they were move from Hanoi and live in the Mekong Delta. The reason she gave was that his seaweed, it had now become his seaweed, he noted, was useless.

Gobbleton was confused. It wouldn't have been so bad if Te' Upp was nice to him. As it was she was worse than living with that bitch of a wife of his. He wondered what the other six families with which Te'Upp had informed him they would be sharing a home, would be like? He thought perhaps a nervous breakdown was in order. But dismissed the idea as he thought that it was unlikely that either Te'Upp, or her masters would understand, or be sympathetic.

Meanwhile, back on the farm, the scientists continued to make more discoveries. The prion had gone and it was the seaweed that effected this miraculous cure. They tested the theory on infected pigs. Fed them sea weed and low and behold they were cured and declared free from infection. They tried it out on other infected animals too. Sheep, goats and cattle all underwent the same recovery.

The seaweed was the panacea for BDS. Would it work on humans? Gerald spoke to Toni. Toni spoke to Meddlesome. The problem was one of getting the seaweed tested on humans and then if it was a success, getting the drug onto the market. Stringent laws were in force with the regard to new drugs. Toni and the New Deal Democratic Party needed to bypass this gate somehow. If the drug could be tested and was proven to effect a cure, the NDDP would be seen as saviours. They needed to involve Willie. A secret message was sent. A message that naturally Bradford picked up too.

Willie could see the problem. It was two fold. First of all the drug needed testing. Then if successful, he needed to bypass the food and drug people. Then there were the Brits. Whilst they could be allowed credit for the discovery of the cure, commercial exploitation and profits were definitely the domain of America. If he pulled this one off, then the pressure would be off him. Also he could shuttle back and fore across the Atlantic and reacquaint himself with Heigar's sexual preferences at the same time. So, first things first, test the drug.

This proved to be surprisingly easy. The prison system of America was bursting at the seams with prisoners on death row. Each time one got shot, hung, fried or injected, there was an outcry. What could be simpler that to cut a deal with these guys? Guinea pig in exchange for life? If they died, so what? If they survived, well both sides came out smelling sweet. 500 prisoners were quietly and deliberately infected with the BDS disease. Then the tests and trials began. All of the prisoners that received treatment were pronounced cured. The drug was a success. The next trick would be to get it past the food and drug boys. The obvious method of achieving this would be to claim that it was a natural product.

Del Minki, who had remained remarkably quiet and patient throughout all of the events since their chief scientist had disappeared, along with their genetically modified sea weed, now saw their opportunity to press their case and claim their share of the cake. They had not been idle in the intervening time but had preferred to maintain a very low profile. If things had gone wrong, then they didn't want any fingers pointed in their direction. There again, if events turned out well, then they wanted their share of any profits to be made. So though keeping in the background, and seeming to take no interest, they had in fact been bringing their not inconsiderable resources to bear in the form of both a thorough investigation and observation of the facts and subsequent events. It was Del Minki that eventually supplied the solution

Though they too had failed to locate their missing scientist and also assumed that he was dead. This was no longer regarded as being important. His original task, that of growing genetically modified seaweed as food, had been a failure. This was however now superseded by a whole new objective. That of obtaining the sole licence to market the drug that could cure BSD. As for having the sole rights to market the seaweed as animal feed? Well that would prove to be difficult, as the stuff only appeared to want to grow on the Blue Stone. They would do some quiet research on that later. Either way they didn't need Kenu Itayaku and since he had absconded with the product in the first place, and subsequently disappeared, presumed drowned. They were not liable for death benefits, or had any responsibilities towards him at all. Del Minki washed its hands of Kenu. Del Minki, via its Washington contacts began to put pressure on Willie Clayton at this stage.

The Brits had the seaweed. Seaweed that had originally belonged to Del Minki. Seaweed that hadn't existed in the Universe until Del Mini produced it. They hinted that it was all a bit like God and Genesis, but on a smaller scale. They could see that now the seaweed was growing in Wales and there was no way that America was going to be able to claim it. Del Minki at this point subtly substituted America for Del Minki, in the conversation. As a source of food for human beings, it was not the best. That they agreed. But as source of food for animals, it was great. So, in the long term, it should not be too difficult to get the stuff to grow elsewhere. But, there again, that was open to exploitation by anybody. All anyone needed was a few cuttings. That would be impossible to stop from happening. No, the real money-spinner was the cure for BSD. Del Minki had the where with all to make this drug. After all, it was only basically ground up seaweed. As such it could be claimed to be a natural product and there fore not subject to federal food and drug regulations. There were no rulings with regard to products obtained from genetically modified seaweed. The stuff had never existed before, so there were no regulations that covered it. Any way, it could be argued that the seaweed was no longer the same plant as the one that had left Japan. In fact the Brits had already used this argument against America when they discovered it growing in their waters. This growth was something that might or might not be connected to their original product. Who could prove what? The lawyers could argue for years and make millions.

No, market the BSD cure now. Market the product as a herbal remedy, called, oh, Kelp Help, or Marine-Aid or something, and pip the Brits to the post. That they could do now. Regulations already existed with regard to not only the validity of herbal products, but with regard to patent laws too. Regulations that were recognised and adhered to by the UK. The market window would only be open for a set length of time. For as long as it took for all sufferers of BSD to be cured. America must strike now, whilst the iron was hot. Get in and get in fast and clean up. Once it became public knowledge that America had a sure-fire cure, it didn't matter if the UK dragged its feet with regard to legislation. As with viagara, public pressure would force the issue.

Willie Clayton could see both the political and economic sense in taking this course of action. Del Minki would make a profit, thus ensuring work for Americans and revenue via tax for the country. There was also the kudos to be gained and no doubt a suitable contribution towards his party's re-election funds from a grateful Del Minki.

America would have the sole rights to produce and market Kelp Help, and some licence could be granted to the Brits to produce the drug, sorry, herbal remedy themselves. The Brits could be left alone to harvest and market their own seaweed. This they could sell as both animal feed and a cure for the animal strain of BDS. They could also sell, at a suitable cost sufficient amount for the herbal cure to be manufactured. This price would have to be sufficiently low for the herbal capsules to be made economically, bearing in mind that America controlled the patent. Since Britain had a state controlled National Health system, then they would not want to be placing themselves in the position of effectively having to buy in the product for which they supplied the raw materials at a cost that was prohibitive.

Hence, they would have to keep down the cost of raw seaweed. Meanwhile, since Del Minki would be receiving the raw seaweed for the production of the Kelp Help, they would be in a position to attempt to grow it themselves and then in turn enter the animal feed market. The Kelp help market would diminish whilst the animal feed market would grow.

Game, set and match.

Willie Clayton agreed. Del Minki received the green light to start producing "Kelp Help Kapsules" as it was decided that the product would be named. Their marketing team would begin to fire up the sales campaign. Maybe at first a few deliberately leaked rumours.

Hints that cure had been discovered. In America. Then perhaps a muddled denial. Just to muddy the waters. Then proof positive, in the form of leaked memos. Then perhaps a Del Minki representative could go on prime time TV. He could make a point of saying that the so-called miracle cure was as yet untested. No need at this point to mention prisons and death row inmates, it hinted of exploitation. Also that it was a natural product an actually really a herbal remedy. Down play the drug side. No need at this to mention seaweed. That could come later, and at no point in the early stages would the fact that the seaweed in question was in fact growing in the UK. Certainly under no circumstances ever, would the words genetically modified be used at all. That should stir things up in Europe. Then a learned paper.

Stating that this was a 100% natural product and did in fact indicate that it would indeed provide a cure for BDS. Public pressure should then be sufficient to over ride any UK Governmental doubts. So once again Willie Clayton found himself looking forward to yet another spell with Heigar, and he would bring along Lulu to keep Toni sweet too.

It was the Vietnamese down on Gerald's farm that made the next discovery, but were so confused that at first they kept it to them selves.

CHAPTER: 11

Sheep are placid, heard animals. The only time that they resort to frenetic activity is when threatened, and then they run. In the opposite direction from the perceived danger. Spring lambs do frisk about for a time but that short period of their lives soon passes within weeks. Kevin and Gyp posed no threat. Gyp was well used to livestock and generally ignored it. She disliked cows due to having been kicked and knocked unconscious as a small pup. The scar from which was plainly visible over her right eye. Cows she avoided. Though her breed was renowned for working with sheep, Gyp was the exception and avoided them too. Maybe thinking that they also were capable of delivering a hefty wallop. Gyp was obviously puzzled and unhappy. She sat down and stared at the sheep, then looked up at Kevin for guidance. Kevin however was also at a total loss. He stared at the sheep in wonderment. They were not behaving as sheep should. Instead of quietly grazing the vegetation, occasionally looking up at their surroundings, and then slowly moving on to graze again. These sheep were active. Very active. In fact, very, very active. They appeared to have rubber bands for suspension and were literally bouncing around the field. Apparently oblivious to Kevin and Gyp, each other and the world in general. They looked like springs on amphetamines, thought Kevin to himself. As if to confirm his thoughts, two of the sheep rolled around the ground and then reinvigorated, proceeded to bounce around like South African antelopes in a wild life film. It was the passing comparison to amphetamines that caused Kevin to look a little harder. The sheep seem to have been grazing on a rather strange weed. It was about knee height, with a dark green colored leaf that had ragged edges. It also had several, small purple flowers, not unlike the bell shaped blooms of foxgloves. Kevin went forward and bending down examined one of the plants. Kevin knew nothing about plants or nature in general for that matter. This was a totally new species for him. It did not however appear to be growing haphazardly. In fact it had certainly been cultivated, and in a very quiet and seldom visited area too. Kevin suddenly had a sinking feeling in the pit of his stomach. He decided to leave the sheep to their own devices for the moment and he hurried back down to the brewery to fetch George.

George had been busy checking the fuel oil supply and getting ready for the next brew. Steam raising being a very vital part of brewing. "Got to maintain the correct temperature." He had instructed Kevin. "Very important is steam. All of the vats are heated during the process and the fermentation depends upon good temperature control." The huge copper vats and their associated pipe work gleamed and sparkled from being hand polished. George was peering into one of the brewing vats through a large inspection door in its burnished, covered top. Just like he is looking into a great big wizard's hat thought Kevin. George meanwhile was testing the great sweeping paddle that moved and mixed the hops and crystal malt within the vat during the process. He looked up as Kevin called him. "George, I think that we have an emergency up in the top field. Some of Farmer Thomson's sheep have broken through the hedge."

"Ah! No big deal." Retorted George, and turned to continue his inspection, saying, "We can chase them back later and fix the hedge. They will just chew the grass for us. Don't worry about it."

"George, I need you to look at these sheep." Said Kevin urgently. "They are not acting normally."

"How do you mean?" enquired George, having emerged from his peering and inspecting. He looked at Kevin with slight curiosity. Kevin he knew didn't know the first thing about sheep. "Bright as a new pin in there." He indicated with his head, as he polished an imaginary smear from the huge copper vat with a clean rag.

"They are dancing around like Michel Jackson on speed." Said Kevin emphatically. He had a sudden thought. Maybe George didn't know what speed was. "You know, they are acting crazy, jumping all over the place. Not only that they have been eating some plant that I have never seen before. Look, please come with me and check. I have a nasty feeling about this and I need your opinion." He looked at George willing him to agree. It never occurred to Kevin to order George to follow him. George, returned his look, and rubbed his chin. Then coming to a decision said.

"OK lad, seeing as how you are all hot and bothered. I will come along and have a look." He took another large rag from the pocket of his coverall and wiped his hands. "Come Gyp." He said, "If I have to walk up there, you can too old gal."

Kevin noted that he had been demoted to lad again, but was grateful that George would accompany him. So together and with Gyp faithfully escorting them, they climbed back up to the top field.

"Bloody Hell!" Exclaimed George with deep feeling as he stopped dead in his tracks and viewed the gamboling sheep.. "What ever has got into those silly buggers?" He stopped dead in his tracks and had pushed back his cap and paused in mid scratch in astonishment.

"This I think." Said Kevin. Bending down and plucking a handful of the strange plant for George to look at.

George took the proffered plant from Kevin and peered at it closely. He scratched his head some more and then dug into the top pocket of his boiler suit and took out his spectacles and examined the plant carefully. Finally, he looked at Kevin and shook his head. "Damned if I know what it is boss. Never come across anything like it before. But they are certainly eating the stuff." He pointed to the sheep that now and again would take a mighty swing at the ground, tear off a clump of the odd plant, and eat it with relish. Then only to increase their cavorting. "They're all drunk." George exclaimed. "Every last blessed one of them!" He turned to Kevin. "Right Boss, first job, get some help and get these few sheep penned until they sober up. We will need some help with that! Then fix the hole in the hedge to stop any more coming through. No on second thoughts, block the hole just temporary like first. We can use some old branches from out of the woods." He pointed with his head towards the nearby tree line. "I'll do that, you get some hands up her fast boss."

Kevin noted rather ruefully that though he had been reinstated as boss, he still was very much under George's command. He started back down the slope again shouting over his shoulder, "OK George, will do." Gyp started back with him, but soon stopped. Then turned and head down and tail streaming behind her, headed back up the slope towards George.

Once again at the brewery, Kevin quickly rounded up the four Kharzi workmen and together, with them, he again began the climb up the slope. When they reached the top however, the Kharzis all looked at the scene in dismay. Then pointing to the sheep and the strange plant, they began an agitated conversation in their own language. "Never mind the babble speak!" Shouted George. "Get them sheep penned. Try to move them to the far end of the field." He pointed to the other corner, bounded by two solid hedgerows. "There are none of those plants down there." He added. "If you can keep them at that end, I will take a couple of the Kharzis with me and bring back some barbed wire we keep for emergencies. We can run a holding pen from the two hedges in the corner. Looks like our lads know all about this plant and you can see that it has been cultivated. Bloody cocaine or something! We will all end up doing 30 years apiece if this lot ever becomes public. Once these sheep are sorted, best get Peter her chop chop and sort this lot out." He returned to closing the hole where the sheep had originally broken through.

Eventually and not without difficulty, the sheep were herded into the far corner of the field. Actually herded was not the correct term. They had no fear at all and had in the end to be bribed with handfuls of the odd plant. Much to the consternation of the Kharzis who broke into agitated conversation each time Kevin pulled a handful. "Maybe I ought to get Beth to brew them some strong coffee." Muttered George, as he looked at the sheep. "They are drunk as lords." The sheep now were definitely looking the worst for wear and had begun to lie down. One by one they fell into a deep sleep, oblivious of the world. "Maybe I ought to call the vet? I don't know what we will do if any of them dies on us. It's this lot's fault." He indicated the Kharzis, "They know all about the weed." He kicked at a clump of purple flowers. "Better call Peter and get him here fast. Maybe this lot knows about the effect upon sheep and what we should do." One of the sheep began snoring gently.

Kevin returned to The Black Badger and called Peter. Leaving George and the Kharzis in the top field to keep an eye on the now sleeping sheep. Sheep that slept at all odd angles. When Vicki asked what was wrong? Kevin briefly explained. Vicki looked alarmed. "I don't want anything to do with drugs Kevin. You know why. For all I know there may be a warrant out for me now in connection to Leroy." She looked frightened.

"I'm sure that there isn't Vicki. If there was, with all the publicity we have had, you would have been picked up long ago. Certainly after the Camberwell Crescent thing."

Vicki shuddered, "Please don't mention that again Kevin. Drugs scare me Kevin. Please what can we do?" She looked at him helplessly.

"Peter is on his way. We will have to find out what it is and more to the point who planted it and for what reasons. I only hope that there isn't or has not been any other crop! Come on let's have a cup of tea. I will tell Beth gently and then we will wait for Peter. It shouldn't take him long to get here."

It took Peter less than 20 minutes to reach them. By which time Beth had been told of the situation. Kevin brought him into the kitchen where both Beth and Vicki were drinking tea. "Sit down Peter please, we have an emergency on our hands and it's very serious." Beth handed Peter a cup of tea and Kevin explained the morning's events. "We could all end up in jail." He stated. "Not only that but if there has been any dealing, then we could lose everything. Brewery, Badger, the lot mate!"

"Calm down Kevin it hasn't come to that and it won't. Now call the girls in. Let's start with the weakest members first. I think that I know what the plant is. They call it zhip, and from what you have told me, it's a pretty good description too. It's not on the proscribed list here in the UK, but from what you said, it damn well should be. There again, since it is not common knowledge, best not broadcast it. It's not plentiful in their country and commands a high price. It's traditional at important weddings. What I can't understand is why it should suddenly become so potent? Obviously it has taken all too well to your rich soil. It's used in small amounts as I said, for special occasions. It's normally a mild stimulant and given to the bride and groom prior to their wedding night." He grinned. "Keeps you awake you see." I had no idea that they were carrying seeds with them. My guess is that they planted all the seeds they had, hoping that just one or two plants would grow. Instead of which you seem to have field full.

"Mild stimulant!" Spluttered Kevin. "Those sheep were flying Peter. Now they are all snoring and who knows? Maybe lapsing into comas by now and going to whatever world dead sheep go to."

"Maybe something to do with your soil. Who knows? I can only tell you about what I know and have seen for my own eyes. Back in their country it's no more intoxicating than betel nut or chewing quat."

"Peter, I have no idea what either betel nut or quat is. I can equally only relate my recent experiences. What are we going to do?" But Mulchi and Vania were ushered into the room by Beth and cut short anything else that Kevin might have wanted to say. Peter turned to the two women and indicated that they should sit. The women had picked up Kevin's agitated state and were nervous. Peter approached them gently and Vicki smiled at them, albeit nervously too. Peter and the girls had a long conversation in Kharzi. Finally, he looked up at Kevin. "Right." He said firmly and in a cheery voice. "It is as I suspected. They planted the stuff for the wedding."

"Oh bloody wonderful!" Exclaimed Kevin. "Yes me Lud. We were having a wedding so I handed around the crack cocaine and needles full of heroin. Sorry about everyone expiring!" Kevin shook his head in exasperation. "Never mind the sociology Peter. What about the sheep? And the crop?"

"They assure me that the sheep will survive. They may have a hangover, but they will survive. As for the crop? Dump it fast." He looked across the table at Kevin.

"I will!" Declared Kevin firmly. "I will pull the lot out and burn it."

"Best not." Said Peter, shaking his head. What happens if the wild life in general gets a lungful? There may be even worse effects from smoking the stuff. Also what about the person doing the burning? Could end up trying to fly or something" Vicki shuddered and spilled her tea. "No, better to just pull it and dump it. Then watch out for any seedlings. Shouldn't have any though. Sounds like it was all too young. I'll come up with you and take a peek. Stop worrying. I will have a word with them and tell them that growing zhip in the UK is a no, no. Doubt that they will understand why, but if the chief says no, then no it is. And you my old son are their chief. So calm down. Let me do the talking and you just nod your head a lot. OK?" He got up, and patting Vania on the shoulder made, Don't worry noises. "Lead me to the scene of the crime Oh Mighty Chief." He laughed, "They are a bunch aren't they?"

"OK for you." Muttered Kevin ungraciously. "It's not your arse!"

Peter turned and placing a friendly hand on Kevin's arm said seriously, "Actually it is Kevin and I am very sorry that I got you into this mess. But as yet, providing Little Bo Peep next door doesn't count his sheep today, there is no great harm done, and no laws have been broken. We can return the livestock just as soon as they are mobile. Block the hole and pull up all of the zhip. OK?"

"OK" agreed Kevin, "Sorry I got all wound up, but things around here are beginning to put me under some pressure and I really don't want any more problems. Come on Peter; let me introduce you to a bunch of junky sheep."

Together they climbed up the bank to the top field. Peter stopped and picking some on the weed, gave it a cursory look. "Yep! That's zhip." He looked around. "Quite some crop you had! I have never seen it so plentiful or so large. It's normally much smaller than this. You know, if you ever decide to give up brewing, you could have a tidy little earner here!" He laughed, seeing Kevin's expression quickly added, "Just joking, just joking. Let's have a look at the sheep." They went over to the other end of the field where George and the Kharzis stood over the prostrate and snoring sheep. "Morning George. What you been feeding this lot on?" He laughed, "Don't worry, it won't kill them, but I dare say they will have a nasty hangover." He greeted the Kharzis and they respectfully replied in their own language.

"You sure that they are going to be alright?" Asked George. "They are sleeping pretty soundly. We don't want to have to explain this to Mr. Thomson. They're his sheep after all. God alone knows what the Min of Ag would say if they saw this lot! Mad sheep disease or something."

Peter spoke to the Kharzis and they all nodded their heads and made It's all OK noises. "They assure me that the sheep will sleep soundly for a spell, and they start to get mobile again. Once they stop staggering, they will push them back through the hedge and block up the hole."

"They will also pull up every single root and blade of Zhip and dump it in the woods. No, on second thoughts, they had better bury it deeply. In the woods too please." Kevin indicated over his shoulder in the general direction of the trees. He was now visibly more at ease. I don't want any animal getting to the stuff. OK? I also need you to impress upon these guys that growing zhip is OUT. Here, or anywhere. Point out to them that any seeds they have should be flushed down the toilet. Also, that if they are caught by the authorities as having any involvement with zhip, or any other little botanical surprises for that matter, It's the first plane back to Kharzi land for them. All of them. George I want you to witness this and I want Peter to translate to us word for word please. Sorry Peter, but this too serious for joking. It's not just Vicki and me, but there is George and Beth to consider too. What would happen to them if we got closed down, or worse still, everything confiscated by the Government as drugs profits? You know how they have tried to shut us down before. This is handing it to them on a plate and believe me they would crucify us." He stopped and looked at them all.

George came forward and put out his hand and taking Kevin's hand in his, he removed his cap. "Thanks boss. Me and the missus knew that you were a chip off the old block. Silas would have done just the same and said the same thing. I know that it's not their fault and they meant no harm, but we have a duty to keep them on the straight and narrow so to speak. And you have a duty in law boss, regarding actions of employees. I recon that we can sort all this out and keep it our secret. Just as long as Peter here spells it all out in black and white."

Peter addressed the Kharzis and explained that their actions, although unwittingly, had placed their Chief and them selves in danger. In addition, should this become public there would be no wedding and that they could well be repatriated to their homeland. This caused visible consternation among them. He explained that zhip, no matter how popular in their country was not allowed in Britain. The reason he said was obvious. It grew far too well and look what it did to sheep. Sent them to sleep. That was certainly not the idea behind giving it to brides and grooms on their wedding night. The Kharzis could see the logic of that and one by one, starting with the eldest asked for Kevin's forgiveness, affirming their allegiance at the same time. Kevin instructed them to watch the sheep and once they were completely recovered, return them to their side of the hedge. Also, to check the hedge line for further weak places and repair same. He then went on to instruct them that all the zhip was to be pulled up and disposed of so that it posed no threat to any other creature, but not to burn it. Finally, that a regular check had now to me made to ensure that no plants survived and that there would be no repetition of drunken livestock.

Timothy Longstanton had been discharged from hospital. He was now a walking wounded. Neck still firmly braced in a plastic collar and his right arm in a sling for comfort. He limped with the aid of a stick and with each painful step cursed the name of Kevin Firkettle. Whilst lying in hospital and sipping the seemingly never ending prune juice, he had developed a method switching off from the outside world. Thus, he could mentally isolate himself from the day-to-day banal ramblings of his fellow patients. So whilst they wittered on about their boring and meaningless lives to Timothy, he remained cocooned within himself. Not being able to nod in agreement, he just lay there and allowed their drivel about football, National Lottery and the price of petrol, to wash over him. He rapidly became known as a good listener. Actually, he was plotting his revenge upon Kevin and was totally oblivious to their chatter. He meticulously went over in his mind, as best he was able, the total destruction of Houghton Springs Brewery. The only time that his reverie was interrupted was when his formidable lady visitor came with fresh supplies of prune juice. A Challenger tank would have been hard pressed to ignore her for long, thought Timothy to himself. So he tolerated her visits and obediently drank the juice.

Timothy had decided that fire was the answer. He was not in least worried that evidence of arson would be found. He fully intended to point all fingers at The Soldiers Of The Divine Order and Maxwell Crump. No, Timothy felt that a major conflagration was called for, and the best day would be on mid summers eve, to coincide with the planned ceremony. Timothy had used a cell phone to send whispered messages to Maxwell and knew that he Maxwell, was now well in Cynthia's good books and had her ear. Cynthia desperately longed for Maxwell to have far more than her ear. In fact, she panted and writhed in lustful thoughts of a hairy Maxwell. A huge, rampant hairy Maxwell who; ripping off her clothes and throwing her to the floor, would plunge deep inside her and satisfy her years of sexual frustration. Each night the dreams became more vivid and each morning Cynthia awoke, totally washed out, in a bed that looked as if a pair of elephants had slept in it. Maxwell, he knew would be close to Cynthia on mid summers eve. In addition, hopefully Cynthia would come along with an elite force of the commando wing of The Soldiers Of The Divine Order. Planning no doubt, to perform a Blitzkrieg operation on Kevin with her assembled force of Bible toting, religious storm troopers. Timothy would then ignite the brewery in secret and the pub too. His weapon of choice? An incendiary device, complete with timer. Details of how to make this little gem he had downloaded from the internet. Timothy decided that two would be required and the subsequent conflagration would leave nothing but a shell. He fervently hoped that Kevin would be included in the blaze, but made contingency plans if he was not. He was at first disappointed that it could not be guaranteed that Kevin would perish, but drew satisfaction from the knowledge that he would be bankrupted. Even with an insurance claim, the brewery would be finished and who knows? The finger of suspicion might even then include Kevin. Bankrupted, broken, suspicion falling around his shoulders and no where to live and no livelihood. Kevin would then take his own life. With a little help from Timothy, that is. Rat poison or weed killer would fit the bill nicely. He would ensure that Kevin swallowed a large dose. Timothy envisioned strapping a hapless Kevin into a chair, in the burned out shell of the brewery. Gagging him and passing a tube up his nose and down into his throat. Then the poison could be administered by using a funnel and gravity. Any subsequent marks on the body being where he, his cousin had attempted to force his mouth open. In of course, a desperate and futile effort to save his dear cousin's life and remove the deadly mixture. Timothy gloated over the idea of forcing a helpless Kevin to swallow the painful poison and then watch him die. He reasoned that both he and Joseph Mengler would enjoy such a scene. It was still too good a death for Kevin. However, it would have to do. Anything else might be difficult to disguise. He had again toyed with the idea of crucifixion, but discarded it as being impractical. It would, he thought, be far too difficult to convince the police that Kevin had committed suicide by crucifixion and knocked all the nails in by himself.

The geology of the area of Houghton Springs and its immediate environs was interesting for anyone having a curiosity in the subject. The land at the surface being ancient limestone of marine origin. Below this lay a huge strata of sandstone. Below which lay a granite bedrock formation. Houghton Springs was surrounded an all sides by high ground. As a consequence of which, rainfall tended to sink into the lime stone and percolate downwards, through the sand stone, until it encountered the impervious granite layer. At this point it began to saturate the sandstone layer, rather similar to a sponge holding water. As more rain fell and the hydrostatic pressure built up, the water, over the years had cut itself a channel underground. This eventually culminating in emerging from a rock face. If one stooped down, one could enter a small cave where there was a deep pool of clear fresh water. The pool itself being Houghton Springs and one could observe the fresh spring water welling up out of its depths. The pool continually overflowed and ran out to form Houghton Brook. The Black Badger had placed two submersible pumps into the depths of the pool and it was upon these and the water supply that the brewery depended. Timothy was well aware of this fact. He reasoned that nothing short of dynamite would move the spring itself. Even then the water would find its own way out. A new bore well could be sunk in a matter of days. As for the pumps? Well new units were available for purchase off the shelf. No, nothing less than total destruction of the brewery and pub would suffice.

The EEC had issued a letter to Kevin informing him that a team of inspectors would arrive in June, on a date that Kevin saw clashed with Mid Summer's Eve. They wrote to him, in legal EEC terminology that all but defied his powers of deduction and command of the English language. The crux of their letter being to inform him that they intended to carry out a full inspection of both brewery and bottling plant. Their stated objective, in long and impressive words and written on expensive paper, was two fold.

To ensure that the water conformed with EEC purity regulations. Also that the brewery and bottling line fell within EEC hygiene standards. There then followed a wealth of information regarding where the appropriate standards could be accessed. Kevin thought that even if he gathered the appropriate documents, it would take a year or more to read them. He began to have sinking feelings about the whole inspection. George however, was not so dismayed.

"Don't worry lad." Was his comment. "The water is crystal and the brewing is the best. It all falls well within any regulations you care to name. You can't apply new regs to a process this old lad. This is traditional brewing and they know we have them by the short and curlies there. It's all been tried before. Mr. Wilberforce will wipe the floor with them." He looked at Kevin in a very confident manner. "No lad, just as long as I steam the barrels properly and I always do. The brew depends upon that. We are home and dry with the brewing. Why, just look how this place gleams. Spotless it is!" He made a wide sweep of his hands that took in the brewing floor. The copper vats gleamed a burnished gold and pipe work reflected sunlight. The Kharzis had done an excellent job of painting the walls white and sanding the wooden floor. Kevin had to admit that first impressions were good. The place was spotless; the walls reflected the light and the pipe work and vats all glowed. All of the windows sparkled too. He had to take George's word that they were an excellent brewery and infringed no food and drink laws. They certainly looked efficient and hygienic.

"No, our problems are with the bottling line. I recon that they could find fault there, if they were picky that is. Even there since we are a live beer, we only have to sterilize the bottles, and we do that. I even add sodium metabisulphide into to the bottle washing water before they get steam sterilized. Just to be certain. Our reputation depends upon our product. Why, I have never had a bad batch yet. Or any complaints either." He added. "Anyway we need a new line and we all know that. Even if they closed the line down pending improvements, we would still be in the business of brewing. It's a lack of production of beer for any length of time that can sink us. We can still produce, but maybe not bottle. The draught production would be unaffected." He smiled confidently at Kevin. "No don't you worry lad, I'll see that we are all ship shape and Bristol fashion."

The leader of the proposed team was a Dutch gentleman named Klaus Van Der Krapper. Billy Boom was a little worried about the credibility of this gentleman. From his point of view Van Der Krapper's qualities being suspect. The Dutch being an honest race and generally regarded as being above taking bribes. Further investigation however, discovered that Van Der Krapper was a stubborn and arrogant little man. He was also a stickler for rules and regulations. It was reputed that he had memorized every single EEC directive regarding food and drink, and could recite them at will. He had a reputation for dotting ies and crossing tees. Furthermore, he had some longstanding, internal European fight going on with the German food and drink ministry. This concerned the correct definition of beer. The Germans being of the opinion that what a Dutchman knew about brewing beer could be written on the head of a pin. This feeling, being almost historical in its origins. The outcome was that the Germans felt very miffed at having a Dutchman in charge and had insisted upon the inclusion of a very large and jolly Bavarian in the team too. Investigation of "Henk the Tank," as he was fondly known, due to his huge beer gut. Revealed that one only had to keep his unquenchable thirst satisfied, for him to agree that there was no such thing as a bad beer, just some that were better than others. Billy strongly felt that Henk could not be relied upon to close down any brewery. Make recommendations for improvements maybe. However, he would never close down an institution that he held so close to his heart.

The third member of the team was some forty-year-old French spinster. Mademoiselle Aughty apparently only drank an occasional glass of wine, knew nothing of beer and hated all Germans per se. Billy reasoned that the Dutchman would automatically assume command. This would upset the German, who would then want to contradict any conclusions that the Dutchman made. Thus canceling him out. Billy was reasonably sure that on Van Der Krapper's past record, he would find every single pernickety

EEC infringement. Also, that he would be opposed to Henk The Tank on principle. The spinster was therefore, the obvious person to be targeted. It subsequently transpired that she was not averse to having her bank account padded. This would be done, providing she condemned Houghton Springs Brewery. Billy thought that the odds were in his favor. It was unlikely that Van Der Krapper would want to give Houghton Springs brewery a clean bill of health, knowing that Henk The Tank would want to. Thus he still held two votes to one. He sat back satisfied. Even if in the unlikely circumstances that the EEC team did pass the brewery as being fit for purpose, he still had the MI5 agents as a fail safe back up. Best to have them go in too and complete their mission, he thought. This way would he be certain of achieving his objective. Billy picked up his phone and quietly informed the MI5 men that it was all systems go.

Charley Buggit and Gerald Shaddow were activated. They had already visited The Black Badger, posing as innocent tourists and were familiar with the Brewery. They had even paid One pound each for the guided tour and free sample. They knew exactly where to plant their bacillus for maximum effect. They went into the web and accessed the site of The Real Beer Drinkers. There they learned of the planned and quiet observation of Mid Summers Day by The Black Badger. Tables would be set outside, a special meal served and a free bottle of crememorative Black Badger given to every diner over the age of 18. They also were informed of the forth coming inspection by the EEC team. Their bacillus could not survive for long periods out of its culture environment. Therefore timing would be critical, if they were infect the bottling plant and brewery. They decided to again visit The Black Badger posing as tourists and at an opportune moment, just prior to the team's inspection, open up the thermos flask that innocently carried the germs and smear them in appropriate places around the plant. The EEC team then taking samples for analysis would be forced into the conclusion that the Houghton Springs Brewery was not just unhygienic by EEC standards, but a positive biological hazard. They decided that they would use a camper van of German manufacturer for both transport and cover. They began their preparations accordingly.

The Kharzies were concerned about their all too successful attempts to cultivate zhip. The strain that had grown so well, had a potency that they had never seen before. It was obviously no use what so ever for the purposes intended. That was a disappointment. That albeit unwittingly they had not only compromised their surrogate chief but also threatened their own existence as a refugee group, had profound effects upon their collective psyche. They had waited anxiously for the sheep to recover, some in the interim period, carefully examining the hedge for weak points. They also set about diligently pulling up the zhip and stacking it in small piles. Then, as one by one and slowly the sheep recovered, they moved them about, keeping them on their feet. The animals however, exhibited all the signs of a major hangover and were reluctant to do anything except lie down and look very unhappy. Once they had returned several very bleary eyed and groggy sheep sheep back to the adjoining field, they repaired the gap with the barbed wire. Next they went into a huddled group to discuss the best method of disposing of the zhip. Since the surface geology was lime stone, there were several places in the woods above the springs where small sink holes had, over the years been formed. This occurring when the lime stone below was slowly washed away by rainwater and had formed a small cave. The roof of which, over a period of time would collapse. Badgers were fond of digging into these areas and making their sets. The Kharzis had found a reasonably fresh collapse, a mere two feet of so across, but perhaps six or more deep. They decided to stuff the zhip into this cavity and push it as far down into the ground as possible. Then they would cover the hole with loose soil and leaf litter. This they set about doing.

CHAPTER: 12

The two weeks or so before mid summer's eve had seen heavy rain. In fact Kevin was beginning to wonder if both ceremony and any outside table usage were ever going to take place, or be washed out? He had visions of a sodden bonfire and a very unhappy Vicki. However, a few days before the planned ceremony the weather, as predicted, changed for the better. A high pressure front swept in and lingered. The ground began to dry out and lights were strung outside of The Black Badger. Flower baskets were purchased, along with some flowering shrubs and a trellis erected and clematis encouraged to climb up it. George cut up some old barrels for the shrubs and the Kharzis worked with a horticultural will.

"Looks like Groundforce has been employed." Said Vicki approvingly, as she viewed the new patio. "The tables look just right." She added over her shoulder as she went back inside the building. They had chosen a modern wrought iron version of a traditional park bench. Somehow the manufacturers had managed to produce a greenish, copper like tone to the metal and had used a dark, polished hardwood that was most attractive.

"They fit as if they have been there for ever." Commented Beth. That and the plants and baskets. Why The old Badger had never looked so neat. The brewery is spic and span too. Old Silas would be really proud of you Kevin." She patted him on the shoulder in a motherly manner. "You and Vicki too. She's a fine lass." She looked at Kevin knowingly. "Worked hard she has lad."

Kevin nodded, saying, "I know, I know. It was a lucky day for me when she crossed my path."

"Lucky day for all of us Kevin." Beth looked at him seriously. "She is part of our lives now Kevin. George and I wouldn't want to loose her."

"Loose her?" Said Kevin in a worried and at the same time questioning manner. "How do you mean, loose her? Has she mentioned anything about leaving? I thought that she was happy here with us and the Badger and everything?"

"Happy enough now lad, but she is looking to the future lad. Her future, she is just your business partner at the moment. Not even that legally as far as I can make out. You are going to have to think very seriously about that young lady Kevin; soon too. Else you might just loose her lad, and none of us want that now do we?"

Kevin looked alarmed. "I certainly don't Beth. I would be lost without her. She knows that too." He stopped and idly kicked at a small stone and than giving a sigh looked at Beth. "Just let me, I mean us, get the EEC out of the way and then decide about the bottling line and I can offer Vicki something substantial. Right now we are still skating on thin ice."

"It's not security in the money way she wants you daft Twollop! UH! You men are all so blind! It's security in the relationship she needs!"

"She knows that I love her Beth!" Exclaimed Kevin hotly.
"So best you carry on thinking along those lines lad and think what you can do to prove to Vicki that you really care for her. Bah! MEN!" Beth turned and walked away leaving Kevin wondering what it was that he done wrong. Later however, when he tested Vickie's reaction towards him, he found no change. She was just as she was normally. He wanted to dismiss Beth's outburst, but he could not and found that worrying.

The day before mid summer's eve a mini van arrived with three girls. Well, young women would be a better description. Each would have been in her very early thirties or late twenties'. They all wore woolen ponchos, had lots of beads and long flowery dresses. They also wore head bands to retain their long hair. Kevin was immediately reminded of pictures he had seen of the Hippies of the sixties. They commented upon the new look Black Badger and asked if it was under new ownership? Kevin told them that he was the new owner.

"Still brewing then?" Observed one of the women as she sipped a pint of Black Badger.

"Uh Huh." Agreed Kevin, as he pulled another pint for her companions. "I took the place over when my father died." He was concentrating on pulling the beer, and not looking at the women. He did not notice the comprehending glances that passed between the women.

"So the previous owner was your father?"

"Yes. Why, have you been here before?" He looked up at them, placing a foaming pint on a tray in front of him.

There was a brief silence, and then the woman who had first spoken to him said, in a non committal manner. "We passed through some years back and met your father. He was an interesting man. He held strong beliefs regarding this place."

"So I gather." Said Kevin, now on his guard, and trying to pull more beer and look at them at the same time. He failed and beer splashed all over his left hand. "Are you aware that five lay lines intersect here?" She and her companions waited quietly and expectantly for his reply.

"Bother!" Exclaimed Kevin, placing the glass down and looking for a cloth. Adding, as he did so, "I didn't know about the lay lines." He had no idea what a lay line was, but realized that it might well have something to do with his late father's beliefs. "But my father was a very spiritual person. He held very firm views." Kevin thought that was a sufficiently non committal answer that covered all of his bases.

"Oh yes." She went on firmly in agreement. "He certainly did. He found that the juzt a position of the structure of the atom so similar to that of our universe." She looked at Kevin as if expecting a comment. Kevin however considered silence to be his best ally for the moment. So he pulled a serious face as if in agreement and slowly nodded his head. Seeing that there was nothing more forthcoming from Kevin, she continued in a school marm manner. "He considered that the sun's relative position and relationship with our solar system mirrored that of the necleus and its electrons. In an atom the relative distances are enormous you know." She looked at him gravely. Kevin returned her look with equal gravity.

"They contain more space than matter, actually." The giggly female obviously did not want to be left out of such an important conversation. Kevin however maintained his silence.

"The obvious leader of the group continued, ignoring her friend's contribution. "Yes, your late father firmly believed that we were but mere atoms in a much larger structure." Kevin had an almost irrepressible urge to say "Oh, you mean something like a huge, cosmic dog turd?" But had the good sense to remain both silent and poker faced.

The leader continued her lecture. "He also understood the full implication of a pentagonal intersection and the area thus enclosed" She said pondeously and her companions nodded as if one. Just like a bunch of nodding dogs, thought Kevin to himself. What the heck is a pentagonal intersection, I wonder? However, his musings were curtailed as she continued, "And he understood so much about natural forces too." She looked at her two companions for support and they both made assenting noises, and nodded some more. Kevin thought that he was on firmer ground with agreeing that Silas was a fund of knowledge in all things mysterious. He made noises to this effect and was met in return with knowing looks and more enthusiastic nodding.

Kevin came over to their table with their drinks. "Right at this spot." She indicated with a steady finger and no argument voice just about where Kevin was standing. "Is an intersection."

"We used GSP to confirm it!" The giggly one butted in again and looked at him smugly.

Kevin automatically looked down at the floor and had a sudden urge to move but instead said in a jocular voice, "I didn't know that a GSP unit could detect lay lines." He studied the polished wooden floor some more, but if it held any secrets, it was keeping them to itself and just stared back. Again his train of thought was interrupted as the woman pressed him some more.

"Are you a believer? I mean, Like your father?" The three of them looked at him expectantly. Kevin paused. But his reluctance was not noticed as the woman confided in him, "We are all New Age Theogodologists." As if that explained everything. "Your late father fully understood about these things." She continued without a break. "Would like us to hold a session and read your fortune?" She looked at him in anticipation. "We have some Tarot Cards in the van you know." She added eagerly.

Kevin knew that he was getting well out of his depth so excused himself with, "Well, not just at this moment, if you don't mind." He demurred and escaped by moving back behind the bar and looking at his watch and improvising. "I'm rather expecting a phone call from some important guests at any moment." As if to bear out his remarks, Beth came into the passageway that connected the bar to the rear of the house. Thus, out of site of the occupants of the bar, she silently hissed and made telephone gestures with her hand. "In fact I think that someone is calling me now." Declared Kevin happily, glad to be able to leave the three rather strange and disturbing women. He disappeared into the back.

The call was from the EEC team and they informed him that they would arrive the next day well before lunch and could he accommodate them? They would require three separate rooms, and had their own transport. Kevin made a mental note and returned to the bar. The women were engaged in a deep conversation, but ceased immediately upon Kevin's return. Each looked at each other and Kevin had the distinct impression that they had been discussing him. He looked at them and smiled in a knowing manner. There was a long pause, whilst they all stared at each other. The one who had spoken to him originally broke a rather pregnant silence. She looked at Kevin directly in a most disconcerting way and asked rather pointedly, "Phone call?" Kevin nodded, saying, "Yes."

"You must have good ears." She observed, "I never heard the phone."

"Oh I got there just before it rang." Said Kevin mischievously. "I'm psychic you know." He nodded his head whilst looking at them in a very serious manner. "The lay lines." He said, as if that in itself was explanation enough. "That pentagonal intersection." He made a face that he hoped would indicate secret knowledge and mysterious power. The three women immediately exchanged meaningful looks at each other, as if his explanation had just confirmed their own thoughts. Kevin laughed to himself. "Important was it then?" Asked the same woman, still pushing. She had put her drink down as was holding her hand to the side of her face, as if being fully aware of something, but just wanting a point clarified.

"Visitors, you know." Said Kevin in a secretive tone, looking around him as if not wanting others to hear him. "Very important visitors." He winked secretively at them.

"Ah Ha!" mused the woman looking at her other two companions, "Visitors eh?" She nodded as if understanding, adding, "On mid summer's eve is it. Special visitors?"

"Oh yes," Replied Kevin in all honesty. "On mid summer's eve and special visitors" He winked at them again and was surprised when she slowly closed one eye and nodding her head tapping the side of her nose, as she did so. Mulchi and Vania came in to the bar at that moment and any other further conversation was terminated. Kevin left them all and out of sight shrugged his shoulders and dismissed his odd guests. He went about his work not giving the three women another thought.

Charley Buggit and Gerald Shaddow had driven their camper van to within easy striking distance of The Black Badger. They had pulled into a secluded lay by and Charley was inside the van brewing a cup of tea on the gas stove. The pathogens were all safely locked up in a thermos flask and stored in the small refrigerator of the camper van. They had brought TV meals with them and intended to heat them in the van's microwave oven. To an observer's view, they were just a couple of fifty year old campers. Their cover was that they were bird watchers. They had taken the precaution of bringing along some well thumbed reference books on the in fact to add credence to their cover.

"Nice to get out of London Charley" Observed Gerald. He was sitting outside in the sun in a small aluminum folding chair favored by campers the world over. He had placed a matching table in front of him and a similar chair for his companion. "Sort of close to nature so to speak. Quite refreshing it is. Isn't that a lark?" He pointed into the adjacent field.

Charley leaned out of the large, open side door of the camper van, and looked in the direction that Gerald was pointing. "Nah, yer Muppet. It's a kestrel. It's hovering, not rising and singing. Gawd! I only hope no one asks you about birds Gerald."

"Yeah, well I didn't have much time to mug up on our little feathered friends." Replied Gerald, in a slightly miffed tone, "I will just stick to the line that I am new at all of this and just along to keep you company. I majored in explosives and dirty tricks, not sweet little birdies. Anyway, it's still nice to away from London and the Adam's family in Number Ten!"

"That's true mate. Not ours to reason why etc. But one can't help wondering at times just how sane this lot are? Paranoid is old Billy Boom, a right little control freak he is. I wonder what friend Billy has against some poor old country brewery. Maybe they served him a duff pint. Mind you, last time we passed through, as I recall, it was a bloody good beer they brewed. Tidy little place too. Seems a shame really. Talking of pints, don't forget to buy a couple of crates on expenses before we do the dirty deed."

"Oh aye, that we will. We'll have few over the bar too before we give them the nasties, at Billy's expense of course." He laughed. "Just to get the feel of the place like. Have you checked out if the telly works in this mobile boudoir? There's football on tonight."

The EEC team arrived early. The team leader Klaus Van Der Krapper was a diminutive, fussy and skinny little man who favored dark suits and bow ties. Steel rimmed spectacles and a severe and unfriendly manner made up the rest of his demeanor. Henk The Tank, was well named, and the exact opposite, Large, friendly and with hands like hams. He had obviously annoyed the Dutchman already and dismissed most of what he said with a huge wave of his hand and a puff of his ruddy cheeks. Each time he did this, his very large grey moustache would wave its agreement too. Mademoiselle Aughty kept a frigid distance from Henk and managed a pretty fair copy on Van Der Krapper's disapproving look. She was a skinny creature with a mousey face and brown hair tied back in a bun. She remained Kevin of cartoon character schoolteachers. He got the Kharzis to take their bags and show them to their room. He offered them refreshments, which were instantly rejected by Van Der Krapper, on behalf of "His" team. However, Henk, again dismissing the Dutchman with a wave, said, "Show me the bar please and put my bag in my room. I vill be happy to take a drink of your most famous beer." He smiled broadly saying, "Ah take no notice of him, he has never forgiven us for invading Holland." And he laughed. Van Der Krapper and Mademoiselle Aughty gave disgusted scowls and disappeared into the interior. Henk sat himself firmly down at an outside table and smiled in content with both the world and his dismissal of his two staid companions.

The three women had also moved outside and Henk had positioned himself so that he could look at them and the countryside. He nodded to them in a genial and friendly manner. "Goot afternoon ladies." He said. I am Henk from Germany. I am a visitor here. You are visitors too perhaps?" The three women looked at Henk and than at each other. The woman who had originally spoken to Kevin, and who seemed to be the group's leader answered.

"Are you the special visitors that the owner mentioned? It's Mid summer eve…." She left the statement hanging.

"Yah, yah, yah, ve are special visitors from Europe." Agreed Henk happily. The women exchanged meaningful looks.

"Oh good." She got no further as Charlie and Gerald drew up in their camper van. Then got down and looked approvingly at the Black Badger.

"Seems a shame Gerald." Muttered Charlie quietly under his breath. "Nice little pub this." He shook his head with a sad look on his face, and closed the van door.

Charley nodded a glum agreement, Muttering a "Bleeding loony is old Billy. Known it for years. Like I keep saying, it's the Adams Family we have at No 10." They walked towards the attractive frontage and looked over at the two occupied tables. Vania was taking orders.

"Come and join us." Offered Henk in a friendly tone, Drinks all round, on me." He looked at the three women, "More gusts." He added. The three women looked eagerly at the two newcomers and indicated that they should join them Charley and Gerald joined them and they drew two tables together and introductions were made all around." Vania brought beer. Henk approved with gusto and ordered another round. Charley offered to buy everyone lunch and they all settled in to be friends and enjoy themselves. The leader of the trio was named Petunia and it was obvious that Henk had taken a shine to her.

"Are you here for the ceremony?" Asked the small excited and giggly one.

"Shhh!" Said Petunia, "You know it's a secret."

"Oh yes." Said Charley in a hushed tone. "We are here for that. Aren't we George?"

George, who had been eying up the giggly one, and like Charley had been briefed about the strange goings on at The Badger, quickly agreed. Thinking, maybe I can get my leg over too. He had already established, that like themselves, the women were traveling in a camper van. He did some quick sums and thought, well old Jolly German can wind Petunia back to his room and me and Charley can have a camper van apiece. It would make the trip worth while he thought. He too nodded in a secret manner and decided to improvise and follow Charley's leads.

"Ohhh! That's so gratifying said the last woman and the quietest member of the trio. "I mean, we can all dance together can't we?" She looked at them expectantly. George and Charley both nodded vigorously. Henk, not wishing to be left out nodded firmly too, finished his pint and called for more beer. The bees buzzed, the birds sang and the sun shone and every one was set to spend as happy afternoon in each others company. The idyllic scene was however blighted by the arrival of Van Der Krapper and Mademoiselle Aughty. Upon viewing the happy and festive mood outside, they treated the group to frigid stares and decided to return within the lounge and eat there.

"The lady is allergic to happiness, or maybe she is jealous at seeing so many beautiful English roses." Henk dismissed the disgruntled pair with a flourish and the three women smiled and the little one giggled.

Next on the scene, but unbeknown to anyone, was Arthur Smallpiece. He approached the Badger from the other direction and carefully hid his car. He had taken the precaution of buying some camouflage netting and wearing ex army dappled brown and green fatigues. He quietly slid into the woods and cautiously climbed the wooded slope. Making his way up to the top field, and remaining within the tree line, he looked for a suitable place of concealment. Eventually he set himself up in a small natural hollow caused by a fallen tree that gave him a good vantage point. He draped the netting carefully over his hide and added a few odd branches and bracken to make it blend in even more. Satisfied, he slipped inside to wait and check his digital camera.

The afternoon progressed. The sun shone, the bees buzzed, the birds sang and the six patrons were fast becoming bosom friends. Maxwell and Cynthia arrived together in her car. Three Soldiers Of The Divine Order followed in a minibus. The leader, a gangly youth with spots and two girls, also about 18 years old. A skinny one and a fattie. They looked at the party in the front of the Badger and sat down primly at the table furthest away and ordered some Crump's Cola. Which The Badger did not stock. Coco Cola was offered and an argument ensued. Mulchi was serving their table and she and had no idea what was the problem. She promptly marched off to find Vania. Meanwhile Van Der Krapper had become increasingly incensed over Henk's approach to the inspection. "Fool will be too drunk to inspect anything other than a bed!" He spat. "Come Mademoiselle; let us drag him from his party." He got up stormed out from the lounge followed by his French Colleague.

"Beast!" she muttered under her breath, "Boch!" Cochon!"

Outside George had arrived on the scene with Vania and was trying calm things down.

"Might as well drink water!" Affirmed one of the "Soldiers." In a loud voice for all to hear. He looked around for support.

"It's very good water, so why not?" Stated George. "Furthermore I'll give it to you free!" He obviously had little time for argumentative lads and showed his feelings.

"So you should. It only comes out of the tap." Retorted the spotty youth. He laughed at scoring a point and looked at his two female companions trying to impress them.

George was getting riled. He took a hearty dislike to the spotty young man and he viewed Cynthia with distain. He was getting annoyed and it was beginning to show. "Actually it doesn't." He declared firmly. It comes from our own springs young man. As anyone with a happoth of brains would know!" He stared the youth down adding as he did so, "I can show you if you like, we can go together"

"WE will go together!" Van Der Krapper had arrived unnoticed and been party to the conversation. He slapped the table for effect. Surprised at both the interruption and the new voice everyone looked at him. Seeing that he now held centre stage, Van Der Krapper exploited the situation and taking the lead he turned to George and imperiously demanded, "Well? What are you waiting for?"

George drew himself up, "By all means." He stood aside and touched his forelock "My pleasure... Sir" He added and with as much dignity as he could muster, led the whole troop out on to the road and turned left up the gentle hill and into the wood in the direction of the springs.

As a group they trooped behind George in summer sunshine towards where Houghton Springs Brook emerged from the trees and gurgled its way down the road in front of them. George turned left into the woods and the dappled sun shine shone through the trees and bathed them in light green and shadow.

"Pump house." He indicated the locked building on his right and moved further into the cool woods following the brook. The path ended at the rock face. George looked up at the rock face covered in moss and ferns and all overhung with trees. Crystal clear water gurgled out from a small cave and formed Houghton Brook. Due to the recent heavy rain, the brook was swollen. "The springs are inside in the grotto." George announced. He pointed at the rock face and the entrance of a small cave, from which the brook emerged. "If you duck down, you can get inside on the right there." He pointed to the right hand side of the brook where it exited from the cave. One by one they all ducked and entered. Electric lamps in bulkhead fittings set in the wall lit up as George flicked a switch. The small cave was cool and peaceful. The atmosphere was pleasant and leaned more towards a enchanted grotto in a pantomime, rather than a commercial water source. Ferns and moss grew on the damp walls and the clear water welled silently up from the springs and was contained in a natural pool that had been reinforced with some cement work and natural stones. It swiftly overflowed via a specially built outlet and bubbled towards the bright light of the entrance. It was all rather like a rock pool in an expensively designed ornamental garden. The three women Ohhed and Ahhed. "Fine water." Declared George, pointing at the pool. It was rather crowded in the cave and the ones at the back jostled and tried to look at the pool. George produced a clear glass beaker, saying in a sarcastic tone, "It's tested by an independent lab quite often you know. Try some, it won't poison you." He held up the beaker for takers.

One of the three women immediately grabbed the beaker. She scooped up about half a pint and drank it down. "Marvelous!" She declared and drank again. Everyone wanted to try the water. George looked at them all vying to grab the beaker and drink. He shook his head and quietly left them in the grotto. He stood outside, and Gyp appeared. He patted her head. "Only one with any sense, he muttered." He sat down on a large stone and lit a cigarette and Gyp lay down at his feet. "Leave them in there gulping water gal." He murmured as he fondled the collie's ears. Gyp lolled a tongue and offered her head for more attention. "Only one with any sense." Stated George again. He patted the dog some more and continued to wait.

Meanwhile inside the grotto strange things were happening. Everyone that drank the water wanted more, and then more again. They became animated and noisy. They started to laugh. George looked back at the cliff face and scratched his head. He looked at his watch and then again at the cave entrance and noise that was emanating from it. He wondered if it might be best to try to get them to come out in case someone fell into the water and drowned. He approached the cliff face and bent down, leaning in to the cave entrance. "Best come out now." He shouted, but he was ignored. There seemed to be some kind of party going on inside the cavern. He stood up and scratched his head again, now puzzled. How could so many previously reasonably sober people suddenly become drunk all at once? Suddenly he had visions of the sheep. Bloody Hell! It's got into the damn water table. But how? He wondered. He stood there pondering this thought. No more zhip was growing; therefore it had to be the last bunch. He thought that obviously the Kharzis had stashed the plants somewhere and the recent rains had somehow contaminated the water. Can't last for long, he thought and must be getting weaker. Most he reasoned would be washed out along with the stream. Might have a few wobbly tadpoles. Who would notice? Can't last long he thought again to himself, as if trying to convince himself. He was about to brew again. How would it affect the brew he wondered? There again, it might add a bit of extra punch. He nodded to himself. Hmmm, well, we wanted a special mid summers brew didn't we? His thoughts on the matter were rudely interrupted by people suddenly erupting out of the cave. Like bloody bats, thought George and stood to one side, as totally ignoring him they rushed by.

"To the ceremonies, to the ceremonies." Cried one of the strange three women and waved her arms vigorously. Ignoring, or being oblivious too George, she led the way around the side of the cave face, and up the slope and through the woods. Ah well mused George, they can all run around the woods if they like and wear them selves out. Kevin won't be doing anything until much later. "Come on Gyp. Home lass, I had better check that all is ready to brew. To brew or not to brew? That is the question." He looked at Gyp seriously and then laughed. "Bunch of nutters!" he muttered to himself and he started back towards the Badger with Gyp following by his side.

Kevin had seen them all troop off in the direction of the springs. He had thought to follow, but reasoned that George could show them all perfectly well and had no need of him. Anyway, there was nothing wrong with the water. He quietly collected Vicki. "Let's do the ceremony now, while it's all quiet. They have all gone off to look at the springs. Then if there are any odd balls about and remember Cynthia is here again, with reinforcements this time too. We will have long finished." Vicki agreed and they went to change and warn Beth.

When Kevin arrived in the top field, carrying his hat, stick and book but without and bags of powder this time, Arthur took notice. He was well concealed within his hide. He had his small digital camera set on a tripod and he quickly zoomed in on Kevin. Kevin appeared to be lighting the fire. He saw no sign of anyone else and was rather disappointed. He was getting all worked up and excited at being a voyeur. Kevin and Vicki had walked up together. Vicki wearing her diaphanous long dress. She had bundled this up around her waist and she wore Kevin's anorak which was far too large, and reached almost to her knees. She also wore Wellington boots and held her clear plastic slippers in her hand. She waited patiently within the tree line and out of sight. Watching, as Kevin, who had taken the precaution of seeding the fire with several large plastic bin bags. Each of which had been filled with scrap paper soaked in diesel fuel. The fire quickly ignited. Kevin began his circling and chanting, throwing his arms about. He had taken the trouble to tie the hat with a chin strap and was sure that it would be secure this time. "Get ready Vicki." He hissed, as he passed her place of concealment.

"I'll just come forward and put the slippers on when I am at the fire." Replied Vicki. "I have already dumped the dress. Let's get this over with as fast as possible please."

It was at this moment that the women burst into the far corner of the field. Hotly pursued by a gaggle of Soldiers Of The Divine Order, and the inspection team minus Henk. He finally appeared along with Maxwell and Cynthia. Kevin stopped dead in his tracks and watched amazed as the three women threw off their clothes, their leader trying to strip off an unresisting and puffing Henke as soon as he had reached the clear grass. The soldiers, that consisted of two girls and the spotty youth, immediately fell upon him and pinned him down and stripped him. Throwing off their own clothes at the same time. Van Der Krapper and Mademoiselle Aughty seemed to want to join in the fun and Cynthia was trying to remove Maxwell's trousers. The now totally nude leader of the three women was now urging them all to join around the fire. The two MI5 men appeared and taking one look at the proceedings threw themselves in with a willingness. Naked they all rushed towards Kevin and Vicki. Kevin was pushed to the front and around the bonfire they all danced in some strange, nude conga. Vicki who had appeared on the edge of the wood wearing only her Wellingtons, stood mouth open as Kevin either led, or followed. Depending upon viewpoint, the group of naked dancers around the now well lit fire. Arthur's shutter clicked away furiously.

"Bloody Hell Kevin!" Shouted Vicki at him, gesturing with her hands, "Have you been selling tickets?" She stood, a rather forlorn and solitary nude figure. Somewhat conspicuous in her Wellington boots.

"No Vicki, I haven't a clue where they all sprang from." Gasped Kevin, as he was continued to be propelled around the fire by the leader of the three women. "I think that they are all drunk."

Breasts bobbed, bottoms wiggled, arms were waved in a frenzied manner and the leader of the women began to chant "Spirits of the earth, fire and air." This was taken up by the rest of the group as they pranced naked around the fire whilst Vicki stood watching amazed. Kevin being caught up in their circle was pushed and shoved around with them. Mademoiselle Aughty had a trance like look on her face and soon all of the others began to acquire the same fixed and happy smile. Quickly pairs began to form. Cynthia and Maxwell. Charley and Gerald each joined up with the other two women. Van Der Krapper and Mademoiselle Aughty gravitated towards each other. The Leader of the trio of woman grabbed Henk, and pushed him in front of her. Henk had been built for comfort, not speed or rushing up slopes and naked dancing. He promptly collapsed on to the ground gasping. There was no respite. Immediately the naked woman, the group leader, jumped on top of him. Long hair, breasts and beads all flying in different directions. Together they rolled away from the frantic circle. All the others then, as if, like a flock of starlings acting upon some esoteric knowledge and as one, took their cue. Each, with a partner, fell to the floor too. Except that is for the fat little girl soldier and the skinny one with no breasts. They first looked longingly at each other and then together at the skinny lad with spots. Just like a pair of cats and as one, they pounced. The spotty youth stood no chance, and like a gazelle caught by a pair of lions, he too fell to the grass. Again like two predators, the girls vied over the carcass. Each wanting the choice meat. They came to a mutual agreement on how to divide their kill. The youth, overpowered, made no attempt to escape.

A very chubby and pink Cynthia sank down, pulling Maxwell on top of her. With a huge sigh of pent up frustration at last released she cried in pure joy, "Take me. Take me." So Maxwell obliged her and doing as he had been instructed, did so with a will and great determination. Click, click, click went Arthur's shutter.

"Gawd almighty! Just look at them." Spluttered a baffled Kevin. "Just like bleeding rabbits. What's got in to them?" Bottoms bounced up and down in the grass, oblivious of all around. The two young girls with the one Soldier were giving him a tricky time. One sat astride his face and the other his hips. Both vigorously bounced and wriggled. The poor lad seemed to be turning blue.

One of the young Kharzis appeared at the end of the field. He gawped, moved forward and stumbled into Arthur's concealed hole. He yelled in alarm. A noise that went totally unnoticed by the sexually gymnasts in the field.

"I'm off." Said Vicki and turned and disappeared back into the tree line.

Arthur however had made a break for it. His only clear line was toward Kevin. He dashed out and dodging writhing and contorted bodies raced directly for Kevin and the fire. Give Arthur his due, he dedicatedly kept hitting the shutter button each time he dodged an entwined and engrossed couple. As he approached Kevin, Kevin for no reason what so ever threw up his hands and his cloak followed like the wings of a bat. "BOO!" He shouted. Arthur gave a sort of strangled sound and dropped the camera. Kevin promptly picked it up as the Kharzi youth steamed past him too in hot pursuit of Arthur. Kevin examined the camera. It seemed undamaged, the tripod having broken its fall. He looked around him at the writhing bodies, each oblivious to anything except their own pleasure. He carefully focused on the spectacle of Klaus Van Der Krapper, minus his steel-rimmed glasses, giving an obvious ecstatic Mademoiselle Aughty a good shafting. Kevin quietly then took his time and photographed a very happy Henk and group leader also an equally delighted Cynthia busy coupling with a vigorous Maxwell. Then in an act of compassion, he then took the trouble to move to the side of the threesome. With difficulty, and his hands slipping on her wet body, he finally managed to physically lift the fat one off the lads face. Which was now going a fine shade of purple. "Time for a change." He instructed and pushed the skinny one backwards and off the lads hips.

"Thank you." Gasped the youth. But his respite was short lived as per instructions, the young girls changed positions. Ah well, thought Kevin, at least you should be able to breath easier with the skinny one on your face.

He turned and humming to himself made his way back down to the black Badger, removing his tall pointed hat as he did so.

Vicki was waiting for him in their bedroom. "What ever was all that about?" She asked him in wonderment. "Regular little orgy going on! Did you see that Dutch fellow and the skinny French bird? There were really going some! What's going on Kevin?" She was dressed again in her normal clothes of jeans and a tee shirt. "For Gawd sake's change, you look like a refugee from a fancy dress party!"

Kevin began to remove his Silas costume. "Well, you remember the sheep incident?" He turned to half face her and Vicki nodded, but still looked puzzled. "I recon that they were all high on zhip!"

"But where did they get it from? And all of them? How?" She looked at Kevin waiting for an answer.

"I don't know as yet. There must be some common denominator. Actually I'm not bothered about the how right at this moment. More, the, what shall we do with the knowledge?"

"How do you mean Kevin?" Vicki still looked perplexed. Kevin tapped the camera that Arthur Smallpiece had dropped.

"All in here." He smiled, "Now just what do you think our EEC friends will do when they receive a copy of these snaps with their respective bills?"

"That's blackmail!" Declared Vicki, very firmly.

"No it's not!" Argued Kevin. "OK, it is if I say or request demands in writing. I wasn't going to say or demand anything. Just sort of leave it all hanging."

"Like old Van Der Krapper's balls you mean?" Vicki giggled, "Let me see them again." She sat on the edge of the bed with Kevin and he flicked through the pictures on the screen on the camera. "Come on Kevin, download that lot in to the PC and get the color printer all warmed up. "What shall we do with others?"

"Oh I think that Maxwell should be included on the distribution list and Cynthia too. The odd ball women and the two guys we can ignore along with the two little girls raping that follower of the dive order. Poor sod was suffocating under the work out he was getting!" He laughed, "Right, get the presses rolling."

Together then went into the office and downloaded the photographs and laughed and joked together. Whilst they were seated at the PC, Kevin heard a noise. He opened the door just a crack. He observed Henk and the leader of the women going into his room. "Looks like they are coming around and still up for action, so to speak." He spoke quietly over his shoulder to Vicki as he silently closed the door. "You finish the printing and I will go down stairs. I want to catch Van Der Krapper and Mademoiselle Aughty. Oh, I expect that you will need to change the cartridge. Only print small size. That will help to save the ink" He left Vicki busy printing the photographs. She ran out of ink and had to change the cartridges, but not before she had made an extra set of prints of Maxwell and Cynthia locked in copulating bliss. These she placed in a brown envelope and using the telephone directory, obtained Maxwell's home ddress. She then addressed the envelope to his wife and stored it safely. I'll teach you to give this little girl problems my son." She thought to herself, and nodded in a satisfied manner.

Kevin had the pleasure of seeing a flushed, but dressed, Van Der Krapper arrive along with a smiling Mademoiselle Aughty. Her hair had come undone and was now streaming out around her head in a very disheveled way and he had lost his bow tie. They both totally ignored Kevin, and with Van Der Krapper being pushed and urged from behind by the French woman, they disappeared into his room. The door closed, then opened again and a feminine hand hung "A Do Not Disturb" sign on the outside door handle. Kevin blinked, shrugged and went back to find Vicki.

Maxwell and Cynthia drove in her car back to her house. The Two young female Soldiers, propelled an almost, on the point of collapse. Spotty youth to their minibus and drove off. Charley and Gerald took the two women back to their camper van, all giggling about "Doing a foursome." And they too drove away.

CHAPTER: 13

Timothy Longstanton had carefully observed people arrive at The Black Badger. He watched as the MI5 team joined the three women and Henke at a neat and charming rustic table. He saw some foreign and attractive young female bring them beer and food. Timothy observed that they were enjoying themselves and that both beer and food met with their approval. Then he saw Cynthia, Maxwell and The Soldiers pull in. More patrons he fumed to himself. The Black Badger is making a profit and attracting cliental. He had to admit that it certainly looked attractive with its baskets of brightly colored flowers and trailing greenery. Timothy noted the smart and beckoning tables and the shrubs in old cut off beer barrels. It all positively reeked of exactly what a country pub on a warm summer's day should look like. He glanced across at the brewery. In the clear hot sunlight, its stonewalls had a charming and countryside air. It's dark, slate roofs glistened and reflected the summer's sun. It all seemed to welcome a thirsty visitor with promises of cool, shade inside, coupled with the smell of hops and a cold foaming pint of Black Badger. All of which was exactly the opposite impression of what Timothy wanted. No, he wanted to see a derelict, depressing and forlorn heap of darkened stone. Preferably with broken roofs and in the middle of a thunderstorm in November. Instead of which he was confronted with this little gem of a tourist's idea of what an English country pub and small, private country brewery should look like. Timothy decided to burn the place to the ground and all who patronized it too. He waited his chance. His hired car attracting no more attention that any of the other parked vehicles. Timothy crouched down inside the car, using a mirror held up in his hand to make his observations unseen. His position was uncomfortable as he still wore a neck brace. He cursed quietly to himself and tried to find a more comfortable position. He watched as George arrived, and then some small skinny guy with a bow tie of all things. The skinny guy was accompanied by a mousey, angular female. Then, to Timothy's surprise, they all trooped off past him and up the slight hill. Then they they all disappeared into the woods.

Timothy had taken the trouble to use his red wig and false moustache disguise. He had also changed the number plates on the car. In a small hold all were his incendiary devices. These consisted of a cheap alarm clock, battery and contacts, coupled to a detonator. The detonator has been secured inside a terracotta flowerpot whose small end had been plugged with fire clay. The large end blocked with a 6mm steel plate and sealed with fire clay. Inside the flower pot was a thematic mixture of powdered aluminum, iron filings and magnesium. The flowerpot in turn had been placed inside a screw top aluminum container. Timothy knew that once the detonator ignited the thematic mixture intense heat would be generated. The steel plate would melt allowing the burning mixture to escape and actually ignite the aluminum container. Such intense heat would last for well over 5 minutes and be sufficient, if placed correctly, to incinerate everything combustible in its immediate surroundings. That in turn should then start a conflagration that would raise The Black Badger to the ground. That it would be obvious to any investigator that an incendiary bomb had been utilized, and thus arson committed, Timothy didn't give a damn. He could not be connected. Let someone prove that he was in the area even. Why, he didn't even fit the description of some mystery visitor with red hair. No, it would be either onto Maxwell or the crazies that suspicion would fall. He would claim that he was sitting in the small cottage that he had rented, 100 miles away, and recuperating from his car accident injuries. He hadn't even been injured on a road that was close to The Black Badger, and was in fact heading in a direction other that one leading towards Houghton Springs, when he had been pushed off the road. Timothy had even gone to the trouble of renting a small and isolated cottage beyond where he had been so rudely removed from the road by the two brothers. He would claim, if questioned, that had been his objective in the first place and he had merely continued with his plan after the accident. Only now he was recuperating, where as before he had planned to write a book about growing up in Africa. So what that he happened to drive a car similar to one seen before the conflagration? A conflagration in which, hopefully, his cousin and girl friend had perished. Just how many cars of that make and color were there in the country? So now he inherited. So what? A blackened and ruined shell? That some of his kin had also died was doubly unfortunate but what could he Timothy do? He had no interest in brewing. No, it was all very sad. In light of these circumstances, he would sell up as fast as possible, and use the money to further finance his writings. Secretly, that he would not make as much money as he had hoped, was annoying, but so be it. The destruction of Kevin Firkettle had become the number one priority in his mind.

Timothy carefully removed his plastic color, wincing as he did so. He dumped the sling and flexed his hand and wrist. Still weak and painful, but they would suffice. He grabbed the hold all and exited his car. He entered the bar of the Black Badger. He found that he was alone. Timothy did a quick scan on the bar, taking in the furnishings and deliberating where best to set his charge. He noted the wooden tables and chairs, curtains and carpets. Then his eyes alighted on a recessed and padded bench in the corner, close to a window. Perfect he thought. Place the bomb below the bench seat, in the corner. It would be out of sight. However, with plenty of combustible material around it. In addition, the padding on the seat would, he suspected be made of foam. That with give off poisonous fumes and thick black smoke. An added bonus. Vania came in and stood behind the bar expectantly. Timothy smiled at her and asked for a pint as he approached the bar. Vania drew his drink and Timothy paid her. He was surprised at how cheap the beer was. He sampled it, it tasted good. Timothy cursed under his breath but outwardly continued to smile. No wonder trade was brisk, he reasoned to himself. "Maybe I will sit outside." He smiled at Vania as he spoke and slowly moved to wards the door. Vania nodded and disappeared back inside the Badger. Immediately, Timothy slipped the bomb out of the hold all. Quickly, he set the timer for one hour. Then in one smooth movement, but being very careful not to jerk his neck at all, he bent down and placed the device under the padded bench seat. He stood up and satisfied himself that it was well out of sight. Then he silently left the bar, taking his drink and the remaining incendiary with him.

Out side, Timothy looked around him and saw that he was alone. He placed his drink on a convenient table and walked across the yard. Slipping into the brewery by its unlocked side door. He paused, and listened, but could hear nothing except a wasp trying in vain to escape through a window. Timothy looked around the brewing floor, he found that he had to rotate his body, rather than his neck and he was beginning to regret having removed the brace. He saw the gleaming copper vats, each with its inspection door open. Beside then stood some sacks of what smelled like dried hops. Perfect, thought Timothy. Those sacks will burn just beautifully and all these wooden floors and supporting timbers. Why the whole place is a tinderbox. He moved towards the sacks and stooped down. He had intended to place the incendiary charge under the sacks, but found to his surprise that they were heavier that he had anticipated. He found that he could only exert any real lifting pressure with his good left arm. He tried again and jarred his neck in the effort. An involuntary grunt escaped his lips at the sharp pain. Timothy cursed Kevin to Hell and back and readjusted his position.

Up stairs, George had been sitting down at a small table that doubled as a desk. He had brewer's tables open in front of him and a small calculator. He was planning volumes of water and quantities of ingredients. He had already lit up the oil-fired boiler some time ago and had a nice head of steam building. George wanted to brew with the minimum of water. Then, having given the springs time to flush through, add more later. This would require some careful juggling with temperatures and he was totally involved in working out the maths when Gyp looked up. She had been lying at his feet, as was her normal position whenever George sat at the table. George looked at her. "What is it lass?" He put down his pen and listened, thinking that maybe one of the customers had entered the brewery out of curiosity. He could hear nothing unusual and was about to dismiss Gyp's low growl, when he heard a noise on the brewing floor below. All the floors in the brewery were wooden, and sound travels well through such a medium.

Gyp growled quietly again. "Shhhh, girl." motioned George, "Best we take a look eh?" He was fully expecting to see some customer on the floor below poking around innocently. George had quietly opened a door that stood at the top of a small flight of wooden stairs that accessed the upper floor where he had been working. He looked down and watched as Timothy took the shiny bomb out of the hold all and set the timer. Gyp poked her head through the simple handrail and growled. Timothy Longstanton realized that he was no longer alone. He slowly straightened up and slipped his right hand back into the hold all again.

George looked at him calmly. "What have you got there my lad?" He asked quietly.

"I suppose that you are George Stoats?" Replied Timothy equally calmly.

"Correct, and just you might be?"

"Timothy Longstanton is who I am George. No doubt you don't recognize me. Just one moment." He pulled a small automatic pistol from the hold all. Tucking the bomb under his left arm and still holding the gun in his right hand, he dropped the hold all. Then he cocked the gun with his left. Slowly and with the gun steadily pointing at George, he stooped down and gently allowed the bomb to slip softly onto the sacks. With his now free left hand, he lifted his red wig. Then he slowly stood up.

"My, my, my. It is you. I might have guessed. Up to no good as usual are you? What is that thing down by your feet?" George pointed with his chin at the bomb that was now lying on a sack.

"Well George, it's not a thermos flask of tea that I have brought you!" Timothy stated sarcastically. The gun still pointed unwaveringly at George. "Hmm, I can see that your rustic brain is too slow to comprehend all of this, so I'll tell you." He looked at George spitefully. "When Silas died, I should have by rights inherited this lot. Naturally, I would have booted you and your stupid wife out ASAP and sold the place to the highest bidder.

That was my right George Stoats. Instead of which up pops Kevin nobody Firkettle and steals my birthrights. So George I am about to burn the whole damn place to the ground. Yes, and The Black Badger too. You along with it naturally and hopefully that Bloody meddling Kevin, his skinny bird and your fat wife too and anybody else that gets in my way. Now is that clear enough for you? Oh yes, and I have planted another one of these little beauties in the bar. So George Stoats say bye to the wicked world, because I am about to shoot you and set the charges." His voice, though hushed carried great menace.

"Do you think that you will get away with it lad?" Asked George quietly and calmly in a unruffled voice. "It will be obvious that it was Arson."

"Good! Well done! Of course it will be arson you idiot and stupid Maxwell can carry the can!" Timothy laughed. As if on cue, and unbidden, Gyp leaped from above down onto him. Snapping at his face as she did so. Timothy stumbled back, throwing up his hand to fend off the dogs body and flashing teeth. The gun dropped as he jarred his neck. Then gracefully he fell into the open door of the vat. Gyp stood looking down in at him and growling. The hairs on her neck and back all standing straight.

George came down the steps two at a time and he stooped and picked up the gun. He moved his dog to one side and looked in the vat. Kevin lay quietly at the bottom with his head at an odd angle. George quietly closed and locked the door. Then he turned his attention to the bomb. He unscrewed the canister and pulled out the detonator and then jerked off its wires in a rather professional manner. Almost automatically and as if he had previously had plenty of experience in such matters. He dropped the now defused charge and carefully placed the detonator on the windowsill. He crossed the yard swiftly and entered the bar. He was alone. He heard someone coming out from the back, thinking no doubt that there was a customer. He called back in a reassuring tone, "Only me, no one else." And Vania replied and went back to whatever she had been doing. George looked around the empty room. It didn't take him long to look under the bench seat and he defused the second bomb too with a equally efficient touch. Then he carried it outside and back to the brewery. The detonators he kept separate. The aluminum cylinders now opened revealed the flower pots. George nodded to himself. He removed the flowerpots and then cracked them open onto a sack. "Nasty" he muttered. Obviously recognizing with what he was dealing. He went to the door and sprinkled the thematic mixture over the yard's cobblestones. Then returning he removed the batteries and separated the alarm clocks. He placed one clock downstairs, as if it was part of the brewing equipment and the other upstairs on the desk. The wires he put in his pocket along with the batteries for later disposal. The detonators he thought could be buried later along with the automatic pistol too. He returned to the vat and opened the door. He looked down at an inert Timothy. Timothy hadn't moved, "Oh well." Murmured George, we may have had to dump this brew anyway. He bent down and started loading the hops and cracked malt into vat. Then he closed the door, turned on the water, paddle and steam. "We'll leave you to cook lad." He said adding, "Then you will get dumped with the rubbish, personal by me and no one will ever find you. I have a nice little sink hole earmarked for you my lad. Come on Gyp lass. Enough excitement for one day. Time for a cup of tea. Throw me and the missus out on the streets would he? Kill the boss and that sweet little Miss Vicki too. Burn us down indeed, and what would have happened to you old gal?" He patted Gyp's head affectionately as they walked quietly across the yard in late afternoon's summer sunshine muttering quietly to the dog, "I never thought all that bloody bomb disposal crap would ever come in useful. Just shows old Gal, one never knows."

That evening the Badger was far busier than usual. Peter Goodbody and Andrew Ashbow also dropped in. Andrew commented on the out side seating and Kevin explained how they hoped to expand, but as he said ruefully, "It will all have to wait until I have managed to buy a new bottling line. Or better still a good second hand one."

Henk and the leader of the group, who now insisted on being called Petunia, appeared and were in expansive mood. "Marvelous ceremony." Declared Petunia to Kevin. "I can't remember much of it, but I ended back here in his bed. So no complaints." She slapped Henk playfully on his large chest. "I haven't been to a ceremony like that for, ohhh." She paused, looking at the ceiling, hand on mouth. "Well, a very long time." She ended lamely. "Far too long in fact! I have no idea what has happened to the other two." She looked about the crowded bar. Off with those bird watchers I expect. Still they are both big girls now. They will turn up." She laughed happily and patting Henk again on his chest added, "He is so strong!"

"Yah it's true." Smiled Henk, "But now the engine needs more fuel. Black Badger Kevin please." He smiled expansively and hugged Petunia with a huge hairy and bear like arm.

Klaus Van Der Krapper quietly ordered room service; for two.

The next day Timothy's car was still standing where he had left it. Kevin wandered over and seeing that the keys were in the ignition assumed, not unnaturally, that one of the revelers from the previous evening had been well over the limit and had been driven home by someone else. He drove the car onto the yard, awaiting its owner's return and thought no more about it.

The EEC team of inspectors were getting ready to leave. Kevin had made their bills up separately and each was presented in a large white envelope. Van Der Krapper turned white when he saw the photographs. Mademoiselle Aughty blushed to her roots and looked wildly at Van Der Krapper. Henk laughed, clapped Kevin on the shoulder and said in a loud voice. "Vonderful! I vill take five copies." He looked at Kevin expectantly and called over his shoulder, "Petunia my lieblich, Kommen sei hier. He smiled at Kevin, "Petunia is coming back to Munich with me."

Petunia arrived, she was talking on a hand phone and laughing. "Oh Henk." She exclaimed, "Guess what. Tilly and Vanessa went off with those two bird watchers. Well then drove into a ditch and the police have arrested Gerald for driving whilst under the influence and all of them for performing lewd acts in public! Isn't it a scream?" She laughed, then taking one of the photographs that Henk held out to her she laughed and exclaimed, "Oh Herr Van Der Krapper, what a marvelous likeness of your bottom!" She turned to Madamoiseele Aughty and pointed to the photograph saying, "Just look how you are enjoying yourself too!" She looked at Kevin. "It really was a wonderful ceremony Kevin. Thank you so much."

Vicki had quietly joined Kevin. "So you all seem to have enjoyed yourselves." She said gaily and turning to Henk asked. "And is our tiny brewery up to EEC standards?" She smiled sweetly at Klaus whilst gently waving an envelope similar to the ones that had contained the photographs.

"Your beer is excellent dear lady." Said Henk graciously and leaning forward towards Vicki said quietly but loud enough for Van Der Krapper to hear, "And I am sure that my colleagues will agree." He winked slowly at her and Vicki tried to hide a smile. "Von't you?" Henk had turned to look patronizingly at Van Der Krapper and Mademoiselle Aughty. "Ve vouldn't vont to upset our good friends and stop them from brewing their excellent beer now vould ve?" He left the question hanging like a sword of Damocles over Van Der Krapper's head. Van Der Krapper looked a little sick but mumbled something about The Black Badger being well with EEC standards. He and Mademoiselle Aughty were obviously wanting to leave as fast as possible.

"Well that is good news and gratifying to know." Declared Kevin happily." I'll get someone to help you with your bags." He called for one of the Kharzis to assist them. As they were leaving Henk quietly cornered Kevin. "Ve had a vonderful time young man. Maybe now my friends regret, but not your friend Henk. You don't have to vorry about those pair." He indicated the retreating Van Der Krapper and Mademoiselle Aughty. "It vill all be fine now. I met my Petunia, and am happy for that. Now, I help you and you help me Yah?" Kevin nodded readily in agreement. "You do nothing to upset the apple cart with photographs yah? It vill be our little secret Yah? You just leave all to your good friend Henk." He looked at Kevin for agreement and Kevin nodded his head. "For me Photographs are no problem, but for our friend...." He left the sentence hanging and looked at Kevin.

"Actually I was never going to do anything else Henk. I will wipe the camera clean too."

"No, better if you keep our friends photographs in secret on a disc. It vill keep them in line. Mit me, you have no problems. I am happy to see the small Dutchman discomforted and that stringy French bitch too. No better ve keep those photographs as insurance. Also, I love your beer! Now the next thing that vill happen is that I vill return soon with my Petunia to drink more of your famous beer. You see, all vill be vell my young friend."

"You and Petunia and her friends are welcome any time Henk and the beer comes free." Stated Kevin with conviction.

"Excellent, excellent. Ve have an accord, as our Miss Aughty vould say." He laughed. "Now I and Petunia vill make our friend's lives a perfect misery until ve return to Brussels!" He laughed again. "I have vaited years to be able to squash that little man. Thank you Kevin and Mrs. Kevin too and Yah, we will be back." He waved and joined the rest of the group by their mini bus. "Just like Arnold Swarzanegger." Murmured Kevin.

All had been quiet at The Black Badger for a week or so. The only event being that Kevin eventually reported to the police that there was still a car parked in his yard that he assumed belonged to some customer. Could the police trace it please? Maybe the customer had had an accident? The police came, looked at the car and then started asking questions. Had anyone seen the owner and could they describe him? No one could. Vania, either from harboring deep and mistrustful thoughts regarding any police force, or because she genuinely made no connection to Timothy, remained quiet. George just shrugged and said he was responsible for the brewery, not customers and he hadn't seen or noticed anything. George had intimated to Kevin that he might have to dump the latest batch. He used the pollution of the water with zhip as his excuse and tapped the side of his nose. "I'll just dump it quietly boss and no one will be any the wiser. It was only a small batch. I was worried that it might not be up to standard, so only brewed a small amount. We don't want to be wasting good malt and hops if the water was a bit iffy. It's all fine again now boss. No I will just swill that lot out and dump the makings myself. Then no one will be any the wiser. We don't want to be giving anyone any excuses to point fingers at us do we boss?" Kevin, having noted that he was once more the boss, agreed and told George to do as he felt fit. So, George carefully emptied out the remains of Timothy Longstanton, along with the usual rubbish left in the vats after brewing. Then instead of bagging it all up for pig feed as was usual, he rather irreverently dumped the lot, in secret, into a well concealed sink hole. Adding several large rocks as headstones and plenty of earth. The woods would soon hide any traces he thought. He had long since disposed of all other traces of Timothy's wig, gun etc. With equal for throughness.

The police were baffled. Some person with red hair and using a false license under the name of Adam Jones, had hired the car. He had then disappeared without trace, leaving only the car behind. A car that had false number plates. The file was left open, and forgotten. Since Timothy had made a point of covering his tracks and had no relations to morn him. Well, at least, none that knew that he had died, he never featured in any police investigation. George went around with a satisfied smile on his face, and was often seen patting Gyp's head and talking to her in quiet and confidential manner. This being put down to the one man and his dog syndrome, and like the mystery car, dismissed.

Vicki had anomalously sent the photographs of Maxwell's infidelity to his wife. The result being that she immediately sued for divorce and sited Cynthia as correspondent. Mrs. Maxwell was out for blood. She wanted revenge for what she openly stated, were all those wasted years. Having of course, conveniently ignored any benefits that she had enjoyed as his wife. She looked toward to ruining Maxwell along with Crump's Cola and reveling in what she and her solicitor saw, would be the lucrative, financial benefits of such an action. She had her eyes set on a small beach side property in The Cayman Islands and a life of iced rum cocktails and the occasional toy boy. Mandy, Maxwell's girlfriend in Birmingham, seeing which way the wind was blowing upped and left. Taking everything that wasn't screwed down at the same time. Maxwell decided on a damage limitations policy and approached Kevin with an offer. Take over the debt on his bottling line and cost of removal and reinstallation at Houghton Springs Brewary. In exchange for all copies etc of any sexually or otherwise, incriminating evidence. Kevin nearly bit his arm off at the offer. The bank loan frightened him and he knew that he would be hard pushed to make the payments. On the other hand, he also realized that he would never have another opportunity to get a virtually new bottling line so cheaply. Maxwell also offered Kevin a whole batch of new bottles. "Do you think that we might use these?" Kevin had asked George.

George examined the bottle. "Can't see why not, but it's not our usual shape and its clear glass too. Do we have access to continued supplies?"

"Yes, but they are a bit pricy. I was wondering if we could just use them for a one off run?"

"We could, but then we would need a small batch of special one off run beer." George scratched his head, pushing back his cap. "I don't know. I'll give it some thought. No rush, those bottles won't eat anything and we have plenty of room to store them." The conversation turned to other topics and the matter was left in abeyance.

It was later next week, when suddenly, out of the blue, Henk turned up with Petunia in tow. "Ve come to see old friends and also EEC business." He declared. I vish to sample the batch of beer that you vere brewing ven ve left please." He added.

Kevin knew that he could do nothing, so called George for support. George told Henk that they had thought to brew a special Mid Summer's brew called Old Silas. He warmed to the theme as Kevin watched amazed at the web George spun. He showed Henk the new bottles, all carefully stored. Henke examined the bottles and remarked upon their quality. "I can see that I am dealing with a serious master brewer." He stated, patting George affectionately on the shoulder. "Come let me sample Old Silas."

Kevin looked at George and George looked back at Kevin. "There is a small problem Henk." Said George sadly. "The brew was not our pure traditional recipe and I fear that it really is not up to standard. I was going to dump it, but needed to tank it and put it on our land, and not allow it into the open drain system. I'm just waiting to borrow a sludge tanker from one of the farms and I will dump it."

"Not up to standard?" Henk was obviously shocked. "My Master Brewer and his apprentice? Not up to standard? Come, I must see this disaster." He waited, adding, "Come, show me. I cannot believe there is a bad beer at The Black Badger."

George shrugged, "As you wish Henk, I haven't tasted the brew for a while and it's still in the fermentation vat. It just looks odd to me." He led them over to a fermentation vessel and taking a glass, drew off a small quantity of a highly diluted Timothy Longstanton's brewed remains. He waited, looking at Kevin and shrugged. "I don't think that you will like it." He said to Henk.

Henk sniffed at his glass, and then held it up to the light. "Needs filtering certainly." He said. Then sniffing again he stated, "The nose is good, strange back aroma, rather like beef soup." He looked at both of them with a puzzled expression on his face. Kevin and George registered non committal attitudes of the, "Upon your head be it." Henk sipped the brew. He looked even more puzzled and then sipped again. "What did you add to this?" He looked at George. "I cannot verk out vot is the back flavor." He smacked his lips and took another deep draught. "It's good, Yah! Very Gut! I like it, but you say it vas no good. Vhy you try to fool old Henk?. He looked at them and smiled. "You vish to joke vith me yah? Come my good friends, another glass for Henk Yah?" He sipped at the glass this time and then held it to the light. "Maybe you put in some secret herbs, Yah? We say nothing only that your beer is full of body." He smiled at them in a secretive manner, winked and drank down another huge mouthful.

"That's for sure." Said George in a matter of fact voice, "Definitely a full bodied beer this one." He handed Henk another glass.

"So you vill filter and bottle yah? I know that everything else is vell in order, but you vill be needing a new bottling line please. Yah?"

"Actually Henk we have one. My problem is staying solvent long enough to pay for it!"

"Money, money, you speak to me of money? Without help you vill sink. Is that the problem?"

"That is exactly the problem Henk. We need the line to stay afloat and the cost may sink us."

"Come my friend." Said Henk genially, and placing a huge and paw like arm around Kevin. "Your friend Henk vill show you how the EEC can help you vith a grant. A big grant. A huge grant. Ve have too many monies in the EEC. Time to liberate a little for a good cause. Henk vill buy the bottling line for his good friends Kevin and George and then excellent beer can be brewed again in Houghton Springs. Poooph! Money! Money is no problem for Henk." He passed his again empty glass for refilling.

Therefore, it came about that Henk arranged for an EEC grant. Timothy Longstanton turned into Old Silas. Andrew Ashbow rebuilt the dray and placed it along with old Morris Minor on display and the Black Badger thrived.

Maxwell, discovered that Cynthia was an excellent cook and that she fussed about him in a most pleasing manner. Totally non reminiscent of either his previous wife or mistress. Since he had been rendered homeless by his wife, her solicitor and Mandy, he had, at Cynthia's insistence moved in with her. Beggars not being choosers, being his feelings. Cynthia quickly forgot all about The Soldiers Of The Divine Order and their views of sex. She was far too preoccupied with pursuing her own view of the matter with a willing Maxwell. As for The Soldiers, they were left to their own devices, thundering Sulphur and Brimstone at each other every Sunday in a mutually pleasing manner. Cynthia also resigned as a councilor and took to breeding King Charles Spaniels. Crump's Cola went into liquidation and the ex Mrs. Maxwell took off for places unknown.

Billy Boom got a breathing space, as Crump's Cola was no longer extracting water. Anyway, he had his own problems. The Foreign Secretary's son, Lawson Squitter was at the moment being detained in some dirty and squalid jail within a small African country. The "Democratic" leader for life, having thumbed his nose at all things British had closed down Her Britannic Majesty's Embassy. Sending the Ambassador and all of his retinue scurrying over the border into a neighboring and more congenial country. Apparently, his countries only export was bark from The Jogubottie tree. This being the main ingredient of "Lawson's Laxative" The new, "socialist" leader, no doubt not wanting to be seen as yet another corrupt black, had decided to nationalize the jogubottie tree bark export business. This way he hoped to hide his personal vested interests in his countries only viable export under a smokescreen of helping the poor people of his nation etc. Thus pushing up prices and making even bigger profits for himself in the process. All of which were squirreled away into various tax haven banks throughout the world. Lawson, instead of following the more usual western approach to such an incident. That is, on the one hand praising the new leader for his efforts in trying to drag his country out of the stone age, whilst at the same time opening a personal Swiss bank account for him. Then offering aid in the form all sorts of things no one wanted, such as mobile phones and fast food outlets. All of which ultimately would be paid for in Jogubottie exports. Thus keeping the leader happy, Lawson's laxatives happy and the peasants impoverished but with a taste for western produce. No Lawson apparently, had got a bunch of mercenaries together and had planned invasion. Not that Billy Boom's problems ended there. His Home Secretary had been exposed by a national tabloid as having an affair with his postman. The latter being some illegal Armenian immigrant whose visa requirement had been fast tracked under instructions issued that had originated from the desk of the Home Secretary. Billy was looking for a cheap diversion that would show him in a good light. He was still struggling with the police over the drinking whilst under the influence charge and that lewd acts in public. He was trying frantically to not only keep a firm lid on that incident, but distance himself from it at the same time. The police having traced the camper van in question as being a MI5 pool vehicle. Gerald and Charley having fallen under the total denial blanket and left to fend for themselves had become thoroughly disgruntled and were singing like canaries. Billy decided that recent news from the Black Badger gave him the opportunity to demonstrate how he was a "Man of the people." A one eighty about face was called for. Spin doctors were organized accordingly.

CHAPTER: 14

The wedding of Mulchi and Vania was due to take place. Arthur Smallpiece, having failed to produce any evidence had no story. Though he knew about Maxwell, he had nothing to back any allegations. Therefore Maxwell's rapid divorce was not really earth shattering news. The wedding consequently was quietly publicized by Peter Goodbody and Andrew via his connection with The Real Beer Drinkers Association. Billy naturally picked this up in Whitehall too. He decided that the time had come for his 180-degree turn around. He would go public and use the celebration to show just how well Britain was treating the immigrant problem. That the Black Badger continued to brew free of excise duty, might also be capitalized upon. More so, since the EEC had given Houghton Springs Brewery, not just a clean bill of health, but commended it upon its standards. Billy knew when he was beaten. His public image ratings were rock bottom. Stuff the fiddling amounts to be gained in excise duty compared to the easing of the water problem and no one inspecting that barrel of governmental blunders and undeclared interests. Anyway, the future looked bleak for his party, so maybe it was time to get out while he was still ahead and hand the whole mess over to the opposition. They were screaming to be given the chance. Billy decided to visit the Black Badger as a guest at the wedding. He could then optimize the event and be seen dressed casually in jeans and open necked shirt, swilling a pint with the locals. Yes, he thought, a pint in a special pewter tankard that he would give to the Black Badger to mark his visit. Far better to bring The Black Badger firmly into the fold and capitalize upon it. He set his spin-doctors to work. The outcome of which was that since the EEC had commended the small brewery, Billy Boom's government needed to top the continental accolade. A new national honor was promptly invented along the lines of the Queens Award for industry. Houghton Springs Brewery being earmarked for the first presentation.

The first shot at a title being, The British Cottage Industry Industrial Recognition Award. This was even too large a mouthful for the quasi-governmental body responsible for dreaming it up. Next came British Rural Amelioration Award. Which certainly had a ring to it and as Billy commented, he had no idea what amelioration meant, but it sounded good and that was what mattered. Naturally, the French, having got wind of Billy's plans and since anything that had British in front of it was sufficient to induce them to start foaming at the mouth, objected. More so since their Mademoiselle Aughty had been an original inspector. A compromise was suggested and European Amelioration Recognition was suggested. That no one had any clear idea of what the title meant, finally dawned and the far more sensible suggestion (from a thoroughly bored Danish representative) of European Rural Industry Award was finally agreed. Kevin was duly notified that the award would be given and the ceremony would held at the Black Badger and that the PM would attend. Somehow, the date clashed with the already published wedding date.

On the day that The Black Badger had official notification, an excited Henk had phoned from Munich. Did Kevin know of the award etc? Kevin did, but was unsure what was entailed. "No problems." Declared Henk confidently. "I shall be there vith my beautiful Petunia. Together. Ve shall see it through. And drink lots of beer." He added as an afterthought.

Vicki and Kevin were discussing the turn of events in their bedroom.

"Seems like we will be OK now." Observed Kevin, "The Black Badger and everything."

"Yes, you have done well Kevin. Your father would have been proud of you."

"It's all down to you really Vicki." Kevin looked at her gently. "I could never have done it without you."

"I wonder what Marlene and her mother are thinking now Kevin Firkettle. Famous you are. PM going to pin a gong on your chest no less." She laughed in a quiet and sad manner.

Kevin picked up on her mood. "What's the matter Vicki? You seem a little down."

"Oh you remember what I told you a long time ago about you growing and me being left behind? Well it's happening Kevin. You are famous now."

"No I'm not and anyway, it was only your pushing me that enabled me to do anything. Honest Vicki." He looked at her kindly. "I do love you Vicki, I really do, so please don't start talking about leaving me, because if you do all of this will have been for nothing."

"How do you mean Kevin, all for nothing?" Vicki looked long and deeply into his eyes as she spoke.

"Well Vicki, if you go then I have no further interest in The Black Badger, or anything else for that matter. I will give the lot to George and Beth, Honest I will."

"What about the wedding and chief giving away the brides and the entire Kharzi thing?"

"Oh George will always welcome them here, you know that. No, I just couldn't live here without you Vicki. It would be too depressing."

"What would you do?" Pressed Vicki.

"I honestly don't know." Kevin looked forlorn. Lost and hopeless

"So you do love me then?" Vicki looked at Kevin again and waited.

"You know that I do."

"Good as your aunty Vicki has a little surprise for you." Shesmiled, "You my son are going to be a father. So best you make that a triple wedding."

POST SCRIPT:

There was a triple wedding and Billy Boom was in attendance, along with Henk and Petunia. The presentation of the award was made and news reporter's bulbs flashed. George was awarded the title of Master Brewer by The British Real Beer Drinkers Association and great play was made by all of how the Kharzis had been integrated into British society. Billy got his press coverage and was seen to be a man of the people. He was photographed quaffing a foaming tankard of Black Badger. A framed and signed photograph of him shaking hands with Kevin was presented and now adorns a prominent position on the wall behind the bar of The Black Badger. A whole new line in bottled beer was brewed named OLD SILAS. Manni was kept happy counting the profits. Mr. Wilberforce retired to a small cottage nearby with Astrophy and frequented the Black Badger. He made a point of only drinking from the tankard that the PM had so kindly left behind. However, he had it engraved in Latin. "To the victors go the spoils" So everyone lived happily ever afterwards. Well, most of the time anyway. Except that is for Marlene, whose mother never forgave her for taking up with that useless, mop wielding scoundrel Roger in favor of that nice and intelligent Kevin.

The End.